Forever Twenty-One * Book One

DEATH DEFYING

J.S. EADES

This is a work of fiction. Names, characters, places, and incidents are either products of the author's imagination or used fictitiously. Any resemblance to actual events, locales, or persons, living or dead, is purely coincidental.

Eades, J.S.
Death Defying / J.S. Eades
ISBN: 978-0-9939582-3-6

Website: www.jseades.com
Facebook: AuthorJSEades
Twitter: @JS_Eades
Instagram: @jseadesauthor

Editorial Assistance: Dina Bielby, Gina Sweet-Ellis, Eva Oktabcova, and Shannon McIntyre
Cover Design: Heather D. Murray

Edition: February 2023

I want to thank Heather, Dina, Gina, Shannon, Mara, Amanda, and my father Fred for all their support. Most of all I need to give a huge thank you and shout out to my writing partner, Eva. Her feedback has been absolutely invaluable and I don't know what I'd do without her.

This book is dedicated to one of my biggest fans and supporters,
Lois Flower (1942 - 2020)
Taken far too soon, you are greatly missed.

Table of Contents

Prologue

June 19, 1973, Toronto, Canada

The big glass doors swoosh shut behind Madeleine Bourreau as she enters the hospital lobby. She looks around with concern at the odd sound. Madeline doesn't like hospitals. She had all of her children at home, as had her mother before her, and her grandmother before that, all the way back as far as anyone can remember. She's never had any use for hospitals. Or doctors, for that matter.

Her daughter Angelique, however, has very different ideas. About childbirth. About an appropriate partner and father of her children. About many things. Angelique seems to enjoy challenging tradition. She's chosen to deliver her firstborn at Mount Sinai Hospital. Madeleine doesn't like coming into the busy downtown either, but today she will put up with the pollution and the traffic and the people. She would put up with almost anything to meet her brand new granddaughter.

The woman behind the reception desk is dressed all in white. A smart white cap stands out in contrast against her dark hair. "Good morning. How may I help you?" she greets Madeleine with a cheery smile.

“I am ‘ere to visit Angelique Bourreau,” Madeleine tells her.

The receptionist flips through a big blue ledger until she finds the right name. “Ah, here she is. Room 1515. That’s up on fifteenth.” She points towards the brass elevator doors. “Your sister?” she asks as Madeleine turns to walk away.

Madeleine frowns, but switches it to a smile before she looks back and replies, “Why, yes. I am so excited to meet the baby.”

She steps off the elevator on floor fifteen and looks around curiously. This is a huge, modern building. Madeleine has never been inside a building as large as this before. So many floors. So many hallways. Which one leads to her daughter? Spotting another white-clad nurse coming her way, she stops her to ask directions.

At last she finds room 1515. Outside the door, she pauses to reach inside her jacket and withdraw a small vial of pinkish-white powder. After uncorking the bottle, she covers the opening with a finger and inverts it, coating her fingertip with a circle of powder. She carefully tucks the vial away, making sure to not brush it off.

Now wearing a genuine smile, Madeleine enters her daughter’s room. Angelique is sitting up against her pillow cradling her day-old daughter in her arms. She looks a bit tired, and her long reddish-brown hair is hanging limply and in need of a wash, but basically she appears the same as usual. No one would guess she’d just delivered a baby last night.

“Maman,” Angelique says happily. “Come meet your new gran’ bébé!”

Madeleine approaches the bed and Angelique shows her the pink blanket-wrapped infant. "Elle est belle,” she says softly. She is beautiful. Then, in a normal tone, “What is her name?”

“Genevieve Agnes,” Angelique says with a smile. Madeleine has never seen her daughter look so happy. Motherhood is going to agree with her. Perhaps it might even temper her rebellious nature. But that is probably wishful thinking on Madeleine’s part.

“Très bien.” Geneviève had been Madeleine’s mother’s name. She’d passed away nearly a decade ago, but she knows Angelique remembers her grand-mère well and fondly. Her daughter pronounces the baby's name *jen-nuh-veev*, rather than the proper French *jahn-vee-ev*. Perhaps Madeleine can nudge her into correcting that. Agnes is the child's paternal grandmother. She also does not pronounce her name the French way. It irks Madeleine, but she understands it's Agnes' choice.

That reminds her, either Agnes or Marcus or both of them could show up at any moment. "May I hold her?" she asks. "So you can freshen up or stretch your legs?"

Her daughter's eyes light up. "Merci. I do need to use the washroom." She carefully hands the child to Madeleine, then throws back the sheets and disappears behind a white-painted door.

Madeleine sits on the edge of the vacated hospital bed and looks down at her tiny new granddaughter. The child has inquisitive green eyes, just like Angelique's. Madeleine hopes that, unlike Angelique, Geneviève will grow up to embrace her destiny. With a little help from her grandmother, perhaps she might even be the one to save them all. Because something must be done. Angelique might not take the threat seriously, living on the far side of the ocean from her people, but the rest of the family, those who remain, understand.

"Ma douce," she whispers to her granddaughter. "I 'ave a gift for you, sweet girl." Madeleine gently presses her powder-coated finger to the baby's forehead. The powder, pale to begin with, becomes translucent before vanishing into Geneviève's soft skin.

"Il est pour toi," Madeleine whispers. "He is for you."

Chapter 1
Happy Birthday

June 18, 1994, Toronto, Canada

Genny Dupont thinks about death a lot. Presumably more than the average twenty-year-old, anyway. She worries about being hit by a car each time she crosses the street. She wonders how it would feel to be electrocuted in the shower. She wonders about things falling off office buildings downtown and creaming her on the sidewalk below. She even sometimes imagines what her funeral will be like. Will her favorite songs be played? Will there be red and white roses on her coffin?

She doesn't know why dark stuff like this invades her thoughts so much. If she had to guess, she'd say it's probably because her parents had died when she'd been seven. But honestly? She's wondered about her own death for as long as she can remember.

On the morning of her twenty-first birthday, she wakes from a strange dream about her mom to find her seventeen-year-old sister Chloe standing by her bed with a big grin on her face and an even bigger cupcake in her hands. Behind her, Peter Murphy glares accusingly from a black and white Bauhaus poster on the wall. Genny concurs.

“Happy Birthday!” Chloe exclaims. She wears baggy ripped jeans and an oversize black Nirvana tee. Because of course she does.

Genny groans. “Remember how you asked me what I wanted for my birthday?

“Sure.” Still grinning.

“And do you recall what I said?”

Chloe brings her free hand to her chin and looks up and to the left as if thinking hard. “A cupcake?”

“No.” Well, yes, but that’s not the point.

“A hug from your awesome sister?”

“Not so much.”

“The big pancake breakfast Gran is making?

That gives Genny pause. Her stomach rumbles at the thought. “Still not it.”

“Well you’re getting all three. So get your butt outta bed. Today is your lucky day.”

“What I wanted for was for you to let me sleep in. I didn’t think it was too much to ask. Was it?”

“Was it what?”

Genny sighs. Sometimes talking to Chloe feels like pulling out her own hair. One strand at a time. “Too much to ask?”

“Genevieve,” Chloe starts and Genny cringes. Her mother always used to call her by her full name. “I hate to break it to ya, but it’s almost ten. You *have* slept in. And now it’s time to get up. Unless you want to spend your entire birthday in bed? But then you’d miss breakfast, and I know there’s no chance of that.”

Ignoring the dig, Genny reaches for the clock on her nightstand and angles it toward her. *Damn.* It *is* almost ten. She can’t very well complain about an early wakeup. Then the smell of frying bacon hits her nose, making her stomach gurgle again. Chloe’s right, she isn’t about to miss breakfast.

Grabbing the cupcake from her sister’s hand, Genny crams the entire thing into her mouth. Frosting coats her lips and chin, but she doesn’t care in the slightest.

Chloe barks out a surprised laugh. “You are *such* a weirdo,” she says, her bleached blonde hair not moving in the slightest as she spins around and leaves. So much gel, so early in the day. Genny shudders.

Her own head falls back against the pillow. She chews the cake thoughtfully as her sister's footsteps fade down the stairs. Genny and her best friend Dawn McArthur have big plans today. First, they're going shopping. Then they're going out for dinner and drinks. And, best of all, after that, they're going to Apothecary to dance their butts off and hopefully flirt with some hot guys. Well, Genny intends to flirt, anyway. Dawn will likely tell Genny she had, but in reality not make eye contact with anyone she doesn't know. Whether she's brave enough to flirt or not makes zero difference, though. Either way, they're going to have a great night.

She licks the frosting from her lips and tries to wipe off the rest with her fingers, but she still feels sticky. With a sigh of resignation, she pushes herself out of bed and crosses the hall to the bathroom. She turns on the tap and then examines her reflection in the mirror. Her chestnut brown hair is a mess, but otherwise she looks the same as always. Once the water is warm, she scrubs the remains of the frosting from her somewhat pointed chin. Although, she's not really sure why she'd bothered. She's just going to get syrupy-sticky again. Breakfast course number two is almost ready.

When Genny comes into the kitchen, Gran sets a plate piled high with blueberry pancakes at her spot at the table. On top, a single candle glows in the middle of a ring of strawberries.

"Happy Birthday, dear!" Gran tells her with a wide smile. Before Genny can thank her, Gran and Chloe launch into the birthday song.

Chloe, of course, has to add the final line: "you look like a monkey and smell like one, too." And, as they do every birthday, they all laugh.

"Thanks, guys." Genny grabs the tongs and piles a small mountain of bacon beside her pancakes. "You're the actual best, Gran."

After their parent's accident, their paternal grand-mère Agnes had taken in Genny and Chloe without hesitation. They've lived with her in North York, a neighborhood of

Toronto, ever since. Agnes has raised the girls as if they are her own children, and Genny will be forever grateful to her, but the truth is that, besides going into foster care, they'd had no other options. Their mother Angelique's relatives are all dead, and their father Marcus had been an only child. Genny's entire family now sits at this table.

Chloe drinks black coffee, but has taken no food. This is not unusual. Sometimes she doesn't eat at all until dinner. It makes zero sense to Genny; breakfast is literally her favorite part of waking up. But if Chloe has decided she doesn't feel like eating, no amount of persuading will change her mind.

"What are you up to today?" Gran asks as she lifts a forkful of pancake.

"Dawn's coming by in a couple hours and we're going down to Queen West." That area has funky, unique little shops and Genny wants to look for something perfect to wear tonight.

"Sounds like a lovely way to spend the day," Gran replies. "What about you?" she asks Chloe.

"Also going shopping downtown. With Kate. But we're looking for CDs, not dresses." Kate has been Chloe's best friend since they'd been small, although Genny wonders how much the two even have in common anymore. Kate is preppy and dates a football player. Chloe went full-on grunge a year ago and spends most of her free time in her room listening to music.

"Have fun," Genny says. While she also loves music, she isn't anywhere near as obsessed as Chloe. Her sister had nearly gone catatonic when she'd found out two months ago that Kurt Cobain had committed suicide. Genny had thought it tragic, but she hadn't gone downtown to the candlelit vigil or anything. Chloe had. And cried about it for a week. Maybe longer. Genny had tried to be sympathetic to her sister's pain, but she hadn't really understood. Mom and Dad dying had been devastating. Some rock star they hadn't known taking his own life at the peak of his success? It'd been sad, but it hadn't affected her day to day life.

Chloe had only been three when their parents had passed away, so she doesn't remember them very well. Genny had been nearly eight. She still dreams of them, still hears their voices in her head sometimes. Though they are no longer with her, Genny feels attached to them. Chloe, on the other hand, never speaks of them unless prompted, and often not even then.

"Do you wanna TTC down to Queen with us?" Genny asks her sister. TTC is short for Toronto Transit Commission, which is what locals call the city's bus, streetcar, and subway system.

"Nah, Kate should be here any minute. We're not waiting around for you." She has another gulp of coffee, then gets up and dumps the rest into the sink. Before Genny or Gran can comment, she vanishes back upstairs, presumably to put on her makeup. Chloe likes to line her eyes with heavy, black pencil. Genny doesn't judge her it, though. At Apothecary, all the girls wear heavy makeup and most of them look stunning.

This reminds Genny that she has less than two hours to finish eating, shower, throw in a load of laundry, and get ready to go out. Stabbing another bite of syrup-covered pancake along with a chunk of strawberry, she stuffs it into her mouth. Unlike her sister, she is not wasting a single morsel of this delicious breakfast.

As Genny pulls open the steel door from the Queen Street sidewalk, a familiar heavy beat hits both girls right in the chest. It's KMFDM's "Godlike," a song they both love dancing to.

"Dammit, we're missing it!" Dawn exclaims, hurrying past her up the steps. Apothecary is located on the top floor above a sewing shop. Genny often wonders what the owners and patrons of that shop think about the goth club upstairs.

"You know they'll play it again in a few hours," Genny protests, although having to rush upstairs isn't nearly as arduous as she pretends it is. Though she always worries about falling, she's climbed these stairs in high heels many times and has never once tripped. But there's always a first time.

After they pay their cover, Genny heads straight to the bar. The bartender approaches her with a grin. "Hey Genny.

What can I getcha?" He has to speak loudly to be heard over the music.

"Hi Stefan. It's my birthday. Can you make me something celebratory?"

Stefan is decidedly hot. And flirting with hot guys is part of tonight's plan. His grin widens. "Yeah? Well, Happy Birthday! Hmm, how 'bout a Zombie?"

Genny slides a hand across the bar top and squeezes his wrist. "Perfect. Make it two."

"Comin' up." Stefan turns to the guy standing to her right. "What about you?"

Just then the KMFDM song ends and she hears him reply, "In honor of her birthday, I'll 'ave the same. And they're on me." The voice has a slight French accent.

Intrigued, Genny turns to see who has just offered to buy her drink, already prepared to decline. Beside her stands a tall, slim, brown-skinned man looking back at her with a shy smile. He looks to be about her age, with thick black hair spiked out at the front and short around the sides and back. Like most other guys at Apothecary, he wears black jeans and a black t-shirt. More importantly, he's cute. Especially his smile. That smile is frickin' adorable.

The next song isn't quite as raucous, so she doesn't have to yell. "Thanks," Genny tells him. Based only on his smile, she makes an impulse decision to not add, "but no thanks."

"You're quite welcome."

She leans closer. "I don't mean to be nosy, but are you French?"

He nods. "I was born in France, but I've lived 'ere, in Toronto that is, for many years." He pauses, then sticks out a hand. "I'm JP. It's short for Jean-Paul, but everyone calls me JP."

Genny looks down at his outstretched fingers with amusement, but takes his hand and shakes. "Hi JP. I'm Genny. My family is from France, too, but I was born here."

JP's brows draw together for a second, but then his expression returns to shy and cute. Before he can say more, Stefan sets three tall glasses on the bar in front of them. "Three Zombies. Fourteen bucks." Pulling his wallet from his jeans, JP hands him a twenty.

Genny grabs two of the drinks and turns back to JP. "Thanks again. My friends have a table over there." She indicates the back of the club with her chin. "Come say hi later."

"Will do," he agrees. He's looking at her curiously again. Does she have food stuck in her teeth? She makes a mental note to pop into the washroom to check.

Genny makes her way to the booth in the back corner to find Dawn and a couple of their friends. As she sets down the glasses and slides in, they all shout, "Happy Birthday!"

"Tell me you didn't have to buy your own drinks tonight?" Jonny says. Genny and Dawn had become fast friends with him and his buddy Flav about a year ago, when they'd first started coming to Apothecary.

"I didn't. Some cute guy beside me at the bar paid. Gotta love free drinks."

"Oh yeah? How cute?" he asks with a mischievous grin.

"Yeah, how cute was he?" Dawn echoes, leaning in.

"Very cute. I told him to come by and say hi later."

"Excellent." Dawn takes a sip of her drink. "Whoa. This is strong!"

"Stefan made them for me for my birthday, so he might've put a little extra in." Genny sucks on her own straw. Yep, lots of booze in that. She'll have to go easy on Zombies tonight. Happily buzzed is her goal, not so wasted she has to be babysat by her friends and poured into a cab later. She turns to Dawn. "Do I have something in my teeth?" She bares them like a snarl.

Dawn, understanding the serious embarrassment of walking around with food stuck in one's teeth, scrutinizes Genny's mouth. "Nope. Why?"

Genny shrugs. "No reason."

The opening beats of a Nine Inch Nails song they all like starts and they all perk up. After another sip from her straw, Genny grabs Dawn's hand and leads her to the dancefloor. Genny has exactly two celebrity crushes and Trent Reznor is one of them. She and Dawn have tickets to see Nine Inch Nails next month and she's already stoked about it.

As they dance, Genny notices Dawn eyeing the dancers in the two elevated cages along the side wall. She knows her friend is just waiting for a cage to vacate so she can climb in. Dawn doesn't care if others watch her dance; she just loves letting the music carry her away. Genny has no idea where her friend goes when she cage-dances, but she suspects it's almost trance-like, sort of like a form of meditation.

The song ends and one of the dancers climbs down from their cage. "See you later," Dawn tells Genny, hurrying over to climb in as a new song starts up. Genny stays where she is on the dancefloor. From the corner of her eye, she notices someone approach her. It's JP.

He flashes her a nervous grin. "Would it be presumptuous of me to dance with you? I mean, *by* you. Dance beside you. Do you mind?"

She doesn't mind at all. "Dance away."

JP starts dancing and Genny has to bite her lip to keep from laughing. He's...not good. His feet move erratically, not even close to keeping the beat. His long arms flail around his body like he has no control over them. He looks happy enough, but Genny has to avert her eyes. She doesn't want to hurt his feelings if he notices her laughing and thinks it's at him. So she dances beside him and focuses her gaze on the floor near her shoes.

When the song ends, Genny decides to put JP out of his oblivious misery. "Wanna come sit with us?" she asks. He follows her back to their booth, where she motions him into Dawn's vacated spot and slides in beside him. After introducing him to Jonny and Flav, Jonny drops her a wink before getting up and vanishing into the crowd. She's pretty sure it means he agrees with her assessment of JP's cuteness.

"So what do you do?" JP asks her. "Are you in school?"

Genny had intended to go to university, but after high school, she'd gotten a temporary job at an insurance office that turned into a permanent position, and she's worked there ever since. She isn't ashamed that she hasn't gone to university, but she isn't exactly proud of it either. "I work downtown," she replies, grabbing her glass and taking a long drink. It's almost time for a refill.

JP doesn't let it go so easily. "What do you do?"

"I'm a secretary. Or admin assistant, as they call us now. It's the opposite of exciting. How 'bout you?"

"I guess you'd say I'm a scholar. Of sorts. Always studying, that's me. You should see all my books. My maman always says I need to be careful with candles or my apartment will go up in flames one day. That's not all I do. I'm also a...I guess you would say a record keeper." He looks like he's about to add more, but makes himself stop. Maybe he thinks he's talking too much. Genny thinks it's kind of adorable.

"What do you study?"

Again his face takes on that odd look and again it vanishes and makes her wonder if she imagined it. "History," he states firmly.

Genny smiles. "I love history! Especially archaeology. What kind of history do you study? French history?"

"Mostly, yes. And Canadian, too, a bit."

Before Genny can reply, Jonny returns and sets another Zombie in front of her. "Happy Birthday, Gen."

Genny gets to her feet and hugs him. "Thanks. You're the awesomest."

"Very true," he laughs. Before she can draw back, he leans close and whispers, "Too bad he's straight. He's a cutie-pie."

Snorting, Genny replies, "How can you be so sure?"

"Because he is super clearly into you, hon. He came here with a couple friends and he's been ignoring them pretty much since you walked in."

She's thankful the loud music masks their conversation. "If you say so." She hopes Jonny's right.

Dawn returns to the table and sits where Genny had been, beads of sweat making her pushed-up cleavage glow. She glances at JP with confusion, then turns back to Genny. "Sorry. Did I take your seat?"

"It's fine. This is JP. JP, meet my friend Dawn."

Once they say hello, Dawn stands back up and beckons to Genny to resume her spot. Instead, JP slides out. "I feel like dancing again. Anyone want to join?" he asks the group, but his eyes stay on Genny.

Yep, he's definitely interested. That's probably why he's been acting sort of awkward. "Why not?" Genny says, grabbing her new glass and taking a drink before following him back onto the now-crowded dancefloor.

One of her favorite Sisters of Mercy songs is playing as they find a spot near the DJ booth. As before, she tries to keep her gaze averted from JP as he dances. Although one bonus to his flailing is that other dancers move away and give them space.

Halfway through the song, Genny suddenly feels all the hair on her forearms rise. Then the back of her neck begins to tingle. Though not painful, it feels sort of like a low-grade current is running over her skin. She stops dancing and looks around, trying to spot the cause, but she can't see anything that might explain it.

JP bends his head to her and asks, "What's wrong?"

Genny scans the room again. "Nothing, I guess. I just felt weird for a moment. It's fine." The strange sensation is still there, but since JP doesn't seem to be feeling it, too, she doesn't want to alarm him. It lasts through the end of the song and all through the next. With still no obvious source, Genny decides it must be a side effect from the Zombies. Odd, but tolerable.

JP excuses himself to go to the washroom. Genny wonders if he also wants to find his friends and explain where he's been. She goes back to the booth and slips in beside Dawn.

Dawn's cheeks are flushed from dancing and drinking. It makes her look extra pretty, and with her nearly black hair and pale complexion, she's always pretty. All the guys in their friend group think so, but Dawn has never dated any of them. Once time last year when they'd been on the bus late at night coming home from the club, she'd drunkenly admitted to Genny that she'd wondered if she might be into girls. Genny had been a bit surprised at first, but had assured her it made no difference to her. Dawn is her best friend. All Genny wants is for her to be happy.

"So? Sparks?" she asks Genny.

Genny smiles. She feels like she's thrumming with electricity. "Oh yeah. Definite sparking."

"He's handsome."

"Yep."

"Seems nice."

"Yep."

"You gonna give him your number?"

Turning to face her friend directly, Genny says, "You think he's gonna ask?"

Dawn laughs. "Definitely. And he's heading this way right now."

Genny looks up to see JP pushing through the crowd toward them. His expression is no longer cheerful. In fact, he looks kind of anxious. "Genny?" He crouches so his face is level with hers. "Look, I know you just met me, and you 'ave no reason to trust me yet, but I really, *really* think we should leave. Right now. There's…uh, some trouble about to start. I already told my friends to take off, and we need to do the same."

Her brows draw in tight. Leave? The night is still young. She's only had two drinks. And, more importantly, it's her birthday. But JP looks dead serious. He wants her to leave with him. It's tempting, but she isn't going anywhere without Dawn. She turns back to her friend.

"JP says we should go."

Dawn nods. "I heard." Now she looks worried, too.

"You want to? I mean…"

Leaning across the table to Jonny, Dawn says, "JP says some trouble's about to go down. You guys wanna stay or go?

Jonny shrugs. "I've seen bar fights before. And the back door is ten feet from here. We'll stay."

Dawn turns back to Genny and JP. She assesses JP for a moment. "Fine. Let's go, then."

JP looks relieved. "This way."

The girls follow him out the back door that leads to a hallway and stairs down to the alley. Considering how well he seems to know his way around Apothecary, Genny's surprised she's never seen him here before. From the back alley, they come out onto a tree-lined side street. They walk it parallel to Queen Street for a few blocks before returning to Queen and jumping on an east-bound bus. As they sit down, Genny realizes the strange tingle she'd felt is gone. When had it vanished? She'd clearly failed to notice during their rush to leave the bar. Does that mean it had been connected to something at Apothecary? Will she feel it again next time she goes?

Dawn and Genny are on double seat together and JP sits on the next seat down, his long legs stretched out across the aisle. Other than the three of them, the bus only has two other passengers, an older Hispanic couple who are probably also on their way home.

"Which way are you going?" Genny asks JP.

"North."

"As in North York?"

He nods.

"So are we." Genny doesn't ask specifically where he lives. She doesn't want to seem too nosy.

They transfer to the subway at Yonge, taking the same route Genny takes every weekday after work. She actually finds the lurching and rumbling of the train soothing, especially at this time of night when it isn't crowded shoulder to shoulder with commuters.

When the girls get off at Sheppard station to grab another bus the rest of the way, JP comes with them. Dawn looks up at him curiously. "You go this way, too?"

"Sort of. I live only a few streets from 'ere. I'm not trying to be creepy, I swear," he tells them with a grin. "I just want to make sure you both get 'ome safely."

"That's just what a creepy stalker dude would probably say," Genny replies, deadpan. JP looks chagrined and she laughs. "Just kidding. C'mon. Here's the bus now."

Before they disembark at their stop, true to Dawn's prediction, JP asks Genny if he can call her sometime. None of them have pens, but he swears he'll memorize her number. Shaking her head in amusement, she tells it to him and they all say goodnight.

Dawn is staying at Genny's tonight, so they start off toward her street. "Too bad the night ended early," she says. "But it was fun while it lasted."

"Totally. I had a great birthday. And, to be honest, I didn't mind leaving."

Chuckling, Dawn replies, "I bet not."

Genny feels her cheeks heat up. "Think he'll call?"

"If he remembers your number, then definitely. If not, I predict he'll show up at the club next weekend."

At the mention of Apothecary, Genny recalls the strange sensation she'd felt earlier. And, maybe coincidently, just for a second she swears she feels it again. It's like fingertips brushing the nape of her neck. But then it's gone.

I must be losing it, she thinks.

Thirty minutes later, Dawn already snoring softly beside her, Genny once again gets that strange tingle. This time it lasts about twenty seconds. Just long enough for her to think, *I am definitely losing it.*

But she is far too tired to dwell on it any further tonight.

Without a sound, she moves through the dark forest. Who would've guessed she could ever walk so quietly in a place like this? The only light is the soft glimmer of moonlight between branches above.

The woods are remarkably silent, too. Why doesn't she hear other signs of life? Mice? Raccoons? Owls? Where are all the nocturnal creatures?

As if answering her question, a twig snaps somewhere up ahead. She quickens her pace, realizing she's not just walking, she's stalking. Her fingers tighten on something in her hand. A weapon. She's holding a weapon and she wants to kill...something.

But what?

Her heart rate is calm, her breath controlled. She's not scared. She's confident and sure. She has a job to do, and it's to kill whatever snapped that twig.

She approaches a clearing in the trees. It's brighter here; the light can reach the ground. A man stands half in the shadows on the other side. He doesn't see her. She hides behind a thick trunk for a moment, calculating each risk.

The time is now.

Leaping into the open, she grabs the man's arm and spins him around. Moonlight illuminates his face and she sees he's not a man at all. He is a monster.

The light hits his glistening white teeth, now bared and threatening. They are long and sharp. He reminds her of an angry dog about to attack. Those teeth are not human, and neither is this creature. He will kill her if he gets the chance.

She smiles at the thought. Because he will not get the chance. He thinks himself an apex predator, but he is wrong. She is the predator tonight.

He lunges at her but she dodges easily. With a frustrated snarl, he tries again. She seems to dance with him, letting him get close, then darting away. She is teasing him, making him angry. Making him hungry.

He reaches for her shoulders. This time she lets him grab her, and as he does he laughs. His laugh is not human either. It's vicious and otherworldly and should send shivers up her spine.

But it doesn't.

In one quick movement, she stabs forward with the object in her hand into the center of his chest and upward, up under his ribcage.

Is it a dagger?

Whatever it is, the strike works. He groans and falls to the ground. She kneels over him, driving it deeper, making sure to mangle his heart. If he has a heart. He must. Because hot blood rushes over her hand and coats her wrist.

She examines his face in the pale moonlight. His eyes are empty, his skin ashen. He is dead.

And she smiles again as she wipes her blood-soaked hand on his shirt and cleans off the weapon on his pants.

Her sense of satisfaction is fleeting as she gets up to continue the hunt.

One more down. Too many more to go.

Genny wakes with a gasp, clutching the sheets with sweaty hands. Dawn is still asleep beside her. Looking at the clock, she sees it's 4:18. A strip of moonlight pierces through the gap between her curtains and she shudders.

What the hell was that all about? she thinks with a sigh as she settles back into her pillow. *No more Zombies for me.*

Chapter 2
New Direction

It turns out JP hadn't been lying about his excellent memorization skills, Not fifteen minutes after Dawn leaves the next morning the phone rings. Genny jumps up to grab it before anyone else can.

"Hello?"

"Would this be Genny?"

She smiles. "Would this be JP?"

"It is. 'Ope you don't mind that I called so soon? I just...I wanted to." He sounds nervous. And excited. Nervously excited. It's still cute.

"Of course not." It's a beautiful sunny Sunday and she has no plans. "What're you up to today?"

She hears JP chuckle. "I think that's supposed to be my line?"

"Oh, sorry. Rewind. Chuckachuckachucka. I'll start over. Of course not!"

Now his chuckle turns into a full throated laugh. "Okay. So. What are *you* up to today?"

Genny's smile grows wider. "Not too much. What did you have in mind?"

"Would you like to meet for coffee?"

"Sure. When and where?" She grabs a pen and poises it over her palm.

"You know The Second Cup at Bayview Village? Is that too far?"

"I know it. It's a quick bus ride from here." Dropping the pen, she adds, "What time?"

"An hour?"

"Perfect. See you in an hour." As she replaces the handset, she realizes she's still grinning. It's been a long time since she's felt this excited about a guy. Her last boyfriend had moved to New York, and they'd broken up over long distance concerns. That had been a year ago. She's ready to move on.

Genny showers and puts on makeup, and after staring into her closet for bit, finally chooses a black knee-length sundress with a small white flower pattern. At the front door, she laces up her favorite black Doc Martens and she's ready to go. Twenty minutes later, she walks into The Second Cup. She's a few minutes early, but she quickly spots JP waving at her from a table in the back. She's pleased to note that he looks pretty good in the daytime, too.

As she approaches, he gets to his feet. "I was going to get you a coffee, but I didn't know 'ow you took it. Or if you even liked coffee. So then I was going to order you a tea. But there are so many kinds to choose from and I didn't know what you liked. And then there's 'ot chocolate. But that seems more like a winter option. So I...well, I didn't order yet."

She can't help grinning at this. "I like coffee."

Together they go up to the counter and order. JP tries to pay, but Genny won't let him, instead slipping the cashier a five while he's trying to explain why he thinks he should treat her. As she carries her mug back to the table, she wonders if he's always so talkative or if it's just because being around her makes him nervous.

Genny blows on the surface of her coffee before taking a tentative sip. When she glances up, she sees JP watching her intently.

"Did you burn your tongue?" he asks.

She shakes her head.

He looks curious. "'Ave you ever?"

"Have I ever what?"

"Burned your mouth on coffee?"

Genny shrugs. "I don't know. Probably. Doesn't everyone?"

"But do you ever recall doing it?"

She thinks about it. "I guess not. Why?"

"I was just curious. I haven't either." Maybe realizing the inanity of the question, he changes the subject. "So do you still live with your parents? Or with Dawn? Or?"

"My younger sister and I live with our grandma. Our parents died when we were small."

JP frowns. "I'm sorry to hear that."

"Thanks. It was a long time ago. I was only seven." Genny takes another sip of coffee. It's definitely hot—steam still rises from it—but it doesn't burn her. Is that weird? "What about you?"

"I live alone. But my mother and uncle live only a few blocks away."

"What about your dad? If that's not too personal?"

"Papa is in France. My parents are still married, but they live separately right now. Maman goes to visit as often as she can. I know she misses him terribly, but Papa's work is important. He is needed back 'ome." Talking about his father makes JP look a little sad.

"You must miss him, too," she says sympathetically.

"Of course. But I understand." His melancholy clears, although he still seems nervous. "So…there's actually something I want to talk to you about."

"Okay."

"Do you mind if I ask you some personal questions?"

One side of Genny's mouth curves up. "How personal are we talking?"

At first he looks surprised by her question, but then he smiles. "Nothing very super personal. I promise."

"Then shoot."

"Do you get sick very often? Like cold or cough or flu?"

"Nope," she shakes her head. "I'm healthy as a horse."

"Do you remember ever being sick?"

Genny tries to think. "Not really. But I'm sure I probably was when I was little."

"What about your sister? Has she ever been sick?"

She shrugs. "I don't remember. Why?"

"Do you recall any injuries? Broken bones? Scrapes? Bruises? Even paper cuts?"

Her brows draw in tight. "I...I don't know. No broken bones. But the other stuff? I must have. Everyone does."

"But not you. Right?"

Genny's confused. What's with these questions? "Why do you wanna know?"

"Because there's something important I need to tell you. And I know you won't believe me, but I assure you it's true."

All humor seems to have left him. In an attempt to break the tension, she leans sideways and bumps his shoulder with her own. "Try me."

"I am..." He stops again, chewing his lower lip. "There's no easy way to tell someone this when they aren't expecting it, but...I am thirty-four years old."

Her brows fly up. "You are not!"

"I am. I was born on November 5, 1959 in Lentemps, France, to Jacques and Marie Levoyant. I have two older brothers and one older sister. And I know I look twenty-one. My siblings look twenty-one. My parents, aunts, uncles, grandparents, great-grandparents all look twenty-one. Because we are immortal. We do not get sick. We are rarely injured, and when we are, we 'eal quickly. And we do not age past adulthood."

Genny's jaw has fallen open. "Is this some kind of joke? Because—"

"No joke. This is who I am. And I wanted you to know."

Oh my God. He's completely serious. Disappointment washes through her. She usually has such great instincts for people, but she's never been so wrong before. JP is clearly insane. She needs to get out of here. But what if he isn't just regular crazy, but dangerous-crazy? If only she'd called Dawn and told her where she'd been going. What's a good excuse to leave?

"That's...interesting." One hand reaches for her purse and pulls it against her thigh.

JP sighs. "I know this is difficult to believe. And you barely know me, so why would you believe me? But before you go, please just listen for a few more minutes?"

Genny doesn't reply, but she doesn't stand up either.

"I am an immortal. And I believe you are one, too."

She exhales an incredulous laugh. "Do you even hear yourself? That's *nuts.* Seriously nuts."

"You are Geneviève Bourreau, yes? Daughter of Angelique Bourreau?"

Stilling, she whispers, "You *have* been stalking me! Was our meeting last night on purpose? Did you plan the whole thing out?"

JP shakes his head wildly. "No! Not at all. I didn't know who you were, at least not at first. I just liked you. And then, as the night went on, I...I guess I kind of recognized you. From the stories. My whole family—all immortals, really—know what happened to your parents. And that you and your sister were still out there somewhere, probably with no idea of your ancestry. My mother was your mother's closest friend. She knew you when you were a child. Maybe some part of you even remembers her?"

Genny's head is spinning. She can't stay here a minute longer. She jumps to her feet, bumping the table with her hip and sloshing coffee over the sides of both mugs. "Look, I don't know how you found out so much about my family, but you need to stay away from me. If I see you again, I'll call the cops."

"Wait. When you get 'ome, see if you can cut yourself. Even just a pinprick. You'll be able to, but only if you really try. Because your skin is strong. It takes a lot of effort to break it. That's why you've never had an injury before."

Snorting, she shakes her head in disbelief. "He must be off his meds," she mutters as she hurries to the door.

JP does not follow her. She does not look back.

When Genny gets home, she makes sure to turn both the regular lock and the deadbolt on the front door.

Gran comes around the corner from the kitchen, a towel over one shoulder. "You're back early."

"Yeah. Bad date. I really misjudged that one."

"Well, that can happen."

"If a guy with a French accent calls for me, tell him I don't live here anymore, okay?"

"Can do," Gran assures her with a smile.

Genny goes up to her room and flops onto her bed with a deep sigh. She'd liked JP. She'd even thought he might be boyfriend material. Never before has she been so wrong about a guy. It's disappointing. Disheartening, really.

Much as she tries to forget about it, bits and pieces of what he had told her keep popping into her head.

We do not get sick. We are rarely injured, and when we are, we heal quickly.

Genny can't recall ever being sick. She can't recall Chloe ever being sick. She doesn't remember any injuries, either. Do they even have bandages in the bathroom cabinet? Or medicine of any kind? She's never given any thought to this stuff before.

Getting to her feet, she goes to check. Gran's blood pressure pills are on the second shelf, along with a bottle of antacids, Advil, some Vick's VapoRub, and a half-full bottle of cough syrup. Those are also Gran's. Other than her toothbrush, toothpaste, and makeup remover, Genny's never used anything else in this cabinet.

Is that weird? She's starting to think it might be.

Bracing her hands on the counter, she stares at herself in the mirror. She doesn't even remember ever having a pimple. In high school, Dawn always used to say how jealous she was of Genny's perfect complexion. And Genny used to laugh and claim she must take after her mother.

My mother was your mother's closest friend.

Can she recall any of her mom's friends? She closes her eyes and tries to think back. She vaguely remembers a lady who used to visit sometimes, a bronze-skinned woman who talked like her mom. Could she have been JP's mother? Could anything he'd said possibly be true?

She trots down the steps to look at the photos on the living room mantle. The big one is her parents' wedding picture, the two of them so young with matching love-struck smiles. Beside it is a framed shot of her father holding her on his lap when she'd been a toddler. Mom isn't in this one, but the next is a photo of the whole family. A shy young Genny stands at her father's side, while her sister is in Mom's arms. Chloe looks to be about two. Genny picks it up and compares it with her parent's wedding picture. Does her mother look older in the one with Chloe? The wedding photo is a bit faded from time and sun, but from what Genny can tell, Mom looks pretty much the same. Still young and happy looking. Dad looks a little older, but Mom? Not really.

She can hear her grand-mère moving around in the kitchen. "Hey Gran?"

"Yes?"

"Where's the old photo album from Mom and Dad's? The one with all the pictures of us as kids?"

Gran's face appears around the edge of the doorway. "Isn't it in the cupboard beside the TV? If not, check your sister's room."

Kneeling to open the cupboard, Genny sees a colorful row of photo albums with a gap where the big blue one used to be. "Chloe must have it," she sighs. "Are there photos of Mom in any of these?"

Coming over to join her, Gran examines the spines. After a few moments, she pulls out an old faded green album with a spiral binding. "There should be a few in here from when Marcus and Angelique first starting dating." She flips to the end and then turns back a few pages. "Here's one. They were on their way out to dinner and I made them stop so I could take a picture. Against your mother's will, if I recall. Like you girls, she was always starving."

Genny takes the album from Gran and studies the photo. Dad definitely looks younger in this one. His face is narrower. Mom wears a polite smile, but Genny can tell she's not into it. Her reddish-brown hair is pulled back into a high ponytail. And her face looks exactly the same as in the picture where she's holding Chloe, taken nearly a decade later. Something drops in Genny's gut. Could JP be right? No. There's no way. Her mother had just been blessed with great genes. That's all.

Frowning, she closes the album and puts it away. Then she heads back upstairs, but instead of going into her own room, she pushes open her sister's door. Chloe is over at Kate's this afternoon and won't likely be home until dinner, so Genny steps inside. It's an act of trespass that would make Chloe blow a gasket, but right now she doesn't care. Her curiosity is burning and she doesn't want to wait until later to ask permission.

A huge poster of Nirvana is taped to the wall over Chloe's unmade bed. Another black and pink one of the cover of Pearl Jam's "Ten" is above her dresser. Rumpled clothes are strewn over most surfaces. Her sister isn't exactly known for her tidiness, and right now that's maybe a good thing. It's not like Chloe will notice if she moves stuff around.

Even with the mess, it doesn't take Genny long to find the blue photo album. It's sitting on the shelf below the night table. Although her sister won't admit it—refuses to talk about it most of the time, in fact—Genny knows she regularly looks at pictures of their parents. It's hard to believe Chloe even remembers them. She'd only been a toddler when they'd died. But even if she doesn't, she clearly thinks about them. This is something Genny understands all too well.

Sitting on the edge of the bed, she opens the album and starts examining each photo. Before she even gets to the fourth page, she can no longer deny the evidence in front of her. Her mother looks the same in every picture. She's not sure she would have noticed if JP hadn't dropped this bomb on her today, but now that she's looking for it, it seems so obvious.

Could Mom really have been an immortal?

But that's ridiculous.

Isn't it?

Flipping the page, another picture catches her eye. This one shows her mother arm in arm with a brown-skinned young woman with straight, long black hair. Their foreheads are tilted together and they wear matching smiles. The woman seems familiar to Genny. She thinks she remembers her from when she'd been small. Is this JP's mom?

She has so many questions, and the only way to get answers would mean letting herself consider the idea that JP might have been telling her the truth.

His voice speaks up in her head again: *See if you can cut yourself. Even just a pinprick.*

That's the test he had told her to try. Frowning even deeper now, Genny puts the album back on Chloe's shelf and returns to her room. After closing the door behind her, she pulls open a dresser drawer. A jumble of items crowd it and it takes her several second's scrounging before she digs out a safely pin. Opening it and bending the pin away from the clasp, she stares at the sharp point. Has she ever cut herself before? Has she ever bled? She knows her friends have—she's seen them suck on their fingers to stop the bleeding—but she has no memory of ever seeing her own blood. The more she thinks about it, the more she realizes how unusual this must be.

She puts the pin point against the pad of one fingertip and tenses. It's going to hurt, she knows that much. She doesn't want to hurt herself, but she needs to be sure JP is wrong. Even if he'll never know it, because she never intends to see him again. Pressing down, she watches her skin dent from the pressure and she waits for the pain. But it doesn't come. The tip of the pin doesn't pierce her at all. She pushes harder, but she can't make it penetrate.

That's strange, she thinks with a deep frown. Something must be wrong with the pin. She tosses it in the garbage and heads downstairs. Gran sits in the living room reading.

"Just grabbing a cookie," she calls out as she passes. No one who knows Genny would ever question that.

In the kitchen, she actually does pick up a couple of cookies. Then she takes the sharpest, pointiest knife from the knife block. Upon further consideration, she also grabs a few paper towels. Just in case. Hiding the knife behind her, she munches a cookie as she hurries back to her room.

At first she just sits on her bed and eats her snack. She's well aware this plan is crazy, just as crazy as the guy who put it in her head in the first place. She should not be letting his crazy rub off on her. But she has to know. Crazy or not, she has to prove this to herself. She'll never be able forget about it until she's sure what JP told her is as insane as she knows it has to be.

Genny wads up the paper towels on her dresser and lays her pinky finger across them, rationalizing that she uses it least. Bracing herself, she places the sharp edge of the knife against her finger and pushes down.

Nothing.

She tries slicing back and forth as she presses, sure that will do it.

Still nothing.

Okay, this is definitely weird. She examines the blade closely. It looks sharp enough. So why won't it cut her? Feeling a bit frustrated, she tries with the tip. It works about as well as the pin.

Genny blows out a sigh. This is getting ridiculous.

You'll be able to, but only if you really try.

She opens her hand on top of the paper towels. With her free hand, she raises the knife and brings it down as hard as she can onto the middle of her palm. Which is an incredibly stupid thing to do. For most people, anyway.

Genny feels a sharp bloom of pain, but it's gone as quickly as it came. It's so fast she barely has time to process the sensation and mutter, "Ouch!" Removing the knife, she sees a dot of bright red blood on her hand. It's so red and round and perfect, and she can't help staring at it in wonder. After a moment, she wipes it away with the paper towel and notices there is no wound beneath. Not even a reddened spot on her skin.

It's already healed.

After finding a free bench at Willowdale Park, Genny watches a couple of kids playing Frisbee with their dog while she waits. She doesn't have to wait long. Soon, JP walks up and sits beside her.

"I take it you tried the experiment I suggested?" he asks quietly.

She frowns, but nods. "I don't know why, but I did." After she'd cleaned up, she'd swallowed her pride and called to ask him to meet her. It seemed like the only way to get the answers she needs.

"Were you able to cut yourself?"

"Eventually. A little. It took a lot of effort, though." She drags her fingers through her hair. "This is...I mean, I can't even..." She stops and sighs. "What the *hell* is going on?"

"I told you. We're immortal."

"I *know* what you said. But how is that even possible?"

JP stretches an arm along the back of the bench, leaning closer but not too close. She suspects he's trying not to scare her away again. "My mother and uncle live close by. I know the 'istory, but that's just facts and dates. I remember your mom, but they knew her whole family. Would you like to meet them?"

Genny hesitates. She's still in shock, and meeting other immortals—if that's even what they are—will only make it worse. "Have you already told your mother about me?"

JP nods. "I had to. You and your family are so important to us. There are entire books written about the Bourreaus."

"Really?"

"Really. Not public books; books kept in the library in Lentemps. And I've read all of them. If you're willing to come with me, my mother really wants to meet you. It's totally up to you. I told her you might not be ready for such things yet."

"I'm not. My mind is reeling. But I want answers." And since they'd been friends, Genny is pretty sure her mom would've wanted her to know JP's mom. "So let's go."

His eyes narrow as he examines her face. "Are you sure? Because I can take you to meet them another day if you need more time to process all this."

She gets to her feet. "I'm sure. Lead the way."

They walk until they come to a white triplex. JP rings the bell of the far right unit, and a few moments later a young Indian woman pulls open the door. Genny's recognizes her immediately. This is her mom's friend from the photo.

JP's mother's eyes light up the instant she sees them. "Oh, Jean-Paul! I did not realize you were coming by today." Turning to Genny, she says, "And you are... Mon Dieu! You must be Geneviève! I should 'ave known. You resemble your grand-mère. I'm *so* glad you came."

"Genny, this is my mother, Marie."

"Hello," Genny greets her. "Just Genny is fine."

"Ever so pleased to meet you, Genny. Please come inside." Marie waves past her and they follow her into the entranceway.

JP leans in to kiss Marie on both cheeks. "Salut, Maman." Marie beams up at her tall son. There is a clear family resemblance, especially in their matching smiles.

It's weird watching them. Marie looks so young and pretty, like any girl Genny might see at the club, or out shopping, or anywhere, really. How can she possibly be JP's mother? Genny can't wrap her head around it.

"Won't you please sit down? I'll make us some tea," Marie offers.

JP ushers Genny into the living room, where a dark-haired guy about their age sits watching television. She doesn't think he's JP's brother, as he is light-skinned like her. The man glances up when they come in, then switches off the television and gets to his feet, extending a hand to her.

"You, my dear, mus' be Geneviève Bourreau," he says with a French accent thicker than either JP's or Marie's. "I am René Levoyant, JP's oncle."

Right. JP had mentioned that his mother lived with his uncle. While he has his mother's eyes and smile, she can see a lot of his uncle in him, too. Both are tall and slim, with a thick shock of hair.

Shaking René's outstretched fingers, she replies, "Nice to meet you. I'm Genny Dupont, actually." It's unsettling that these strangers already know who she is. Does everyone in JP's family know about her? Everyone in that French town he'd mentioned? Unreal.

"You do not 'ave your mother's name?" René asks as he resumes his seat. "Why ever not?"

Genny shrugs. "In Canada most children take their father's last name." She's surprised he doesn't already know this.

René nods. "Yes, but your family 'as always followed this tradition. The Bourreau women were...are...special." He pats the arm of the couch next to him and Genny and JP take a seat. "Do you know nothing of your family, Geneviève? Your legacy?"

Glancing at JP, she shakes her head. What does she know of Bourreau traditions? Not a damn thing. "My parents died a long time ago. This is all brand new to me."

Marie enters the room with a tray of cups and a teapot. "I'm sure she wants some answers, René. She must be feeling over...what is the word?" She looks to JP.

"Overwhelmed?" JP offers.

Marie sits in the vacant chair across from them. "Overwhelmed, oui. And who could blame her?" She pours out tea into the cups. It smells fragrant and floral.

"This is definitely overwhelming," Genny agrees. She's starting to feel like she doesn't know who she even is anymore. To think she'd woken up this morning excited about the new guy she'd met the night before, never guessing that meeting him would change her life—and her understanding of her family, herself—forever.

"You and my mother were friends?" she asks Marie. "Can you tell me about her?"

"Of course. What do you remember?"

"I can still recall her face, and her voice. I remember helping her with my little sister, and her reading us French children's stories that I only understood parts of. But, please, tell me what she was really like, if you can?"

Marie takes a sip of tea and leans back in her chair. "Angelique was my dearest friend. Losing her was one of the most painful losses I've ever been dealt. We came to Canada together, you know. In 1971. JP was just twelve and his brother, Thierry, nineteen. My older son Claude chose to remain in France, and my daughter Bea lives in London with her family."

"Gran told me my mother met my father here."

"Yes, she did. Your grand-mère Madeleine was quite displeased about your mother's choice to marry a non-immortal. It would've caused them such difficulties later, if they'd been able to live out their lives. Your father would've aged and died while Angelique stayed young and perfect. Rules for marriage and children are very strict in our community, as you might understand. We need to keep the immortal bloodlines pure, or someday our descendants will no longer be immortal at all. You and your sister are the only half-immortals we are aware of."

Genny frowns. "What does that mean? That Chloe and I are half immortal? Neither of us has ever been sick or injured. My skin is nearly impenetrable. Will that be temporary? Will we still grow old and die someday?"

"We do not know," René says. "Perhaps you 'ave more of your mother's genes. Perhaps more of your father's. From what you say, you 'ave all the traits of an immortal. Right now. But only time will tell."

"Your mother didn't care about our rules," Marie continues with a wistful smile. "She liked to do things her own way, much to your grand-mère's despair. Angelique had been engaged to a local man, but they broke things off after a big argument. Angelique broke things off, I mean to say. That was one of the reasons your grand-mère agreed that she could come with us to Canada. She was just supposed to stay with me a few weeks and then return 'ome, but she met Marcus and..."

"The rest is history," Genny finishes with a small smile.

Marie nods. "Oui. They married and were blessed with you and your sister. And for a while everyone was 'appy."

Genny's smile vanishes and a soft sigh slips out. "Until the accident."

"Until the accident."

"It was no accident!" René states vehemently.

Genny turns to him with surprise. "What do you mean? They died in a car crash."

"They did," Marie says, shooting her brother-in-law a disapproving look. "But we believe that it might not have been an accident. There is much more to tell you."

"Maman, maybe we could save this for another day?" JP says. "Genny's got a lot to process already."

"No," Genny brushes her fingers against his forearm. "Let her speak. I want to know."

"Your family, the Bourreaus, they are more than just immortal," Marie says. "Some, although not all, of the women could use magic. Your mother and grandmother could, but your mother's sisters could not. Do you recall ever causing anything peculiar to occur that you could not explain?"

Genny shakes her head. "Not that I'm aware of. But magic? Are you seriously telling me my mother could, like, cast spells and stuff?"

René replies, "Oh yes. She was quite talented at it. Not as talented as your grandmother, but still, she was very strong."

"My mom was a *witch*?" Genny looks to JP. He just shrugs.

"She was," Marie continues. "Although we do not use that word. We prefer to say *mage*. Angelique was so much more than a mage, though. She was a true warrior."

"What d'you mean?"

Marie glances at René, then back to Genny. "Your mother, and her mother, and her mother, going back many centuries were defenders of peace. Slayers of evil. There are dark creatures out there that feed on and murder 'umans. And the women in your family, they kill them."

Both Genny's eyebrows fly up. "You're joking!"

Marie shakes her head.

Genny has accepted a lot of insane things today, but this is a step too far. "C'mon! Evil creatures that feed on humans? Are you talking vampires? Demons? Ghouls? Because none of those things are real."

"Correction," René says. "Two of those aren't real. Vampires, 'owever, are very real. They are our natural enemies. And you, my dear, are a vampire hunter, just like your mother was before you."

Genny stares at him wide-eyed. She is about to tell him he's crazy, that they are all crazy, and walk out the door, when she remembers that perfectly red drop of blood on her palm. And the cut that healed in seconds. If she's really an immortal, how much bigger of a stretch is it to believe in vampires?

"Unfortunately he speaks the truth," Marie said. "I wish it were not so."

Something occurs to Genny and she whips her head back to Marie, "You think my parents were killed by vampires?" she asks, her pitch rising.

Marie's gaze shoots to René's again. "We believe so."

"Why?" Genny can feel her pulse racing. "What makes you think that? Were there bites marks on their necks? Can vampires even bite through immortal skin?"

"They have extremely sharp teeth," Marie said. "I imagine it's more difficult than regular 'umans, but yes, they can bite us. But your parents did not die from vampire bites. Their car caught on fire. Fire can kill us, and vampires, too, if our bodies are burned to ash. We believe they caused the accident and made sure the flames incinerated them both."

Sighing, Genny leans forward, bracing her elbows on her knees. "Okay. So vampires are real. If my mother's family was immortal, and yet they are all dead, did vampires kill them all?"

"Oui," René spits. He looks disgusted. "The filthy creatures have targeted Bourreaus for over a century. And if they find out about you, you will also be in danger. You and your sister both."

"My uncle is right," JP says. "And there are vampires here in Toronto. Not many, but a few. I've seen them myself."

Genny squares her shoulders defiantly. "But I'm a vampire slayer, right? You said I was born one? What does that mean? How am I different? And how can I kill them?"

"You need to be trained, and there are no slayers left to train you," Marie says sadly. It's obvious how much she misses Genny's mother. "What it means is that you are stronger than others. 'Ave you noticed this?"

She thinks about it. "Maybe. I've accidentally broken things before."

"And you are probably quite agile and dexterous," JP tells her. "I think you would learn combat skills quickly."

"Well, that's great. But there's no one left to teach me to fight or kill vampires. Should I sign up for a karate class or something? Or sword fighting? Maybe crossbow? Crossbow looks like it could be fun." She's starting to sound frantic.

"All those things are great ideas," Marie agrees. "But we will help you. I used to spar with your mother to help her practice. I will try to train you as best I can. She would want me to."

Genny shakes her head in amazement. "This is...a lot." *Understatement of the year.* "I think I need to go home now, but thank you so much for your hospitality." She gets to her feet and JP follows.

Marie walks with them to the front door. "I 'ope to see you again soon, Genny."

"I'm sure you will," she replies, forcing a smile. As she reaches for the doorknob, Genny notices her fingers trembling.

"You've really seen vampires in Toronto?" she asks JP. He's walking with her back to her house.

"A few times. There was one at Apothecary last night. That's why I got you out of there so quickly."

She stops and looks up at him. "*What?* You're kidding?"

His expression is not that of a guy who's kidding. "I didn't want him to spot you. It's important they don't learn how to find you."

Something important occurs to her. "How can you tell which ones are vampires?"

"We have auras. Supernatural beings, I mean. Immortals have a golden glow about them. Vampire's auras are a kind of pinkish-red."

Supernatural beings? Is that what she is? It still sounds so insane. Genny stares up at him. "I don't see any gold light around you."

JP smiles. "Look closer. You're not used to seeing it."

Squinting, she tries to focus. "Nope, still nothing."

He looks behind him, then moves to the other side of the sidewalk into the shadow of a tall hedge. "Sorry. I was backlit. What about now?"

Genny takes a few steps backward and studies him. Could there be a slight yellowish glow around his face? "Maybe? I think I see something."

"It will get easier the more you look for it. And once you're used to seeing it, it'll just become normal."

"So my aura is how you knew I was an immortal?"

"Yes. You and the vampire both. It was a busy night."

Genny just shakes her head as they continue walking. "I can't believe I actually have vampires to worry about along with all this other stuff."

"It's good you met me then, because my family and I will assist you. And once you're trained, you will be able to protect yourself just fine, I think."

"Hope so." Then something else occurs to her. "So are werewolves real, too?"

JP snorts. "Men that can turn into wolves at the full moon? Pure Hollywood fiction. Although I 'ave read ancient tales of shapeshifters, but I've seen no evidence they were anything more than legend."

She shrugs. "After today, I have no idea what's real and what isn't anymore."

"Well, when you think of more questions, just call. I'll do my best to answer them."

"Thank you." She flashes him a warm smile, realizing he's been incredibly patient with her today.

When they get to Gran's, Genny decides against inviting him in. Promising to call her later, JP leaves and she heads inside, once again turning both locks behind her. After grabbing a cookie from the kitchen, she finds Chloe on the living room couch with textbooks spread out around her.

"Another exam tomorrow?"

"Last one, finally. But it's Geography." Chloe sighs. She's been struggling with Geography in her final year, and Genny knows she's worried a poor grade will bring down her overall average.

"Good luck. I can't help you with that." Pausing at the bottom of the stairs, Genny turns back to her. "Can I ask you a question?"

Her sister looks back up. "Shoot."

"You ever remember being sick? Or me being sick? Because for the life of me, I can't."

Chloe frowns. After a moment, she replies, "Not really. But we must've been, right?"

"Right," Genny agrees. "We probably just forgot. Because we are just so super healthy." She takes a huge bite of her cookie and they both laugh. Although she knows she'll have to eventually, she has no plans to tell Chloe any of this until she gets it figured out herself.

When she hits the top of the steps, as she always does she immediately imagines what it would be like to fall down them, and how it would feel to break her neck. But then she stops herself.

I am immortal. I'm not going to break anything. I can never die that way. I may never die at all.

Holy shit.

Chapter 3
By Your Side

Quinn Sinclair is restless. It's nothing new. Quinn is often restless, often paces the floors of his house, or goes for long walks through the city. His mind is nearly always on overdrive, although most around him wouldn't know it. Reticent on the outside, he frequently has rapid-fire thoughts flying around within. Except when he sleeps, of course. Sleep is his only refuge from himself. But sleep is a long way off right now.

This time it's not his usual preoccupations. He's wondering about the two immortals he'd spotted at the club last night. The man, he's seen around a few times, but the woman is new. Quinn is sure he doesn't know her, yet she'd seemed so familiar. There had been something about her he couldn't quite figure out. So he'd followed her home. Discreetly, at a distance, until she and her human friend had gone inside. Then he'd moved closer.

The girls had gone to bed in an upper floor room. Quinn could hear her friend snoring, but the immortal had still been awake. Listening closely, he'd even been able to detect her heartbeat. It had started to slow as she, too, had been about to drift off. So he'd left.

He can't seem to stop thinking about her. She's not like other immortals. Her aura isn't yellow like her male friend's; it's paler, like moonlight. It had given her a rather ethereal glow. He's never seen a being with an aura like hers before.

When Cassandra had come home in the hour before dawn, he'd told her about the immortals he'd seen. She had no explanation for the woman's strange aura, but she hadn't seemed too interested in it, either. She'd just excused herself to go upstairs. Quinn had heard her on the phone before he'd gone to bed, but he hadn't bothered listening. It had probably been Assembly business, and he has little interest in any of that. Not unless circumstances force his involvement, anyway.

The back door swings open and, think of the devil, in walks Cassandra. When she sees him, she greets him with a smile.

"Quinolin! What's up? No, wait, let me guess. Brooding? Journaling? Some other form of self-flagellation? All of the above?"

Quinn regards her skeptically. "You have a wee bit at the corner of your mouth. Messy supper?"

Cassandra smirks, her tongue darting out to lick away the splotch of red. "Breakfast, actually."

Quinn has known Cassandra for nearly sixty-five years. They'd met in Chicago back in 1929, just weeks before the stock market crash. Over the decade he'd spent in the windy city, they had become friends, confidants, and even lovers for a while. But that had been a long time ago. Now they are partners in this long and often pointless life. Sometimes one of them will leave for a few months or years, but they always find one another again. They are each other's anchors. And though he doesn't always agree with her, he can't imagine his life without her.

"Did anyone call while I was out?" she asks, her long red curls bouncing off her shoulders as she strides over.

Quinn's brows arch. "No. Who are you expecting?"

As if by magic, the phone on the kitchen counter starts to ring. Cassandra hurries to grab it, cradling the handset between her shoulder and her ear while she washes up at the sink. "Danforth Dungeon. We've got shackles in every size," she says cheerfully. There's a pause while she listens, then: "Oops. You'll hafta picture me saluting."

Having no interest in eavesdropping, Quinn grabs his journal—still open to the blank page he'd turned it to before he'd begun pacing—and goes up to his room.

A few minutes later, Cassandra bursts in without knocking. "That was Kellan. He has a job for us."

Quinn sighs. Kellan Lahaine is the General and right-hand man to Lillabeta, Grand Mistress of the Assembly. He is not a man to be trifled with. Well, truthfully he's not a man at all. But while Kellan is both powerful and dangerous, the Grand Mistress is downright terrifying. It puts Quinn and Cassandra in a precarious position. They can't very well refuse a job from Kellan or risk the wrath of the entire Assembly. They'd made a life for themselves here in Toronto the past nineteen years. It'd be a shame to have to leave it all behind.

"Great." He glares at Cassandra. "I assume this is because you reported what I told you?"

"I had to. You know as well as I do that staying in the Assembly's good books is the only way we can keep living free and safe. And that means sometimes doing work for them. They don't ask all that often."

He grits his teeth. "I am well aware. And when they do ask, it tends to be something unpleasant so they keep their own hands clean. I'm tired of us being their lackeys."

She sits beside him on the bed. "I know you are. Believe me, I am too. But it's important we stay under their umbrella. The consequences of refusing…"

Quinn nods. "I know. So what does *General* Kellan want this time?"

Her face brightens. "It's actually not so bad."

Genny rolls over on her bed, the phone cord stretching around her bicep. "He's taking me out tonight."

"Where are you going?" Dawn asks. She sounds excited for Genny.

"No idea. He didn't say."

"Well, did you ask him what you should wear?"

"I did, but he said it didn't matter, that I'd look good in anything."

"Good? Not pretty? Not amazing? Just *good*?"

Laughing, Genny says, "Good is good." She doesn't care where they go, although she hopes it will involve dinner.

"What did you guys do on Sunday?"

"Met up for coffee. Hung out in the park. Went to meet his mother." All of these things are true, but Genny doesn't tell her all the unbelievable information she'd learned while doing them. She's nowhere near ready to explain it to anyone. Not yet.

"You met his *mother*? On day two? Holy crap, Gen. That's fast!"

"I guess. He asked me if I wanted to meet her, and I figured why not? She's nice. You'd like her."

"And you must really like JP."

"Maybe," Genny replies, deadpan. "Don't you?"

Dawn chuckles. "Yes, although I don't really know him well enough to have much of an opinion. He's cute. And he's into you. And you're my best friend, so I'll have to get to know him better. If you guys aren't out doing something romantic, maybe we can all go back to Apothecary on Saturday?"

"I'll ask." Glancing at her watch, Genny frowns. Time is growing short. "I'd better run. I'm still in my work clothes and I gotta get changed before he gets here."

"Call me tomorrow and tell me how it went?"

"Obviously!" Laughing, she hangs up.

Right at six, the doorbell rings and Genny rushes to get it. When she pulls open the door she finds a smiling JP on the front porch. It's that shy smile again, the same one he'd given her at the bar that had piqued her interest. She wonders if he's nervous about their first official date.

"Hi," she greets him. "C'mon in for a minute while I run and grab my purse." Gran appears in the doorway to the kitchen, wiping her hands on a dishtowel and looking at them curiously. "Gran, this is JP. Mom was friends with his mother. Be right back." With that, she dashes up to her room.

When she returns, she finds Chloe peppering JP with questions while Gran watches with an amused expression.

"And she really used to visit us when I was small?"

JP nods. "She remembers when you were born."

"Does she have any baby photos of us?"

"She might. I'll 'ave to ask."

"Yes, ask her. And bring her over sometime soon so we can meet her."

Behind Chloe's back, Genny shoots JP a look. Meeting Marie is *so* not going to happen until she figures out how to explain all the craziness to her sister and Gran.

"I'll mention it," he replies, but his eyes are now on Genny.

"Ready to go?" she asks him. "Thanks for entertaining him," she says to Chloe. "I hate to break it to you, but he's all mine now." She takes JP by the elbow and guides him out the door.

"Sorry about that. My sister can be kind of intense sometimes."

"Nothing to be sorry for. I like her."

They seem to be walking toward a car at the curb. "Wait," Genny says. "You have a car?"

JP chuckles. "Yep."

"You never mentioned it?"

He shrugs, but he's still smiling.

"So we don't have to take the bus tonight?"

Unlocking and opening the passenger door for her, he replies, "Not tonight. But I do use the TTC a lot. It's much easier in this city to use mass transit than deal with traffic. And parking can be difficult." The car is a black, late 1980's Buick Regal, probably built in the nearby city of Oshawa. "It's actually Oncle René's car," he explains as he starts the engine, "but he lets me borrow it when I need it."

"Well I'm glad you borrowed it tonight. So where're we going?"

His eyes are on the road as he makes the turn onto Sheppard Avenue. "You like Italian?"

"Food, men, or salad dressing?" Genny replies, laughing.

He shoots her a glance. "That depends. I'll need to know the answer to all three."

Genny pretends to think about it. After a moment, she says, "Yes, yes, and yes."

"You like Italian men?"

"I don't know. I've never dated an Italian guy. I might."

"Do you want me to see if I can find you one? So you can find out?" Genny can tell he's trying to keep his face serious, but he's mostly failing.

"Nah. I like the guy I'm dating now."

JP looks over at her again. He's now smiling widely. "Good to know." The sight of that smile makes her chest tighten in the best possible way.

He takes her to Il Fornello on Eglinton Avenue. They each demolish a big plate of pasta, plus garlic bread, plus tiramisu for dessert. Not once does he comment on the amount of food she can eat, something her previous boyfriend had loved teasing her about. Maybe all immortals have huge appetites? Genny still has so much to learn.

After dinner, they decide to go for a walk along the street. Some shops are closed for the day, but music blasts from the open door of a record store near the corner of Yonge Street.

Genny perks up. "Want to go in?"

"Lead the way."

They browse the racks, shelves, and boxes until Genny pulls out a vinyl copy of The Mission's *God's Own Medicine*. "Oh hey! I've been looking for this. And it's only four bucks."

JP offers to buy it for her, but Genny refuses. "Thanks, but no. You got dinner. I can buy my own record." Catching the hurt look on his face, she adds, "I'm a self-sufficient girl. You don't have to buy me stuff to earn my affection. Just be yourself. It's already working."

"Is it?" he asks, his grin now mischievous.

"Try me and see."

Once they're back outside, JP reaches for her hand. His palm is warm against hers, and she can't help wondering what it would be like to kiss him. They walk around for another half hour, but since it's a weeknight and Genny has to work in the morning, they decide to call it a night. During the drive, they chat mostly about music. She's surprised to learn that JP is into classical music and he can even play the piano. He hasn't heard of a lot of the bands she likes, but when she mentions specific songs he might have heard at Apothecary, he recognizes them.

"If you're not into goth music, why do you even go to that club?" she asks as they pull up in front of her house.

"My friends like it. There are always lots of pretty girls there. And I should know, because I met the prettiest one in the whole place."

Genny laughs. "Cheesy. But charming."

He leans closer. "Is it still working?" he asks softly.

"Is what still working?"

"Earning your affection?"

"Try me and see," she repeats.

His nervous smile flashes across JP's face for a second, but then it disappears as he gazes intently into her eyes. Lifting a hand, he gently brushes the side of her face with his fingertips, sending a shiver up her spine. He tilts his head slightly, closes his eyes, and shifts forward until their lips meet.

Unlike his dancing, it turns out he's very good at kissing.

Twenty minutes later, Genny slips under the covers and closes her eyes, remembering her date with JP. Specifically, remembering kissing him. And holding his hand. And their goofy conversations. But mostly the kiss.

That should be fodder for some great dreams tonight, she thinks, reaching to turn out the lamp. Just as the room darkens, she gets that weird tingling sensation she'd felt on Saturday night. All the hairs on her forearms rise and the ones on the nape of her neck immediately follow. It's strange, but not unpleasant. It's like her entire body is lightly vibrating. Switching the light back on, she gets up and goes into the hall. Carefully opening Chloe's door, she looks around the room. Her sister is sound asleep in a huddle, breathing deep and even. Next she goes downstairs and looks in the living room and kitchen. She peeks out into the yard. She even inches open the door to Gran's bedroom and checks in there.

Nothing is amiss. She can find no source for the feeling. As she tiptoes back upstairs, the thrumming vanishes. This time it had lasted longer. Clearly it hadn't been from the Zombies.

So weird.

Genny gets back into bed and again switches off the light. Even stranger than the sensation itself had been, she kind of misses it now that it's gone.

Rolling over, she puts it out of her mind and drifts off to sleep thinking of JP's lips on hers.

Rain drums on the roof as the car moves through the night. It's so dark that the headlights' twin beams illuminate little but raindrops, with barely a glimpse of the pavement below.

Turning to the man driving, she's surprised to see it's her father. She opens her mouth to greet him, but instead says, "I 'ave done everything I can think of to protect them. You know I 'ave."

"I know. But if something does happen to us, and they're discovered..."

"They won't be. Not for many years. Perhaps not ever."

He sighs. "I hope you're right. But I still think we should tell my mother the truth."

She presses her lips together and doesn't respond. If anything happens to them, Agnes will take the girls, but she doesn't need to know the real reason why. The fewer people that know, the better. With any luck, all this worry and preparation will have been for nothing.

The radio is playing REO Speedwagon's "Keep On Loving You." She reaches to turn it up and starts to sing along.

Suddenly two men appear on the road in their path, abruptly silencing her off-key singing. Dad slams the brakes and swerves, jolting them both forward in their seats. She gasps and looks to him, then back out the windscreen. The men have vanished. Her father tries to course correct, but another man appears. Then another. The car starts to fishtail and spin on the slick surface. Reaching for her father's arm, she clutches it as their car leaves the highway and hits something. Hard. The impact drives the air from her lungs.

Something digs into her chest, making it difficult to breathe. It's the seatbelt. She tries to undo it, panic swelling inside her. Finally freeing herself, she sucks in air as she turns to her dad. His face is against the steering wheel. Blood pours from a gash on his forehead. She finds his wrist and checks his pulse. Thank God. His heart still beats.

"Marc? Marcus!"

His eyelids flutter.

She smells something acrid and reaches for her door handle, but the door refuses to budge. Cracks like spider webs cover her window, spreading wider as she watches. Out of the now thinning rain, she sees a man materialize. He's staring at her. She opens her mouth to scream at him to help them, but before she can speak, she spots the tell-tale pinkish glow around his head.

A vampire.

Reaching to the floor by her feet, she tries to locate her bag. Inside are wooden stakes and sharp knives. Finding it wedged under her seat, she pulls it onto her lap and looks up to see if the vampire is still there. But he's gone.

With a loud whoosh*, the engine catches on fire.*

Genny jolts awake with a scream stuck in her throat and her body drenched in sweat. Shoving off the sheet, she lies gasping in the dark. Had that been how her parents had died? Roasted to death in their car while vampires watched?

She may be only one of two slayers left, unprepared and untrained, but Genny vows she will make them pay for what they have done.

Every last one of them.

Chapter 4
Face to Face

"So how do you kill a vampire?" Genny asks JP. They're sitting holding hands on Gran's back deck. Chloe isn't home and Gran is napping, so Genny assumes she can talk freely about this. "Stake to the heart? Sunlight? All the usual stuff?"

"Yes to stakes. Not sunlight, although they do avoid it as it's apparently quite painful. Vampires and immortal are actually very similar. Except they are cruel, undead things that drink blood to survive."

Genny snorts. "How are we similar?"

"Both can only be killed by destroying the 'eart or brain. Or by being burned to ash, which destroys both organs."

"What about garlic or holy water? Crucifixes? Silver? Any of those work?"

"Garlic is a myth perpetrated by vampire fiction. They can also cross running water without issue. For reasons I don't really understand, contact with silver and blessed objects like crucifixes and 'oly water burns them much like sunlight does. It only weakens them, though. It won't actually kill them. And they recover fast like we do, so, like us, any non-lethal damage is only temporary."

Nodding, Genny mutters, "Got it. So focus on the heart or the head." Then she thinks of something else. "What about the needing an invitation to enter thing?"

"True, but only for private residences. Not public buildings, which you probably already guessed from the vampire at Apothecary on Saturday. So you are safe inside your 'ouse. Or mine."

"Good. At least I only have to worry about Chloe and Gran when they're out."

JP sighs. "Only if you're discovered. With any luck, you won't be. And if you need someone to keep an eye on your family, please let me know."

She leans her head on his shoulder. "I might just take you up on that."

"Anytime." He squeezes her fingers.

"Has your mom said anything about when we could start training?"

He chuckles low in his throat and the sound of it gives her a sudden urge to end to this conversation and kiss him instead. "Eager to get started? I'll give her a call when I get 'ome."

"I keep having weird dreams about vampires lately. I know this sounds crazy, but they almost feel like messages from my ancestors. It's like they want me to take over the slayer reins for them."

"Really? I've read of Bourreaus having odd dreams before, like ancestral consciousness or something."

Lifting her head up, she looks at him. "What does that mean?"

"If I understand it correctly, it's like being able to share memories. But the book was pretty vague."

"These books about my family history? Can you show me them?"

He smiles. "Only if you come to Lentemps with me one day."

"Could someone ship them over?"

Shaking his head, he says, "All the books on immortal families are in the restricted section of the Lentemps library. If the librarian doesn't know you, you don't get access. Those books do not leave the library."

Genny sighs. "Well, that's a pain. I can't afford a trip to France anytime soon. But someday."

JP squeezes her hand. "Someday. I'd be 'appy to go with you when you're ready. Whenever you want."

She moves her face closer until they're nearly touching. Whatever cologne he's wearing smells so good she wants to lick him. "Right now, what I want is this," she murmurs, and presses her lips to his.

On Saturday evening, Dawn calls Genny to say she's already downtown. She got called into work to cover a shift, so she'll meet Genny and JP at Apothecary later. Genny tries to call JP to let him know, but gets no answer. Strangely he does not have an answering machine.

She blows out a frustrated sigh. He had mentioned he'd be at his mom's most of today, so she assumes that's where he is. Last night they'd gone out to a movie and afterward he'd told her somewhat apologetically that his friends also wanted to go to the club again. He'd asked if Genny would mind terribly if he just met her and Dawn there. Of course she'd agreed. It's no big deal. Much more importantly, he'd promised he'd go home with her after.

Genny knows he'd meant he'd see her to her door, but she's kind of hoping he'll invite her back to his place tonight. It's been a week now and they'd seen each other nearly every day since they'd met. Kissing him is great, awesome actually, but Genny is ready for more. She's pretty sure JP is, too, especially after last night's marathon make out session in his uncle's Buick. She'd gone inside flushed and unsatisfied, but happy. Maybe tonight she'll be able to fall asleep without the middle condition.

She puts on her cutest bra and underwear, dons a sexy black dress with a plunging V-neck, and curls her hair. Once again, she tries calling JP to tell him she's heading downtown alone, but there's still no answer. Maybe it's for the best. He'd only worry about her going by herself, and there's no need. She knows the route perfectly well, as she takes the majority of it every day to work. So after applying deep red lipstick, she sprays on a touch of perfume—Calvin

Klein's *Obsession* naturally—and heads out to catch the bus.

The bus stop is two streets over, only a five or six minute walk. There's still some light in the sky, but the sun is rapidly setting and the mature oaks lining the street cast deep shadows over the sidewalk. As she approaches a particularly dark section, she moves out into the road, and as she does, she gets the now-familiar tingle.

She stops and looks around, again searching for the source of it, and again spotting nothing out of the ordinary. Increasing her speed, she steps back into the shadows. It's only about twenty feet until the streetlight brightens her path again. Twenty feet isn't that far.

Or so she thinks.

Before she can reach the relative safely of the light, a hand snakes around her neck and a damp cloth is pressed over her nose and mouth. She has just time to register a chemical smell.

And then nothing.

Genny comes back slowly, shifting in and out of partial awareness for who knows how long. She registers that she's lying on something hard and cool. There's a pillow beneath her head and a blanket seems to be partially covering her legs. She opens her eyes, but it's too dark to see anything. Where *is* she? The last thing she remembers is...is walking to the bus stop?

Wait. Did someone grab me? Panic bubbles up in the back of her throat. She takes a deep breath and tries to remind herself that freaking out won't help. Instead, she tries to assess her surroundings. The surface below her feels like concrete. Although it's hot outside, it's chilly enough in here to have her pulling the blanket higher. And there's a musty odor. Could she be in a basement?

Has she been kidnapped? By a vampire? JP had told her he'd seen one at Apothecary last weekend. Maybe the creature had spotted her that night after all. But even if it had, how would it have known who she was and how to find her?

The blanket is soft against her bare shins. If she's been kidnapped, why would the kidnapper provide comfort like a pillow and blanket? And she's not bound. She shifts onto her knees, feeling along until one hand hits a vertical metal bar. Beside it is another one. And another. Her heart sinks. No wonder she's not tied up. She's in a cage.

She really *has* been kidnapped. How much time has passed? JP and Dawn will notice when she doesn't show up at the club. She's confidant JP will quickly guess what happened. But how will he ever find her?

This is bad. Very bad.

"Hello?" she calls, shaking the bars hard enough to make the entire cage rattle.

There's no reply.

She gives the bars a few hard kicks, but they don't even bend. Exhaling hard in frustration, she follows them around until she understands her prison is about four feet by seven. Big enough to lie down in. Had this specifically been designed to hold humans? She suspects it might have been.

The back of the cage is against a wall. Genny puts the pillow behind her head and leans against it, unsure what she should do. Time passes, although she has no idea how much. She finds herself dozing in and out of sleep as she waits for someone to return. *Or something*, she thinks with a shudder.

The sound of footsteps crossing the floor above brings her back to alertness with a start. Her heartrate quickens. Something very bad might be about to happen. Seconds later, a bright rectangle opens high up and the silhouette of a person moves into view. As they start down the stairs, Genny scrambles to her feet.

Are they a vampire? Coming to kill me?

The answer to the first question is undoubtedly yes. She presses herself against the wall as they approach, desperately hoping the answer to the second is no. Or at the very least not right now.

Her eyes have adjusted to the dark, but the figure is backlit by the light from the open door above, so she's unable to make out any features. Remembering what JP had told her, she squints, examining their outline. Is that a faint reddish glow around the head? She's pretty sure it is. So it's a vampire.

"Are you gonna kill me?" she asks, shocking herself by voicing her fear.

She hears a snort. "Not me." It's a woman.

Genny's throat goes dry. "But someone is?"

"Obviously. You're not here for your scintillating personality. But don't fret. You have some time. They'll probably torture you for a while first."

"W-why?"

"D'uh. To get information. Why d'you think?"

"I d-don't know anything." Genny wishes she could stop the quiver in her voice, but her body isn't listening to her brain's commands right now.

"Not my problem." The vampire tosses something between the bars that hits Genny on the thigh, bouncing off and rolling away in the dark. Then the woman turns and speeds back up the steps. Genny gets a quick glimpse of red hair before the door is shut and the light is gone.

Stepping forward, she reaches out until her fingers hit the front bars and then feels around for the cage door. Once she finds it, she realizes it has a padlock on it. She tugs at it, knowing it won't open, but needing to try anyway. It doesn't budge. Her captor is not that stupid. Carefully she explores every inch of the cage, but she can find no possible point of escape. The bars are strong and unyielding. She has nothing she can use for leverage. Or for a weapon. Which means she's screwed.

She feels around for whatever had been thrown at her. It's a bottle of liquid. Could it be water? She twists off the cap and has a sniff. No smell. They'd given her a blanket and pillow. It's not that much of a stretch that they might give her water as well. If someone else is coming, they clearly need her alive and fairly well. Her throat hurts, probably from stress, so she throws caution to the wind and takes a drink. It's water, and its coldness on her throat feels like heaven right now.

Sitting on the pillow, she pulls the blanket back over her legs and lets her head fall against the bars. Someone is apparently coming to torture and kill her and she has no idea what to do with her feelings about that. She's terrified.

And worried for Chloe. But she's also wondering about the creatures who want her dead. She's never seen a vampire before. Though she'd tried, it had been too dark to make out the woman's features. No matter the danger, she can't help being curious. Are they like Anne Rice's vampires? Or more like Dracula? It's a stupid thing to focus on, but it's better than sitting here waiting to die.

And then there's JP. Will he be able to find her before it's too late? She wishes she had a way to get him a message. Blowing out a frustrated sigh, she closes her eyes and listens closely to her surroundings. The only thing she hears is a small creature—a mouse, probably—scurrying in the far corner. Maybe the woman left. If so, Genny's glad she's gone. She takes deep, slow breaths, focusing on the air passing in and out of her nose. It's a trick she sometimes uses when she's too wound up to sleep. It doesn't always work, but this time she can actually feel her body start to relax, bit by bit, muscle by muscle, working its blessed way up from the tips of her toes.

She doesn't even try to fight it.

Genny doesn't know if sedatives had been added to the water or if it had just been her over-stressed brain giving up and shutting down, but somehow she'd managed to fall asleep. When she wakes from her uneasy doze and remembers where she is, she notices that the tingling sensation has returned. Then she recalls that she'd felt it right before she'd been grabbed. Is it caused by being near a vampire? Like some sort of slayer Spidey-sense?

But no. The woman is a vampire, and there had been no tingle when she'd been here. Yet Genny can feel it now. Strange.

She detects the rising and falling cadence of people talking on the floor above, but it's too faint to make out any words. From the tones, she thinks it's a man and a woman, possibly the woman from before. Abruptly the talking stops, and moments later she hears the unmistakable slam of a door.

All is silent for a few minutes and she dares to hope they've left. Her tension shoots up when she hears footsteps start across the floorboards again. Not the same ones as before. Surer, swifter. The door at the top of the steps is pulled open and this time she sees the outline of what she thinks is man. He closes it soundlessly behind him and descends the stairs in the dark. His feet on the steps are softer than the woman's had been. If Genny hadn't known he's there, she might not have even heard him. The faint pink glow around his face is the only way she can tell where he is. With a sinking heart, she confirms he's another vampire.

Her entire body seems to be vibrating. She's terrified of course, but this isn't just fear. It's that strange sensation she's been feeling off and on all week. Suddenly she realizes the tingle is connected to this man. No, not a man, a vampire.

She hears a scraping sound. Before she can say anything, a low, sort of raspy voice says, "You are Genevieve Bourreau?" He pronounces it the English way like her parents used to. She detects just a hint of an accent. Not French. British? Or maybe Scottish?

"You clearly already know who I am," she says. "I think I deserve the same courtesy. Who are *you*?" She sounds a hell of a lot braver than she feels.

"My name is Quinn."

Although she isn't sure why, Genny understands he's told her the truth. Why would a kidnapper admit his real name to his kidnappee? Because she's going to die soon, that's why.

"Are you the one who grabbed me?"

Is that a soft sigh? "I had no choice."

Interesting. A contract kidnapping? Is he also a hit man—or hit vampire? A torturer? "Who do you work for?"

Exhaling a chuckle, he says, "You ask a lot of questions."

"Can you blame me?"

"Not really."

The scraping sound comes again and she realizes it from chair legs shifting across the concrete. He's taken a seat and pulled himself a bit closer.

"D'you really not know why you were taken?" There's that slight accent again. She's pretty sure it's Scottish. *Who knew there were Scottish vampires? Let's be real, who knew there were vampires at all?*

Genny shakes her head as she leans back against the bars. "I honestly don't know much of anything. But I think I'm starting to figure it out. I assume you work for the ones who killed my parents?" She can't even bring herself to say the word *vampires* out loud, which she realizes is ridiculous at this point. They're very real. And they're going to kill her soon if she can't figure a way out of this.

Quinn is silent. Before either of them can say more, there's another slam upstairs and the clomp of heavier footsteps. Genny just has time to think that the woman has returned when the basement door is pulled open.

"Seriously?" the now familiar voice calls down. "What the hell are you doing? Get your ass back up here. There's no point talking to her. They'll be here soon and then she'll no longer be our problem. And not long after that, she'll be dead."

Quinn blows out another low sigh, so soft Genny almost misses it. Without a word, he goes back upstairs and she's once more left alone in the dark.

They're both gone. The tingle had vanished about an hour ago and Genny's pretty sure both vampires had left together. She's all alone, left waiting for some psycho to come kill her.

At least she knows her future torturer-slash-murderer isn't either Quinn or the woman. They're just her captors. The middle men. Or middle vampires. She'd first felt the tingling sensation that night at the bar, so she assumes Quinn must've been the vampire JP had spotted at Apothecary.

Oh God! JP!

Will she ever see JP again? He must know she's missing by now. Genny has no idea what time it is, but her best guess is that it's somewhere in the early hours of Sunday morning. He's probably out combing the streets frantically searching for her. How will he ever find her in a city of two and a quarter million people?

She feels around for the pillow. Once located, she props it behind her head so she doesn't have to lean against the hard metal bars. Which of her captors gave her a pillow and blanket? A little comfort for the soon-to-be-dead girl? JP and his family had described vampires as vicious and heartless. Evil. Why would evil creatures care about her comfort?

Soft footsteps upstairs startle her, and the pillow falls to the side. Only one set of steps this time. The woman has a heavier stride, so it's either Quinn returning or someone new. Maybe it's her murderer? This plastic bottle won't be enough to fend them off.

The door at the top of the stairs opens and closes again, and again someone descends in the dark. When Genny hears the scrape of chair legs, she says, "Quinn?"

"Yes."

Whew. Then she scolds herself. Why is she relieved? He's still a vampire. "Have they come for me?"

"Not yet."

She sighs. How much time does she have left? And what does Quinn want? He's clearly come down to see her, but he's not very talkative. She decides to initiate. "Can I ask you a question?"

"Yes."

"You're a vampire, right?" The word feels alien on her tongue, and her cheeks warm.

He's quiet for a moment before replying, "I am."

She really wishes she could see him.

"Prove it."

Once more there's silence. Then: "How?"

Genny's hands are trembling. She's pretty sure she's being extremely stupid right now, but she has to know. "Show me your face."

She hears him moving around. Can vampires see in the dark? JP hasn't mentioned it, but based on tonight, she's pretty sure they can.

Suddenly a light appears. She sees a hand holding what looks like a camping lantern. A dark shape sits back down, the lantern resting on his knee. She can make out the curve of a cheek, the hard line of a nose. But that's it.

"Turn it brighter, please," she asks, not sure if he'll comply.

He does. A soft yellow glow illuminates him. It's not natural light, and there are still so many shadows, but she can see his face now. A dark swath of hair falls across his forehead. He has full lips and a straight nose. His eyes are too deep in shadow to be seen, but she can tell he's looking at her.

"You can see me just fine, can't you?

Quinn nods.

"It's a bit creepy that you can see me in the dark, but I need light to see you. Not really fair."

He chuckles and she sees a flash of teeth. They don't look like vampire fangs; they look like normal human teeth.

In for a pound, Gran likes to say. "Do you have fangs?"

His expression immediately turns serious. "When I need them."

"Show them to me."

Quinn regards her without answering. She suspects he doesn't really want to. She's about to speak again when he opens his mouth and raises his hand. Pointed canines suddenly extend, glinting in the light, and he bites into his own palm. Grimacing, he withdraws and the wound heals right in front of her. She's so fascinated by the blood on his hand that when she shifts her gaze back to his face he looks normal again.

"Ouch," she exclaims. "You didn't have to do that."

He shrugs. "You asked to see."

"I heal that fast, too. I just learned that last weekend. I poked myself with a kitchen knife until I drew blood, and it healed right away. It was totally surreal!"

His brows draw in as he stares at her. "Did you not know you were immortal?"

Genny shakes her head. "Not until a week ago."

"Your parents—"

"Died before they could tell me anything. I was only seven."

Something flashes across his face. Is that sympathy? If so, it surprises her. But it must be an act, because he's handing her over to vampires who will kill her. He's no better than they are, and she needs to remember this. She thinks of something else she wants to know. "Were you at Apothecary last Saturday?"

"Yes."

"My friend saw you. And I assume you saw us?"

Another nod.

Should she mention the tingle? If she's going to be dead soon, then why not? She might as well learn whatever she can. "Why can I sense when you're around, but not the woman?"

Now he looks surprised. Again, he inches the chair closer. "What is it you feel?"

"Like my skin is vibrating. Like a low-grade electric current is running over me. It doesn't hurt, but it's noticeable."

He frowns. For a moment he looks like he's about to say something, but then his face shuts down, all expression gone. "Do you need more water?"

Genny picks up the half-full bottle. "I'm good."

"Food?"

"No, thanks."

Without another word, Quinn turns off the lantern. A moment later she hears his footsteps ascend the stairs.

If she stays here, she'll die. It's as simple as that. But what can she do? She tugs on the lock again. It doesn't move. She shakes the cage door, but it only rattles. She has no weapons and no way to get a message to anyone. All she can do is wait for them to let her out and hope she can figure out a way to escape. But they're strong, and they're fast, and they can see in the dark. What chance does she have against a group of vampires?

No chance at all.

She opens the water and takes another long drink. Even if it makes her fall asleep again, what does it matter? Finding the pillow, she lies on the floor of her cell. Time feels like it's slipping away, pouring out like sand through an hourglass. She can visualize it, can count each grain as it falls. It's the middle of the night and her brain and body both crave sleep. With nothing else to do, she gives in.

Genny has no idea how long she's been asleep, but it's still dark when she wakes. Maybe there are no windows down here? Maybe it's broad daylight and she doesn't even realize it? But no, that makes no sense. If other vampires are coming to collect her, they'd come at night. Unless they've been delayed and she's stuck here until evening? If that's true, she doesn't know whether to be relieved or frustrated. If it's daylight, Quinn and the woman won't return for hours, either. No wonder he'd asked if she'd wanted food. Apparently she should have said yes.

Feeling around, she finds the water bottle on its side near the outer bars and has a sip. There's only a little left, and it might have to last her many more hours. As she sets it back down, she feels that she's right at the cage door. Although she knows it's pointless, her hands slide up the bars to the lock once more.

What?

It's hanging open. Genny goes still, listening for any sounds in the building. Not even the mice are moving now. Is this some sort of trick? As quietly as she can, she unhooks the lock and pushes on the door. The hinges squeak as it swings open and she stops again, waiting for a reaction from above.

Nothing.

As she rises from her knees, she feels something on the floor beside her. It's her purse. It hadn't been in the cage with her before. Had whoever opened her lock also given her back her purse?

Okay, this is super weird.

But she doesn't let herself question it for long. Even if this is some sort of trap, she has to try to get out of here. If she stays, she'll die.

She makes her way out of the cage, feeling in front of her for the chair Quinn had been sitting on. It's a good thing she's moving slowly, because the toe of her boot hits the leg and the chair scrapes a few inches over the concrete.

Still no sound upstairs. Can she find the stairs without tripping over anything? If only immortals had night vision like vampires. She goes around the chair and moves in what she thinks is the right direction. A few long moments later, her outstretched hand touches something wooden. She feels above and below the board. It's definitely the side of a step.

As softly as she can, Genny climbs the stairs, feeling ahead until she touches the door at the top. Her fingers close around the doorknob and she pauses to listen again. There's a soft clunking noise that sounds like it could be a refrigerator. Nothing else.

Carefully, gently, she pushes open the door. It's still night. Soft light from either the moon or a streetlight through a window shows her she's in a short hallway. It's dim, but after so much time in the dark, she can see pretty well.

It's a lot warmer on the main floor. No air conditioning here. Vampires probably don't care about things like that. Something about the way the house smells makes her wonder if anyone even lives here. It has a disused air to it.

Since the sun hasn't yet risen, that means the vampires could show up at any moment. Another door is in front of her, its window covered by a thick blind. She pushes it aside and looks out to see the jagged outline of trees. The backyard. Hoping against hope that no one is out there, she unlocks the door and slips outside.

A light breeze brushes her hair off her face. Although it's hot and humid outside, just the feel of that breeze invigorates her. She tries to be quiet as she makes her way around the side of the building, but doesn't succeed. Twigs crunch under her boots. Branches from the untrimmed hedge smack against her arm. No upkeep has been done on this property in a long time. If someone does lives here, they don't bother much with appearances. There are so many trees around the house that it's probably in the shade most of the time, which would be good for vampires.

Once she reaches the sidewalk, she looks both ways down the deserted street. A streetlight glows half a block away. The one closest to the house is conveniently—or maybe purposely—out. A car is parked along the curb several houses down in the other direction. It looks empty but she can't be sure. What if someone is watching the house?

Panic tries to rise, but Genny shoves it down. She has to get away from here as fast as she can. Taking a deep breath, she throws caution to the wind and begins to run down the sidewalk in the opposite direction from the car.

She doesn't stop to look back until she's three blocks away at an intersection with another residential street. When she at last glances behind her, she can see no one following. But would she notice them? They can see her in the pitch dark, after all. She turns right and starts to run again.

After two more blocks, she spots a corner store with a pay phone outside. With relief she digs in her purse for a quarter, plugs it into the coin slot, and...*crap*. She can't remember JP's number. She's dialed it enough times this week that she should know it, but it just won't come. It starts with two-four-eight, so she punches those buttons. Then a one. What are the last three digits? With her finger hovering over the keypad, she tries to recall. Is it seven-nine-two? She tries that.

"We're sorry. That number is not in service," a robotic woman's voice says.

Genny groans and hits the handset cradle to hang up. Her quarter clatters down into the return cup. She fishes it out and jams it back in.

Okay. Think. She poises a finger over the numbers again. Two, four, eight, one. But not seven, nine, two. Seven, nine, *three*. A relieved sigh slips out when she hears the line at the other end begin to ring.

What if he's not home? What if he's still out looking for her? She doesn't even know where she is, or how far away she might be from home. If he doesn't answer, she might be looking at a very long walk.

Five rings. Her throat aches with the panic threatening to return.

Then: "'Ello?" He sounds breathless.

"JP? Please, I don't have time to explain, but can you come get me? Right now?"

"Oh thank God," he sighs. His relief is palpable. "I'm coming. Tell me where you are."

Genny looks around, but she can't see a street sign. The trees in this area are all thick and tend to block signs, especially in the dark. As she spins back to face the wall in frustration she spots the name of the store.

"I'm at a payphone in front of Little Joe's Convenience. I don't know what street, or even what neighborhood I'm in. Can you find me?"

"I'll find you. Be there as soon as I can."

Genny hangs up and looks around again, realizing just how exposed she is. She notices a large bagged ice freezer along the side of the building. It's not a great shelter, but she can kneel behind the far side so anyone passing on the street won't see her. Unless they're really looking, anyway. She's fully aware she's still in grave danger.

She's not wearing a watch, so she can't check the time, but she crouches behind the freezer for what feels like an hour. Once a car goes by and her heart leaps, but it doesn't slow. The first glow of dawn has just begun to lighten the sky when a familiar Buick Regal pulls up in front of the store. Genny jumps from her hiding spot and rushes over, dragging open the passenger door and scrambling inside. After pushing down the lock button, she turns to JP and he pulls her into his arms.

"Are you okay?" he mumbles into her hair. He sounds so worried.

"I am now."

"What 'appened?"

"I'll explain everything, I promise," she says. "But please, let's go. I wanna be far away from here."

In response, JP gives her a squeeze. She can tell he doesn't want to let her go. Then he quickly starts the car. She's never felt so much relief as they speed away

During the drive, Genny recounts all she can remember. He keeps shooting her concerned glances, interrupting only occasionally with questions, most of which she can't answer.

When he turns onto her street, she shakes her head. "They know where I live now. Can I go back to your place?"

"Of course."

JP's apartment is a third floor walkup, and although it's not a big deal to have to climb them, he slides an arm around Genny's waist and helps her up the stairs.

"This is a serious problem," he says after closing and locking the door. "If they know where you live, you and your sister are both in danger. I'll speak with my family today. We'll figure this out."

"They can't get inside without an invitation though, right?"

"Right. Do your grand-mère and sister know not to invite strangers in?"

Genny sighs. “I haven’t told them about vampires yet. Guess I need to do that. But on principle they don’t tend to invite just anyone in.”

“Do you want to call them now?”

It’s not even six-thirty in the morning. They will both still be asleep, and Chloe will side with the vampires who want Genny dead if she wakes her sister up this early. “Not yet. Do you mind if I rest here for a few hours before I go home?”

JP steps forward and wraps his arms around her, pulling her against his chest. “Of course you can. God, I was *so* worried about you!”

“I was, too.” She pulls back a few inches and looks into his eyes. “I thought you’d never be able to find me. I thought I’d never see you again.”

His eyes soften and he bends his head and kisses her. Just a sweet kiss. Neither of them tries to intensify it this time. They’re both far too exhausted.

He gives her a t-shirt to put on. It’s so long it fits her like a dress, but it smells like him and she kind of loves it. They climb into his bed and he pulls her back against him, one arm draped protectively around her waist. Leaning over, he kisses her on the cheek. “Goodnight,” he whispers. “You’re safe now.”

And surprisingly, even after everything she’s just been through and everything she now knows, she believes him. Even more surprisingly, she feels herself start to drift off in his arms.

Chapter 5
Jumping Someone Else's Train

Quinn comes in the back door of the safehouse to find Cassandra waiting for him. She does not look pleased.

"Did you let her out?" she asks, glaring.

Inside, he's impressed. Genevieve figured it out, and fast. Clever girl. Outwardly, his only reply is a frown.

Cassandra scowls for a few more seconds, then turns with a huff and strides into the kitchen. "Fine," she says, her tone sharp. "Let me rephrase. I *know* you let her out. The padlock was open. My question is: *why* would you let her out? Are you trying to get us killed?"

He follows her, bracing a hand on the table. "Of course not."

"Kellan will be here soon. And we no longer have the Bourreau girl to hand over to him. How d'ya think he's going to react to that news?"

"I'll tell him she escaped. While you weren't here. I'll take the blame."

"Well that's just great Quinn, because it's entirely your fault!" Cassandra swipes a hand over her eyes. "And then he'll rip your fucking head off."

"Maybe. Maybe not."

She rolls her eyes. "Don't be stupid. Even if you lie and say it was an accident—which we both know damn well it wasn't—it still makes us look like fools. How do you think Kellan reacts to incompetent subordinates?"

Quinn's face is impassive. He knows this mess is on him. It hadn't been his plan to release her. But then he'd talked to her. She doesn't deserve this. She's an innocent. He can't just let Kellan take her.

With a sigh, Cassandra says, "Let me talk to him. He knows me better than you. I'll try to smooth this over." She pauses, shaking her head. "I know you hate being involved in shit like this, but it'd be great if you didn't actively try to get us both executed. That's all I'm asking."

"I don't mind taking responsibility for my actions."

"And you may well end up having to. But let me try." She steps closer and takes him by the shoulders, forcing him to look her in the eyes. "You've only delayed things for her. You know that, right? He won't give up, because Lillabeta won't give up. Not until every slayer is dead."

Quinn bristles, shrugging out of her grasp. "She's not a slayer. She didn't even know she was immortal until a week ago. She's no threat to any of them."

Cassandra frowns. "Don't let yourself get attached. They don't care if she knows the pointy end of a stake from the dull one. She's a Bourreau, which means she has to die. Once she's gone, there will be no more slayers and this stupid vendetta will finally be over."

He doesn't reply, instead turning to leave. He no longer wants to be here when Kellan arrives. He'd only make things worse. Cassandra can take care of herself, and if they need him, she knows where to find him.

What she doesn't know, because he hasn't told her, is where Genevieve lives. Or that she has a younger sister.

Chloe's eyes narrow as she regards her sister in confusion. Then she laughs. "Are you guys still drunk from last night?"

"I never made it to the bar last night. And believe me I know how crazy this sounds. I didn't buy a word of it either, at first. But just watch. I'll prove it," Genny tells her. She takes the knife she's holding and stabs it hard and fast into the back of her forearm. "Ah! Really hurts for a sec," she says to JP.

"What the *hell* is wrong with you?" Chloe asks, snatching the knife from Genny's fingers. "Have you gone completely mental?"

JP hands Genny a napkin and she wipes away the spot of blood. "Look. See?" she says, holding out her arm to show Chloe. "There's no wound. It healed. And you would too, because you're the same."

Chloe frowns at her, the knife still clutched in one hand. "How'd you do that?"

"It's not a trick. Our bodies heal super fast. We never get sick and we never age past twenty-one. Right?" She turns to JP for support.

He nods. "It's true. Your sister will never look a day older than she does now."

Chloe's eyes are wide as she glances between them. Then she focuses on JP. "So how old are you claiming to be?"

"I'm thirty-four. And your mother was fifty-one when she died."

"She was?" Genny says. "I didn't know that."

JP nods again. "She was born in 1930."

"You're nuts," Chloe states matter-of-factly. "Mom had just turned thirty. It says so right in the obituary!"

Genny's surprised her sister even knows what's written in their parent's obituary. It's a subject Chloe rarely talks about.

"Dates can be faked," JP says. "Our documents all have adjusted birth years once we grow too old to match the proper one. I was born in 1959, but my driver's license says 1970. In a few years I'll need to get a new one with a more recent birthdate."

Sitting back against the couch, Chloe blows out a puff of air. "You guys are really serious about this immortal stuff, aren't you? Like, I thought you were trying to pull a fast one on me, but then you went and stabbed yourself. And there's no hole in your arm! Unless you've suddenly turned into David-fricking-Copperfield—which I highly doubt—then I don't think you faked it."

"I didn't. And I totally get it. It took until I did it myself before I started to believe what he told me. I *know* how crazy it sounds." Genny bobs her chin toward the knife in her sister's hand. "Feel free to try, if you're feeling brave."

The smile that crosses her sister's face at the suggestion creeps Genny out a little. Instead of bracing her hand against something or grabbing napkins to stop any bleeding, she just lifts up the knife and jams the tip into her palm. It bounces back, her skin undamaged.

"What the hell?" Chloe exclaims, clearly disappointed.

"Our skin is quite thick and difficult to penetrate," JP tells her. "You'll need to stab forcefully."

Chloe snorts, one eyebrow arching. "You do realize you sound like a psychopath, right?"

JP chuckles. "Just wait until you 'ear the rest of it."

Before he's even finished speaking, Chloe stabs herself again, this time using all her strength. "Ow!" she cries. The second she sees blood, she presses her hand to her mouth and sucks it away. "Tastes like pennies. How weird is that?"

That her blood tastes like pennies is the part Chloe finds weird? "Look at your hand," Genny suggests softly. "Is there a mark?"

Chloe examines her palm. "Nope. Nothing." Her eyes rise to her sister's. "I'm really immortal? Like, I'll never die?"

"It's not quite as simple as that."

And though she wouldn't have thought it possible, Chloe's day then gets even better, because they spend the next thirty minutes explaining to her all about immortals and vampires.

"So the bottom line is: don't invite anyone into this house that you don't know and trust. And be very aware of your surroundings when you're out after dark. Or even better, just stay home." But Genny knows her sister. Chloe's smart enough, but she's stubborn. She'll do what she wants.

"Can't. I have a date tomorrow night," Chloe tells her. She'd been smiling before about the immortal stuff, but now she's positively glowing.

"Oh yeah? New guy?"

"He just started working at The Second Cup. I was there with Kate and Amy last night to drop off an application and he asked me out."

JP frowns. "Do you know 'im? Or do any of your friends?"

Shrugging, Chloe says, "Yeah, I think Darry's one of Amy's friends. Pretty sure she said he goes to her school." Amy goes to a Catholic high school, while Chloe attends a public one, but they've been friends since they'd met at summer camp.

"Well, just to be safe, don't invite him in," Genny says. "And make sure your friends are around when you're hanging out with him."

"Sure, *Mom*," Chloe rolls her eyes. She's fully aware calling her sister that is a low blow. It rarely stops her.

Genny flinches, but she chooses to ignore it. "Just be careful. We can't stress it enough. And stay close to home. I'd suggest you be home by ten, but I know you'd just ignore me."

Genny and JP leave Chloe to process all the information they've just dumped on her. On their way downstairs, JP says, "Do you want to start training tomorrow evening?"

She turns to him with a smile. "Definitely."

"We could go to my place after you're done work? I can make us dinner."

"You had me at training. Dinner only sweetens the deal."

"I might be able to think of one or two other things to sweeten it," he says with a wink.

Her smile grows wider. "Such as? Are you talking chocolate cake? Because I would call in sick for cake."

JP laughs. "Noted. I was thinking I'd show up 'ere in the morning and ride in with you. And then come meet you after work. You could bring a change of clothes with you to the office, couldn't you?"

Genny knows he's offering to chaperone her tomorrow both so she feels safe after her ordeal last night and to ease his own worries. "Works for me," she tells him as they reach the front door.

Before he leaves, he takes her into his arms and kisses her. She doesn't intend to deepen the kiss with her sister upstairs and her Gran in the living room, but it happens anyway. Kissing JP is her new favorite thing to do. When they finally pull apart, he's grinning from ear to ear.

"See you in the morning," he says.

"Call me before bed anyway," she replies.

After brushing her teeth, Genny changes into a nightgown and flops on her bed. She can hear Chloe on the phone in her bedroom, so she knows she'll have to wait a while before she can talk to JP.

Propping up her pillows behind her shoulders, she lies back and stares at the ceiling. So much has happened in the past twenty-four hours. It's kind of insane. If she hadn't napped at JP's until two in the afternoon, she'd be exhausted right now.

Telling Chloe had been one thing, but after dinner she'd sat down with Gran and tried her best to explain everything she'd learned about immortals and vampires. To her utter shock, Gran had believed her. Even though Genny's dad had never told his mother anything about this world, Gran had still believed her—although she'd refused to let Genny cut herself to prove it. She'd asked lots of questions, requested to meet Marie and René as soon as possible, and had told Genny something she already understands: she has a responsibility to protect her sister. Even the vampire stuff hadn't fazed Gran as much as Genny had expected, but to be fair, she'd left out the part about getting kidnapped. She hadn't want to freak Gran out too much.

In the end, Gran had told Genny how lucky she is not to have to worry about illness or aging and then changed the subject, asking her about her relationship with JP. So all in all, it had gone a lot better than it could have. Small as it is, Genny knows she's lucky to have the family she does.

She's especially lucky to have such an awesome boyfriend. Tomorrow she's going to start training with his mom. If only she'd already been trained last night, she could've…

Could've what? Killed Quinn before he could grab her?

Yes, a voice in her head answers. *That's exactly what you would've done. Then you wouldn't have been kidnapped. No kidnapping, no traumatic experience.*

And it *had* been a traumatic experience. Hadn't it? Then why doesn't she feel more traumatized? Is bouncing back from scary stuff just part of being an immortal? Or a slayer?

Genny thinks about it. Since waking up this afternoon beside JP and then coming home and telling Chloe and Gran, she hasn't felt scared once. Other than being locked up in the dark and told she'd be tortured and killed, what really awful thing had happened? The woman had thrown a water bottle at her. That had been it. She'd been terrified at first, but the longer she'd been there, the less scared she'd felt. It must be a slayer thing. Anyone else would probably hole themselves up in their house and refuse to leave.

And who had opened the padlock? Not the female vampire; Genny's sure of it. It had to have been Quinn. But why? And why does she feel that strange sensation every time he's near? At least he'll never be able to sneak up on her again.

She blows out a frustrated sigh. No matter how much about this weird new world she learns, she still seems to have way more questions than answers.

At four-thirty, Genny powers down her computer, grabs her bag, and takes the elevator to the lobby. She spots JP sitting in one of the chairs near the revolving doors to the street. The moment their eyes meet, he jumps up with a grin.

"How was your day?"

"Better now." She reaches for his hand. "So what're you making for dinner?"

His grin falters, but only a little. "There's actually been a slight change of plans. We've been invited to dinner at my mother's. Is that all right? I promise I'll cook for you soon. Rain check until tomorrow?"

Genny shrugs. "Works for me."

They take the subway up to Sheppard station and walk the three blocks to JP's mom's house. Marie greets Genny with kisses on both cheeks, just like she does her son. Although she's only met Marie once before, Genny already feels like she's considered part of the family.

After changing into shorts and a t-shirt, Genny, Marie, and JP go out to the fenced-in back yard. It's not large, but it's all open grass, which should help cushion her anticipated falls.

"Let's start by exploring what your natural instincts are," Marie says. "One of us will try to attack you. You will not know which. When we do, just react with what feels right."

Chuckling, Genny says, "So fall to the ground unconscious, then? 'Cause that's what happened Saturday night."

Marie frowns. "What do you remember about being taken? Anything?"

"It all happened so fast. Someone grabbed me from behind. Next thing I knew I woke up in the dark." Genny doesn't mention the Quinn tingle she'd felt right before. "Wait," she adds. "I think I remember a chemical smell. What's that stuff they use on TV shows? Chloroform? Maybe it was that."

JP nods. "Probably. That would explain why you were unconscious for a while. It will work on immortals, but not for long. And vampires can move extremely fast."

Before Genny can reply, Marie attacks her from the side and knocks her to the ground. Genny rolls over and Marie straddles her, pinning down her arms. Genny starts laughing. "See? Clearly I don't have much instinct for this."

Marie gets to her feet. "Try again. Think about defending yourself. Do whatever comes naturally to you. Don't worry about punching or kicking. You won't injure us, so please fight."

JP extends a hand to help Genny up. She hears the sound of the screen door opening and turns around. It's René.

"Come to laugh at my humiliation?" Genny asks him.

René smiles. "Oui. Amuse me." He sits on the patio step and lights a cigarette. Lung cancer is clearly not a concern for immortals.

As she turns back to JP, he tries to grab her from behind. Genny ducks and manages to slip out of his grip, but he lunges forward again, hitting her on the shoulders. Once more she falls to the ground and JP lands on top of her.

"Fight back," he whispers. "Give me all you got."

Genny draws in a breath, then braces her palms on JP's chest and shoves him off as hard as she can. He flies backward, landing on his ass and laughing. "Nice one!" he exclaims.

She gets up and starts to come at him, to attack him back, but before she can, another hand grabs her around her neck. Without even thinking about it, she reaches up and yanks the hand away, spinning around and knocking René to the ground. Everyone smiles but Genny. She's still stunned she'd been able to do it.

"Excellent!" Marie exclaims. "Great reflexive response!"

"The girl is a natural," René says to JP. JP is beaming with pride.

They practice for another half hour or so before Marie and René go inside to get dinner ready. JP and Genny sit on the grass. "I'm impressed," he says. "You definitely 'ave good instincts."

"Thanks. It was kinda fun," Genny says. "Can we practice again later?"

"I don't see why not." He wraps an arm around her shoulders and pulls her into his side. "Maybe just the two of us next time?"

After a delicious meal of roasted chicken with a thick cream sauce, Genny thanks Marie and René and she and JP walk back to his apartment. He's invited her over to watch "Buffy the Vampire Slayer" with him so they can both dissect and make fun of a Hollywood vampire movie before she goes home.

When they get inside, Genny glances toward the bathroom. She still feels kind of gross from all the exercise. "D'you mind if I grab a shower first?"

"Be my guest. Towels are in the cupboard. Turn the dial all the way to the left or you won't get enough 'ot water. And if you need shampoo—"

"I'll find it. Thanks."

Stripping off her clothes, she steps into the shower. The hot spray drumming against her skin feels heavenly. As she soaps herself, her mind begins to wander. She tries to imagine what JP's hands would feel like on her body. He dances awkwardly, but kisses amazingly. Would making love to him be like the former or the latter? Or somewhere in between?

She rinses and turns off the water, wrapping herself in the biggest, fluffiest towel she can find. Instead of putting her sweaty clothes back on, she emerges from the steamy bathroom wearing only the towel.

JP appears in the hallway. His eyes widen when he sees her standing there. They walk toward each other, coming together in the middle of the hall. Her hands go to his waist. His slip up to cradle her face. He looks like he's about to say something, but whatever it is can wait. Genny silences him with a kiss.

Neither of them hesitates now. Lips and tongues meet, hands roam. JP's shirt gets unbuttoned. Genny's towel falls to the floor. Without pulling away from her, he reaches out blindly and pushes open his bedroom door, guiding them both to his bed.

And it turns out, much to her delight, it's definitely the latter.

Chapter 6
Some Kind of Stranger

Quinn's bedroom is what Cassandra likes to refer to as an unnatural disaster area. She keeps telling him it's a fire hazard, but he loves it like this. Every spare bit of wall space that isn't interrupted by a door or bed or dresser has a bookcase along it. And each shelf is stuffed with books. Books are stacked on top of his bureau, along the wide headboard of his bed, and on the floor in front of most shelves. Quinn has been a vampire for 112 years. As a human prior to that, he hadn't been able to afford books; the only one he'd owned had been his Bible. But since turning immortal, he's accumulated quite the collection. This room is his cocoon and he wouldn't have it any other way.

The bottom two shelves of the bookcase nearest his bed are lined not with books, but leather-bound journals. Some of these are so old the leather has turned dark and brittle, the pages within yellowed. Quinn never pulls out the oldest ones. He knows what's written in them as well as if it's written on his own heart.

He sits on his bed trying to read as he waits for Cassandra. She hadn't returned last night, but at least she'd left a message saying she'd see him tonight. He's having difficulty focusing on the page in front of him. His mind keeps straying to other things. Like wondering how Kellan had taken the news of Genevieve's escape. And what the Assembly's next plan for her will be. And if he will stand aside and let them take her next time, or stick his neck on the line—both his and Cassandra's necks, let's be honest—and try to stop it. The answer to that last one should be easy. It should be obvious.

But, conflicted as all this makes him feel, it isn't.

At the sound of the door opening downstairs, he drops the book and speeds down to meet her.

"Miss me?" Cassandra asks him with a smirk.

He ignores this. "Where did you sleep?"

"At the safehouse. By the time I could feed, it was almost dawn. The house was close, so I used it."

Quinn takes a seat, resting an ankle across the opposite knee. "So? What did he say?"

"Kellan didn't show. Instead he sent two of his minions. One of whom, after hearing we'd lost the girl, actually pulled out a fucking mobile phone if you can believe it and called him. Then he passed the damn thing to me!"

"And?" Quinn doesn't care much about the phone. It's typical Kellan. He's always enjoyed showing off the latest technology.

"And he stayed in New York. He didn't say why." She comes over and perches on the arm of the couch. She's smiling.

"That's not what I meant and you know it," Quinn says.

"He wasn't happy about it, but he didn't demand our heads on a platter either. I'd call that a win. He asked me a few questions about her, most of which I couldn't answer because I barely spoke to her. And in case you're wondering, I didn't mention your little chat with her. I figured you'd prefer to avoid an interrogation. It doesn't matter anyway. As I told you, they have a Plan B."

"And it is?"

"No clue," she replies.

Frowning, he shifts his foot back to the floor. "How much time?"

"Until what? They come for her again? How should I know?" She goes over to the kitchen, opening the freezer door and peering inside. "We need more blood bags. I'll get some tonight. You finish them too damn fast. They're not Capri Suns, you know. They're for backup."

Quinn shrugs. "I stayed in last night."

"Waiting for me?"

There's that smirk again. He should find it irritating, but he doesn't. "Yes."

"Why? Were you worried about me, Quinceañera?"

If anything had happened to Cassandra, it would have been his fault. So of course he'd been worried about her. But she already knows that.

"Will they let you know what they're planning?" he asks, getting up and following her into the kitchen.

"Only if they need us to play a part. Which I highly doubt, since we fucked up Plan A."

"You mean I did."

She snorts. "If the shoe fits." Grabbing a box of cookies from the cupboard, she edges past him and returns to the couch.

Quinn knows he should let this go. It would be safest for both of them if he forgets all about Genevieve. But for some reason he can't. "Can you find out?"

Cassandra turns back to him. She looks like she's about to lecture him, but then her face softens. "No promises," she says. "But I'll see what I can do."

After work on Wednesday, Genny immediately feels the Quinn tingle—as she now thinks of it—the moment the elevator doors open. Her heart starts to race. It's still broad daylight. He shouldn't be out and about yet. She looks around, but spots neither Quinn nor JP. Since JP had told her he'd be here, she takes a seat to wait for him. Her eyes scan the lobby nervously, not resting until JP comes through the revolving doors and strides toward her with a smile. Strangely, the moment he appears, the tingle vanishes.

Putting it out of her mind, she takes JP's hand and they head out and make their way to the steps down to the subway platform. JP has been riding back and forth with her all week. She knows he's trying to be protective of her, and although she loves spending time with him, she doesn't love feeling like she's being babysat. She's been tempted to tell him she doesn't need a chaperone since yesterday, but she worries it might hurt his feelings. Their relationship is still so new to risk making waves.

They get off at Sheppard and go straight to JP's apartment. Although she's supposed to train with his mom again, they have made sure to give themselves an hour's buffer before they need to go to her house.

Yesterday's training with just the two of them at JP's had been quite a bit shorter than planned. Knocking each other down on his living room rug had quickly led to other, more pleasurable activities. It's no surprise they can't get enough of each other at this early stage, but today Genny's going to make sure they limit their fun to an hour and then go to Marie's. She is determined to learn how to be the strong fighter her mother would want her to be.

The next morning's train has just pulled into Dundas station. One more stop until she needs to get off at Queen. Genny has been procrastinating telling JP that he doesn't need to commute with her every day, but so far hasn't quite gotten up the courage to do it. Time's almost up. She'd better just spit it out.

"So," she turns to JP, pulling their joined hands into her lap. "It's been four days. While I appreciate the company, I don't think it's really necessary for you to ride with me to work and back every single day."

His brows draw in. "I want to."

Sighing softly, she replies, "I know you do. And I like spending time with you. Very much. But I'll be fine commuting by myself like I always have. I can call you when I leave the office and again when I get home if you want. And I can still come to your place after work a few days a week."

JP looks unconvinced.

Before he can protest, she continues, "I like to use my train time to listen to music, or read, or just tune out the world. Don't get me wrong, I love that you've been coming with me this week. I just think..."

"I know," he says. "Absence makes the 'eart grow fonder, right? We've been seeing each other every day. You need some space."

Genny brings their hands to her lips and kisses the back of his. "Just a little space. Not too much space. Do you mind?"

With a tight smile, JP asks, "Are you still coming over after work?"

"Absolutely," she nods.

"Then I don't mind. And this is your stop, so give me a kiss and I'll see you later."

Genny leans in and kisses him. Then she kisses him again. "You're the bestest boyfriend ever."

JP laughs. "That's my goal."

As she rides the elevator to the lobby at 4:45, Genny wonders if she'll feel the tingle again today. She'd admitted to Quinn that she could sense when he's near. Would he dare show up here again? Especially since JP isn't around? JP had said that sunlight is extremely painful to vampires. So why had she felt the tingle yesterday afternoon?

The moment the doors slide open, all the hairs on her arms stand up. Her skin starts to resonate and she smiles to herself. He's nearby. But why? Is she in danger? Should she find a phone and call JP?

Of course you should! the voice in her head says. Yet she doesn't get back on the elevator. Instead of being alarmed, like she knows she probably should be, she's curious.

Genny goes out onto the sidewalk, but it's crowded with people and although she looks around, she doesn't spot any familiar faces. Then again, would she even recognize him? She'd only seen his face in shadows. She doesn't have a clear picture of what he'd look like in normal light. He could honestly be any of the men around her and she probably wouldn't realize.

She makes her way into the subway and as usual, looks down at the tracks and wonders what it would feel like to be electrocuted by the third rail. Or hit by an oncoming train. So many people pick this traumatic way to end their lives. Not that Genny would ever do that. And even if someone pushed her—a fear she's regularly harbored—she now knows she wouldn't die. It would just hurt like crazy. She shudders at the thought.

The tingle stays with her even after she gets on the train. She scans the people around her again. None of them are looking at her. But he has to be here somewhere. Maybe she should've called JP after all.

She lucks into a vacant seat when a woman gets up as she approaches. After sitting down beside a middle-aged guy in a suit, she pulls her book from her bag. She pretends to read, but she's hyper aware of the crowd of commuters surrounding her. The car jostles from side to side as it starts moving down the track. Her view is limited to elbows and jackets and hands clutching briefcases. But the tingle persists, which means Quinn is still near.

All of a sudden, the man beside her rises and pushes his way through the crowd. They're in-between stations, but she assumes he intends to position himself closer to the door. No one immediately fills his seat, which seems a little odd. Genny knows empty seats never stay empty long at this time of day.

She's right. Another man sits down not five seconds later. From the corner of her eye, she can see his jeans and black lace-up boots. Not business clothes. It's a bit hot out for jeans and boots, but to each their own.

Then she notices that the other commuters have shifted a few feet away from them. She's not sure if they've even realized they've done it. The tingle is surging over her now. Suddenly she figures it out.

Before she can confirm, the guy beside her softly says, "Hello Genevieve."

"Quinn," she whispers, knowing he can hear her. Her heart is racing and she's sure he can probably hear that, too. "Have you been following me?

"Just a wee bit."

Genny takes a deep breath and turns to him, at last seeing him in good light. His hair is light brown and cut short, with longer bangs coming to a point over his forehead. Thick, dark lashes frame the most unusual pale gray eyes—eyes that are currently looking right into her own. He's not what she'd expected. From the shadowy look of him in the basement last weekend, she hadn't really known what to expect, but this isn't it.

"Why?" she asks.

He looks away, quiet for a moment. Then he says, "You're still in danger."

"I'm well aware. It's all everyone keeps telling me."

"They want you dead."

Genny nods. "Do you?"

The train lurches to the side, gravity making her leg bump into his. A jolt of electricity shoots through her entire body and lands in the pit of her stomach. It's not at all unpleasant, but definitely inappropriate. She quickly moves away.

"No," he says.

She's momentarily flustered. *No what? Oh right.* "Why not?" she asks quietly, although she's nearly positive no one else is listening to them. "From what I've been told, you should."

"You're in no danger from me."

It doesn't answer Genny's question, but it does make her feel better. She's always been a good judge of people. Maybe that's why she isn't as frightened of Quinn as common sense says she ought to be.

"Who then?"

He sighs. "I don't know yet. But they will send someone."

"Who're *they*?"

"The Assembly." Genny has no idea who the Assembly is, and Quinn doesn't volunteer any further information.

"I've started training," she tells him, sitting back in her seat and pretending to read her book again. "I'm learning to fight back." She knows she still has so much to master, but it's important he understands she's not just some helpless victim.

"Good."

They're both quiet for a few stops, but he doesn't make a move to leave. She has to keep reminding herself that he's a vampire, not just some intriguing guy sitting beside her on the train. She has a million questions, but isn't sure he'd be willing to answer any of them.

Closing her book again, she turns back to him. "How are you here?" He looks confused, so she adds, "The sun is out. I thought...I mean I was told that you stayed inside in the daytime."

"I won't burst into flames, if that's what you mean." He says this with a smile. It's a nice smile.

"Yeah, but doesn't it hurt?"

"It does. But I keep to the shadows. And I carry gloves and a cap." He pats the bulging pocket of his blazer.

"Ah." Question after question pops into her head. Where to start? "Can I ask you something a bit more personal?"

He nods.

"How old are you?"

Quinn blinks, surprised. Whatever he'd been expecting, this clearly hadn't been it. "Since birth? One hundred and thirty-nine."

Genny's eyes flare. "Holy cow. Really?"

"Yes."

"So how old were you when...?"

Something akin to pain flashes across his face for a second. Frowning, he replies, "Twenty-seven."

Genny does some mental math. That means he'd been born in 1855 and turned into a vampire in 1882. She can't even imagine the things he must have seen in such a long life.

"You have a bit of an accent. Can I ask where you're from?"

"Edinburgh." He pronounces it *Eedin-bra.*

"Scotland?"

Quinn nods again.

She smiles to herself. She'd been right about his accent. "I've heard it's really beautiful there. Do you go home often?"

His face goes wooden. "Not since 1883."

Oops. Clearly she's hit a sore spot. "Sorry, I was—"

"Don't apologize," he cuts in. "I just...I can't talk about that."

They are just pulling into York Mills station, one stop before Sheppard. She realizes the car is much less crowded now. As the train comes to a halt, Quinn gets to his feet and exits the door across from them without saying goodbye or looking back. Before the train even begins to move again, the tingle is also gone.

That night in bed, Genny tosses and turns. Between thoughts of her training session with Marie, which had gone well this time, and reminiscing about being in JP's arms, not to mention her peculiar subway conversation with Quinn, she feels like she'll never fall asleep.

She'd completely forgotten to ask Quinn why he'd unlocked her cage. Such an important question and it had slipped right out of her mind when he'd actually been beside her. Why doesn't he want her dead, like all the other vampires do? Why would he presumably risk his own life by letting her go? He must have a reason, an ulterior motive of some sort, but for the life of her she can't begin to guess what it might be.

He'd told her he's no danger to her, and for some crazy reason she believes him, but she can't tell if he's on her side or simply trying to stay out of it. She can't tell much of anything about Quinn, and he doesn't volunteer much. Having a vampire ally would definitely help her and her sister stay one step ahead, help them to stay alive. If he really is an ally.

Can a vampire slayer even have a vampire as an ally? He's supposed to be her enemy. Their instinct should be to want to kill each other. Yet he clearly doesn't want to kill her, or she suspects she'd be dead already. And if she's being honest, she hopes she's never put in a position where she would have to kill Quinn.

As if he knows she's thinking about him, the tingle starts up again. Genny jumps out of bed and rushes to her window, pushing aside the curtain to peer down at the street below.

He's nearby. In fact, he can probably see her looking out, although she can't see him. Smiling, she gives a little wave at the darkness and lets the curtain fall back into place.

Once she's back in bed, the sensation vanishes. This time when she closes her eyes, her overactive mind mercifully quiets and she finds her way to sleep after all.

Quinn walks the deserted streets in the dark, thinking. He can't seem to get Genevieve out of his head. He keeps picturing her on the train, those curious green eyes looking at him. At first she'd been afraid of him, as she should be. But then she'd started asking questions and before long he'd realized she hadn't been scared anymore. Is that just the slayer part of her? Or is it simply Genevieve?

She'd been so close. He'd been able to hear the pounding of her heart, the rush of blood through her veins. Yet not once had he felt the pull of it. He's never tasted immortal blood before. Could that be why? Maybe it isn't as tempting? Genevieve doesn't make him hungry, she makes him...fascinated. That's the best way he can describe it.

He *is* hungry right now, though.

Quinn doesn't kill humans, not for more than a century. He either feeds on them, heals them with his own blood, and then hypnotizes them to forget, like he'd been taught by a very old friend a very long time ago, or he drinks animal blood. Both of these options are still wrong, still theft, just like the blood bags Cassandra steals, but at least this way he can live with himself.

He heads east, into the wooded area along the Don River. Deer can often be found in these woods. Also, just before dawn sometimes ambitious joggers run the paths. Although Quinn considers himself an abomination against nature, he can admit being an apex predator has its perks. Not only does he have enhanced hearing and the ability to see in the dark, but he can also move much faster than other creatures. He can even slow his own heartrate and breath to the point where animals can't detect him. It makes for pretty easy hunting most of the time.

Tonight the woods are quiet. Often wee creatures, like birds or mice, can sense danger even if they can't pinpoint what or where, and right now they're all in hiding. It's hot and still and clouds blanket the moon. The air is heavy with humidity, making all the natural odors that much stronger: the rich earthy scent of soil below his boots, the must and mildew of a nearby squirrel den, the sweet perfume of trilliums, their petals closed up for the night.

He closes his eyes, lifts his chin, and draws in a deep breath. Little is more peaceful than being in the woods at night, just him and the squirrels. And maybe a deer. It's too far away to detect scent, but he catches the sound of an animal in the distance drinking by the water's edge.

Carefully not to step on any fallen twigs, he makes his way down to the river. When he gets closer, he spots the deer. *No, wait.* There's actually two: a doe and her young fawn. The mother is nudging her baby to drink more. They're hot and thirsty, and it's dangerous for a fawn out in the open.

Quinn backs away. He can't feed on a mother or child.

He continues along the well-trodden path. It's getting late. He'll need to feed soon or head home and make do with another blood bag. He has about thirty minutes before he'll have to go. Thirty minutes to find the sustenance his cursed body needs.

Then he hears it, the rhythmic *thump, thump* of running shoes hitting the dirt. A jogger. Part of Quinn flinches, wishing he hadn't detected the sound, but another part comes alive with anticipation. Human blood. Pumped right from the vein. He starts to salivate at the thought. Before, he'd been hungry. Now he's absolutely ravenous.

He slips into the trees, blending into the shadows as he watches the path. The shoe beats are getting closer. He can detect the jogger's elevated heartrate, hear each metered inhalation and exhalation. A woman comes into view about twenty feet away. She's short, with blonde hair pulled back into a tight ponytail. Early forties, maybe. All her focus is on the path ahead. She just wants to get home.

And she will, but a wee bit low on iron this morning.

He's so hungry, he swears he can already taste her. Just before she reaches the place where he's hidden, Quinn steps back out onto the path, blocking her way.

The woman comes to an abrupt halt, her pulse spiking, her breath now coming in short, ragged gasps. "Excuse me," she says, trying to get around him. She's terrified. He'd better put a stop to that.

"Look at me," he commands, and although the sky has only just begun to lighten, he makes sure she can see his eyes. "Don't be afraid."

Her own eyes flare as she stares back at him. "Okay."

“I need something from you. It won’t take long. And after, you will forget all about it and go straight home.”

There’s a flicker of nervousness, but it fades away. “Will it hurt?” she asks.

“Just for a moment. May I?”

“Yes,” she nods. She’s calm now. Fear taints the taste of blood, makes it wild and kind of bitter. A willing, relaxed human donation is the very best a vampire can hope for.

“Thank you.”

He slips his arms around her, drawing her into his embrace as his canines extend. Her skin is hot and salty with sweat as he pierces it. And then for a few delectable minutes, Quinn ceases to think at all.

Chapter 7
Scared to Dance

By the time Quinn gets home, it's started to rain. Though the sun's not out, he knows he probably shouldn't go downtown again today. He also knows he hasn't been listening to that inner voice much lately. But first, sleep. Setting his alarm for three, he crawls into bed.

He'd healed the jogger and sent her off on her merry way, no wiser about the slight weakness she might feel for the next few hours. Quinn, however, feels absolutely rejuvenated. Feeding on human blood directly from the source is a whole other experience to drinking from blood bags. It's hot and fresh and alive, and it makes him feel fully alive, too, at least for a while. It gives him so much energy, he's not sure he'll be able to sleep.

He can hear Cassandra's clock ticking from two rooms down and he wonders if he'll have to lie here and listen to it for the next six and a half hours. He needn't have worried, though. The next sound he hears is the voice of the afternoon DJ on CFNY excitedly telling listeners about the Nine Inch Nails and Soundgarden show up at Molson Park next month. He switches off the radio just as "Rusty Cage" starts playing and gets out of bed.

Vampire sleep isn't like human sleep. They don't toss or turn, they don't dream, they just kind of turn off. At least that's how Quinn thinks of it. He's grateful for the lack of dreams. If he had to regularly relive the horrors his subconscious would undoubtedly drop him into, he thinks he would have found a way to kill himself over a century ago.

He isn't sluggish when he wakes like humans are, either. He doesn't need coffee to perk him up, although he does enjoy a cup sometimes. He just switches from off to on and that's that.

It's still overcast, but the rain has let up. After showering and changing into fresh clothes, he heads out again.

On her break that afternoon, Genny gives JP a call.

"'Ello?"

"Hi. It's me."

"I was 'oping to 'ear your voice." She can tell he's grinning. It makes her grin, too.

"I think I'm going to head home after work."

"Ah." Now he sounds disappointed.

"Because I thought maybe I'd grab my pajamas and toothbrush before I came over. If you don't mind some overnight company, that is?"

"Ah!" It's amazing how a simple change of inflection on the same word can convey a completely different reaction. "Of course I don't mind. You're always welcome. Although I suspect you don't need to bring the pajamas."

Genny laughs. "Because it's hot out, right?"

"Yes," he chuckles "Definitely because of the temperature. So what can I make you for dinner? What's your favorite meal? I'm off to get groceries soon."

Her smile grows wider. "Surprise me."

"I'd be delighted to. See you later."

Sometimes Genny can't tell at all that JP is thirteen years older than her, and other times it's glaringly obvious. Not too many guys her age would be so excited to grocery shop to plan a meal for her. She wonders what her mother would say if she knew her daughter was dating Marie's son. Genny thinks she'd be pleased.

Mom would not, however, likely be so fine with her burgeoning friendship with a vampire. If that's even what she and Quinn are. Are they friends? She doesn't know how to define their relationship, but they definitely aren't the arch enemies they're supposed to be.

She hasn't even told JP about her conversations with Quinn yet. She probably should, but she's been avoiding it. She suspects he won't understand. He and his family hate vampires. They would want Quinn dead. Heck, they'd probably expect her to kill him. And though she's not sure if she and Quinn are friends, she's pretty sure she doesn't want to do that.

Genny senses he's back the moment she steps into the lobby, but she doesn't actually see him until she comes out onto the busy sidewalk. Glancing to the left, she spots Quinn leaning against the wall. At least he's not skulking in the shadows this time.

Their eyes meet and she can't help smiling. "You again. Waiting for me?"

"D'you mind?"

Genny shrugs. "No. Just don't take off without a word this time. It's kind of rude."

He falls into step beside her. "My apologies." The line of his mouth twists sheepishly. "I'm not used to spending much time with humans."

"Your kind doesn't care about manners?" She's hesitant to use the v-word with so many people around.

"My kind?" He chuckles.

"You know what I mean." They descend the stairs and join the crowd waiting for the next train. Like before, people move away from Quinn and they're able to walk right to the edge of the platform. "Why do they do that?" she whispers.

"Unconscious self-preservation instinct, I would think. It's sort of nice, isn't it?"

With a loud screech of brakes, the train pulls into the station. They're the first to board, but the car is already full of commuters. Quinn walks up to two well-dressed men and within seconds they vacate their seat and move to the far end of the car. Genny shakes her head as she sits down. "It really is."

"You said you only found out about your immortality two weeks ago?" he asks.

"Yep. The day after my twenty-first birthday."

"That night at Apothecary? You were with another immortal the first time I saw you."

Since Quinn had recognized immediately that she and JP are immortal, she wonders if vampires can see auras, too. "That was JP. I just met him that night. He told me the next day."

"That must've been quite the shock."

He's being chatty today. It feels like he's said more to her this afternoon than he ever has before. "I thought he was a lunatic." Dropping her voice, Genny adds, "But then I went home and tried to cut myself and couldn't. It took a hard stab with a sharp knife to even draw a dot of blood." She turns to Quinn, her face serious. "That was the first time I'd ever even seen my own blood."

"And you believed him after that?" His strange gray eyes hold hers.

"What choice did I have? And then I met his mother, who it turns out had been friends with my mom. They explained everything to me. You have no clue how much my life has changed in the past thirteen days."

He tilts his head a little. "I might have some idea."

Oh right. "I guess maybe you would. But that was a really long time ago, right?"

His lips press together. "Some things never fade," he says softly

Genny remembers he doesn't like to talk about his past, so she changes the subject. "I've been meaning to ask you something. Why did you open the padlock and let me out?"

He frowns. "I told you yesterday. I pose you no danger."

"And for some crazy reason I even believe you. But you took me, whether it was on someone else's orders or not. So you clearly weren't too concerned about my wellbeing then. What changed?"

Shrugging, he replies, "I was following orders, but after talking to you, I realized you didn't deserve to die."

She blinks, her brows narrowing, but she thinks he's telling the truth. "Thank you," she murmurs.

"You're welcome."

They reach a stop and some people get off. No one new boards their car and the circle of space around them grows wider. "So you work for them? The, uh, Academy?"

"The Assembly. No. They just request favors from time to time. It's prudent to stay on good terms with them."

"And they want me dead?"

He nods.

"Does the woman who was with you?"

"Cassandra? She was just doing the job."

"That doesn't answer my question."

Another shrug. "She doesn't care either way."

So why does Quinn? "And she's your…partner?"

"Something like that. Partner, companion, housemate. We've been friends for decades."

Genny nods, interpreting his words to mean *girlfriend.* "So is she an ally or an enemy? I'm just trying to get all this straight."

"She's neither. At least not right now."

They're silent for a few moments as the train pulls into the next station and more commuters exit. Only two more stops until Sheppard. "What are you up to this weekend?" It feels weird to ask Quinn this like he's just one of her regular friends. Last weekend, his plans had been to kidnap her and hand her over to be murdered. A lot has changed in a week's time. Hell, everything has changed since two weeks ago. God only knows what will happen to her next week.

He looks surprised by her question. "I'm not sure. How about you?"

"JP and my friend Dawn and I are going to Apothecary tomorrow night."

"Do you go every Saturday?"

Shrugging, Genny says, "No, but since I missed last week, I thought I'd try again."

"It's a weird place."

She snorts. "I would've thought you'd fit right in."

"Hardly." One side of his mouth curves into a half smile.

"What, all those drunken humans obsessed with fake vampire culture not your thing?"

His small smile widens and turns into a full on laugh, and it makes his entire face light up. She's taken aback by how handsome he looks. She'd noticed before, of course, but now it's like she's just seen a whole different side of him. A more human side.

The train comes to a stop and an automated voice over the speakers says "Sheppard station."

Already? "This is my stop," she tells him, getting up. "See you around?"

Quinn remains in his seat. He holds her gaze for a moment and nods. "See you."

As she disembarks and walks to the stairs, Genny feels her heart beating faster than normal. And though she tries not to, she can't help grinning.

When Quinn gets home half an hour later, he finds Cassandra sitting at the kitchen counter with a glass of whisky in her hand. She looks like she's been waiting for him.

"This is three afternoons in a row you've vanished. Two of them sunny. I can't help wondering where you've been going."

He shrugs. "Downtown."

"Why?"

"Stuff to do." He knows he's being evasive and he knows she knows it.

"On sunny days? Stuff that's worth the searing pain?" She looks skeptical.

"I keep to the shadows. You know the drill. It's bearable."

"But unnecessarily masochistic when you could just wait for dusk. Although to be fair, you and masochism are longtime bedfellows. Tell me why you keep going downtown."

He holds her gaze. "Tell me you don't already know the answer."

Narrowing her eyes, Cassandra says, "Of course I do. I know you better than you know yourself most of the time. What I don't get is *why*. Did Kellan ask you to keep an eye on her and you just forgot to tell me? Is that it? Because if it's that, then I get it. But if it's just you being all weird and stalkery I think I deserve to know why. Especially since your last stupid move could've gotten us both killed."

"I know," he sighs. He flops onto the couch.

She comes over to sit beside him. "Quincy, baby, I love ya." She pats him on the thigh. "You know I do. But unless there's a really good reason for this strange obsession you seem to have developed with the immortal girl, I'm gonna have to ask you as a friend to cut it the fuck out. I value my pretty little head staying right where it is on my pretty little neck. And I'd prefer if your pretty head stayed where it belongs, too."

"She's..." He stops, exhaling long and low. "I can't really explain it. She's just...different."

"Yeah? Different how?"

"I just said I don't know how to explain. You know I'm not good at making connections. For the past six decades there's really only been you. But there's just something about her. She...she reminds me of someone I used to know long ago." He stops, raking a hand through his hair. "I know it seems stupid to you that I'd try to help her, but she doesn't deserve to die because of crimes her ancestors committed."

"I don't think you're stupid. I think you've decided to fight a fight you can't possibly win. Because her guilt or innocence makes no difference. She's a slayer by birth. The Assembly has a zero tolerance policy for slayers."

"I'm well aware." He leans forward in his seat, bracing his elbows on his knees as he looks over at her. "How many times in the past have I dug my heels in on anything? How many times have I ever interfered with what they wanted, even when I didn't like it?"

"Never."

"Never," he repeats with a nod. This isn't quite true. He had, once, although his attempt had failed. It still haunts him. "And there's been some horrific things, things I'll never forgive myself for. But this time I just can't. I won't go along with it."

Cassandra considers him for a moment. Then, with a sigh, she also nods. "Fine."

Quinn frowns. "I'm not asking you to risk your life for a stranger. If you wanna leave town, I'll understand. I'll come find you again once this all blows over."

"Don't think it hasn't crossed my mind."

He chuckles. "I'd expect nothing less."

She takes a drink of whisky, and then settles back into the couch. "I have some news actually. I found out Kellan's sending an assassin."

Quinn's eyes flare. "Why didn't you tell me that before?"

Shrugging, she flashes him a grin. "I just did."

"Wait. Who are they sending? Tell me it's not Juliette."

"To take out the Bourreau girl?" Cassandra laughs. "That'd be like shooting turtles with machine guns. No, it's some eastern European dude named Gruhn. Apparently he's humungous. Still overkill, in my opinion."

Quinn is relieved Kellan hasn't sent Juliette. She has the deserved reputation as the most skilled vampire assassin on the planet. She's basically Lillabeta's one-woman Special Ops team. If Juliette had been tasked to kill Genevieve, he doubts he'd be able to prevent it. But Gruhn? Quinn has heard rumors about him, that he's a dangerous giant of a vampire. Stopping him will be difficult, but Quinn doesn't think it's impossible.

"Any idea when?"

"He'll be in town sometime before dawn. So probably tomorrow."

He turns to Cassandra. "Wanna come to a goth club with me tomorrow night?"

She snorts. "As much as that sounds highly entertaining, I can't. I have a date."

"Oh yeah? With whom?"

"Wouldn't you like to know?" She gets to her feet. "It probably won't go anywhere, and I'm not even sure I want it to, but if it does, you'll be the first to know. Well, second anyway."

Cassandra has an active sex life, but she hasn't had a true partner in nearly a decade. She dates, both women and men, merely to release sexual tension. And to facilitate feeding Quinn assumes, although he doesn't ask.

While Quinn himself isn't exactly celibate, he rarely hooks up with humans these days. And when he does, he never feeds on them. If he did that, he'd have to hypnotize them to forget, and that would make any intimacy feel nonconsensual. So, unlike most vampires, he keeps the two things strictly separate.

It's been a long time, though. If he really wanted to, he could return downtown tonight, go to a club, and probably leave with a willing partner. But the truth is, he's just not interested enough to bother. Sex with strangers is unfulfilling. Back when he'd still been human, before he'd met his wife, he'd considered going into the priesthood. Although he'd lost his faith a long time ago, he has often wondered if celibacy might still be the right life for him after all.

Yet, if he's being honest with himself, as of late that thought no longer crosses his mind.

On Saturday morning, Genny wakes up to the feel of JP's lips on her shoulder. She smiles and rolls over, but when he leans in to kiss her, she pulls back. "Hold on a minute." Getting up, she heads to the bathroom to pee and brush her teeth.

When she slips back beneath the sheets, she greets him with a kiss. "Morning."

"Morning. I was just wondering, do you like omelettes?"

That's not at all what she'd expected him to say. "Sure."

"Great!" He throws back the sheets and starts to get up.

Before he can leave the bed, she grabs his arm and pulls him back. "What's your hurry, mister?"

"I thought I'd make you breakfast. Why? Do you have something else in mind?" His dark eyes are twinkling.

Genny loves how happy he always seems to be. His good moods tend to rub off on her as well. "For the record, you are amazing," she says, smiling. "Do you treat all your girlfriends this well?"

JP props his pillow against the headboard and leans back into it. "I know you're going to find this difficult to believe, but I actually only had one before you. Well, two, but primary school doesn't count."

"Really? You're right, I definitely find that hard to believe."

He shrugs. “She wasn’t immortal. When I realized I was starting to fall for her, I decided to break it off. It wouldn’t ‘ave been fair to stay with her when there was no future.”

“Why not?”

A soft sigh slips out as he thinks about the other girl. “It wouldn’t have worked out. You remember what Maman told you?”

She recalls all too well. “Immortals can only marry and reproduce with other immortals. But my mom broke that rule. You can’t help who you fall in love with.”

“The uproar over your mother’s marriage to your father impacted everyone. It was a very big deal. My own mother has stressed the importance of that rule my entire life. I would’ve probably moved back to France to live with my father soon if I ‘adn’t met you.”

“Seriously? You were considering moving back?”

JP nods. “It would’ve been my only option to meet another immortal woman. As far as I knew, my relatives were the only ones in this area. Until I met you, that is. And what a wonderful turn of events that ended up being.”

Snuggling into his side, Genny says, “I agree. I would’ve just kept on living my life completely oblivious to the truth about my family and myself if Dawn and I had decided to celebrate my birthday at a different club.”

“Yes. And if you’d done that, you might’ve been killed, because the vampires might’ve found out about you anyway.”

“Maybe.” Here’s an opening to broach the Quinn subject. “Have you ever considered that not all of them might be evil? Just like not all immortals are probably as kind as you and your family?”

Shifting his head so he’s looking at her directly, he says. “I love that you try to see the good in others, but please don’t be naïve, Gen. Vampires are evil by their very nature. Once they’re turned, all their ‘umanity is lost. We’re just food to them. Nothing more.”

She opens her mouth to protest, to admit she knows one who is neither evil nor lacking humanity, but she closes it again. She doesn’t want to get into a philosophical discussion about human and vampire nature right now, especially not one that might lead to an argument.

Maybe all other vampires are as JP describes them, but she knows Quinn is not. He's different. She may still have lots to learn about both vampires and immortals, but she's sure about that.

"You two look happy," Dawn says.

She and Genny are nursing drinks at a booth at the back of the club. Jonny and Flav are up dancing, and JP has just excused himself to go to the washroom.

"We are," Genny admits, smiling.

Dawn smiles back. "Good. I thought you'd never get over your last guy. I'm glad to see you've finally met someone interesting."

Chuckling, Genny thinks of all the stuff she's found out since she'd met JP, stuff Dawn still has no idea about. "*Interesting* doesn't cover it." A big part of her wants to tell her best friend everything, but JP and his family have cautioned her on the importance of keeping the truth about them under wraps. "What about you?" she asks. "We haven't talked much the past few weeks. Which is totally my fault, since I've been spending nearly all my free time with JP. Sorry."

"That's okay. I know you've been busy. Not much is new. Work is the same. Watched a bunch of movies. Hey, did you hear that they made a movie of Anne Rice's *Interview with the Vampire*?"

"No way!"

"Starring Brad Pitt and Tom Cruise. It'll be out this fall. We'll have to get a group together to see it."

Genny nods, but inside she wonders if Dawn would still be as excited if she found out vampires are real. She also can't help wondering what Quinn would think about the movie.

Jonny and Flav return to the booth at the same time as JP. Before they can talk more, "Fascination Street" by The Cure starts up. Jonny breaks into a grin and grabs onto Genny's hand. She and Dawn get up and follow him back to the dancefloor.

Genny has already finished one drink and is working on her second, although she's avoiding Zombies. Her goal tonight is to put all thoughts of vampires, slayers, and life-threatening danger out of her head and just have some fun with her friends.

And she gets to for a solid two hours before the hair on the back of her neck rises and she gets an involuntary shudder. *Quinn*, she thinks, rising onto her toes and trying to see over the heads. She starts toward the entrance. As she's working her way through the crowd, someone grabs her elbow. She spins around, expecting to find Quinn, but it's JP, looking worried.

"That vampire's 'ere again," he tells her. "We need to go."

Genny sighs. There's no way to avoid telling JP the truth now. Craning her neck, she looks around again and finally spots Quinn at the end of the bar. "It's okay," she tells JP, resuming walking toward Quinn.

"What do you mean it's okay?" JP says from behind her. She doesn't reply.

When she gets to him, Quinn's eyes meet hers, flash to JP, then back to her again. He's not smiling.

"You decided to show up," she says.

JP steps in front of her protectively. Then he processes what she'd said and turns back at her, brows narrowed. "Wait. You know 'im?"

Genny looks up at him and sighs. "Yeah. We're..." She stops, glancing back at Quinn. "We're friends."

Shaking his head, JP scowls. "You're friends with a...with *him*? When did *that* 'appen? And why am I just learning about it?"

She's fully aware that, loud music or not, Quinn can hear every word. She needs to defuse this situation before it escalates. "Quinn, this is JP. JP, meet Quinn."

Looking at JP again, she takes hold of his hand and squeezes his fingers to try and placate him. He doesn't say hello to Quinn.

Quinn, on the other hand, looks amused. "I didn't come for the entertainment," he says to Genny. She can barely hear him, and has to move closer, dragging JP a few steps closer as well.

"I have information. Can we speak somewhere a bit quieter?"

Genny frowns. "Follow me," she tells both of them. She releases JP's hand and heads for their booth without looking back. She knows they'll come.

She passes Dawn blissfully swaying in one of the cages and Flav doing his artful writhing in one corner of the dancefloor. Jonny holds down their booth by himself. When he sees both Quinn and JP, he raises an eyebrow at Genny.

"Sorry, Jon," she says, "But could you please give us a few minutes?"

He slides out, appraising Quinn before flashing Genny a wide smile and a thumbs up behind the guys' backs.

"What's up this time?" she asks Quinn as he takes a seat across from her and JP. JP is still scowling.

"Cassandra found out the Assembly has sent an assassin." Quinn tells her. "He's already in the city. So you need to be extra careful."

"Who's Cassandra?" JP asks. "And who's the Assembly?"

Genny takes his hand under the table and gives it a reassuring squeeze. "Cassandra is Quinn's friend. I'll explain everything later, okay?"

"I should 'ope so." He still looks unhappy.

"Do you know anything about this assassin?" she asks Quinn.

"He's huge. Eastern European. I've never met him, but he has a reputation for brutality."

"What a shock," JP mutters.

"Thanks for telling me," Genny says. She turns to JP. "Should we go? It's a big city. There are a million places I could be."

"Why should we believe any of this? It's probably a trick so you'll leave with him." He bobs his chin toward Quinn.

Quinn is ignoring JP, presumably not surprised by his hostility. He's looking only at Genny, waiting for her response. "They know I saw you here. You're in danger if you stay. You need to get home. Or at least to somewhere he'd need an invite to enter."

"I think you're the one who needs to leave," JP says to him. "You're not welcome 'ere."

"JP!" Genny says, shocked. "Don't be an ass. He's trying to help."

"And I'm trying to keep you safe," JP replies. He's still glaring at Quinn.

"So am I," Quinn says. He gets up and disappears into the crowd.

Genny turns to JP. "I'll tell you everything once we're back at your place, I promise. Can you please just go with it for now? You may not trust him, but I do."

"Why? At least give me one damn reason why you trust that guy. Because none of this makes a lick of sense to me."

Genny clutches JP's hand in both of hers. "Because he let me out last weekend. Remember I told you the lock on the cage was open when I woke? Well, it was Quinn who unlocked it. Now please, let's go before some monster assassin shows up and tries to kill us."

As they stand, Genny spots Quinn returning. Before he can say a word, she hears JP mutter, "*Shit.*"

She turns to him. "What?"

"We need to go," Quinn says as he gets close. "Right now."

JP wraps an arm around Genny and ushers her toward the back door. When they reach it, he spares a glance behind him. "Good God! That guy is massive!"

"You saw him?"

"He just came in," Quinn replies for JP. "Go. Now."

JP pushes open the door, but before Genny goes through, she turns back to Quinn, beckoning him closer.

"My friend Dawn is dancing in one of the cages. She has dark hair, blue eyes and is wearing a black dress. Can you get her? We're parked in the lot just south of here off Richmond. Meet us there? Please?"

Quinn just nods as he shuts the door behind them.

They hurry down the back stairs. "I hope he didn't spot us," Genny says as they slip out into the alley.

"I 'ope your so-called *friend* didn't just send us into a trap. But I'm sure you didn't think of that when you asked 'im to get Dawn, did you?"

Genny sighs. "I don't wanna argue about this right now. Let's just get to your car and wait for them."

JP is silent the rest of the short walk, but he keeps a firm hold of Genny's hand. When they reach the car, they both climb inside and he locks all the doors. She's on high alert, twisting her head to watch out the windows in every direction.

After a few strained moments, JP says, “Did you even once consider that maybe the vampire let you out and...and did whatever to befriend you so that you'll trust ‘im? So it will be easier to take you next time?”

Genny's stressed about their safety, especially Dawn's right now, and can feel her irritation rising. And she really doesn't want to be irritated with JP. She's been keeping things from him, which is her own fault, so she understands why he's confused and suspicious. “Of course I've considered it,” she says, holding her temper. “But I trust my intuition. And my intuition tells me I can trust Quinn.”

“Well you just put your friend's life in the ‘ands of your intuition,” he says. “So I sure ‘ope you're right.”

“I wish you...” She stops as she feels the tingle again. Looking around the lot once more, she spots Dawn and Quinn hurrying toward them between a rows of cars. Though she hadn't doubted Quinn for a moment, anything could have happened with that huge vampire. She exhales a sigh of relief as she reaches behind her to unlock the rear door for Dawn.

“Why'd you guys leave without me? And why have I never met your friend Quinn before?” Dawn asks Genny as she gets into the car.

“Good question. Just what I'd like to know,” JP responds dryly.

Genny ignores them both, rolling down her window to thank Quinn, but he's already walking away. For reasons she can't explain, she calls his name in her head: *Quinn!*

He stops and turns back to her.

Did I say that out loud? But no, in the mood JP's in right now, he would have surely reacted. Quinn looks expectant, like he's waiting for her to say more. How could he have heard her? His turning back must've been a coincidence. Mouthing the words “thank you,” she waves.

He gives a small nod, lifting a hand to her before vanishing into the night.

Chapter 8
Nowhere Fast

JP drops Dawn off at her apartment building and then they silently head to his. Both he and Genny have been unusually quiet during the drive, but Genny knows they need to talk this out soon. She can tell he's hurt and angry she'd kept a secret from him. Especially *this* particular secret. She should've told him every time she'd spoken to Quinn, but she knew he wouldn't like it, wouldn't understand. Now she's stuck in the awkward position of trying to fix this mess she's made.

Once they're inside his apartment and he's locked the door, she expects him to turn and confront her about it, but instead he kicks off his shoes and walks to the bedroom.

"JP?" she says, following him.

"What?"

"We need to discuss this."

"Clearly. But I don't even know where to start. The fact that you're friends with a fucking *vampire*?" He spits out the word like it burns his tongue. "Or the fact that you deliberately didn't tell me? We've been together for all of two weeks and you're already keeping secrets." Sitting on the edge of his bed, he slumps forward and drags his fingers through his hair, making it stick up in thick black clumps.

"I know I should've told you. I'm sorry."

He lifts his gaze to meet hers. "So why didn't you?"

"I guess because I knew you'd react the way you're reacting. But that's no excuse. I should've told you anyway. We can't keep secrets from each other if we want this to work. And I do."

JP sighs. "I do, too. But I think you're being dangerously naïve. You don't know the 'istory like I do. You're new to all this. One vampire pretends to be nice to you, and you're swayed into thinking they're not all evil? They killed your parents! And your grandparents, and aunts, and uncles, and nieces. They killed your whole family! And they'll kill you, too, the moment they get a chance."

She feels her anger rising again. "Don't think I'm not fully aware of that. Maybe you're right. Maybe every other vampire is evil. But Quinn is not."

"What makes you so sure? Can you explain that beyond merely saying it's your intuition?"

"If he wanted to kill me, I'd already be dead. He's had plenty of chances."

That had clearly been the wrong thing to say. JP's eyes narrow. "Just 'ow much time 'ave you spent with this vampire?"

Genny blows out a long puff of air and sits beside him. She reaches for his hand, but although he lets her take it, he doesn't thread his fingers through hers.

"He...he came downtown after work a couple days this week and we talked a bit. In a public place. There were lots of people around and I was in no danger." She doesn't mention the subway rides and she doesn't mention the tingle. JP's already worked up enough as it is. "I was exaggerating when I said he's had lots of chances. But he could've killed me last weekend and he didn't."

"What did you talk about?" His voice is still icy.

"I asked him why he unlocked the cage and he said he realized I didn't deserve to die. He and his...girlfriend Cassandra do jobs for the Assembly sometimes. That's the group of vampires who run things in their world. They were told to grab me and hand me over, but instead Quinn, presumably risking his own life to do it, let me go." JP starts to say something, but Genny keeps right on talking.

"If he was as cruel and merciless as you say, he would've killed me himself or just let them take me. It would make no sense to let me go, then spend time earning my trust just to kill me later. And tonight he got Dawn out of the club for me, no questions asked. He's proven he's trustworthy."

Standing up, JP braces a hand against the wall and runs the other over his face. "Okay. So one vampire 'elped you. I still don't understand why. Why would Quinn release you, a total stranger? Especially an immortal slayer who they'd surely been told would kill them if she could?"

Annoyance flares up again. "Oh, I don't know," Genny says. "Maybe because he's not evil? And if he's not, then I can only assume there are other vampires who also aren't evil. Maybe they're a lot more like us than we want to believe, because it's easier for us to kill them if we see them as evil?"

"You mean like 'ow they've killed your entire family?"

"Enough," she groans. "Please. I don't have all the answers. I barely know any answers at all."

With another long sigh, JP sits back on the bed and puts his arm around her, pulling her against him. "Fine. I trust you, and you obviously trust Quinn, so…fine. I'm done arguing about this. But please don't keep major stuff like this from me anymore. I…I care about you so much, and I want this to work. But it only can if we're honest with each other."

"I know and I agree. I'm sorry again for not telling you."

"I guess I understand. I did kind of lose my mind there for a bit. Most of it was because of the whole vampire thing, but I admit there was also a part of me that was jealous."

Genny lifts her face to look at him. "You were?"

"Totally. I'd just found out you'd kept your friendship with a vampire a secret from me. I couldn't 'elp it. All kinds of negative thoughts flew into my mind."

"You have nothing to feel jealous about. I'm all yours."

He bends his head to kiss her. "That's good. Because I don't want to lose you."

"You won't. But I have to ask: if we did break up, would you really move back to France?"

JP shrugs. "Probably."

With a smile, Genny teases, "So you're only with me because I'm immortal?"

He grins back. "Oh yes. Absolutely. It's definitely not because of your laugh, or your pretty green eyes, or how sexy you look wearing nothing but my t-shirt, or that thing you do with your—"

"Stop," she laughs. "Or I won't do it tonight." Before she can say more, he kisses her again. And then there's no further talking for a while.

For the past hour, Quinn has been prowling the streets searching for any sign of Gruhn, but so far has found no trace of the huge vampire. He's pretty sure Gruhn had spotted him ushering Dawn out Apothecary's back door, and he'd half wondered if the assassin might come looking for him. But apparently not. For all Quinn knows he may be far away by now. Hopefully he doesn't find Genevieve.

Quinn hadn't followed them to ensure they got back okay, not wanting to lead Gruhn to where they live, but part of him wishes he had. Hopefully she's home safe in bed now. If anything happens to her because of one of his bad decisions, he'll never forgive himself. And his list of unforgivable offences is already long enough. It's not the time to let himself dwell on that, though. He has to focus on finding Gruhn.

Some vampires are excellent trackers, some not so much. As far as Quinn can tell, it's because age improves their already enhanced senses. He's good at prey tracking, but tracking another vampire in this dirty, smelly, busy part of the city is proving difficult tonight.

At last he stops at a payphone and calls Cassandra. She had a date earlier, and if it had gone well she might not be home. But after two rings, she picks up. "Thrills, chills, or kills? To what do you owe the pleasure?"

Typical Cassandra. Though he's heard most of her shtick before, it still brings a smile. "It's me. How was your date?"

He hears a chuckle. "Total bust. What's up?"

"The assassin showed up at the club tonight. I got Genevieve and her friends out, but now I can't find him.

Look, I hate to ask, but you're a better tracker than I am. Will you come help?"

She pauses for a second. Only a second. Then she simply says, "Where are you?"

He tells her and hangs up, appreciating that she hadn't questioned him further before agreeing. He knows she'll get here as fast as she can, so he blends into the shadows along the side of a nearby store and waits.

Earlier at Apothecary, Genevieve had introduced him as her friend. He'd also overheard her tell JP that she trusts him. Quinn knows he doesn't deserve either her friendship or her trust, but still, hearing her say those things makes him feel a sort of pleasure he hasn't felt in longer than he can remember. If she knew the truth about the things he's done, she'd offer him neither. In fact, she'd undoubtedly stake him. And if she ever tries, he's pretty sure he won't fight back.

Not ten minutes later, Cassandra steps into the glow of the corner streetlight. Her long red hair is perfectly coiled, her makeup impeccable. How she'd managed to speed down here and not muss her hair is beyond Quinn.

He joins her, and as they start down the street she quietly peppers him with questions about what Gruhn looks like, smells like, how long since he'd left the club, and which areas Quinn has already covered.

"You should've called me right away," Cassandra chides. "This'll be next to impossible now."

"I know. I didn't want to get you involved."

She snorts. "But you got desperate enough to change your mind? Or did you just miss my company that much?"

He doesn't reply, but again he smiles.

"I'm gonna go with both," she answers herself.

They move silently through back streets and alleys for another hour, but still find nothing. Eventually they end up on the waterfront. It's a lot more peaceful down here. Quinn can hear the waves lapping against the dock and the groan of ropes rubbing against boat hulls.

"Ready to call it a night yet?" Cassandra asks. "There's no trace of him. Maybe he has access to a mage and is using a cloaking spell."

"I saw him at the club."

"Yeah, but you were expecting him. If he's using a spell, you wouldn't have noticed him at all if you hadn't known he might show up."

Quinn frowns. "That could be problematic."

"What, you thought keeping tabs on a vampire assassin would be easy?" She's giving him that look again, the one he knows means she's questioning his sanity.

"No. But maybe between the two of us…"

"One of the two of us is ready to find a snack and head home."

"Fine," he sighs. "Let's go."

They start walking north toward Union station. As they're passing through another graffiti covered alleyway, Cassandra spots a couple making out against the wall.

"Dinner is served," she mutters under her breath. She takes two silent steps closer to the lovers, then looks back. "Joining?" she asks so softly only Quinn can hear.

He shakes his head.

"Your loss." Cassandra glides up to the couple and sets a hand on the man's shoulder. "Interested in a threesome?"

Both humans reek of beer. The guy takes one look at Cassandra and smiles drunkenly. "You serious?"

"Serious as death by exsanguination."

He doesn't understand, doesn't get the joke. Quinn's only half-sure it *is* a joke.

Cassandra turns to the woman. "What about you, doll?" She stares into her eyes as she speaks. "You're not afraid of little ol' me, are you?"

The girl shakes her head.

The guy laughs. "Afraid? Of you?"

Turning back to him, Cassandra also holds his gaze. "How 'bout you shut up and just enjoy?"

Then she pulls them both close and bites into the man's neck. He grunts, but does not cry out. The girl watches, fascinated. Perhaps she thinks Cassandra is just kissing her lover's throat. Perhaps she doesn't care either way anymore.

After a minute, Cassandra lifts her head from the man and buries her face into the skin behind the girl's ear. Quinn hears a soft moan. He knows that sound well. If a vampire is precise and gentle when they feed, the act can cause the donor intense pleasure. It's why so many vampires combine sex and feeding.

Quinn watches them for a few minutes, but although he's also hungry, he makes no move to join in. He doesn't let himself have fresh human blood too often. Last night's indulgence had been enough for a while. He'd better wait until he gets home and can drink from a blood bag.

Cassandra finishes her meal and heals them both, carefully licking up every drop of spilled blood. It's an innately sexual act, a personal moment of connection between predator and prey, and Quinn looks away.

"Look at me," Cassandra commands the couple, and their eyes instantly dart to hers. "You're both going to go home now and fuck each other silly. And you'll have no memory of meeting me."

The woman nods. The guy just stares at Cassandra in awe. She pushes them toward the street-lit sidewalk and slips back into the shadows with Quinn.

"Enjoy the show?" she asks, smirking as she wipes off the corner of her mouth.

He doesn't reply; he just turns and continues walking.

"So I wanna ask you something," Cassandra says as they head for the far end of the alley. "The other day you said the immortal girl reminds you of someone you used to know?"

Quinn nods.

"An old flame?"

"An old friend."

"You sure about that?"

He picks up his pace and she has to speed up to match his stride. "Very sure. She was betrothed to another. We were only ever friends."

"Did you love her?"

He nods again. "Yes. But not the way you're implying. Why are you asking about this?"

"Have you *ever* loved anyone the way I'm implying? I know you never loved me that way. Which was fine, I wasn't looking for that anyway. But in all the time I've known you, this is the first time I've seen you—"

"*What*?" Quinn snarls. It's one thing to talk about Madeleine, but he definitely doesn't want to talk about past loves. Love. Singular. There had only ever been her.

Cassandra holds up both hands in mock surrender. "Sorry. Touchy subject, I know. Can I just say one more thing and then I'll shut up about it?"

Quinn exhales a bitter laugh. "Do I have a choice?"

"Not in the slightest. Look, if after a century you've finally gotten your head out of your ass enough to let yourself fall for someone, I'm all for it. But you couldn't have made a worse choice if you'd tried. Not only is this girl marked for death, but also, let's face facts. She has a boyfriend. She's not gonna return your feelings. If that's even what's going on behind that thick skull of yours. Feelings."

At first he doesn't reply. But after another minute of walking, he says, "She's a friend. A friend I don't want to die. That's all."

Cassandra side-eyes Quinn as they reach one of the many entrances to Union station. "If you say so."

Marie frowns, looking from JP to Genny and back again. "Mon Dieu! 'Ow terrifying. Are you sure you are all right?"

"We're fine," JP assures his mother. He squeezes Genny's hand.

They had just explained to Marie and René what had happened the night before. At Genny's request, they'd agreed to leave out Quinn's role, not wanting a rehash of last night's argument with JP's family.

Marie is clearly worried. "I cannot believe they sent an assassin after you."

"I can. Those freaks are ruthless," René says with disgust. "We will 'ave to be extra careful. Tell me more about this assassin. Other than big, what did 'e look like?"

"I didn't really see him," Genny responds. "JP did."

"The vampire was very large, over six and a half feet I'd say, and built like a tank. Dark 'air and beard. Black jacket. That's all I could tell. It was really crowded."

All René's attention is on his nephew. "Think carefully. Is there any chance he saw you?"

JP frowns. "I don't think so. There was no sign of 'im when we left for the car."

"You both need to promise me you'll be 'ome by dusk and not leave until dawn every day. No more going dancing. Take no chances," Marie says. She looks worried.

"Of course," Genny immediately agrees. "We were just talking about that on the walk over."

"Forgive me for being indelicate, but where did you sleep last night?" René asks.

Genny and JP glance at each other. "She stayed at my place," JP admits.

"That is fine. But wherever you choose to stay, Geneviève, make sure you are inside before the sun sets. I know it is not your intention, but please keep in mind you are also putting my nephew's life at risk."

Genny sighs. "I know. I've thought of that, believe me. We'll be very careful."

"Please do. Now I think we need to increase your training time. Come," Marie says, extending a hand to Genny. "Let's get started."

They all follow Marie out the back door and onto the lawn. Genny spars with them for the next forty-five minutes, and she's amazed to realize she's getting pretty good at fighting. Though Marie and René manage to knock her to the ground a few times, for the most part she's able to avoid their attacks and take them down herself. And much to JP's delight, she vanquishes him every time he tries.

After another delicious Marie-cooked meal, instead of going back to his place, JP borrows René's car and drives Genny home.

"Do you think I should tell Dawn? She was in danger last night and didn't even know it."

"Can she keep secrets?" JP asks. "Will she be able to deal with such an incredible truth as ours?"

Genny considers. "Dawn has always been pretty open-minded. And I hate keeping who I really am from her. Considering the risk now just for being my friend, I think I should fill her in."

"As long as you trust her not to tell anyone. When are you planning to talk to her?"

"As soon as I can. This week. I'll see if she'll meet me for lunch one day."

"If you want me to join you for support, just let me know. It's a good excuse to come downtown and see you during the day." Their eyes meet and he smiles.

A minute later he pulls up in front of Gran's and Genny turns to him, taking both his hands and threading her fingers through his, palm to palm. "So are we okay? After last night, I mean?"

JP gives her what might be the softest look she's ever seen. "Completely."

"That's good. I hated that you were mad at me."

"Fighting sucks," he agrees. "Let's never do it again."

"How about kissing instead?" she says with a grin.

"Now there's a concept I can get behind." JP pulls her into his arms and it's another ten minutes before she goes inside.

"You can live without me for one day," Genny teases.

"Nearly two if I won't see you until after work on Tuesday." JP's trying to sound pouty but she can tell he's grinning. "That's the longest we've been apart since we met."

She'd called to tell him she's going to spend the evening at home with Gran and Chloe. Since they'd started dating, she feels like she's been neglecting them, not to mention her chores. If she doesn't do some laundry soon, she's going to run out of clean clothes to wear to work. Between training and spending time with JP, she's let a lot slide, and although she's had good reasons, she still feels guilty about it. "You'll live I think."

"Yes, but will you?"

Laughing, she promises she'll talk to him tonight, then hangs up the phone, turns off her computer, and heads for the elevator bank.

One of the other secretaries joins her on the way down and starts to complain about one of their annoying coworkers. Genny's absorbed in the conversation until they reach the lobby and she realizes Quinn is once again nearby.

Her workmate is still grumbling as they approach the doors leading out to the street. Conscious of the situation,

Genny makes an excuse to turn back while the other woman leaves. She does a mental countdown from twenty, then steps outside and looks to the left.

Sure enough, he's waiting in the same spot as last time. The sidewalk along King Street is in the shade at this time of day, but it's hot and sunny and she spots a cap clutched in one hand. He risks painful burns to come and see her and for the life of her she can't understand why.

"Making this a habit?" she asks playfully as she joins him.

Quinn shrugs, but he smiles back. "Maybe. Would you prefer I didn't?"

They start down the steps to the subway platform like this is just what they do now. Last week she'd told JP she hadn't needed a chaperone. Why is this any different?

"No, it's fine. Unless you're doing it to babysit me. I've already had my fill of that."

He raises a brow, but doesn't ask for clarification. "I wanted to discuss what happened Saturday night."

Genny glances over at him. "The, uh, *big* thing or the thing just before you left?"

"You mean the returning your friend thing?"

Does he not realize what had happened? Maybe not. "Thanks again for that."

He nods. With a gust of wind, the train pulls in and once again they board and find seats vacated for them. Genny could definitely get used to this.

Dropping her voice, she leans closer to him, keeping her eyes fixed on her bag in her lap. He smells like soap, a little. Nothing more. "You were walking away from the car. And then you turned back to me and I waved. Why did you turn around?"

Frowning, he replies, "You called me."

Like this? Genny thinks. She projects the words at him the same way she'd projected his name Saturday night. It's kind of like mentally tossing a thought to someone.

Quinn's eyes shoot wide. "How'd you do that?"

"I don't know. You really heard me?"

He nods, looking thoughtful.

After a few moments of silence, Genny wonders if he's trying to reply the same way. "Can you do it, too?"

"Did you hear me?"

She shakes her head. "Try again. Really try to project it at me."

He stares at her, concentrating. Looking back into those pale eyes, she's once more distracted by how unique they are. But she hears nothing. "Did you?"

"Yes."

"Nada. So it only works one way? Weird."

"I guess so." After a moment, he adds, "The first night I met you, you told me you could feel a sensation when I was around?"

"Yeah. I've started calling it the Quinn Tingle."

They share a smile.

"So it alerts you to my presence?"

Genny nods. "Every time."

He breaks eye contact. "Then I believe I owe you an apology. You must think I've been stalking you."

Chuckling, she says, "Haven't you?"

Leaning forward on his elbows, he looks sideways at her. "It's not that I..." He stops and suddenly smiles back. "You're teasing?"

"Yep. I know you know where I live, and I know you come by at night sometimes. Maybe that should freak me out, but...it doesn't. Because I also know you're just making sure I'm safe. I'm not scared of you, so it doesn't bother me any more than if it was JP doing it. Although I feel like I should just give you my phone number so you can call and check in. It'd be easier."

He's clearly surprised by her words. "You'd do that?"

"Sure. We should practice how far this mental connection thing goes anyway." She pulls her notepad from her bag, jots her number on a page corner, tears it off, and hands it to him. As he's tucking it into his jacket pocket, she adds, "I'm home tonight, so call me later and we'll see if it works from your place."

He seems amazed that she's not bothered by any of this. "I can't help wondering if the—I'm sorry, I can't say *Quinn Tingle* with a straight face, and Cassandra will never let me hear the end of it if she finds out about that—anyway, I can't help wondering if the two things are somehow connected?"

The more time Genny spends with Quinn, the more relaxed and cheerful he seems. He's a far cry from the tense, reticent guy she met not even two weeks ago. She wonders if he even realizes this. "I assume so. Do you think it could be a slayer thing? But if so, why just you and not Cassandra?"

"I don't know." He pauses, thinking. "It seems more like a spell to me."

"You think? Why would anyone cast a spell to connect us? Who would've even known we'd meet?"

Quinn tilts his head. "I wonder," he says softly.

The train shakes and lurches as it goes around a bend and comes into a station. Genny is again thrown into Quinn's side, and again she gets a jolt of energy through her entire body. "Sorry," she says, feeling her face redden as she quickly moves away from him. "What do you wonder?"

He smiles. "It's fine. Do you mind if I ask you a few questions about your family?"

"Go ahead. I don't know much, though. JP's the expert, although I doubt you asking him would go over very well right now." She rolls her eyes.

Quinn ignores the JP comment. "Your mother was Angelique Bourreau, correct?"

"Yes."

"What was your maternal grandmother's name? And her mother before that?"

"I was named after my great-grandmother, so that one's easy." She pauses, trying to think. "I'm sorry, I can't remember my grandmother's name. Gran told me she died when I was just a baby. She doesn't know much about my mom's family either. I'd have to ask JP. Why?"

"It's probably nothing. I was just thinking of possibilities for the origin of the spell."

"JP's mother told me my mom knew how to do magic. I guess she was a witch, although Marie says they don't like that word."

"They don't. Too much negative connotation thanks to idiot religious fanatics over the centuries. They prefer to be called mages."

"Did you know a witch—I mean, a mage?"

"I did. I knew some religious fanatics, too. I actually almost became one. Before..." He waves a hand toward his face. Before he'd been turned.

Now it's Genny's turn to be shocked. "No way!"

He nods. "My entire family was very devout. I had planned to be a priest."

"What changed your mind?"

Quinn's face goes serious again. Not quite devoid of emotion, but close. "I met the woman who became my wife."

Is he actually talking about his past? "Oh wow. I had no idea," she says. She now has at least a dozen more questions that he probably won't want to answer.

"How could you know?"

Before she can say anything else, the train pulls into at a station and she looks up, surprised to see they're already at her stop. "Oh. Time to get off." She stands up, turning back to him. "Any chance you feel like taking the bus with me today, or...?"

Quinn doesn't reply, but he puts on his cap and follows her off the train and down the escalator. Before they go outside, he also dons leather gloves and sunglasses and turns up the collar of his jacket. Only the lower half of his face is left exposed. It's an odd look on a hot July day, but Genny figures it's better than getting burned.

The bus is already waiting, so luckily Quinn isn't subjected to sunlight for long. He does his usual trick of vacating a seat for them and they sit down near the back.

"You're a bit overdressed. I guess it's hard to be discreet when you're trying to avoid sunburn."

"It is. But I don't care. It's better than staying home. And there's a lot more shade than you'd think, especially downtown with all the tall buildings."

"Right. So you said you wanted to talk to me about what happened on Saturday?"

He drops his voice. "Yes. Did you see the guy they sent?"

"No, but JP did. He said he was huge, with dark hair and a beard."

Quinn nods. "I tried to find him after you left, but I had no luck. But he won't give up. He'll come for you again."

"I know. JP and I talked about that yesterday. I'm not going to leave my place, or his if I'm there, between dusk and dawn. Not until this situation is resolved."

Frowning, Quinn says, "That's a good start. But he could be out in the daytime like me. You need to always be aware of your surroundings, especially when I'm not around."

"Do you think he knows where I live? Does the Assembly?"

Quinn turns to face her. "Not from me. I wish I'd never said anything about spotting you at all."

She debates saying she wishes he hadn't either, but there's no point. She knows he regrets it. So she simply says, "I know."

When the bus pulls up to her stop, she stands up and looks back at him questioningly. With a small smile he follows her off the bus.

Deliberately she crosses to the shady side of the street. It's so easy to forget he's a vampire.

"Does it hurt?" she asks.

Quinn shrugs. "A wee bit. I can handle it for short bursts."

"You sure? Because I feel kind of bad asking you to walk with me. I wasn't thinking about the sun."

He looks surprised by her concern. "No need to feel bad. I'm fine."

During the walk home, they keep to the shadows as much as possible. She tells him how well she's been doing with her slayer training, and that she's planning to enroll in a lunchtime karate class.

"Good. Keep it up. At this rate you'll be able to take him out yourself without any help."

Genny grins. "That's my hope. Although I'd take any help I can get."

When they reach her house, she hesitates. He's come all this way with her, but she knows JP would lose his mind if he found out she'd invited Quinn inside. She wonders how long it will take until JP understands what she already knows: that Quinn is on their side.

Before she can apologize for being rude, one corner of his mouth curves up. "Don't worry. I don't expect an invite."

Her face falls. "I would, but..."

"I know."

"Call me tonight, remember?"

At that, his smile grows wider. "I will." Quinn turns and walks off into the shade of the big maples that overhang her street.

Genny watches him until she can no longer see him, then turns and unlocks the door. She can't help thinking how much she likes his smile. And then she feels guilty for thinking it.

But only a little.

Chapter 9
Everything but the Girl

At 9:32 Genny fumbles to answer the ringing phone. Chloe had been talking with her new boyfriend for the past forty-five minutes, so Genny assumes this call is for her. But is it JP or Quinn? As she grabs the receiver, she asks herself which of them she's hoping for.

"Hello?"

"Miss me?" It's JP. And Genny flat out refuses to acknowledge her slight sense of disappointment. Because she isn't disappointed. She's happy to hear JP's voice, and she'd be even happier if he was here beside her.

"Definitely," she says.

"Did you get everything done that you wanted to?"

"Yep. Most of it. At least I have some clean clothes now."

"Good. Does this mean you'll come over after work tomorrow? For training, of course."

"Of course. What else?" she laughs.

His voice drops an octave. "I could maybe think of one or two other things."

"You mean like dinner?"

"Yeah. That's definitely what I meant. 'Ow was your day?"

Genny's smile fades. But she'd promised him honesty, so she has to tell him. "Quinn showed up after work."

JP is silent for a moment. Then: "Oh yeah?" She can tell he's trying to control his reaction.

"He wanted to talk about what happened Saturday night. Make sure we were being cautious, staying in at night, etcetera."

"So 'e's just concerned for your well-being? That's the only reason 'e keeps coming to see you?"

"JP..."

"What? I'm just curious why the vampire would show up at your office yet again."

Genny's annoyance is rising. "Okay, so you remember the part about me and Quinn being friends, right? And friends are allowed to talk without one friend's boyfriend getting all grumpy. Right?"

"I suppose." He doesn't sound convinced.

"I can't keep having this conversation with you. The way I see it, this can go one of two ways. You either accept it and stop trying to make me feel bad about it, or I stop telling you when I see him. Your choice."

She hears him blow out a puff of air. "I don't want you to keep secrets from me."

"And I'm not. I just told you I saw him." She pauses, and then adds, "Do you trust me?"

"Of course. It's not you I don't trust."

Genny sighs. "Fine. Distrust him as much as you like. But if you trust me, then you need to quit getting upset every time I talk to him."

There's silence for a few seconds. "I'll try my best. I don't want you to feel like you can't tell me stuff. You can tell me anything. Nothing you could say could change how I feel about you."

"Good."

"So we're done fighting?"

"That's up to you."

"Two and a half weeks and two fights behind us already?" He chuckles. "I don't know if that's a good thing or bad."

Genny laughs. "I guess we're both just passionate people."

"I think that's an understatement."

They talk more, but in the back of Genny's mind she's thinking that Quinn will probably call soon, if he hasn't already. Her Gran doesn't have call waiting or call display or any other features on her line, so Genny has no idea if he's already tried to get through. Then she realizes she's being dense. She has a way to talk to him right now. Well, maybe.

Quinn, don't call yet. I'm on the phone, she thinks as intensely as she can. She has no idea if it works, because she can't see him. This time she has no face to project the message to. Hoping he's heard, she tries again. *I'll let you know once I'm done.*

"...like tacos?"

Oops. "Pardon? Sorry, I missed a few words there."

"I was just asking if you like tacos. For dinner tomorrow?"

"Right. Yes, definitely love tacos. I like pretty much everything. Except onions. Skip the onions and we're good."

JP laughs. "Noted." His voice softens. "I can't wait to see you."

"Me, too. But if you don't mind too much, I'm gonna let you go. I should get ready for bed."

"What if I do mind?" He's kidding, but Genny is getting kind of anxious to hang up.

"You'll see me tomorrow. Then we can talk face to face."

"Talk, yes. And other things. Will you stay over?"

She frowns. "I'd like to, but I think since it's a weeknight I'll come home before dark. I'll sleep there Friday, though, okay?"

"Okay. I'll buy you your own toothbrush so you don't have to bring one. And—"

Laughing, she cuts in, "We'll talk tomorrow. Goodnight, JP."

"G'night."

She puts the receiver back, still smiling. One of the things she likes best about JP is how much of a big goofball he can be, at least when he's not acting all weird about Quinn. That reminds her. If Quinn had heard her message, he's probably waiting for her okay to call. She heads to the bathroom to quickly brush her teeth, then puts on her pajamas and crawls into bed.

You can call anytime, she thinks at him. And she has exactly enough time to wonder if he's even getting her messages when the phone rings again.

Snatching up the receiver, she says, "Hello?"

"Is this Genevieve?"

"Yes. Did you hear me tell you to call?"

"I did. So now we know you can reach me over at least five or six kilometers."

She smiles. "That could maybe come in handy." She's tempted to ask where he lives, but she decides not to. He's a pretty private guy. If he wants her to know, he'll tell her.

"I agree. Although it would be better if it worked both ways."

"True. And we should test to see how far away we can do it. Maybe tomorrow I can try to send you a message from downtown? Oh wait. You sleep during the day, right?"

"Usually. Although it's not mandatory. I can go several days without sleeping at all and it doesn't really impact me. Why don't you try to contact me about three? I usually get up by then anyway so I can be downtown by five."

To see me, she thinks.

"Yes."

Whoops. She hadn't actually meant to send that thought to him. She'll have to be more careful in the future. "This might be a dumb question," she asks. "But why? Not that I mind. I don't. I'm just curious." And so is JP. In fact, he's significantly more curious about it than she is. Except replace the word *curious* with *suspicious*.

"I enjoy your company. I've mostly only had Cassandra to talk to for the past seven decades. So meeting you has been...refreshing. And none of your questions are dumb."

Holy cow! They've been together for seventy years? That's like an old married couple, albeit one who still looks young and perfect. The phone cord twists around her arm as she rolls onto her side. "I enjoy your company, too. We must be doing this all wrong. Aren't we supposed to be mortal enemies or something?"

She hears a snort. "So I'm told. But I've learned to make my own decisions about who to trust."

Genny wishes JP would adopt the same attitude. How he can be so positive vampires have no humanity is beyond her. If he would just give Quinn a chance, get to know him the way she's doing, he'd understand.

Although Quinn can't see it, she nods. "Me, too. But back to what you were saying before. Can you really go without sleep for days? I'd be a mess."

"The longest I've gone is eleven days."

"That's insane! You weren't a total wreck?"

He pauses. After a second or two, he says, "Not for lack of sleep, no."

"I have so many questions about your life. JP told me some stuff, but...do you mind if I ask you?"

There's a soft chuckle. "Go ahead."

"Do you eat and drink, like, actual food? Or just blood?"

"I can eat whatever I like. Including garlic. But we need to have blood regularly or we'll wither. It doesn't have to be human, though. Animal is fine, although not as...invigorating."

Morbidly curious, she asks, "So do you hunt animals, or...?"

"I don't kill, if that's what you're asking. Nor does Cassandra. It's not necessary when we can just take some blood and then heal the donor."

Genny assumes that means he drinks mostly human blood. *Of course he drinks human blood*, she chides herself. *He's a frickin' vampire*. She needs to stop forgetting that. "But if you do that, how do you prevent the, uh, *donor* from freaking out and running off and telling everyone?"

"Oh. I assumed that was something JP would have told you. Vampires, at least ones who've been taught how, can use a form of hypnotism. We can compel people to forget they ever saw us."

"Seriously? You could make someone do your bidding? That's not creepy *at all*."

Laughing, he says, "I didn't say it wasn't creepy. But it can come in handy. Just think of all the situations you could use a skill like that."

Her mind flashes to her argument with JP after they'd gotten home on Saturday. But no, hypnotizing him to get over being angry with her wouldn't have been right. Convenient. But not right. "Like what?"

"Well, for example, Cassandra and I keep blood bags in the freezer for when we need them, like on days we don't go out. She gets them from clinics or hospitals or bloodmobiles.

We could break in, but it's a lot easier to just use hypnotism to get what we need. It's not ideal. I despise that the only way I can survive is by stealing blood, but there's no choice. Humans aren't just going to willingly donate it to us."

"No, probably not. It's a better solution than killing, though."

"That's what I keep telling myself. But I still don't like it. What I am...it's unnatural. We're monsters. Your family was right to want us dead."

Genny frowns. This conversation has taken an unexpectedly dark turn. Where had cheerful, laughing Quinn gone? "You're not a monster," she tells him firmly.

Another long pause. Then, softly, he says, "If you really knew me, you wouldn't say that."

"So tell me."

He sighs. It's a mournful sound. "I'm sorry. I just...I can't."

All humor has gone from his tone and Genny wishes she could rewind a few minutes and start over. "Quinn, listen to me please? You don't have to tell me anything about your past that you don't want to. I can only imagine that you've lived through some awful stuff, stuff you'd rather not remember. I can't pretend I understand, but I can promise I won't ask you to talk about things that make you uncomfortable. Okay?"

"Yeah."

"Good."

"I should let you get to sleep now." Much like their first subway conversation, they've hit a sensitive topic and his reaction is to disappear.

"Okay. I'll send you a message at tomorrow at three."

"Goodnight Genevieve."

"Goodnight. See you to—" The line goes dead before she can finish.

She hangs up the phone and rolls onto her back, staring up at the ceiling. Quinn's mood had changed so fast. Whatever had happened to him years ago had clearly been quite traumatic. She wishes he'd open up to her, but she knows that's probably too much to hope for, especially so early in their friendship. Still, before the dour turn, they'd been having another good talk. She really enjoys talking to him. Even if there are landmines to avoid.

And now she knows how he feeds, and about vampire hypnotism. She needs to find out more about that. Are immortals susceptible to it, too, or just humans? Because if the assassin can hypnotize her to not fight back, that could be a big problem.

She decides to ask Quinn to try it out on her next time she sees him face to face. If it works, she'll have to see if she can figure out a way to prevent it.

On Wednesday at a quarter to noon, Genny takes the elevator down and heads out onto the sidewalk. Even though she knows he won't be there, her eyes automatically go to the spot where Quinn often waits for her. He's not there, of course. It's the wrong time of day. And after how their last conversation had ended, she's not sure if he'll even show up today.

She walks a block to Richmond Street. Dawn had agreed to meet her for lunch at a little park hidden among the tall office buildings. Finding an empty bench near the fountain, she sits and waits.

Dawn had said she'd come at noon. She isn't always the most prompt, so by 12:10, Genny starts to eat her sandwich. At 12:20, she begins to get a bit irritated. Has Dawn forgotten their plans? Maybe she's sick? If she is, Genny's sure she would've called to cancel.

The park is pretty and the sun feels good on her skin, so Genny waits another twenty minutes before giving up and heading back to work. When she returns to her desk, she sees the red voicemail light flashing on her phone. Hoping it might be from Dawn, she checks the message, but it's just a reminder from her boss about a report that needs to go out.

She calls Dawn's work and the woman who answers tells Genny that Dawn hadn't shown up this morning. She hadn't called in sick; she just hadn't come in at all. The first inklings of worry bubble up, but before she can dial Dawn's apartment, her boss shows up at her desk and calls her into a meeting.

An hour later she gets back to her desk, types up the minutes, and then calls Dawn The phone rings six times before her friend's answering machine kicks in. After the beep, Genny says, "It's me. Missed you at lunch today. Are you sick and asleep? Call me when you get this."

Then she tries Dawn's parents' house. They both work, so unsurprisingly there's no answer, although Genny had been hoping her friend might be there. It's not like Dawn to not show up at work with no call to explain why. Genny's intuition tells her something's wrong.

She decides to call JP.

"'Ello?"

"Hi."

"Oh, hi. I just got back from the store. I got avocados to make us guacamole for the tacos."

"Great. So…I'm worried about Dawn."

"Why?"

"She was supposed to meet me at lunch so I could tell her about…you know. But she didn't show up. And she didn't go to work. And there's no answer at her place."

"That could mean any number of things. Maybe she forgot she had an appointment today when she agreed to meet you?"

Genny's fingers drum on the edge of her desk. "Yeah, maybe. But she wouldn't just not show up to work without calling to explain why."

"Do you want me to go over to 'er place and knock on the door?"

"Could you?"

"Of course. I'll go right now. Call you back soon."

"Thanks. Appreciate it."

After disconnecting, Genny tries to focus on work, but she's having trouble concentrating. Thirty minutes later her desk phone buzzes and she snatches it up on the first ring.

"No answer," JP tells her without preamble. "I knocked for several minutes, but I couldn't detect any movement inside."

"Damn." Genny blows out a sigh. "I really hope nothing's happened to her."

"Me, too."

"Would you mind terribly if I didn't come over after work? I wanna go home and see if I can reach her or her parents tonight. I need to know she's okay."

He doesn't hesitate. "Of course. Should I come over?"

"Maybe. I'll call you later. Sorry about dinner. Rain check?"

"Absolutely. Whatever you need from me, just let me know."

"Thanks, babe. I'll talk to you soon." As Genny hangs up, she looks up at the clock. It's 3:04. *Crap.* She needs to message Quinn.

She heads to the washroom, locking herself in a stall and sitting on the toilet lid. Closing her eyes, she pictures Quinn's face. And with the same intensity as if she'd been calling him out loud, she thinks: *Quinn!* She imagines him turning to look at her like he had on Saturday night. *I'm sorry about last night. I didn't mean to upset you. Hope I'll see you this afternoon.*

She debates telling him about Dawn, but since she has no idea if he can hear her, she decides to wait and see if he shows up after work. Hopefully he hasn't decided he's done with her.

It turns out she needn't have worried. Quinn is waiting for her in his usual spot when Genny steps outside. She can't help it; even as worried as she is about her best friend, she smiles the moment she sees him.

"It's me who should apologize," he says as she approaches.

Before he can continue, she cuts in. "No, you already told me you don't like to talk about your past. I shouldn't have asked. But hey, you heard me! That's crazy!"

He mirrors her smile. "It's pretty cool, yeah."

"So cool. There's actually another experiment I wanna try with you today." He arches an eyebrow. "But before I get to that, I need to tell you something. I'm a bit worried Dawn might be missing."

The smile vanishes. "Why?"

As they start down the subway steps, Genny explains about Dawn. "I've tried calling her like a dozen times and there's no answer. JP even went over and knocked on her door. I'm gonna try her parent's place when I get home. One of them should be back from work by then."

The northbound train pulls in and they board. When they sit down, Quinn turns to her. He looks troubled. "I think Gruhn might've spotted me leaving the club with her on Saturday."

Genny shuts her eyes for a moment. "That's not good. Not good at all." But then she remembers the aura thing. "If he saw you, he would have known you're a, uh…" She drops her voice. "A vampire. But he couldn't have mistaken Dawn for me. She has no aura."

"Right. But I suspect you didn't either before you turned twenty-one. Your sister doesn't."

Her eyes flare. "You've seen Chloe?"

Quinn nods. "I saw her go into your house a few times. I could tell you were related. But don't worry. I didn't tell anyone about her."

"I've never thought to look closely at her to see if she has one. But then again, I'm not very good at spotting auras yet unless I'm trying. Why wouldn't we have one until we turn twenty-one? JP didn't mention that."

"You said your mother could use magic, right?"

"That's what I was told."

"She might've put a concealment spell on you both when you were children. Presumably it wears off on your twenty-first birthday. It would explain why JP never noticed you before."

That hadn't crossed Genny's mind, but it makes sense. The night she'd met JP hadn't been his first time at Apothecary. "You think the Assembly told the assassin that my aura might be concealed by a spell?"

"I think Gruhn himself might be, which is why he may have assumed I was getting you out of the club and not Dawn. It's just a possibility. Neither Cassandra nor I have been able to track him down since I left you guys that night. And we've been trying."

"You have?"

Quinn holds her gaze, his face serious. "Of course. I want to stop him before he finds you."

“Wait. If he saw you leave Apothecary with a woman he thinks might be me, wouldn’t he have told the Assembly that you’re helping me? Doesn’t that put you in danger?”

He shrugs. “Possibly. But it doesn’t matter. I’ll take the risk. Besides, you’re their priority right now.”

Yours too, she thinks.

He nods. “Mine, too.”

Damn it. She’d done it again. She really needs to get better at controlling this. “It does matter if it means you and Cassandra might be in trouble now.”

“Don’t worry about us. We can take care of ourselves. And soon enough, you’ll be able to as well from what you’ve told me.” He smiles and she feels herself relax a little.

“So what about Dawn? What should we do?”

“Once you get home, I’ll call Cassandra. See if she has any idea yet where the assassin might be holed up. The Assembly has a few safehouses around the city. You know about one of them, and she’s trying to find out where the others are.”

“If they suspect you’re helping me, they won’t tell her anything,” Genny says, sighing.

“She can be very persuasive, not to mention persistent when she wants information.” He looks like he’s speaking from experience.

“I really hope Dawn will just answer the phone next time I call and all this worry will be for nothing.”

“Me, too.” He slouches back in his seat and focuses on her. “So what did you want to experiment on me?” There’s that grin again, like he can read her mind or something. Which he can’t, thank goodness. She just needs to get better at not thinking thoughts at him that she doesn’t mean to.

“Oh yeah. So last night you told me you could, like, hypnotize people, right?”

“Yes.”

“Do you have any idea if it works on, uh, people like me?” Genny asks.

“Immortal humans? I don’t know. I’ve never tried.”

“Can we try? Because if…Gruhn, right?”

Quinn nods.

"If Gruhn can hypnotize me, he could compel me to not fight back. Or invite him into my home. Or tell him stuff about my family."

Frowning, Quinn says, "I should've thought of that. You're right, we need to find out."

"Should we do it right here on the train? Or wait until we're somewhere a bit more private?"

Quinn glances up at the subway map. It has little lights that show the upcoming stations. "We're nearly at your stop. Let's wait until we get off the bus."

"Okay."

When the train arrives at the station, Quinn and Genny disembark and walk over to the bus. Clouds have rolled in and she notices he doesn't pull his gloves from his pocket this time.

Again, they sit in the back. Genny splays her left hand and starts to check off things on her fingers. "So I've learned about your diet, and sunlight, and hypnotism, and how to kill both your kind and mine. What else? Do you have a reflection in mirrors?"

Quinn chuckles. "Yes. Same as you. That was just a figment of Bram Stoker's imagination."

"Makes sense. How else could you guys get such great hair?"

They share a smile.

"We have enhanced senses, hearing, sight, smell, taste," Quinn tells her. "Even our emotions are amplified. Although with some of us, you wouldn't know it. Some have learned the trick of tampering down their feelings so they don't feel guilty about their choices."

"Really? That's a thing?"

He nods again.

Holding his gaze, Genny asks, "Why don't you?"

"I..." Quinn stops, breaking eye contact to look out the window. "I want to feel. Everything, both good and bad. Even if it hurts. If I didn't have my emotions, I wouldn't be me anymore. There wouldn't be anything left. I can't let that happen."

Genny has no reply to that. She reaches for his arm, wanting him to look back at her, wanting to tell him she understands, but the truth is that she doesn't. How could she? She drops her hand back to her lap.

When they get off the bus, they make a detour onto a residential street only a few blocks from Gran's. There's a small park down at the bend in the shade of several big oak trees. When they get there, Genny's happy to find it deserted.

They sit on a bench and Quinn turns to face her. "So, I'm going to look into your eyes. And you're going to focus on me and listen to my words. Okay?"

"What are you gonna make me do?" Genny asks with a nervous chuckle.

"How about I tell you to touch your nose? And you try to not do it. Try to keep your hands down."

"Okay." She can feel her heart rate increasing and wonders if he can hear it. Of course he can.

Quinn's eyes hold hers. His pupils seem to expand and contract as he says, "Don't be nervous. Just relax. I want you to do exactly as I say. Touch the tip of your nose with one finger. Do it now."

His eyes are so pretty. She can see why a potential victim might be mesmerized looking into eyes like that. She feels her hand start to lift up. But then she remembers. She instructs it to return to her lap. It goes right back to resting on her thigh.

Smiling, Quinn says, "Excellent. You resisted."

"I almost did it though. Maybe we should practice a bit more?" A twinge of guilt hits her. Is she just saying that because she likes the feeling she gets when they hold prolonged eye contact? *Don't be silly*, she chastises herself. It's important to be absolutely sure that vampires can't hypnotize her. Nothing more.

Quinn tries again. He tells her to clap her hands and they don't even twitch this time. Next he instructs her to stand up and jump into the air.

"Not a chance," she laughs.

He looks pleased. "I think you're safe from hypnotic persuasion. That's a relief."

They walk the rest of the way to Genny's house. When they get there, she doesn't hesitate. "Please come inside, Quinn."

His brows draw in. "Are you sure?"

"Very."

Nodding, he follows her inside. Chloe's out with her boyfriend, but Genny introduces him to Gran. Gran doesn't know he's a vampire, of course. Genny figures she'll probably tell her at some point, but she doesn't want to risk Gran freaking out in front of Quinn.

They sit in the living room while Genny calls Dawn's apartment again. Still no answer. Then she calls Dawn's parents. Her mother picks up, but Dawn isn't there, either. Not wanting to worry Dawn's mom, Genny makes an excuse for where she thinks Dawn might be and hangs up.

She looks up at Quinn worriedly. "No luck. Can you see if Cassandra can find out anything?"

He nods and she passes the phone to him. Once he hangs up, he says, "She thinks she has a lead on where he could be staying. Apparently he's not working alone. She's going to make another call, then come pick me up and we'll go check it out."

"I'm going too," Genny insists.

Quinn's eyes dart toward the kitchen where Gran is washing up. They've already been talking softly, but he drops his voice even lower. Genny has to lean in close to hear. "You're their target. It's far too risky for you to come. You're much safer here."

"I don't care. It's Dawn." Genny picks up the phone again and dials JP's number. As quietly as she can, she updates him.

"The vampire is *there*? At your 'ouse with you right now?" JP asks incredulously.

"That is so far from the point right now," Genny tells him. She'd been expecting that reaction, although hoping maybe he'd focus instead on the more important part of her news. "If you don't like it, then get your butt over here, too, and all four of us will go."

JP is silent for all of two seconds. Then he says, "Do not go anywhere until I get there."

She hangs up with a sigh.

"Everything okay?" Quinn asks.

"He's just...he's been raised to..." Genny stops, again glancing toward the kitchen doorway. Lowering her voice, she continues, "To hate what you are. I'm sorry."

He brushes this off with a wave of his hand. "It's understandable."

"He's wrong about you," she says firmly.

A tight smile surfaces. He opens his mouth, but then closes it again. After a moment, he says, "I don't want to cause trouble between you."

"You won't. Once he gets to know you better, he'll get over it."

Quinn shrugs. "We'll see."

A few minutes later, there's a knock on the door. Genny goes to answer it and finds JP standing there. From the expression on his face, she can tell he still has plenty to say about her inviting Quinn into her home.

"Not now," she whispers. "We need to find Dawn. Once I know she's safe, you can lecture me all you want. It won't change anything, but if it makes you feel better, I'll listen."

JP sighs. "Fine."

"Wait here."

She tells Gran she's going out with her friends for a couple of hours, and then she and Quinn join JP outside to wait for Cassandra.

Genny's heart is racing for multiple reasons. One, she's about to spend time with Cassandra, who, last she'd seen, doesn't care if Genny lives or dies. Two, she's standing between JP and Quinn. JP's tension is radiating off him and Genny doesn't like it one bit. She just wants things to be right between them, to be back to the way they should be. But most of all, she's terrified that her best friend in the world might be dead, killed by a vampire that's after Genny. If anything happens to Dawn, it will be all her fault.

"This is a terrible plan," Quinn says. He has his hat and sunglasses on, but it looks like he's staring at the street. "Genevieve is the one they're after. She should not be coming. Let Cassandra and I take care of this."

JP clears his throat and turns to Genny. "For once I agree with the vampire. You really should stay 'ome."

"Not a chance. Of the three of us, I'm the slayer, right? I just need some stakes. Where can I get stakes on short notice? Or, like, a sword or something?" She tries to smile but neither of them finds this situation even remotely funny. "Fine, I'll do it myself." She walks across the lawn to a tree on the edge of the property and tries to pull off a branch. She's strong, but the tree is stronger. The branch doesn't budge.

"Genny, please," JP begs. "We don't even know 'ow many there are. If anything 'appens to you…"

She turns around to find he's followed her. "No offence, but if any of us is gonna be a liability, it's you. But four of us are better odds than three. If we have any hope of getting Dawn back safe, we need all the help we can get."

Quinn stays where he is at the end of Gran's driveway. She thinks he's watching them, but she's not sure.

With a sigh, JP takes Genny's hand, brings it to his lips, and kisses it. "Just be careful."

"Ditto."

Before they can say more, an old silver Toyota Tercel pulls up to the curb right in front of them.

Cassandra reaches across and pushes open the passenger door. Ignoring Genny and JP completely, she looks up at Quinn and says, "Let's go."

Chapter 10
Dead Souls

"We have company," Quinn tells Cassandra, bracing a hand on the top of the door and indicating over his shoulder at Genny and JP.

Genny leans her head to see into the car. All she'd glimpsed of Cassandra last time had been a flash of red hair. Now all that hair is tucked up under a black knit toque. Her face is pale and pretty, with a pointed chin and thinly arched brows that are currently drawn in tight as she scowls. She looks like a woman you'd be smart not to mess with.

Cassandra eyes the two immortals. "Nope. Not gonna happen." To Genny, she says, "If you want your friend back alive, you need to let us handle this."

Shaking her head, Genny replies, "Dawn is like a sister to me. And I'm the only slayer you've got. I'm coming."

"I don't think you understand. We can move silently. They'll hear you both coming and we'll lose the element of surprise."

Genny's jaw hardens. "Then we can split up and come at them from different directions. I'm not taking no for an answer." She grabs the door handle, but the rear doors are locked.

Cassandra smiles, her gaze shifting back to Quinn. "She's got spunk, I'll give her that. Here's hoping it doesn't get any of us killed." She unlocks the doors and Quinn, Genny, and JP climb inside the car.

It takes almost thirty minutes to drive to the eastern outskirts of the city. Most of the drive, they are quiet, lost in their separate thoughts. JP keeps Genny's fingers entwined in his, his thumb rubbing the back of her hand.

Without warning, Cassandra pulls over onto the side of a deserted road and parks beneath a grove of mature willows with long, hanging branches. She swivels in her seat to face Genny.

"This is how this is gonna go down. We'll split up, like you suggested." Then she turns to JP. "What's your name?"

"Jean-Paul, but you can call me JP. I'm—"

"Okay, JP, you're with me. We'll come in from the front. Little Miss Slayer here will go with Quinn and they'll enter from the back. If we—"

"No way. Genny and I stay together." He tries to make his voice sound firm, but Genny can hear the edge in it. He's scared. So is she. But there's a part of her that's weirdly excited, too.

"Not this time, big guy. We need to split our strengths evenly. Strongest with weakest, one vamp per team. I'll give two mourning dove calls, one to get ready, and one to go in. Then we go through the doors at the same time. They'll probably hear us coming if they're paying any attention, 'cause you two can't lower your heartrate or breathing like we can. But maybe we'll get lucky and not die. You never know." She flashes a sardonic smile.

Genny looks to JP to gauge his reaction. He's scowling at Quinn with distrust. She squeezes his fingers. "I'll be fine," she tells him softly.

His eyes shift to hers. "You don't know that. You should've stayed 'ome. I really wish—"

"You'd both not come?" Cassandra interjects. "Me, too. And yet here we are." She opens her door and gets out. Quinn glances back at Genny before doing the same.

"I don't like this," JP says the minute they're alone.

"I know." She gives him a kiss. "Be careful. I mean it."

"You, too."

As Genny climbs out, Quinn hands her two wooden sticks with pointy ends. "They're not as strong as a crafted stake, but they might work in a pinch. If you use one, make sure you jam it in with all your strength."

She nods, tucking them into the back of her shorts.

JP comes up beside them. "I just need to say one thing to you," he tells Quinn. He's using his authoritative voice, and Genny has to cover her mouth to hide a smile.

Quinn turns his attention to JP, regarding him silently.

"If anything happens to 'er, I'm holding you personally responsible."

Inside Genny groans. If JP knew Quinn the way she does, he'd know there's no need to say that.

"That will make two of us," Quinn replies.

"I'll be fine," Genny assures JP, squeezing his hand. "Now go. I'll see you soon."

JP pulls her to him and kisses her. When he steps back, he looks miserable. Sighing, he hurries to catch up with Cassandra, who has already started down the road.

Genny can feel warmth in her cheeks. She wonders if JP had been trying to mark his territory by kissing her in front of Quinn. Male egos can be so fragile.

Turning to Quinn, who's waiting for her with an amused expression, she says, "Which way do we go?"

"Through the woods. We should end up behind the house. The sun's beginning to set, but it's not dark yet. They'll still be inside. Try to keep as quiet as you can."

He starts into the bush and Genny follows. She tries her hardest not to make noise as she walks, but it's so dim among the trees and she doesn't have enhanced eyesight like he does. When a twig snaps below her shoe, she stops in her tracks, mortified. Quinn glances back at her and beckons her to keep going.

Sorry, she thinks at him.

Instead of replying, he simply shrugs.

Several minutes later, they step into the backyard and hide from view behind an old shed. Quinn tilts his head toward the house. She can tell he's trying to hear what's happening inside. After about five seconds, he holds up three fingers.

Three vampires?

He nods. Then he drops two of his fingers and waves the remaining one, smiling.

And a human? Dawn?

He nods again accompanied by a shrug. He can't tell if it's Dawn or not, but there's a living human in there. They're not too late. Then he moves the finger to his lips. They need to keep super quiet now. And hope no one is looking out any windows.

The natural light is fading. It's almost time. Genny can feel her energy spiking as they wait for Cassandra's signal. She's never rushed into a dangerous situation before. This could go extremely wrong in so many ways, but still, she's excited. If rescuing Dawn means taking out three vampires in the process, she's ready.

From the far side of the house comes a soft cooing and Quinn perks up. He looks to her and arches a brow as if to say *you ready*?"

She nods. She has no idea what's about to happen, but she's as ready as she'll ever be for it.

They bend down and scurry to the back door. Quinn's entire focus is now on the house. Without thinking about it, she reaches for his hand and squeezes it. His fingers are cool to the touch, but the shock she gets from skin to skin contact with him is anything but. She drops his hand and jolts back in surprise.

He looks at her with a questioning expression.

I'm fine. Just...be careful, okay?

One corner of his mouth curves up as he nods. Then the second coo sounds and Quinn immediately throws his shoulder hard into the door. The poor door doesn't stand a chance; it smashes inward and Quinn steps through, quickly looking in both directions. He hadn't needed an invite to enter. Does that mean this house is publicly owned? Or the owner is dead? Probably the latter.

He disappears from Genny's sight and she steps over the threshold after him. The room to her right is empty. She turns toward the room on the left, the kitchen, just in time to see Quinn thrust his hand into a man's chest and tear out his heart.

She sucks in a sharp breath, frozen in place as she watches the man—no, not a man, a vampire; she can see his fangs—fall to the floor. His face goes ashy and gray. Without even flinching, Quinn drops the dripping red mass into the sink. After wiping his hand on a rag, he calmly says, "Now they know we're here."

Genny just stares at him with huge eyes. She realizes she's stopped breathing and has to command her lungs to release the air trapped inside. A second later, Cassandra appears beside her and takes in the dead vampire on the floor. "One down, two to go. We'll take the one upstairs and meet you in the basement."

Quinn nods, walking past them to look for the basement door. He's a man on a mission, focused and determined. Genny's never seen this side of him before. She needs to force herself to focus, too. They have to get to Dawn before it's too late. As she follows Quinn, she tries to shake off her shock.

Around the other side of the stairs, Quinn wrenches open a closed door and disappears. A stab of anxiety makes Genny pause. It's pitch dark down there, a situation she is all too familiar with. She pats around the wall until her fingers hit a switch and a light comes on below. She heads down, her heart throbbing in her chest as she wonders what she'll find.

At the bottom of the steps, she turns a corner and comes face to face with an absolute giant of a man. He's holding Dawn against his chest, her head pulled to the side exposing her neck. Both her hands and feet are bound, and tears stream down her face, but when she recognizes Genny, her eyes flare.

"Run!" she yells. "Don't—"

Gruhn's hand clamps over her mouth. As the massive vampire stares at Genny, a cruel smile slides across his face. "*She* may not be Geneviève Bourreau," he says in a thick Eastern European accent. "But *you* are."

"Let her go," Genny demands. Her voice comes out sounding strong and determined. She barely recognizes it.

"Oh I think not." He laughs and it sends a chill up Genny's spine. "I may, however, be willing to make a trade."

Anger flares inside her. She reaches behind her back and grabs the end of one of the makeshift stakes Quinn had given her, but she doesn't pull it out. "No deal. Let her go. *Now.* And maybe you'll get a quick death."

Clearly, this had been the wrong thing to say. He promptly bends his head and bites into Dawn's neck.

All Genny's attention has been on Gruhn and Dawn. As she gasps in shock, she notices Quinn standing in the corner watching the assassin warily. "Cassandra. Basement. Now," he says as he reaches inside his jacket and pulls out a vial. Uncorking it, he tosses clear liquid at the other vampire. The second it makes contact with his skin, it starts to hiss and bubble. Howling, Gruhn drops Dawn to the floor and clamps both hands to his face. While he's distracted, Quinn grabs Dawn by the ankles and pulls her limp body to Genny, who kneels to take her friend in her arms.

Tearing a strip off the bottom of her t-shirt, Genny applies it to Dawn's neck, holding it firmly in place as her friend groans. She looks up in time to see Gruhn stagger backward, but before he falls, he grabs Quinn's arm and takes him down with him.

Quinn looks at Genny. "Stake," he manages before Gruhn's mammoth hands close around his neck.

Stake? Oh, right. She pulls one from her waistband. Does he mean for her to attack Gruhn? She props Dawn against the wall and gets to her feet. Her heart is now pounding so hard she can hear it throbbing in her ears. It sounds like restless natives getting ready to attack. Gruhn pushes himself up, dragging Quinn with him. As he does, Quinn's hand reaches out to Genny and she tosses the stake into his outstretched fingers.

Quinn is so much smaller than Gruhn. He looks like a ragdoll in the huge vampire's hands. She can't bear to watch this, so she turns back to her friend. Dawn's eyes are closed. Is she still breathing? Genny presses her finger to Dawn's wrist and tries to find a pulse. At first, she can't, but after a few tries, she finally gets one. It's very faint.

Dammit, I can't just sit here and watch my friends die! Where are JP and Cassandra?

"Help!" she shouts.

There's a thump and a grunt behind her and she turns to see that Gruhn has thrown Quinn to the floor. The giant straddles him and starts to throttle him again. It looks like he's trying to rip Quinn's head right off.

Panicking, Genny pulls out the other stake and lets instinct take over. She leaps on Gruhn's back and with all her might drives the stake into his body just below the ribcage but aiming upward toward his heart as she's been taught. The big guy shudders and at first Genny thinks she's failed. Then he goes still and collapses onto Quinn. She's unable see his face so she can't tell if the assassin is dead or not. Sliding off his back, she tries to roll him over. As she shoves, he rolls to one side and she sees that Quinn has staked him in the chest as well. Gruhn's face is gray. He's dead.

"Are you okay?" she asks Quinn.

"Been better," he groans. "But we did it. You did it."

It's her first kill, but Genny doesn't even take a moment to revel in it. She hurries back to Dawn. Dropping to her knees, Genny pulls her friend into her lap and cradles her head against her chest. Her worried eyes find Quinn's. "I think she's dying."

Quinn crawls over to examine Dawn.

"Can you heal her?" Genny asks. She can't let Dawn die.

His gaze lifts to Genny's. He looks stricken. "I…I can't." His eyes flash to the ceiling and he yells, "Cassandra!"

Oh shit, Genny thinks. She'd been so distracted down here she hadn't even considered what they might be dealing with upstairs. Why are they taking so long? Has something happened to them? What if JP's hurt? Or worse? "You can still hear them, right? Tell me they're okay?"

"They're alive. They were fighting the other vamp, but they're coming now."

Genny strokes Dawn's face. The blood glares violently red against her pale skin. Struggling to speak around the sobs that threaten to break her, she looks at Quinn pleadingly. "I c...can't lose her. Please don't let her die!"

His face is so pained. Had Gruhn hurt him? But that can't be it; any injuries would've healed by now. Something is clearly wrong, though. The assassin may be dead, but at what cost? Genny doesn't know how much more she can take.

With a soft sigh, Quinn nods. "Give her to me." He takes Dawn's limp body into his lap. Gently holding her with one arm, he raises the other to his mouth, in one fast motion extending his fangs and biting into his wrist. Blood gushes from the wound and he quickly presses it between Dawn's lips.

Genny watches with amazement as he holds his wrist against Dawn's mouth. Red rivulets overflow her lips and run down her chin to join the scarlet mess on her neck. After just a few moments, Quinn pulls his arm away.

"Is she...will she live?"

There's a scurry of footsteps descending the stairs as Quinn bends his ear to Dawn's chest. When he raises his head to look back at Genny, his eyes are sadder than she's ever seen them. He looks devastated "I couldn't save her," he whispers, shaking his head. "It was too late."

Genny's heart sinks. A sob erupts and she covers her mouth with both hands. Tears start to cascade down her cheeks.

At that moment, Cassandra and JP rush into the room. Cassandra's attention is focused on Quinn. "Did you do it?"

Quinn nods without looking up. His gaze is fixed on the drying blood on his wrist. The wound has already healed. Getting to his feet, he passes Dawn's body to JP without a word. Then he heads up the stairs.

Genny starts to go after him, but Cassandra grabs her arm and holds her back. "Let him go," she says quietly. "Your friend will be fine."

She frowns and swipes away her tears. Dawn doesn't look fine. She looks the opposite of fine. Another sob bursts out. "Can you h-hear her heartbeat?" she asks Cassandra. "We need to...to get her to a hospital."

Cassandra's eyes soften. All the hard-ass vampire attitude is gone. "Sit down," she says, pointing at the steps. Genny sits. "It's Dawn, right?"

She nods.

"The thing you need to focus on is that Dawn is gonna be okay. But right now, she's... well, there's no way to sugar coat it, and that's not my style anyway. She's dead. But only temporarily."

JP sucks in a breath, eyes wide as he studies Dawn's still face. "Mon Dieu," he mutters.

"How can she be both okay and d-dead?" Genny asks. Fresh tears are threatening to fall.

"Quinn didn't get to her in time to heal her. But he did get his blood into her before she died. And that means she'll wake up in a while. But she won't be the same. She'll be like us. Do you understand?"

Genny's eyes go from Cassandra's to JP's and back again. She feels numb, like her brain has taken in so much excitement today that it's just shut off. "Like you?"

Cassandra lips form tight smile. "It's not so bad. We'll teach her how to adapt to her new life. She'll still be your friend, same as always. Just less interested in hanging out on sunny days."

What? Genny thinks. Then it finally clicks. "Oh."

"She'll be a vampire," JP says sadly.

"I got that." She turns her full attention to him, finally. He has blood on his hands, the side of his jaw, and pant leg. "Are *you* okay? What happened?"

"I'm fine. Expedited healing is extremely useful sometimes. We had a bit of a fight on our hands with that guy. He was strong, but Cassandra is stronger. She kicked his ass." JP's eyes flick to Cassandra with genuine admiration in them, surprising Genny. He focuses back on her. "What about you? We heard you guys calling, but we couldn't come until he was dead." He shudders and Genny wonders how messy the kill had been.

"I'll live." She sounds beaten. Exhausted. All she wants right now is to go home. But she doubts that's going to happen anytime soon.

"C'mon," Cassandra says to them. "Let's go. There's nothing left here."

JP carries Dawn all the way back to Cassandra's car. The girls walk on either side of him, but nobody talks. When they get to the car, Genny climbs in the back, and JP lies Dawn on the seat with her head cushioned in Genny's lap. He gets in the front with Cassandra.

"How long until she wakes up?" Genny asks as they pull out. She gently strokes Dawn's dark hair. Parts of it are sticky with matted blood.

“A few hours.” Cassandra says, glancing back at her in the rearview mirror. “Tomorrow morning at the latest. Don’t worry, I’ll be with her. She’ll be in good hands.”

“Where did Quinn go?”

Cassandra shrugs. “I don’t know. But he’ll be back. Eventually.”

Chapter 11
No Time to Cry

Genny cradles Dawn's bloody body as Cassandra drives them through the dark and mostly empty city streets. Tears continue to trickle down her cheeks. She can't seem to stop crying. Though Cassandra has repeatedly assured her Dawn will be fine, right now she just looks dead.

Because she *is* dead. Genny needs to face facts. And soon she'll be undead. If—when—she awakens, she'll be a vampire. It's far from ideal, but it's a hell of a lot better than the alternative. The whole thing had just happened so *fast*. There'd been no time to weigh options. Genny's sure if she could have, Dawn would've chosen undead over dead-dead. But Genny had been forced to make that choice for her. All she can do now is hope Dawn understands. And forgives her.

Of all the times Genny has imagined the various ways she herself might die, she'd never once pictured anything like what had gone down tonight. She'd seen two vampires killed right in front of her. One of them she'd actually helped to kill. How is that even possible? It sounds more like penny dreadful fiction than real life. Yet this seems to be her life now.

She glances down at Dawn's lifeless face again, tracing the curve of her cheek with a gentle fingertip. There's drying blood around her mouth, making it look like Dawn's been eating berries. Her friend's skin is cool to the touch.

Like Quinn's.

No. Genny can't let herself think about that. Not right now. Probably not at all.

Here's another first—she's holding a body in her lap. She's never seen a dead person before. Her parents had been cremated. All she remembers of their funeral are two matching urns, both of which are now buried at Mount Pleasant Cemetery. It's dark in the backseat of Cassandra's car, but Genny remembers all too well how Dawn had looked down in that creepy basement. Not just pale—her skin has always been pretty pale—but kind of grayish-white. Dawn's lips have turned purplish, a gothic shade she'd surely approve of. The blood isn't just around her mouth; it's also all down her chin and neck. The first thing Genny wants to do when they get to Cassandra's is to clean her up. It feels super important that Dawn not see this mess if she wakes up. *When* she wakes up, Genny corrects herself.

At last they pull into a driveway off a tree-lined street. Genny straightens up and looks out the window, trying to see where Quinn and Cassandra live. It's dark, so all she can make out is that it's an old, two-storey home. She barely glimpses the front of the house before Cassandra drives past it to park near the back.

JP gets out and opens the back door. Though Genny thinks she could probably carry Dawn on her own, JP carefully picks her up and takes her into the house.

"Where would you like 'er?" he asks the moment they're inside.

Cassandra tugs off her hat and tosses it onto a round papasan chair. Curly red hair spills down her back. It's glorious. *No wonder he fell for her,* Genny's internal voice whispers. *Shut up,* she tells it.

"Upstairs." Cassandra points to the staircase along the far wall. "Spare room is the first door on the left. Put her on the bed."

JP heads up the steps and the girls follow. Once he lays Dawn down, Genny turns to Cassandra. "Is it okay if I use a damp facecloth to clean her up?"

Cassandra doesn't reply, but she disappears into the hallway and Genny soon hears running water in the room next door.

"Are you okay?" JP asks Genny softly.

Genny's about to remind him Cassandra can hear him no matter how quietly he speaks, but then she realizes he likely already knows. She meets his eyes and shakes her head. "Not even a little."

"I know." He pulls her to him. The warmth of his body is soothing and Genny closes her eyes, wishing they were anywhere but here, wishing none of this had ever happened. "I'm proud of you, Gen. You killed your first vampire! Wait until Maman and René learn about this. They're going to be so excited!"

Genny leans back so she can look at him. A tiny smile surfaces. "I guess I did, didn't I? Well, Quinn and I did, but still. It's unreal."

Cassandra reappears and JP and Genny jump apart. She hands Genny two facecloths, one wet and one dry. "Need anything else?"

"Yes. A rewind of the past two days."

"What's done is done," Cassandra says in a no nonsense tone. "Her life will be different, but once she adapts—and she will—she's gonna be just fine."

Genny's not so sure about that. She sits on the edge of the bed and starts to gently clean blood from Dawn's face and neck. Her shirt is also heavily stained. Turning back to Cassandra, she appraises the vampire. Dawn is bigger, but not by a whole lot.

"Actually?" she ventures.

"What do you need?"

"Dawn's clothes should be thrown out. Is there any way you could lend her something to wear until we can go to her apartment and get clean stuff?"

The vampire swipes a hand through the air in a *no big deal* gesture. "Don't worry about that. It doesn't matter."

"It matters to me. I don't want her to see all this blood when she, y'know, comes back."

A sigh. "Fine. I'll change her. But she'll probably remember what happened."

"Yeah, but at least she won't have a bloody reminder all over her. Burn her clothes. I don't even want her to see them."

Cassandra rolls her eyes. "Whatever."

JP has been silent throughout this exchange. "Can I use your washroom?" he asks suddenly.

"Next door." Cassandra takes a seat on a chair in the corner. She doesn't offer to help clean Dawn, and Genny doesn't ask. It's Genny's fault this happened to her best friend in the world; she has to do this herself.

As she works, she asks, "So what will happen when she wakes?"

"She'll be in transition. She won't actually become a vampire until she drinks blood."

"Human blood?"

"Ideally. It will make her stronger. I have some here, in case you're wondering. No need to volunteer a donation."

Genny removes the last smear off Dawn's chin and starts on her neck. "I know. Stolen blood bags. Quinn told me."

"Oh yeah? What else did he tell you?"

"That you can drink human or animal blood, but human is more...what word did he use? I think it was energizing?"

Cassandra snickers. "Yes. Definitely more energizing."

JP comes back into the room and leans against the wall.

"So do you only drink human then?" Genny asks. She's almost done now. The thicker dried blood is harder to get off, but she's pleased to see the wound has healed. There's not even a scar. She guesses that's a good sign that Quinn's blood really is working inside Dawn. "He told me you guys can heal and then hypnotize the person to forget."

"Is that what you do?" JP asks Cassandra. He sounds intrigued.

Genny glances up in time to see Cassandra arch an eyebrow. "Not that it's anyone's business how I feed, but yes. I don't see the point in killing. Why remove your blood supply when you can just heal and potentially tap that vein again someday? Seems wasteful."

JP clears his throat in a way Genny suspects means he's uncomfortable with this subject. She wonders how tonight has changed his opinion of vampires. It's presumably a lot harder to hate them if they don't actually kill humans.

Dabbing at Dawn's face and neck with the dry cloth, Genny then sets them on the floor beside the bed. "I did the best I could. I guess now we just have to wait."

"Now you two should go home and get some sleep. I'll stay with her."

"I want to—"

"I know," Cassandra interjects. "You feel guilty. You want to be there for her. But the best thing you could do right now is leave her with me until we know how it's gonna be with her. Your blood, immortal blood, doesn't smell as strong to me as human blood. But for a new vampire every sense is extra heightened. It's been a long time since I've taken care of a baby vamp, and there were no immortals hanging out with us when I did, but I do remember how volatile they can be. I don't think you should see her in person until I've helped her transition and she's more used to her cravings. Give me at least a day. Maybe you can come over on Thursday."

Genny's face falls. "But—"

"She's right." JP's sets a hand on Genny's shoulder. "You being around when she's all confused and thirsty and stuff…it would only make things more difficult for her."

"Listen to your boyfriend," Cassandra says. "Call tomorrow and I'll let you know how she's doing. I'll put her on the phone with you and you can ask her yourself, if she's up for it, which I'm sure she will be."

With a sigh, Genny relents. "Fine. I'll call tomorrow." She is beyond exhausted. Getting a few hours' sleep would probably be smart.

JP goes down to the living room to call a taxi.

Genny hesitates at the door to the spare room, then turns back to Cassandra.

"Something else?" Cassandra asks.

Dropping her voice, Genny says, "You think he'll be back soon?"

The vampire's lips flatten into a line. "No idea. But I hope so."

Quinn hasn't driven a car in years, but he figures much like riding a bike, he'll remember how once he starts. After checking nine driveways, he finally finds one with unlocked doors and hotwires the engine. At least it has an automatic transmission so he doesn't need to worry about shifting gears. He takes it to an all-night Walmart, buys a dozen plastic shower curtains, an axe, some rope, and a saw.

The bored-looking clerk at the checkout cracks a lame joke about disposing bodies while he bags up Quinn's purchases. Quinn just humors him with an indulgent smile. If the guy had even the vaguest clue of what Quinn actually needs to do tonight and why, he's sure he'd instead have run off screaming.

One of the reasons the Assembly had chosen this particular safehouse is because of its privacy. It's located on the end of a dead-end street with lots of mature trees and no other nearby buildings. Quinn senses no sign of humans anywhere in the proximity, but he refuses to take unnecessary risks. He backs the car around the house to the rear door.

In a closet, he finds some tools, and uses them to re-secure both broken-in entrances. After locking the front door, he gets to work on the nearest body: the heartless one on the kitchen floor.

Disposing of vampire bodies is far less messy than human ones, as vampires desiccate upon death. They turn hard and dry, kind of like kindling. Using the axe and saw, Quinn makes short work of the first one. It takes two shower curtains to wrap up the pieces, including the heart still in the sink, and he loads them into the trunk of the car. He feels no guilt whatsoever over taking this vampire's life. If he hadn't, the guy would have surely killed him and possibly Genevieve, too. Killing other vampires doesn't faze Quinn at all. They are monsters. They deserve to die.

The body upstairs is larger and there's a lot more blood here than in the kitchen. He'd clearly given Cassandra an intense fight. Quinn had heard them from the basement, but now he sees how much difficulty she and JP must've had taking him down. Well, that she must've had. Quinn can't imagine JP had been much help. Whatever had happened, the final outcome had left the vampire's head separated from his body. It lies on its side in the corner of the room, eyes wide. They seem to glare at Quinn reproachfully.

"Go ahead," he mutters as he crouches in front of it. "Judge all you want. But what choice did I have?" He sighs, reaching to close the eyelids so he no longer has to endure their accusing stare. Opening another shower curtain, he wraps the head in plastic and before long this body, too, is stashed in the car.

One more left. He's saved the worst for last. Disposing of Gruhn will not be an easy task. As Quinn descends the stairs, he tries only to think of what needs to be done: cut the big vampire into manageable chunks, stash the pieces in the car, clean up the blood in all three rooms, drive to Lake Ontario and dump the pieces, then find a safe hiding spot to spend the daylight hours. By breaking it down into smaller tasks, it helps him focus just on the next step. And it keeps him from dwelling on other things. At least for now.

It takes him over an hour to finish up at the safehouse, but when Quinn closes the back door behind him, he is confident the evidence of what had taken place that night is gone. He needs to hurry now. Time is starting to run short. A little over an hour left until sunrise and he still needs to dispose of the packages and then locate a place to hole up for a while.

He drives down to Ashbridges Bay, approaching the shore from behind the waste treatment plant and bringing the car as near the water as possible. Before tossing the packages into the lake, he loads each one down with rocks. Twelve splashes out into the deepest part of the bay, and then Quinn is forced to accept that tonight's work is done. But he can't allow himself to rest yet. He drives the car all the way back to the driveway where he'd found it, then speeds off into the brightening gloom of approaching dawn.

Perhaps instinctually he returns to the wooded trails along the river. The sun is about to rise, so he'll have to forego feeding until later. That's okay. He doesn't care about nourishment right now. He just wants to sleep, to shut off his brain.

Quinn finds a hollow under some bushes in the shade of a group of trees. It smells like a fox den, but it's deserted. He tucks himself into it, getting his clothes even dirtier, but right now he doesn't care about that either.

He feels sick. At some point, he knows he'll have to go home. He'll have to face up to what he's done, take responsibility for her, do the right thing. But for today, he's just going to trust Cassandra to do what needs to be done. She has experience with this, after all. He doesn't.

Try as he might not to go there, he pictures Genevieve's tearful face begging him, pleading with him. *Please don't let her die!*

There had simply been no choice. He couldn't possibly have refused her. So he'd done it. He'd broken the biggest promise he's ever made to himself since waking up into this cruel undead life.

Back when Quinn had been human, he'd been very devout. Everything he'd done, he'd done to honor God. Raised in a strict Christian family, his faith had been a fundamental part of him. But he's no longer the man he used to be. He hasn't been since that chilly autumn night in 1882.

Something is tickling Quinn's nose. It smells musty. Earthy. As he swats it away, he realizes it's a leaf. Wait, make that leaves, plural. He's covered in crunchy leaves. And he seems to be lying on the cold, hard ground. Opening his eyes, he sees it's still dark. Where *is* he?

He looks up and is immediately mesmerized by the dazzling array of stars beyond the twisted maze of barren branches above his head. They're so beautiful. They form patterns he's never noticed before: a seated maiden here, a dog there. That cluster just above the spire's silhouette resembles two crossed bones, much like the ones engraved on his father's wee headstone. How has he never noticed before how beautiful the stars are?

A loud hiss startles him and he sits up. Next he hears an angry screech he well recognizes. Two cats are fighting somewhere close. Looking around, he realizes he's in a kirkyard. Not in a grave, thank the Lord, but under a pile of dead leaves along one ancient stone wall.

He frowns. How in Heaven had he gotten here? Had he been sleepwalking? How long has he been gone for? Elspeth will be worried.

His stomach rumbles. Pushing himself to his feet, he brushes off the remaining leaves and sees his shirt is covered in something dark and crusty. It smells pungent, like copper. Is it blood? He lifts his sleeve to his nose and grimaces. Definitely blood.

Quinn whispers a quick prayer as he checks himself over. No injuries. Nothing seems to be amiss at all. Just a ruined shirt. Elspeth won't be pleased. She'll have to make him a new one, and they can ill afford the fabric. Not with a third child gracing them soon. It's difficult enough to feed the four of them some days.

At the thought of food, his belly again growls. Dear Lord he's hungry. Where can he find something to eat in the middle of the night? Will any of the inns still be open? Quinn shudders at the thought of going into one of those ungodly places, but they will have food. Not to mention plenty of drunks, especially at this late hour.

Hold on. Has he been robbed? He feels for his leather pouch, and exhales in relief to find it still at his waist. Inside are a few pence and shillings. Enough for an oatcake, if he can find one.

He starts across the kirkyard. It's amazing how well he can see with just starlight to guide him. He doesn't trip over a single stone between the rear wall and front gate. Incredible.

The road is deserted, but further along he can hear laughter and the rapid tinkling of a piano. An inn. Complete with requisite drunken fools.

And food. He raises his nose and sniffs. Something delicious. Completely forgetting he's covered in blood, he starts off toward that delectable smell.

Then he comes to an abrupt stop. A man stumbles along the cobblestones toward him. An extremely drunk man. Quinn can smell the combined odors of whisky and sour sweat from here. On instinct, he backs into a narrow alley and waits.

It strikes him that he should be nervous. He's alone late at night in a part of the city he doesn't spend much time in.

He should be home in bed with his wife, the curve of her warm belly pressing against his back. He should not be standing here in the shadows, hungry and hopeful and waiting. Waiting for what, he isn't quite sure, but he can feel his anticipation rising.

The drunk comes closer. He's singing to himself. Quinn recognizes the tune well. It's "Ally Bally Bee," a lullaby Elspeth often sings to the bairns.

The smell of the man grows stronger with every passing second. Piss and whisky and sweat, and it's repellant. But there's another scent, faint at first but growing stronger, that's having the exact opposite effect on Quinn. It's metallic and tangy, this smell, and as he inhales anew, he feels two sharp stings at the front of his upper jaw.

This vanishes as fast as it had come and he promptly forgets it. That tangy scent is so much more important. He steps out from the darkness and blocks the man's way.

Lord God in Heaven he reeks. But there's also that other. It lingers below the whisky, below the sweat. It calls to him like a siren, and though a voice in Quinn's head speaks up that whatever this is, it's wrong, it's a mortal sin and he needs to resist, he simply can't. The pull of it is too strong. He's too hungry.

He grabs the drunk by the shoulders and with a strength he shouldn't possess, Quinn drags him into the alley.

"Who are ye? What d'ye want?" the man asks, terror rising with each word.

Quinn does not answer, because he does not care. He hears, but he doesn't register. It's like the buzz of flies about his head. Just a nuisance. Nothing more. The hunger is all he knows, all he is.

Running his tongue over his teeth, he feels another prick and tastes his own blood. The ravenous lion inside him growls and he lunges.

The next few minutes pass in a blur as Quinn loses himself in the sweet relief of satiating the beast. When he returns to his senses, he realizes he's holding the ravaged body of a dead man, the neck ripped open. Hot blood is everywhere. And God it smells *so* good.

In horror, he drops the corpse to the ground and presses his back against the wall.

My God. How could he do this?

Before he can register another thought, he gets an intense pain at the base of his throat and smells the acrid stench of burning flesh. Tearing open his shirt, his fingers close on the silver crucifix his mother had given him when he'd come of age. It had been her father's, passed down for generations. The metal burns his hand as he rips off the cross. He tosses it to the ground and the pain abates. A moment later it stops altogether.

There's no burn marks on his chest or fingers. It's like it had never happened at all.

Quinn's gaze lands back on the dead man.

I did that, he thinks. *What happened to me? What have I become? Am I a monster?*

Gingerly he runs the pad of one finger over his teeth. They feel normal. Now. Yet he could swear they hadn't been normal a few moments ago.

Growing up, Quinn, like most Scottish children, had heard tales of monsters. His mother'd had a variety of bedtime prayers she had said with him and his brothers, but the one that had most unnerved him as a wee boy is this:

From ghoulies and ghosties
And long-leggedy beasties,
And things that go bump in the night,
Good Lord, deliver us!

He'd used to huddle beneath his blanket and listen for all the things that go bump in the night, imagining Kelpies and Wraiths and the terrifying Baobhan Sith. Baobhan Sith are said to be beautiful female vampires who wear long green dresses to conceal the deer hooves they have for feet. They use their alluring beauty and powers of persuasion to seduce men and drain their blood. This, to Quinn's impressionable young mind, had meant not just killing people, but dooming them to an eternity in Hell. He'd feared Baobhan Sith most of all.

A shudder wracks his frame. Is that what he has become? A male version of Baobhan Sith? Falling to his knees, he covers his eyes with his hands.

I am a monster. I killed that man. I'm an abomination against God. My soul is doomed to burn forever in the deepest pits of Hell.

But how has he become this? As he lowers his hands, his gaze lands on the crucifix, glimmering with starlight on the cobblestones by his feet. Carefully, using just his fingernails, he picks it up and tucks it into his pouch. The cross may burn his unholy flesh, but he refuses to discard it.

Suddenly another, sharper fear grips him. His family. Are they still asleep in their beds, peacefully dreaming, unaware he's no longer with them? Or…?

Quinn can't even finish the thought. In a panic, he rushes from the alley and heads for home. He doesn't even notice he's moving faster than any human should be capable. All he can think of is Elspeth and the bairns.

They live in a basement room below a millinery shop. When he gets there, he finds the door to the street wide open and his gut drops. He rushes down the steps and into their flat. What he finds inside is a sight he'll never forget no matter how many centuries he's cursed to walk the earth.

Quinn had stopped believing in a compassionate God the moment he'd found his wife and children slaughtered in their beds. At least that's what he'd told himself. In truth, a part of him had held on to some last vestigial remains of his faith for many years after. Maybe faith hadn't even been the right word at that point. Maybe it had simply been some slight spark of hope deep inside of him that he hadn't quite been able to extinguish. He doesn't know exactly when it had disappeared. He only knows he no longer believes in a higher power. There is no God. How can there be? A just, loving God would never allow such atrocities, could never allow such abominations as vampires to exist.

That dark night in Edinburgh, weeping over the bodies of his loved ones, he had sworn he would never create any more monsters. But tonight he'd broken that rule.

It's just one more thing he'll never forgive himself for.

Chapter 12
Kick in the Eye

The loud buzz of Genny's alarm clock wakes her with a start. Smacking the Off button, she rolls over and reaches for the phone to call in sick. She's never taken a sick day before, but after everything that had gone down last night she thinks she's earned the right to stay home.

She falls back asleep for another two hours. When she wakes again to the grumbling of her belly, she reluctantly throws back the sheets and trudges down to the kitchen to pour herself a bowl of cereal. When she takes it out to the back deck to eat, she finds Chloe sitting outside listening to her Walkman.

Pulling off her headphones, Chloe stares at her with confusion. "Why aren't you at work?"

For a second, Genny considers telling her sister what had happened. Chloe will learn about Dawn soon enough; there won't be any way to avoid it. But if she tells her, then Gran will find out, too, and both of them will be upset. And Genny doesn't even know for sure yet what Dawn's situation is. Rather than freak them out without any concrete answers, she decides to wait a day or two and see how things go. Later, once Dawn is able to control her blood cravings, they'll be able to see for themselves that they don't need to be afraid of her.

She hopes that's not just wishful thinking and things will work out for Dawn the way Cassandra had told her they should. Because Dawn will also want to spend time with her parents, and it would be awful if she had to avoid them for weeks or even months. Genny knows Cassandra won't leave Dawn alone with humans until she's sure Dawn won't be any danger to them, though.

"It was a pretty late night last night. I decided to use a sick day and sleep in."

Chloe stretches out her legs into a patch of sunshine. Crows caw loudly from the treetops at the back of the yard. "Well, you picked a great day for it."

"So how're things with your new guy? Darry, right?"

With a smile, Chloe replies, "Things are awesome! He's so sweet! He's actually making me dinner tonight."

So much has been going on in Genny's life the past few weeks that she's clearly let checking in with her sister slide, or she'd already know what she can see on Chloe's face: she's fallen for this boy.

"He sounds great," Genny agrees. "I'd like to meet him, if you're at the point where you're willing to introduce him to your annoying sister."

Chloe considers, but only for a few moments and presumably just to irritate Genny. "Why don't we invite both guys over for dinner one night? We can cook for them. Show them we aren't completely useless."

Laughing, Genny says, "Problem is, I *am* pretty much useless. But I guess I can try. I'm sure JP would come."

"I'll ask Darry tonight. So how's it going with JP? Everything still good?"

"Absolutely."

Chloe leans back and sets her book aside. "Has he said he loves you yet?"

Feeling her cheeks heat up, Genny says, "No."

"Well he does. Anyone can see it. Maybe he's just waiting until he's sure how you feel about him."

"It hasn't even been a full month. It's still way too soon for that."

"No, it's not. When you know, you know." Chloe sits up straighter so she can look directly at her sister. "So how *do* you feel? Are you in love with him?"

Genny hesitates. "I…I don't know." Then she smiles. "I kinda think I might be."

Both sisters smile at each other. "Who would've thought we'd both be in happy relationships at the same time?" Chloe says. "What are the chances?"

"Slim to none, I'd bet." Genny gets to her feet with the empty cereal bowl in one hand. "Hey, listen, I need to go call Dawn. She…uh…she might not be feeling the best after last night and I wanna check in."

Rolling her eyes, Chloe says, "Jeez. How much did you guys drink on a Tuesday?"

Genny has a flash of Dawn drinking Quinn's blood and shudders. "You'd be surprised," she mutters before heading inside. After rinsing off her dish, she goes up to her bedroom.

It's broad daylight. Will Cassandra even be awake? But then Genny considers that Dawn probably only just woke up a few hours ago. It's doubtful she'd be back asleep so soon, which means Cassandra will be up with her.

She grabs the phone and dials Quinn's number. She hopes he'll answer so she knows he's back safely, but on the third ring, Cassandra's acerbic voice picks up.

"Bloodbath and Beyond. How can you help me?"

Genny laughs a hard, startled laugh. "Um. It's Genny. I'm just checking in."

She hears Cassandra tell someone, "It's Genny. You wanna talk to her?"

Deep relief washes over Genny when she hears Dawn's voice in the background. It had worked. She's alive. Well, sort of. She's not dead anyway, and that's all that matters.

A second later Dawn comes on the line. "Genny? Oh my God. *Genny.*"

"Dawn, thank goodness. You've no idea how happy I am to hear your voice. I was so worried! How do you feel?"

There's a short pause. "I don't know. Weird? Super weird. It's crazy. It feels like everything's happening all at once. I can hear every little sound. There's a family of mice in the walls and I swear I can hear their whiskers twitching. It's absolutely nuts!"

Genny hears Cassandra in the background say, "You'll get used to it. You learn to tune it out."

"Wow," she says. "Guess you'll be able to hear if anyone's talking about you behind your back now."

Dawn laughs. "True. Work will be a lot more interesting." She sighs. "But I guess I won't be going back to work. I'll have to quit and look for a night shift somewhere or something. I don't know."

"Yeah. That's probably a smart idea. I can help you find something when you're ready. So what's it like, with all your senses so heightened? Do you feel like Supergirl?"

"It's pretty overwhelming, but like Cassandra said, I guess with time I'll get used to it. I can smell *everything*, good and bad. Like the first thing I did after I, you know, ate. Or drank, whatever. The first thing I did was ask if I could use her shower. Because I could smell *me*. And I was rank!"

"Welcome to my life," Cassandra pipes up again. "Just wait 'til you take the subway."

Genny's thoughts instantly return to Quinn. She's never considered all the awful things he likely hears and smells every time he rides with her. "It might take a little while, but you'll figure out how to ignore what doesn't matter. I hope I can come see you soon. Maybe tomorrow? You can let me know what you think."

"Tomorrow might be okay. I think if Cassandra's around, it'll be fine."

She has to ask. "So I take it Quinn isn't back yet?"

"No. I didn't even realize he lived here, too, until about an hour ago."

"Huh. Well I'm sure he'll be home tonight. I'll see you tomorrow then?"

"Yeah, definitely." There's another brief pause. "Hold on, before you go Cassandra wants to talk to you."

"Sure. Call me later."

"I will."

Cassandra comes on the phone. "So listen. You and Quinn have talked a lot the past few weeks, right?"

"I guess."

"I don't know how much he's told you, but do you understand why what happened with Dawn last night is a massive fucking deal for him?"

Genny had definitely sensed he'd been upset, but she has no idea why. "No. He doesn't like to talk about his past, so I don't know much of his history. Only some bits."

"That's a massive understatement," Cassandra says. "Getting Quinn to open up about that stuff is like pulling teeth with rusty pliers. But with you...well, I wasn't sure if maybe he'd told you."

"Told me what?"

"Well, for starters, he hates being a vampire. Have you figured that much out by now?"

She'd have to be a fool to miss that fact. "Yeah."

"After he was turned, he promised himself he'd never make another one. And he never has. Not until last night."

Genny's heart sinks. "Oh shit."

"Yeah. He's probably in a pretty bad place right now. Literally no one is harder on Quinn than Quinn."

"But it's not his fault. It's mine. I begged him to. Maybe if I explain—"

"It doesn't matter what you explain. He did it. It's done. It can't be undone. Now he's gonna have to figure out how to live with the guilt."

Genny shakes her head, although Cassandra can't see it. "I'm not sure I understand. If he's never made another vampire in all these years, why would he break his own rule now?"

"He called for me. He wanted me to come do it so he wouldn't have to. But your boyfriend and I were tied up with the other vamp. I couldn't get down in time."

"I know." Genny sighs. "And don't get me wrong, I'm so glad he saved her, but why didn't he refuse? He barely knows Dawn."

Cassandra snorts. "Don't be stupid. He didn't do it for her. He did it for you."

That night, after JP has gone home and Gran has turned in for the evening, Genny goes out to the back porch and sits in the dark, thinking about what Cassandra had said.

Quinn is hurting. He's out there somewhere blaming himself, hating himself, and Genny can't stand it. She needs to talk to him. But will he want to talk to her? Maybe he resents her for asking—no, *begging*—him to help Dawn? Maybe he never wants to see her again? The thought makes her chest ache. She doesn't know if she can help him feel better, but she has to try.

He did it for you. Those had been Cassandra's words, Cassandra's opinion. Is she right? Had he really broken a century-long personal mandate just for her? He needs to know how much that means to her. Maybe, if she explains just how incredibly grateful she is, it will ease his guilt a little.

Quinn? she thinks, imagining his face. The Quinn her mind pulls up wears the heartbroken expression she'd seen last. And now she understands why, and it kind of breaks her own heart. *I hope you're okay. If you're feeling up to it, will you come see me please? I'd like to talk to you.*

Now all Genny can do is wait. She glances up at her sister's bedroom window. It's open to let in the night breeze. If he does come, they can't talk back here. She walks around the house and sits on the front steps.

After twenty minutes, she decides he's not going to show up and gets to her feet to go inside. Before she can even put her hand on the doorknob, however, she feels the tingle and whips around with relief. Soon a gray outline materializes out of the dark and walks up the path toward her. When Quinn steps into the circle of porchlight, she sees he still looks unhappy. Of course he does. Why would he be happy to see her after what had happened?

"Is she okay?" he asks.

Genny assumes he means Dawn, which means he hasn't checked in with Cassandra yet. "She seems to be. The important thing is she's not dead." Sitting back on the top step, she pats the wood beside her, but he doesn't come closer. "How're you doing?"

"Fine."

He's back to being reticent. Genny doesn't like it. "No, you're not. Look, I know you might not wanna be here right now, but let me just say thank you. I can't tell you how grateful I am for what you did. Don't be mad at her, but

Cassandra told me how you feel about it. I'm sorry I asked you to do something that went against your beliefs, but I need you to understand that it means more to me than I could ever possibly say."

"You're welcome." His eyes are downcast. And his clothes are dirty. Quinn is never dirty, and it makes Genny wonder if he'd slept outdoors.

With a sigh, she stands back up. "If you won't sit, how 'bout we go for a walk?" She heads to the sidewalk, hoping he'll follow. At first she worries he's left, but after a few moments, she hears his footsteps as he catches up to her.

For a while they walk in silence. Then Genny says, "I'm glad you came. I was worried you wouldn't. I thought maybe you blamed me for asking you to do it."

"Of course not. You did nothing wrong."

"Neither did you. I know you feel guilty about it, but you really shouldn't. Dawn is gonna be fine. She's got you and Cassandra to help her learn to do things the way you both do. She's not going to turn into a mass murderer."

As they round a corner, he says, "You don't know that."

"I do. You know why? Because *you* didn't. Becoming a vampire didn't change you that much. You're still a kind, honorable man with a conscience who hates to see anyone get hurt. I know having to steal blood bothers you, but if that's your biggest sin, you really need to give yourself a break."

They are approaching the park where they'd tested if he could hypnotize her. Quinn sighs. Genny can hear a century of sadness in that sigh. "There's something I need to tell you. I was hoping I wouldn't have to, but...you deserve to know the truth."

Her brows draw in. "Of course. You can tell me anything."

They sit on the same bench as before. Quinn is facing her, but she can't see his expression very well. Leafy branches diffuse the light from the streetlamp. He reaches inside his jacket and pulls out something long and thin. When he hands it to her, she realizes it's a stake, an intricately carved wooden stake.

"Wow. This is beautiful." She runs her fingers along it, tracing each notch and groove.

"It was your mother's."

Genny frowns. "What?" Why would Quinn have one of her mother's stakes?

"If you decide to use it, don't hesitate. Aim fast and true like you were taught."

Her frown grows deeper. "I don't understand."

Another small sigh, no more than a hard exhalation really. "As you well know, sometimes the Assembly gives Cassandra and I jobs to do for them. Whether we like the assignment or not, we do these things to stay in their good graces."

She nods.

"Thirteen years ago, during one of the periods when she and I were apart, I got a call from them. They were sending three vampires to me and we were..." He hesitates. It's like the words are too painful to say.

"You were what? It's okay. You can tell me."

"It's far from okay. We were told to...to kill your mother. And to make it look like an accident."

Genny sucks in a breath. Whatever she'd thought he'd been about to confess, this isn't it. Not by far. Her body goes rigid.

"I didn't want to do it," he continues. She can't tell if he's still looking at her, but she doesn't think so. "I tried to get out of it. But once the other vamps showed up at my door, I realized I had no choice. We found out where they were going to and waited for them. It was mid-March, on a dark country road, and there was freezing rain, so conditions were slippery. Perfect for a car to lose control."

"I've seen it," Genny interrupts. Her voice sounds as wooden as the stake she clutches. "I dreamt this. I didn't know it then, but the face my mom saw out the window that night was yours, wasn't it?"

Quinn nods. "Yes. We caused the crash by making them swerve. Their car caught fire. Once the flames shot up, we took off. But as soon as I could I separated from the others and went back."

"Why? To make sure they were dead?" Her words are no longer just wooden. They are ice cold.

He's quiet for a few seconds. Then, softly, he says, "To see if I could save them. It was too late for your father. He was human and he succumbed quickly. But your mother was still alive. I ripped off her door and pulled her out, rolling us both in the snow on the side of the road until the flames were out. I carried her into the woods with the intention to revive her if I could. But too much damage had been done. Her heartbeat had been faint to begin with, and it stopped as I held her. So I took her deeper into the forest and buried her. That stake you hold was in her hand. It's a wee bit charred, but still strong and solid. Perhaps she'd spelled it for protection. I'm quite certain it will still do the job."

Quinn goes silent. Genny isn't sure if he expects her to say something now. She doesn't. It feels like she's been kicked in the head. What could she possibly say?

"I have many regrets, but that night is one of my greatest. If I could go back and change things, I would. I'm so very sorry, Genevieve. If it makes you feel any better, I'll surely burn in Hell for what I've done."

A question pops through Genny's shock. "There were two bodies found in the car. How?" Is that her voice? She barely recognizes it.

"I…I took a body from a nearby mortuary and put it in your mother's seat. If the Assembly had discovered she didn't die with your father, or that I'd interfered in any way, it would have been bad. The news had to get back to them that both your parents had died. Which they did, unfortunately."

Genny stands. Even if she had more to say, she doesn't think any other words will come. So she turns and starts for home.

This time he doesn't follow.

Chapter 13
This Corrosion

When Genny gets home, she goes straight upstairs to bed. She drags the covers over her head and curls into a ball, but she's far too riled up to sleep. Flashes of her dream of her parents last moments keep playing in her mind. She misses them *so* much. And now it turns out that Quinn—

My Quinn, that annoying little voice in her head interrupts. Her throat tightens and she balls her hands into fists. *Don't be stupid. Not mine. Never mine.*

It turns out he'd played a role in her parents' deaths. How is that even possible? Sweet, stoic Quinn? She'd thought she'd known him. How could she have been so wrong?

He'd told her if she knew the truth of what he's done she wouldn't want to be his friend. So now she knows. But what should she do with this knowledge? Should she tell Chloe and Gran? JP? Dawn? Or should she keep it to herself to protect him?

Even *he* doesn't think he deserves protection from the consequences of his actions. So why should she? Why should she offer him any mercy at all? She's a slayer, like her mother. Her dead mother, who, because of him, isn't here to train her or offer advice. But Genny's pretty sure she knows what advice her mom would give her right now: Slayers show no mercy. Slayers slay.

Her throat aches and tears rise to the corners of her eyes, but they don't fall. How can she even consider that? The very idea makes her feel all panicky. He's not just any vampire. He's her friend.

At least he had been. How can they continue to be friends now that she knows the truth? She feels betrayed. She's not sure she can even look at him anymore.

Genny's heart is racing, her pulse throbbing in her ears. She's so angry she can barely acknowledge how hurt she also feels.

So she tosses and turns, heaving frustrated sighs and occasionally punching her pillow. The sky outside has begun to brighten when she at last manages to fall into a fitful sleep.

An hour later, Genny's alarm goes off, and again she decides to call in sick. Before she can reach for the phone, she realizes she's holding something. It's her mother's stake. Examining it in the light of day, she sees it's blackened but still solid and strong. Just like he'd said. As she thinks back on what he'd told her, something hits her hard.

Don't hesitate. Aim fast and true.

A knot tightens in her belly. *Oh my God.* He'd expected her to stake him. He'd given her permission to kill him. And she'd been so upset. She hadn't been thinking straight. What if she'd actually done it? Her stomach rolls. She knows he bears guilt for what he's done, and for turning Dawn into a vampire, but is he actually suicidal?

No, she decides after a moment. If he truly was, he would have done it himself. And he hasn't. She doesn't know if it's their weird connection or just her intuition, but she knows he's still out there somewhere. Hating himself.

Although she's sure she doesn't want him dead, she's less sure there isn't some part of her that hates him, too, right now. It's not a nice feeling. It's not something she's proud of. In fact, it only makes her feel worse.

Everything is such a mess and Genny has no idea how to deal with any of it. So she doesn't. After a quick trip to the bathroom, she calls work, then tucks the stake under her pillow and goes back to sleep.

The phone rings just after noon and when Genny groggily answers it, JP is on the other end.

"Skipping work again?" he asks.

"Terrible sleep again."

"I'm sorry. Nightmares about the other night?"

In some ways the answer is yes, but she's not ready to tell him what she'd learned yet. The last thing she wants to hear from JP right now is an *I told you so*. "Something like that," she mumbles.

"Is there anything I can do?"

Genny sighs. "I think I'm just gonna stay in bed today. But I'll come over tomorrow if you want?"

"Of course I want. Weren't you supposed to go visit Dawn later today?"

Oh right. "I haven't heard from her yet. But she's probably sleeping. I'll see how I feel this evening, but I might wait 'til tomorrow. Maybe we can go visit her together?"

"Works for me. I 'ope you're able to get some rest."

"Me, too. Talk soon."

After they hang up, Genny drags herself out of bed and goes downstairs. She finds a foil-covered pan of Gran's lasagna in the fridge and dishes up a section, heating it in the microwave and taking it back up to her room to eat.

Chloe is out. Gran's car is missing, so she's probably gone to the mall. Which leaves Genny alone with her thoughts, and she doesn't particularly want to think right now. Thinking just makes her angry, which in turn makes her frustrated with herself for being so angry. Once she finishes lunch, she crawls back between the sheets.

She wakes later to a knock at her bedroom door. Rolling over, she glances at the clock and is surprised to see it's already five-thirty.

Her sister comes into her room. "I *thought* you'd stayed home again today. Why're you still in bed?"

Genny sighs. The secrets are starting to pile up. Though she's definitely not ready to tell Chloe what she'd learned last night, it is time to explain about Dawn. "I need to tell you something."

There's something I need to tell you. His words last night. She shoves the memory away.

"Sit down." Genny pats the side of her bed.

Chloe frowns, taking a seat. "What's up? You okay?"

"I'm fine. It's just, well..." Genny stops with a sigh. She wants to tell her sister what's happened to Dawn, but how can she do that without explaining about her new vampire friends, and her own kidnapping a few weeks back? What she really should do is tell her all of it, but the truth is Genny can't bring herself to talk about him right now. She knows if she does, she'll break down and tell Chloe the truth about their parents' death. Then everything would be out in the open and she'd have to face it head on and deal with it.

And since Genny can barely even think about last night's conversation—think about *him*—without her throat tightening and her mind going cold, she knows she isn't remotely ready to talk about it yet. With anyone. Not even the people she trusts most in the world.

Isn't he one? that stupid, annoying voice pipes up. Genny has to repress a sudden urge to scream.

Instead she takes a deep breath. And then another. And then she tells Chloe that Dawn had been attacked by a vampire Tuesday night and that she and JP had tried to rescue her but Dawn had been bleeding too badly. Genny explains that another two vampires had shown up and one of them had saved Dawn's life, but the only way they'd been able to do it had been by turning her into a vampire, too.

Chloe's eyes are huge. "Holy. Shit."

She nods. "Holy shit is right. But at least she's alive. Sort of. Basically. I know the whole thing is freaky, but please don't worry. Dawn's with a friend who's teaching her how to manage her transition without hurting anyone. She'll drink blood from animals or blood bags. We need to be cautious at first, but once she gets the hang of things, I think we should be able to spend time with her like usual."

Frowning, Chloe says, "What friend? JP?"

Genny sits back with a sigh. "No. JP and I actually know a…a vampire who doesn't kill humans. She's taking care of Dawn and she'll make sure she learns how to do things right. It won't be easy, but Dawn's smart and tough. She'll be okay."

Chloe's mouth drops open. "Hold on. *What*? You guys have a vampire friend? Why didn't you tell me? That's pretty massive!"

"You're right. I should've. I don't know if I'd call Cassandra a *friend*, exactly, but she's not an enemy. She's helping Dawn, and that means a lot to me."

"And you trust her?"

"Trust her not to kill me and my friends? Yes." Genny smiles. "You'd like her, actually. She's funny, in a sarcastic kind of way."

Her sister shakes her head, like she's still trying to process all this. "So let me get this straight. Dawn's seriously a vampire now?"

Her smile vanishing, Genny nods. "And you can't tell anyone. Dawn's parents don't even know yet. And I'm worried about JP's family finding out, because she's still my best friend and I have no intention of staking her."

Chloe makes an X over her chest. "I won't tell." A grin suddenly stretches across her face. "Did you really kill the vampire that attacked her?"

"I did." She doesn't mention that she had help.

Smacking her on the shoulder, Chloe exclaims, "Wow, Gen. You really *are* a vampire slayer! Who would've ever thought? And I guess I am, too. Or will be someday. Maybe you should start training me?"

"You're welcome to come with me to Marie's. I know they'd love to meet you."

"Maybe next week. Let's set up a time. Look, I gotta go. I'm meeting Darry at work before his shift."

"Remember, not a word."

"Yeah, yeah." With that Chloe disappears across the hall.

Genny glances at the phone on her dresser. If Dawn calls when she wakes up, Genny wants to make plans to see her. But if she doesn't, Genny decides she's not going to call. Not tonight. Probably not tomorrow, either. She wants to talk to Dawn, but if she calls there, there's a chance he might pick up the phone. And she's not even remotely ready to talk to him yet.

Right now, she's not sure if she ever will be.

The phone rings that evening just as Genny and Gran are settling in to watch television. When she picks up the cordless receiver, Genny is relieved to hear Dawn's voice. She takes it upstairs.

"How are things?"

"Better," Dawn says. She sounds a lot more like her old self. "Do you still wanna come by tonight?"

It's not like Genny's tired. After sleeping most of the day, she doesn't think she'll be able to fall asleep for hours. However, she doesn't feel comfortable going over there right now. "I don't know…" she starts, but she trails off when she hears Cassandra speak to Dawn in the background.

"Wait," Dawn says. "Actually, Cassandra and I will come to you. You feel like a walk maybe? Or we could sit out back?"

"Works for me. See you soon," Genny replies, relieved she doesn't have to make an excuse to not visit.

Dawn must have been practicing her super-speed, because the girls show up at Genny's door not even ten minutes later

"Not gonna invite us in?" Cassandra says the moment Genny steps outside.

Genny fakes a smile, but doesn't reply. At some point maybe she will, but not tonight. The one vampire she'd invited in had let her down in ways she can't even wrap her head around yet. It's still too fresh.

"She's kidding," Dawn pipes up, noticing Genny's reaction. "It doesn't matter."

"Maybe next time," Genny says. She deliberately turns down the sidewalk in the opposite direction to the route they had taken last night. Dawn starts off walking between Genny and Cassandra, but after a few minutes Cassandra switches places with her.

"Have you heard from him?" she asks Genny.

Genny doesn't want to answer that, so instead she says, "You haven't yet?"

Cassandra shakes her head. "Not a peep. Maybe he's left the city."

"Are you worried?"

"Nah. He'll come around. He always does."

Even if Cassandra won't admit it, Genny can tell she's concerned. Of course she is. She's been with him for decades, and she knows he's not in a good place right now. She deserves to know he hasn't gone far.

With a reluctant sigh, Genny admits, "He hasn't left. At least not as of last night."

Halting in her tracks, Cassandra faces her. "He came to see you?"

Genny nods.

"And?"

"He's feeling guilty, like you said he'd be."

"No shit. What else did he say?"

Genny starts walking again. "I…I don't really wanna talk about it."

Cassandra catches up to her and grabs ahold of her elbow. The three of them stop in the shadow of a big oak tree. "Yeah, no. Unless you two were getting down and dirty, I wanna know what he said."

Heat floods Genny's face. "Of course not! Don't be ridiculous. I have a boyfriend. And he has you."

One of Cassandra's eyebrows arches and she chuckles. "Quinn and I aren't a couple. He's my closest friend in the world, and yeah, we used to fuck way back when, like *eons* ago, but no. I love him to pieces, but we're not lovers."

"Sorry." Genny's cheeks feel like they're on fire. "I guess I just assumed."

"Oh honey. You're clearly more naïve than I figured if you thought he was in love with me. Or maybe it was just easier to think that?"

Genny doesn't reply. She doesn't want to talk about last night, but she can see that she's going to have to anyway.

"So. Now that we've cleared that up, tell me what he said to you. Because I'd really like to know what mental space he's inhabiting at the moment."

Exhaling a deep sigh, Genny tells Cassandra and Dawn what he'd admitted. When she finishes, Cassandras face is drawn, her eyes narrowed.

"Let me get this straight. He handed you a stake and told you to use it? Are you fucking kidding me? You didn't think that was important enough to call me about the very second you got home?"

Genny shrinks back from her. "I…no. That didn't even cross my mind." Then her own anger flares up. "I was a bit distracted by the fact that someone I'd considered a friend helped kill my parents! Sorry if calling you wasn't on the top of my thoughts."

Cassandra's eyes widen. "He was on a mission, one that he hated with a passion, but had no choice about, because when the Assembly asks you to do something and you'd like to keep your head intact, you do it. They sent three older vamps to him to make sure the job got done. And afterward he felt so awful about it he rushed back to try to save them. He didn't know you, or them. But he tried to save them anyway. You have no idea the amount of guilt he carries, especially now that he's met you and knows those people were your parents. It eats him up inside."

Dawn's eyes flick between them. Genny remains silent.

"No, I take it back. You *do* know how bad he feels," Cassandra continues. "Because he gave you a fucking *stake* and told you to kill him! Jesus!" She blows out a sigh. "I can't believe he did that."

"He said it was my mother's." She's not sure why she'd bothered to say this. It would make no difference to Cassandra.

"He must've snuck home and got it while we were out. At least he didn't use it on himself." Cassandra frowns. "Although now that he's told you, I'm not sure what he'll do."

Genny hesitates. It's clear how worried Cassandra is. "He's not dead, if that's what you mean."

"Yeah? And how do you know that?"

She hadn't planned on telling them this, but it just slips out. "Because I'm pretty sure I'd know."

"How? How could you possibly know for sure?"

"We have a…I don't know how to describe it, but we have a connection. He thinks it's a spell. I have no idea. But I can feel when he's around."

"Hold on. Wait. You have a *what*?"

"I get a weird tingle whenever he's near. Like low grade electricity running over my skin."

Cassandra chuckles. "That's not a spell, that's chemistry. Hormones. Did you tell JP about this?"

"No. It's not. I felt that he was around that first night he saw me at Apothecary, and I didn't even meet him until a week later. And no, JP doesn't know. I didn't intend to tell you guys either, but…" She stops with a sigh. "I'd appreciate if you didn't say anything to JP. He…well, let's just say he wouldn't take it well."

"Because he's jealous of your relationship with Quinn." Cassandra says. Not like a question, like a statement of fact.

Genny nods.

"Well look. However messy your romantic life may be, that's not what's important right now. Quinn's out there somewhere thinking you're never gonna forgive him. And possibly feeling suicidal. I get that you're upset, and you have every right to be, but if you could see it in your heart to forgive him sooner rather than later, it would be a huge benefit to everyone involved. You *know* it wasn't his fault."

Genny turns away from them and blows out a hard exhalation. "It's not that easy. I'm gonna need some time."

Dawn squeezes Genny's arm. She's been quiet this whole time just listening to them, but now she says, "Of course you will."

"Sure. Take all the time you need," Cassandra says, a caustic edge to her voice. "But make it quick, will ya? Because the way he's feeling right now, he may just leave town for good. And then it might take me years to find him again. I know the whole thing sucks, but just, could you try to maybe see it from his point of view?"

"I'll try," Genny concedes. She doesn't feel much like either walking or talking anymore, so she turns around and heads back toward home. The girls follow. Dawn, in an attempt to lighten the mood, tells Genny that Cassandra is teaching her how to control her new strength and speed. "Do you think I could practice hypnotizing you sometime? It won't work on vampires."

Glancing over at her, Genny says, "It doesn't work on immortals, either."

Dawn frowns. "How do you know if we don't try?"

"Because she and Quinn have obviously experimented with it," Cassandra cuts in. "Right?"

Genny just nods. She doesn't want to relive those memories either.

When they get back to Gran's, Genny gives Dawn a hug and promises she'll see her on the weekend. Cassandra shoots her a look that clearly says *fix this* before they turn and go.

If only it were that simple, Genny thinks as she heads inside.

Later, lying in bed, she realizes she should probably send him a mental message to get in touch with Cassandra and ease her worries.

She should, but she doesn't.

On Saturday morning, for the first time ever, Genny actually wishes it was a workday. She needs a distraction badly and working would help, at least for a while. Tasks would have stacked up in her absence. She could go downtown for a few hours and put a dent in her To-Do pile. She calls JP and tells him she'll come over later this afternoon, then fills a Thermos with hot coffee, gets dressed, and heads out.

It turns out there's enough work waiting for her at the office to keep her mind successfully occupied until after three. Mostly, anyway. When unwanted thoughts try to sneak in, she swats them away like pesky flies. This tactic only works until she comes down to the lobby to head home and there's no tingle, and no one leaning against the wall outside waiting for her. Her throat starts to tighten and she frantically digs in her bag for her headphones. Once they're on, she hits play on the Discman stashed in her bag. The Cure will help distract her.

The music helps, but her commute still feels a lot longer than usual. One and half CDs later, she rings the buzzer at JP's apartment.

He greets her with the wide smile she adores and her tension relaxes a little at the sight of it. Immediately taking her in his arms, he closes the door with his foot as he kisses her. "Missed you," he murmurs.

“Missed you, too.” She kicks off her sandals and heads into the living room. She knows he’s thinking about leading her down the hall to his bedroom, and although she’s not opposed to that, she sits on the couch instead.

He takes a seat beside her, pulling her legs into his lap and starting to rub her tired feet as she leans back against a throw cushion. “How’s Dawn doing?”

“Much better. I saw her last night. Cassandra’s teaching her lots of stuff.”

“Good. Just Cassandra? What about Quinn?”

Genny sighs. “He’s been AWOL since the night it happened. Well. Mostly.”

“What do you mean?”

“He hasn’t been home.” She knows she’d promised JP she’d be honest with him. Although she hasn’t wanted to talk about it, she wonders if maybe it would help if she told him. He isn’t capable of being fully impartial, but he’s a lot more removed from the situation than Cassandra is. And she really needs to share this burden with someone who will see it from her point of view.

It’s not easy to talk about. In fact, it’s remarkably difficult. But she tells JP anyway. Not just everything she’d found out Wednesday, but also what Cassandra had said to her last night about why she needs to forgive him.

To Genny’s surprise, JP listens intently and refrains from any judgy comments, which considering the subject matter means a lot to her. When she finishes, he releases her foot, slides an arm around her shoulders and tugs her against his side. “But it’s not that easy, is it?” he says softly.

“No. Not at all.”

“Don’t beat yourself up about being upset. You have every right to be. They were your *parents* for God’s sake! Of course you’re furious. And you considered Quinn your friend, yet ‘e didn’t even tell you about this until ‘e felt ‘e had to. Sure ‘e feels guilty. And so ‘e should! And you feel angry, you feel betrayed, and you’re naturally going to need some time to process all this. It isn’t fair of Cassandra to expect you to just get over it, to track ‘im down and fix things. You haven’t done anything wrong.”

Genny feels a sudden wash of emotions quite different from the volatile ones she’s been drowning in lately. JP understands. She'd been so worried he might lash out and be angry, too, and it would only make her even more miserable. But instead he gets exactly how she feels.

Straightening up, she sets a hand on the side of his face and looks at him. "I love you," she blurts.

His rich brown eyes flare. He smiles, but instead of repeating it back to her like she'd expected, he says, "You take that back. You weren't supposed to say it first. You've ruined all my careful planning."

She mirrors his grin. "Sorry. Rewinding. Chuckachuckachucka. Let me start again. Thank you for understanding exactly how I feel. You're the only one who really gets it."

His large warm hand closes over hers and squeezes. "You're welcome. So, the thing is…I wanted to make you a nice dinner first, get you in a great mood, maybe go for a walk to the park and find a deserted bench and kiss you like you've never been kissed before. But there's no point in waiting for the moment to be perfect. Anytime I'm with you it's perfect. Because I'm completely in love with you."

Genny leans in and kisses him softly. "That *was* perfect. Am I allowed to say it now?"

"Please do. Or I might burst into tears."

She laughs. They both laugh. She brings her face close again, until their lips are nearly touching. "I love you, too."

Genny and JP spend most of Sunday morning in bed, save for a quick break for breakfast. She finally feels like some of the weight has been lifted. Not all of it, but some. Being with JP is just the distraction she needs. He makes her happy even when other parts of her life seem to be crumbling. Loving him is easy, one of the easiest things she's ever done.

She decides to opt out of going to Marie's after lunch to train. After everything that's happened, she's just not in the right headspace to practice taking down vampires. Instead they rent a movie, spend more time in bed, and order in pizza for dinner. After they eat, she tells him she's ready to head home.

"Why? I was kind of hoping you'd stay over again."

"I know. But I think maybe there's something I need to do."

JP's quiet for a few seconds. Then he asks, "Where will you find 'im?"

Genny's eyebrows arch in surprise. Of course he knows why she wants to go. Thankfully he doesn't sound jealous, simply curious. It's a welcome change. "I'll ask Cassandra." A lie, but only a tiny one.

"Well, even if she doesn't know where 'e is, she'll be relieved to know you're ready to talk."

Sighing, Genny says, "I guess. I don't know if I am, but I think I'd feel better if I at least reached out. We'll see. I'll talk to you tomorrow, okay?"

"You bet you will. In person if I 'ave my way. Love you."

"Love you, too."

She kisses him goodbye. Instead of catching the bus, she decides to walk the seven blocks home. She has a lot to think about.

It's another hot July night. Genny opens her window to let in the breeze, switches on the fan, and climbs into bed. Gran had gone to bed over an hour ago and Genny had noticed Chloe's light had been out when she'd come out of the bathroom. Soon everyone else in the house will be asleep.

She's let herself be angry for three days now. Three extremely long days. It doesn't sound like much time, but to Genny it feels like an eternity. She's tried hard to distract herself from thinking about it—and sometimes, like last night and a good part of today, she's mostly been successful. But it always comes back.

No one's harder on Quinn than Quinn.

That's what Cassandra had said to her. She knows it's true, knows he's out there hating himself. And whether Genny had been ready to hear it or not, the other stuff Cassandra had told her is also true. He hadn't wanted to do it, hadn't known who her parents were, and had even returned to try to save them.

It eats him up inside, Cassandra had told her. And at the time, a part of Genny had thought, *Good.* But it's not good. It's been eating her up inside, too.

It's not that she's over it. Maybe she'll never be completely over it, but she thinks it might be time to try to fix it. Like JP had said, she hasn't done anything wrong, but she knows she'll never be able shake this sick feeling in her gut if she doesn't try to fix things anyway. It's only been three days. Three days is nothing in the grand scheme of things. But there's a massive hole in her insides without him, and that hole aches more than any amount of anger ever could.

And, really, it all boils down to one thing: does she want him in her life or not? The answer to that comes surprisingly easy.

She glances at her clock. It's almost midnight. The house around her is quiet. For the first time what she's about to do makes her nervous. She can feel her heart pounding as she pushes her head into her pillow and tries to lie still. Closing her eyes, she brings his face to mind. Not the sorrowful face she'd seen the last two times, but the relaxed, smiling one from some of their transit conversations.

She focuses on his smile and thinks: *Quinn. If you can, if you're willing to, please come see me. My bedroom window is open. Knock twice and then come inside so we can talk.*

And then she waits.

It takes almost an hour. Genny has actually given up and started to doze off when she's startled by two soft knocks on the glass.

"Come in," she whispers. The window sash creaks as it's pushed higher, and then she hears the thump of his boots on the floor.

Hi, she thinks.

"Hi," he whispers.

We need to talk. Come lie here with me.

"Are you sure?" He sounds uncertain.

I'm sure.

Two more thumps. Those same boots coming off. Her mattress shifts as he sits on the edge. He doesn't make a move to lie down, so she pats the other pillow. *Please*?

There's a low sigh. A moment later, she feels him stretch out beside her. She's on her side facing him, and although she can't see much more than his outline, she knows he can see her.

Where've you been?

"Around."

Cassandra's worried about you. She needs you to come home.

At first he doesn't reply. Then he just says, "I know."

Will you? Or at least call her?

"Yes." She doesn't know if he means he'll return or call. Probably the latter if this conversation doesn't go well.

Good. This is harder than Genny had expected, and she'd expected it to be difficult. She's not sure how to even begin. So, taking a deep breath, she just starts. *As for me, I needed some time to process everything. But I've given it a lot of thought, and I want you to know I understand why you did what you did. I know you didn't want to hurt them, and that you were forced to participate against your will.*

"Genevieve..."

Let me finish. You tried to save them and I'm deeply grateful for that, even though you couldn't. What I'm trying to say is that I forgive you.

He sighs again. "I don't deserve your forgiveness."

Genny reaches across the space between them until she finds his hand. The jolt of electricity she recalls from before they'd entered the safehouse hits her again and she shudders. Not with pain. The exact opposite. She doesn't let go this time; she just lets herself savor the simple pleasure of touching him. JP's hands are so warm, hot even, and she can't help noticing how nice Quinn's cool skin feels against hers on such a warm evening. Pulling his hand into the middle of the bed, she curls her fingers around his.

You do deserve it. Do you feel that? The current where we're touching?

"I do." His voice sounds different now. Still soft, but no longer tentative. It almost sounds like awe.

I've decided that I am stronger than my anger. What we share, our connection? I don't want to lose it. It's good that you told me. Sometimes the truth hurts, but I'd still rather know it.

He's quiet, but he doesn't pull his hand away. That in itself amazes her.

Do you agree? Genny asks. *Can we move past this and be friends again?*

"Yes." His acquiescence is so simple, yet powerful in its simplicity. Because she can tell he means it, and she knows that's a big deal for Quinn. Three nights ago, he'd been willing to let her stake him for his crimes. Accepting her forgiveness would not be easy for him, yet somehow he's managed to do it. It feels like a small miracle.

She tells him how Dawn's doing, and what Cassandra said the other night, and they chat one-sidedly for over an hour.

"Should I go?" he whispers when she starts to yawn.

Don't. Please stay.

He doesn't ask if she's sure this time. He just lies beside her while she drifts off to sleep, a hint of a smile playing on her lips.

Neither of them lets go of the other's hand.

Chapter 14
Something I Can Never Have

When the darkness starts to lighten outside Genevieve's window, Quinn reluctantly releases her hand and slips out onto a nearby tree branch, closing the sash behind him. He jumps to the ground and, with only a brief look back, heads for home.

He attempts to open the back door quietly, although he's well aware there's no point trying to sneak in. If she's awake, she'll hear him. Even if she's not awake, she'll hear. Cassandra is just that good. And he's not wrong. Two seconds later, she speeds down the stairs and comes to a stop in front of him. She looks relieved. But only for a moment; then her face twists into a scowl. Grabbing him by the shoulders, she shoves him into a nearby chair.

"The *fuck* did you think you were doing?"

Quinn flinches. She's even angrier than he'd expected. "I know. I'm sorry."

Her eyes are flashing. "*Sorry*? You're sorry? That's *rich*. You were gonna just leave me without even a motherfucking goodbye and you're sorry? Sorry doesn't cut it this time. Not by half."

He frowns. "We've been apart before. We always find each other again. If I'd decided to leave for any length of time, I would've let you know."

"Oh yeah? And when exactly would you have let me know? Sometime between handing a slayer a stake and telling her to use it?"

His face falls. Genevieve must've told her. "I..." He stops. She's right. He's got no defense.

"You what?" She braces her hands on her hips. "So it's true? You really told her to kill you?"

Quinn glances up at the ceiling. "Is Dawn...?"

"Asleep," Cassandra replies with a dismissive wave. "She's new to this. She won't hear unless I call her name. Or scream at you. Which is not out of the question right now." Her shoulders slump as she sits on the arm of the couch. "Tell me the truth. Do you want to die?"

"Sometimes," he admits with a sigh. The night he'd told Genevieve of his part in her parent's death, he'd thought he deserved it, like he was placing himself before his executioner and confessing his crime, ready and willing to accept his sentence. He can't even count how many times over the years he's wanted to die, craved death like some sweet relief to the torture this agonizingly long life has inflicted on him. But then he recalls how it had felt to hold Genevieve's hand and talk for hours. "If it makes you feel any better, I don't anymore."

Cassandra's head tilts. She still looks concerned. "She talked to you?"

Quinn nods.

"And is everything back to copasetic between you two?"

"I think so. I don't really understand why, but she says she's forgiven me."

"Maybe it has something to do with your *connection*?" A knowing grin finally surfaces.

Chuckling softly, he says, "She told you about that?"

"She said she feels a—now what word did she use?—oh yeah, a *tingle* whenever you're around." Rolling her eyes, Cassandra adds, "I'll just bet she does."

"And this is exactly why I didn't tell you."

"She also said you think it's a spell. Hate to break it to ya, but that's no spell, Quinolin. That's called lust. You've just avoided it so long you've forgotten."

He shakes his head. "It's not that. She..." With a sigh, he stops. He can't tell when Genevieve is nearby the way she can with him, but he definitely feels a spark when she touches him. The truth is, he's not sure he wouldn't feel it anyway.

"I know, I know. She said she felt your presence at the club a week before she met you. Fine. So it might be a spell. Have you looked into it? I mean, who in their right mind would spell a connection between the two of you? What would even be the point?"

"I have no idea." But if he ever finds out, he'll owe them a debt of gratitude.

"It could be important."

"Maybe." He shrugs.

"Maybe whoever did it knew you'd protect her?"

"I didn't even know her before the night we took her. Why would anyone assume I'd protect her?" Most vampires would sooner kill Genevieve than help her. Whoever chose him would've had to have known him really well to know a spell like this would work. And there's no one left who knows him that well but Cassandra.

"No clue, but it might be worth investigating. Too bad all the mages I've known are dead."

Quinn frowns, thinking sadly of the only one he'd ever known.

You were just gonna leave me?

Those had been Cassandra's words when she'd confronted him. He'd thought she'd meant him leaving town, but now he understands she'd meant leave her forever. He gets to his feet and takes one of her hands in his. "I'm really sorry. I wasn't thinking straight the other night and I didn't consider the impact of my actions on you. Can you forgive me?"

She smiles. "You sure spend a lot of time brooding on forgiveness, or the lack thereof." Standing, she pulls him into a hug. "Of course I forgive ya. But don't let it happen again. You and me, we're a team. Even when one of us gets involved with someone else, we always have each other's backs. That's our deal. And I expect you to hold up your end of it."

Quinn squeezes her, then steps back. "I will. Anyway, it's always you getting involved with someone, then running back to me when it doesn't work out. I'm the boring, steady one, remember?"

"Oh, I remember. All of them. And you waited out every last one until it went tits up and I came and found you again. Sometimes I think I'm incapable of maintaining a lasting relationship with anyone but you."

"That's not true. You just haven't found the right person yet. And when you do, you'll probably move to some far off destination and we'll see each other a few times a year on holiday. And I'll still be here, same as always."

Cassandra shakes her head, but she's still smiling. "Maybe. Maybe not. I'm no mage, but I sense change in the wind."

"That's a very un-Cassandra-like thing to say."

"What can I tell ya? I'm adapting. It's the only way to survive. You should look into it."

Quinn chuckles.

"On that note, it's time for me to get some beauty sleep." She heads for the stairs.

"I should probably do that, too. See you tonight."

She levels him a cool look. "You'd better."

"I promise." He crosses his heart.

About halfway up the steps, she pauses and turns back to him. "Hey, you wanna know something else weird? Genny was under the bonkers impression that you and I were a couple. I set her straight, of course."

Quinn keeps his face impassive as he replies, "I'm sure you did." Once she's gone, he sits for a few more minutes longer, thinking. Did learning he and Cassandra are just friends have anything to do with Genevieve calling him over last night? And taking his hand? Maybe not. She probably would have acted the same either way. But he can't help wondering.

With a sigh, he buries those thoughts and heads up to his room. Ideas like that just lead him to places he shouldn't go, places she can't possibly follow. He sits on his bed, but instead of going to sleep, he picks up his latest journal and begins to write.

Genny is startled awake by a voice speaking in French. A wide-eyed blonde girl maybe a few years younger than Chloe is standing over her.

"Wake up, wake up! Why are you still sleeping? I'm much too excited to sleep. Aren't you excited, sister?"

Genny's surprised to realize she understands every word. How has she suddenly become fluent in French? Also, had that girl just called her 'sister'?

"I'm clearly not as excited as you, Lucie," she replies, also in French. Lucie. Right. Because Lucie is her younger sister's name. Next youngest is Marie-Claude, and Annie is the baby, only five years old. Maman had told her their family always has daughters. Maman also expects her to start having her own baby girls as soon as possible, something she's not particularly excited about. She's not ready to become anyone's mother yet; she's still so young, and has much more to learn. Maybe Armand won't mind if she delays it for a while? It's not like it's a rush. Although the longer they wait, the more often she'll have to listen to Maman ask her if she's with child yet.

Genny looks around the small room. It has one lace-curtained window wedged partially open with a block of wood. Her eyes land on a long, cream satin and lace dress hanging over a bureau against the opposite wall.

Suddenly this all makes sense. It's her wedding day. That's what Lucie is so excited about. Today she will marry Armand.

The thought of her wedding brings both excitement and sadness, and Genny doesn't understand why. She's been betrothed to Armand for nearly three years. It's an arrangement set up by her mother, but unlike the marriages of some of her friends in the village, this is a union she is quite happy about. She loves Armand, and knows he loves her. She is confident they will make a good life together.

So why the sadness?

Genny throws back her down-filled coverlet and sets her bare feet on the wooden floorboards. After laying the dress across the end of the bed, her sister pours a pitcher of steaming water into a large bowl. "You need to wash. Do you want me to help?"

"No, thanks," Genny says, puzzled by the question. She's more than capable of washing herself.

Lucie smiles and hands her a sugar-dusted pastry. "I brought you this. Eat it now," she whispers. "You won't likely get anything else for hours." Then she leaves the room, the wooden door thumping shut behind her.

Genny takes a bite of the pastry. It's heavier than she'd expected, but decidedly delicious. Pulling her nightgown up over her head, she tosses it onto her pillow. She has to stifle a laugh when she sees the white ruffled bloomers she has on beneath. Why on earth would she bother wearing those to bed?

Using a clean rag and a wedge of yellow soap she finds in a dish, she washes herself as best she can. Once finished, she looks around. What is she supposed to wear? Should she try to put the dress on now? Or should she wait until later? She has no idea. She scans the room again until her gaze lands on her discarded nightgown. With a swish of her fingers, the garment flies into her hand. Her mouth falls open in surprise. How on Earth did she do that? But then she smiles to herself, as if it's no big deal at all.

As she pulls it back on, there's a knock on the door. "Are you ready?" It's Lucie and Maman, with Annie right at their heels. Annie is adorable. She's a miniature Lucie, all plump rosy cheeks and blonde ringlets.

When she looks at Maman, a part of her is startled. She looks very much like Genny. Same wide green eyes, same wavy, thick brown hair, although Maman's has been wound into a bun at the back of her head.

Before she can think too much about the resemblance, they lead her into another, larger room. Her parents' room. The window in here is larger, and the curtains are tied back to let in the sunshine. A stool has been placed in front of her mother's bureau, and Genny takes a seat before the mirror. It takes her a moment to realize what she's looking at is a mirror, because the face staring back at her is not the face she'd expected. Although there's a similarity, this girl is younger, with sky-blue eyes and more defined cheekbones than Genny's. This strange face should probably freak her out. Yet it doesn't.

Her mother goes to work tying up sections of her hair while her sisters watch from the bed. The process of creating curls is painful, but Genny restrains each urge to wince, knowing Maman will disapprove. And, of course, it doesn't hurt for long.

Lucie hands Maman a necklace, which is fastened around Genny's neck. She smiles as a silver balanced cross within a circle, sort of like a plus sign with flared ends, comes to rest against the hollow of her throat. It's her grand-mère's cross, and Genny is thrilled to be allowed to wear it today.

Next comes make-up. As a child, she would often sit in here and watch Maman apply creams and powders to her face until she looked like an entirely different woman. It had seemed like magic, to her youthful eyes. Though she hasn't been allowed to wear anything more than a touch of rouge before, she's confident her mother knows just what to do. Thick white cream is slathered onto her entire face and massaged in small circles until it's absorbed. It smells kind of nasty and Genny can't help wondering what it's made from. Next her mother dusts her with powder and rubs pink rouge onto the apples of her cheeks. Maman then uses a silvery powder on Genny's eyes and lastly applies a perfect pout of red lipstick. Now she understands Lucie's comment about not being able to eat anything. The lipstick also smells and tastes strange. She hopes she'll get used to it.

Maman blots her lips with a rectangle of thin paper and sprays Genny with floral perfume from one of her beveled bottles. She steps back and scrutinizes her work for a few moments. With an approving smile, she says, "You are beautiful."

Genny barely has time to admire herself before Lucie brings in the wedding dress and all three of them begin helping her get dressed. And, yes, full outfit, right now. Corset and stockings and crinoline, then the beautiful satin gown overtop. Next comes elbow-length button-up gloves and high laced boots that make her grateful for the invention of zippers. Finally Maman turns her around and presents her before the mirror.

"You look absolutely radiant. Armand will love it. Do you love it?"

"Do you?" Annie pipes up. "Do you just love it, Maddy?"

Genny smiles, but inside she feels that pang of sadness again. "Yes," she assures them. "Thank you. It's perfect."

In her mind, she can hear another voice, a strangely familiar one speaking French with a Scottish accent, telling her how beautiful she is and how happy she's going to be. Though he's right, she is happy, it still breaks her heart a little to know she'll probably never hear that voice again.

Genny's alarm startles her out of a deep sleep. At first she's confused and not sure where she is. Then she realizes she's in her own bedroom, not getting ready to get married in some French village. It had just been another of those weird dreams.

She wonders if she should tell someone about it, and that thought triggers a memory of last night. Rolling over, she sees the other side of the bed is empty. Had she also dreamt Quinn's visit? Then she notices her window is closed and she knows she'd gone to bed with it open. He'd really been here. Remembering brings a smile.

It's no surprise he's gone. He'd probably left before dawn to avoid the sun. It's more surprising that he'd even showed up at all. But she's so glad he had. This morning her heart feels lighter than it's felt in days.

After work, Genny goes to JP's place. The plan is for them to go to his mom's for more training. It's another sweltering day, but Genny hasn't trained since before Dawn's kidnapping and she needs to start up again. As they leave his building, she's surprised to see his uncle's car in the parking lot.

"Thought I'd drive us today," he says as he opens her door for her. "Save us walking in this sauna."

"You are still officially The Best." Genny stands on her tiptoes to kiss him. She's feeling a little guilty right now. Not because Quinn had spent most of last night lying on her bed beside her—they hadn't done anything wrong. It's more that she doesn't intend to tell JP about it, because it will only make him needlessly upset. She does want to let him know she's no longer avoiding Quinn, though.

"I talked to Quinn last night," she says nonchalantly as they get into the car.

JP turns to her, surprised. "You did? So 'e finally came back?"

Genny doesn't know for sure, but she assumes he's gone home by now. "Yes, and we talked things out. Things are—well, they're not totally fixed, because something like that doesn't just go away—but things are better now. I told him I understood why he did what he did."

"Well, that's good, I guess. So you don't feel an urge to use your mother's stake on 'im anymore?"

She doesn't laugh. Although she knows he's kidding, nothing about that sentence is even remotely funny. "No," she replies simply. There's so much more she could add, but she chooses not to. Her feelings on that are complicated, intense, and most of all, her own.

Instead she changes the subject. "I had another one of those weird dreams last night. The ones where I'm in the body of one of my ancestors? What did you call them again?"

Starting the car, he glances over at her. "Ancestral consciousness?"

"Yeah! That. I don't know how it's possible—magic I guess—but I had another one. In it, I woke up in a strange bed in an old-timey looking room, and it was my wedding day. My mother and two younger sisters were helping me get ready. We were all speaking French, and I understood every word—can you believe it? And I was going to marry a man named…Arnold? No, wait…Armand I think. And—"

JP's eyes dart her way again. His forehead furrows. "Armand? Your grandfather was Armand St. Jean."

Genny's eyes fly wide. "Mom's dad?"

He nods. "He died before you were born."

"Killed by vampires?"

JP nods again as he steers them around a corner. "What else?"

That sick feeling in her gut returns. "Yeah." Then she recalls something. "In the dream, my little sister called me Maddy. Was that my grandmother's name?"

His eyebrows arch. "Yes, of course. Madeleine Bourreau. You don't know that?"

"I know nothing! Well, slightly more than nothing now thanks to you. I did ask Gran, but she couldn't remember their names. I actually meant to ask you a while ago, but I forgot. It feels like Madeleine wants me to know her." Genny sighs, turning to look out the window. As they enter the parking lot at Marie's, she asks, "Did your mom know her?"

JP pulls the car into René's spot. "She did, although I don't think they were close. I'll see what I 'ave about her in my notes."

When they go inside, Marie greets them both with a hug. "Genny, mon Dieu! JP told me you killed your first vampire a few days ago?"

Genny nods. "It was completely terrifying, but yeah, somehow I did."

René steps into the hall. "Incroyable! So soon! You are a natural. We are so proud." He's grinning widely at her, and it feels almost paternal. Or maybe she's just missing her parents more than usual lately. Either way, it's nice to hear they think she's capable of handling her mother's legacy.

"Thanks. It honestly all happened so fast. And mostly all I was thinking about was rescuing my friend Dawn."

"Ah yes. Your friend." Marie gestures toward the living room. "Please sit down for a few minutes. I've got fresh lemonade. We would like to hear all about it, if you don't mind?"

"Sounds delicious." Genny and JP take a seat on the couch and a minute later, Marie and René join them. Genny explains what happened to Dawn, although JP has obviously already told them his version of the story. When she gets to the part where Quinn gives Dawn his blood, she notices Marie and René exchange a look. Whether that look is about her friendship with two—now three—vampires, or something else, she's not sure. Thankfully neither of them suggests that it's now her duty to kill her friends, although she suspects they may be thinking it.

After a rigorous training session in the cool basement instead of out in the hot backyard, and another wonderful meal, Genny and JP thank them and start walking back to his apartment.

JP is in a great mood. He's cracking stupid jokes and making himself laugh and just being a big, cute goofball. *Her* big cute goofball. She watches his face as he talks animatedly, hands waving, volume rising. She notes the way the skin around his eyes crinkles when he smiles, the way his grin stretches impossibly wider every time he glances at her. Their lives have been so full of danger lately that she worries she's missing out on appreciating the small things. Later, she will look back on this moment and remember it with such painful fondness it will make her chest ache.

She stops in her tracks and he stops too, pausing midway through a sentence to look at her quizzically. Rising on her tiptoes, she puts her hands around his neck and pulls him down into a kiss.

"What was that for?" he asks when they break apart. "Not that I mind."

"Just because. Because I love you."

"I love you, too."

"Then let's hurry back to your place so you can prove it," she says with a devilish grin.

He laughs again. "Now I need to prove it to you?"

"Need to? More like you *get* to. C'mon," she tugs on his hand. "Time's wasting."

Though Genny intends to sleep in her own bed again tonight, she's definitely up for an hour or so in JP's before going home. Thoughts of her strange dream and finding out more about her grandparents have completely slipped from both their minds.

Quinn comes downstairs that evening to find Cassandra and Dawn sitting on the couch, heads close together, talking softly.

They both turn to look at him. "See? Told you he was back." Cassandra says to Dawn.

Dawn looks good. Well-rested. Pink-cheeked. No sign of anxiety or depression, like so many new vampires experience. Cassandra has clearly done a great job helping her adjust. Now it's time for Quinn to take responsibility for what he's done to her.

He makes himself a coffee, then carries it into the living room to sit across from them. Exhaling a sigh, he raises his eyes to Dawn. "I believe I owe you an apology," he says.

At first she seems surprised, but then she smiles. "You don't. Cass has been taking good care of me. She told me you were going through a thing, that's why you weren't here."

Cass? He's never heard Cassandra let anyone refer to her as Cass before. Quinn darts a curious glance her way. She looks like she's trying to restrain a smile. He'll have to ask her about that later. Turning back to Dawn, he says, "No. I mean yes, I'm also sorry for not being here, but that's not what I meant. I'm sorry for…for cursing you to this life. To an existence of avoiding sunlight and having to drink blood to survive. For making you one of us."

Cassandra snorts. "You make it sound like our lives are sheer hell. There's way more awesome shit than bad, and I'm trying to show her this. Don't scare the girl, Q-tip. She's just starting to get used to it."

"You have nothing to apologize for," Dawn says to him. "You saved me from a horrible death. You gave me immortality, so I'll have you guys and Genny and JP forever, if we all stay friends. I'll never get sick. I'm strong and fast and can hear conversations spoken a block away if I try. As far as I'm concerned, the pros far outweigh the cons. And I was always more of a night owl anyway. So thank you."

"I don't regret saving you. But…" He stops. He'd been about to say he had turned her into a monster like him, a monster who can never have a normal human life, never have children, never know the joy of watching them grow. But he realizes maybe he shouldn't project his feelings onto her. She will make up her own mind as the months and years pass. If he tells her why he thinks it's a curse, it will only bring her down and there's no point doing that. "But you're welcome."

"Quinn has a tendency to get all caught up in the negatives. He's a bit maudlin, but you get used to him," Cassandra stage-whispers to Dawn.

“Hey. I’m sitting right here.” Quinn chuckles, taking another sip of his coffee. It’s not blood, and he’ll need some of that soon, but it still tastes pretty good right now.

Cassandra grabs the remote control and turns on the television. When Angela Lansbury’s skeptical face fills the screen, the girls smile at each other and settle back to watch a rerun of “Murder, She Wrote.”. They look comfy on the couch, but Quinn doesn’t much feel like watching TV. Giving them some privacy, he carries his mug up to his room, lies on his bed and grabs the book he’d been reading. It feels like forever since he’d last read it, but it had actually been less than a week ago, back before everything had gone to Hell.

After a few pages, he sets it aside. Maybe he should call Genevieve? He glances at the clock. It’s not even 8:30 yet, and they’d just seen each other last night. Although she’d told him she’d forgiven him, maybe it would be better to let her be the one to initiate contact for a wee while? Just to ensure she’s truly comfortable staying friends with him after learning about...well, what she’d learned.

He picks the book back up and tries to focus again. He gets about halfway down the next page when he hears her voice in his head.

Quinn? Call me at nine, okay?

And he smiles.

Chapter 15
Fear (of the Unknown)

Things go back to normal for a while, at least to this weird new version of normal that is Genny's life now. She goes back to work, hangs out with JP in the evenings, checks in with Dawn when she's able, and talks to Quinn pretty much every night. She doesn't let herself get comfortable, or assume the danger is over—she's fully aware that it's not—but she does allow herself to just try to be happy in the small moments. Moments like training with Marie and JP and kicking his ass, then stealing a kiss when his mom isn't looking. Moments like late night phone conversations with Quinn and sometimes managing to make him laugh out loud. It's not an easy feat, and Genny has been making it a personal challenge.

The hollow fear that something horrible could happen at any time to herself or one of her loved ones never really goes away, but she tries her best not to dwell on it. If she lets her worry run rampant, she'd never leave her bed or allow her sister or Gran out of the house.

Genny knows it won't last, but she refuses to let that stop her from living. Gran tells her it's a very mature attitude for her age. Genny isn't so sure about that, but she also knows she can't allow her enemies to control her, or they will win, plain and simple.

When the phone rings on Wednesday, Quinn gets up to answer it, thinking—or rather, hoping—it might be Genevieve. Instead, a deep-voiced man he doesn't recognize asks for Cassandra.

He holds the receiver out to her, but she opts to take the call upstairs. When she returns a few minutes later, she's frowning.

"Who was that?" Quinn asks.

Cassandra glances at Dawn before turning to him, shoulders squared. "My contact. Kellan's furious about losing the three vamps he sent for Genny. This is far from over."

"So what's Plan C?"

"He didn't know. Kellan's keeping things close to the vest now. He thinks he might even be coming to collect her himself, since using minions hasn't worked out so well. And speaking of minions, shockingly it seems he doesn't trust us anymore." She sighs. "I knew this would happen."

"Knew what would happen?" Dawn asks.

"That we'd fall out of the Assembly's good graces if we helped your friend."

Dawn's brows draw in. "What does that mean?"

"Remember what I told you about the Assembly and their mission to kill all slayers?"

Dawn nods. "So we're still in danger then?"

"We weren't in any danger before. Genny was. But now? Now we might all be fucked."

"I can't just stand by and let them kill my best friend," Dawn says.

Quinn pipes up. "Cassandra's right. We'll all be marked now. It was a risk taking out those vamps and we knew it. But it had to be done."

"So now what?" Cassandra's eyes are on Quinn.

"Genevieve has proven she'd capable of defending herself, and she's still training with JP's mother. I don't care if I'm on the hit list now. I'm not going anywhere. But I wouldn't blame the two of you if you decided to leave town for a while. I'd hate to see you get hurt because of my choices."

Dawn and Cassandra look at each other.

Before either of them can respond, Quinn says, "Think about it seriously. Talk it over. I'm going out to get some breakfast. Back in a few hours."

He stalks the river trails, eventually allowing himself an unsatisfying meal from a lone deer. The full moon is high above, providing plenty of light for humans and animals alike. The buck had heard him coming and tried to run, but Quinn had been faster. The adrenaline released by panic taints the taste of the blood, making it bitter, so Quinn doesn't take much. He just needs to get through the next few hours. Once he's home, he can grab a blood bag if he needs to.

Once the poor deer flees into the underbrush, he heads back toward Genevieve's house. He stands by the tree he'd climbed last night and listens, but it doesn't sound like she's home.

Although it's not something he's proud of, he had followed JP back to his apartment one evening a few weeks ago. Creeping in the shadows and silently watching is a skill vampires excel at, although Quinn suspects Genevieve wouldn't be impressed with the stalking of it all.

Telling himself he needs to let her know what Cassandra had found out, with some unease, he heads for JP's building. He's not even on the property yet when he recognizes her laugh. She's up there. With him. And although Quinn does want to talk to her, he can't bring himself to take a single step closer.

Instead, he turns around and heads for home. He'll meet her after work tomorrow and they can talk then. It's only a day. A day will be fine.

Because the thought of getting any closer to that apartment, of not being able to prevent himself from hearing what they're saying—or, God forbid, doing—makes a weird sort of panic fly around in his chest like a trapped June beetle.

He's loath to identify the feeling as jealousy, but he supposes it must be. Before a few weeks ago, it had been so long since he'd felt like this that he'd completely forgotten the emotion. He'd been a human teenager the last time he'd been envious. An older boy had tried to court Elspeth, but she'd only had eyes for Quinn, and the creeping jealousy whenever he'd spotted Jimmy MacLaughlin flirting with her hadn't lasted long. Besides, envy is a sin, and Quinn had fought the feeling with every morsel of his being. Elspeth had been a woman of her own mind. She could choose whomever she'd wanted, and she'd chosen Quinn. It should have been the beginning of a happily ever after for both of them. At least they'd had ten wonderful years together before…

Before everything had gone to Hell.

He can't allow anything like that to ever happen again.

Right now, striding down this tree-lined street, he's irritated with himself. He doesn't want to be jealous, doesn't want to have these kinds of intense feelings—also long forgotten until a few weeks ago—for anyone, but especially not for a vampire slayer who's in love with someone else. He badly wishes he could simply turn them off. It would make things so much easier.

But then he rethinks this. The bond he and Genevieve share is real, strong, and as evidenced last night, only growing stronger. He knows no matter what happens he can't walk away from her, won't leave her to her fate. He's always been a steadfast, loyal man, and becoming a vampire hasn't changed that. As long as her life is in danger, he will not leave her.

And if he's being honest with himself, probably not even once it's not.

The following day starts off pretty regularly, as days that change everything tend to do. Genny says goodbye to Gran and heads to work, same as usual.

Her workday itself is inconsequential, but when the elevator doors open to the lobby after she finishes, Genny smiles to herself. Quinn is here. This means things are truly back to normal. Well, their normal, anyway. The normal she's been missing.

She hasn't seen him since Saturday night—well, technically early Sunday morning—and she's glad he's decided to come downtown and commute with her again. The ride had felt lonely without him.

The grin that surfaces when she steps outside and sees him waiting for her in his usual spot almost exactly matches the one on his own face the moment he spots her.

"Hi," she says. Her voice sounds a bit shy. That's not normal. Things feel a bit different between them now.

"Hi."

"I wasn't sure if you were done with our ride-and-chats."

He falls into step beside her as they walk to the subway. "Do you want me to be?"

Genny glances at him from the corner of her eye. She can feel her cheeks heating. "No."

"Well, just let me know if you change your mind."

The crowd gathering on the platform parts for them like the Red Sea. As they move to the front, she thinks at him, *I won't.*

"Won't what?"

Change my mind.

Another quick smile flashes across his face. She thinks he looks relieved.

With a gust of wind, the train pulls into the station and they board, as usual easily finding a vacated seat.

"Cassandra got a call last night from one of her contacts in the Assembly," Quinn says as they sit down. The smile is gone. He's all business now.

Genny sighs. She knew this lull wouldn't last. "What's up now?"

"That's the problem. We don't know. Kellan isn't sharing his plans anymore. Her contact thinks he might even come for you himself."

Turning to look at him, she asks, "Who's Kellan?"

Quinn looks surprised. "Have I not given you the rundown of the Assembly yet?"

She shakes her head. "I guess we've been too busy stopping them from killing me and my friends."

"True. But still, I apologize. I really should've explained all this already. They're the group of vampires that basically run things in our world."

"I kind of figured. Like your government?"

"Sort of. More like an autocracy. The Assembly is ruled by the Grand Mistress Lillabeta and Kellan Lahaine is her second-in-command, her General. At least that's what he calls himself. Lillabeta makes the rules, and Kellan enforces them."

"Oh yeah? What are some of her rules? Other than all slayers must die. I already figured out that one."

He grimaces. "The biggest one is that if the Assembly asks you to do something, you do it."

"What happens if you refuse?" Genny knows Quinn has already broken that rule several times. Do they know what he's done, or, more correctly, not done?

His gaze drops to the dirty floor between his boots. "Nothing good."

Frowning, she persists. "What does that mean? Will they come after you?"

He turns back to her again. His gray eyes look defiant. "It's possible. But I don't care. I'm quite done doing their dirty work."

"I know you are. Can I ask how you guys got involved with them in the first place?"

"I never wanted to be," he sighs. "I was fine staying completely under their radar. But Cassandra felt it was important to have connections. And protection, if we ever needed it. She's a social person. She needs more than just me in her life. She thought if we joined the Assembly, we'd make those connections."

Genny studies his face. She can only imagine the lengths Cassandra probably had to go to convince Quinn to join. "And did you? Make connections?"

He chuckles. "I suppose. She definitely did. I'm..." He breaks eye contact. "I'm not good at stuff like that. I'd rather watch from the shadows than be in the middle of things."

This is no surprise. "I get that," she says. "So is there anything else I need to know about the Assembly?"

"Don't underestimate them. Lillabeta and Kellan are extraordinarily dangerous. Ancient vampires are a lot more difficult to kill than us regular ones. Over time, our bodies eventually harden like stone. You can't just pierce them with a wooden stake or cut off their heads, at least not easily. Believe me, if Kellan himself comes, you need to stay hidden. He will show you no mercy. And if you do meet him in person, do not look him in the eyes. One of his strongest weapons is his ability to plant suggestions in your head."

"I thought hypnotism wouldn't work on me?"

"Kellan is special. I've heard he can use his powers to sway anyone. Don't take it for granted that you are immune."

"Crap. So what will that mean? Hiding in my house for weeks? And what about Chloe? Won't she be targeted, too?"

Quinn frowns. "Neither of us has told them about your sister. They may have found out by now through other means, though. You'd both best be extremely careful. Stay in after dark."

The train pulls into a station and Genny looks up. The next stop is hers. This ride seems to be going by faster than usual. "Oh, she's just gonna *love* this. She has a boyfriend now. Telling her she can't leave the house at night is *not* gonna go over well."

"I can help you explain the seriousness of the situation to her if you like?"

"I might take you up on that." She sighs, running her fingers through the hair at her temple to lift the longer strands off her face. "Maybe you can bring Dawn over to visit me while I'm on house arrest? She's still staying at your place, right?"

He drops his voice and leans closer, like he's conveying a secret. "I think she's basically moved in."

"Yeah? Is that okay? I mean, it's your house too, and you didn't ask for another roommate." She feels a little guilty. Dawn wouldn't be living there if it hadn't been for her.

"It's fine. The two of them seem to be growing quite close."

"I'm glad. Dawn needs all the support she can get."

He smiles and looks like he's about to say something more when the train pulls into Sheppard station. They get off, neither of them even hesitating as he continues with her to the bus stop.

"Chloe's gonna be so pissed about having to stay in," Genny reiterates after they find a seat near the back of the bus. "Did you have sisters?"

He shakes his head. "Four older brothers. No sisters."

"Really? You were the youngest of five boys?"

"I was. That's actually why I was named Quinn. It means fifth son."

"Huh. I didn't know that." She's staring out the window at the passing shops, but not really seeing them. "Genevieve apparently means woman of her tribe, or family. Now I understand why a Bourreau would choose that name for their daughter."

"I like it," he tells her. "It suits you. Did you know the Celtic version of Genevieve is Guinevere? And Guinevere is made up of a combination of the words for fair and blessed, and magical being. Both of which describe you perfectly."

Genny turns to stare at him. "Seriously? That's actually pretty awesome. How come I didn't know that? And how come you do?"

He shrugs. "I read a lot. It's one of my favorite ways to pass the time. And I've had a *lot* of time."

"Right. That makes sense. JP's a big reader, too. He calls himself a scholar."

Quinn doesn't respond to that. A minute later, the bus pulls up to Genny's stop. Something has been weighing on her mind since he'd first mentioned it. "So back to what we were talking about before." she says once they disembark. "Has helping me made you a target?"

He looks surprised. "Don't worry about me. You have enough to be concerned with right now. Cassandra and I can take care of ourselves."

Genny stops, turning to face him directly below the shade of a stand of maples. "That's not an answer. Is your life at risk?"

Sighing, Quinn shrugs. "I don't know. Maybe. Probably. But like I said before, I don't care. I don't regret helping you. I'll do it again. And I'll keep on doing it until you're no longer in danger."

"I..." Genny stops. As it always does, her throat gets tight just thinking about it.

"What?" he asks softly.

"Thank you. I just...I don't want anything to happen to you." After a brief pause, she adds, "To anyone I care about."

Quinn breaks eye contact. His gaze is on the sidewalk as they continue walking. He seems lost in his own thoughts.

When they near Gran's, she stops again, and when he glances over at her, she thinks, *I missed this. Last week. I missed you.*

He blinks, surprised. "I did, too."

"Promise me you'll be careful. I mean it. I like having you around." Then she turns and heads up the walkway to the steps. *See you tomorrow*, she thinks as she slips her key in the lock and opens the door. She doesn't need to look back to know he's still watching to make sure she gets inside safely.

As Genny slips off her sandals, Gran comes into the front hallway. "Do you know where your sister is?" She looks concerned, and Genny gets an instant stab of worry.

"No. Why?"

"She didn't come home after work today, and she didn't call to tell me where she was going."

"That's a bit weird. But she's probably at her boyfriends. Do you have his number?"

Gran shakes her head.

"Okay, let me look in her room and see if I can find it. Or one of her friend's. I'm sure someone will know where she is."

Genny goes up to Chloe's bedroom. Moving aside the rumpled black t-shirt draped over the phone extension, she looks for slips of paper that might include phone numbers. Unfortunately she finds nothing but a jotted note of The Second Cup shifts. Chloe had been scheduled to work from ten to two today.

Trotting back downstairs, she finds Gran in the kitchen. "Did you happen to notice what time Chloe left this morning?"

Gran frowns. "I don't know. I assumed while I was out in the garden."

Genny realizes with dismay that she hadn't seen Chloe last night either. It had been after nine when JP had dropped her off, and she'd just assumed her sister had been in her room. But she hadn't checked. "Do you remember hearing her come home last night?"

Gran looks surprised. "She wasn't back when I turned in. Do you think maybe she stayed at one of her friends?"

"That's what I'm wondering. Maybe she decided to sleep at Darry's. I wish I knew how to reach him."

"She's young and newly in love," Gran says with a small smile, but Genny can tell she's worried. "She probably forgot to call and will show up any minute."

"Probably," Genny agrees. But Chloe should know better than to vanish without a word like this. Genny had warned her about the dangers they face as immortals and how careful she needs to be. Sure, her sister can sometimes be a little scatterbrained, but she doesn't think Chloe would forget to call Gran if she'd planned to sleep elsewhere. Not knowing how worried it would make her family.

Genny heads back up to her room. The moment she closes the door behind her, she leans against it, shuts her eyes, and thinks at Quinn: *Hey, can you come back here or call please?*

Ten seconds later, the phone rings. She grabs for it before Gran can pick up.

"Hello?"

He doesn't waste a moment. "What's wrong?"

She tells him she doesn't think Chloe had come home last night, knowing he'll share her concern. "Can you please ask Cassandra to try to find out if the Assembly knows about her?"

"On it. I'll call you back soon."

"Thank you." Genny hangs up and lies back on her pillows with a sigh. She reaches for the phone again to call JP and tell him, but then she pulls her hand back. Better wait until Quinn calls back so he won't get a busy signal. Chloe's probably fine, she tries to convince herself. They don't actually know anything bad has happened. Yet.

It's another ten minutes before the phone rings again, ten long minutes during which Genny's brain torturously imagines every worst case scenario. She snatches up the receiver halfway through the first ring.

"Quinn?"

"She couldn't get a straight answer," he tells her. "Which I think we can safely assume means they know about your sister."

Shit.

"Yeah." Quinn had heard her again. Genny wonders how many other times that might have happened. He keeps talking. "You said she has a new boyfriend?"

"Yeah. They've only been dating a few weeks. I haven't even met him yet."

"Tell me everything she's told you about him."

Genny thinks for a moment. "I don't know much. They both work at The Second Cup. I think she said he went to school with one of her friends. She told me he's super sweet and treats her really well."

"Did she say what he looked like? What's his name?"

"Nothing about looks that I can remember. His name is Darry."

The line goes quiet for a few seconds. Then Quinn says, "One of Kellan's lieutenants, one of the ones who came here and forced me to participate when we were tasked with your parents'...well, you know...is a very old Italian vampire named Darius. But he looks young, like maybe twenty."

Genny's eyes shoot wide as raw panic surges up inside her. "Oh my God. You don't think they sent him to...to what? Seduce my sister? Kidnap her and hand her over to Kellan? What do I do now? How do I find her?"

Quinn exhales a deep sigh. "Hold on a minute. Let me talk to Cassandra." Genny can hear their muffled voices, but she can't make out what they're saying. "Okay, she's going to try to see if she can find out more. Stay right there. Don't go *anywhere*. If they do have Chloe, they're probably going to use her to lure you out."

Tears well up in Genny's eyes. She doesn't know if she can promise him that, so she just says, "Call me back as soon as you can."

"Will do." He hangs up.

Instead of putting the phone back, Genny dials JP's number. When he answers, she quietly tells him everything, including what Quinn suspects about Darry.

"Don't you worry," he says. "We will find your sister. I'm going to call Maman and let 'er know about this, and then I'll be right over. See you shortly."

When Genny goes downstairs, Gran tells her she's going out to the grocery store. Once she's gone, Genny heads back up and searches Chloe's room again, taking far less pains to be careful not to disturb her sister's mess. She still can find no clue to Chloe's whereabouts. Genny returns to the living room, but she's too worried to sit down. She wishes either Quinn would call or JP would show up so she wouldn't be forced to be alone with her thoughts.

Thankfully, JP rings the doorbell a few minutes later. The moment she answers, he sweeps her into a hug. "We'll find 'er," he says into her hair.

Genny gives him an appreciative squeeze and then steps back. "What did your mom and René say about it? Do they know who Darius is?"

"Maman is quite worried. She wants to assist any way she can. René was out, but she will tell 'im soon. Did Quinn call back?"

Genny shakes her head. "Not yet. And before you start, I'm sorry I called him before you, but Cassandra's the only one who might be able to find out info from the Assembly. Although it sounds like they're not telling her much anymore, since we killed those vamps while rescuing Dawn."

"Vamps?" JP raises an eyebrow at the term.

"Vampires, sorry. You know what I mean."

"Of course. It just sounds strange coming from you."

She knows he means she's talking the way Quinn and Cassandra talk, but it doesn't matter. None of that matters right now.

Genny takes the cordless phone with her as they go out back to sit on the deck. She curls into JP's side on the padded bench and tries to let his warmth comfort her. Even though there's nothing he can actually do to help right now, he knows she's anxious, and he's here for her, and she loves him for it.

When the phone rings in her lap, Genny grabs it up and presses it to her ear. "Quinn?"

"Is this Genevieve Bourreau?" It's a young man's voice, confident and without any discernable accent. She doesn't recognize it.

"Not Bourreau, Dupont," she corrects. "But yes."

"Hold on."

There's a brief pause, and Genny hears the sound of crying. She sits up, spine rigid as Chloe comes on the line.

"G...Genny?" her sister sniffles.

"Where are you? Are you okay?" Genny angles the phone out a few centimeters and leans closes to JP's ear so he can hear.

Another gasping sob. Then: "You...you need to listen to me and...and do exactly as I say if you want to see me alive again." Chloe's voice has gone wooden. "Come alone to 3115 Marsden Road. If any immortals or vampires are spotted with or near you when you arrive, I will die. You are being listened to right now. Do not tell anyone where you are going. Come immediately. Go around back of the building. Answer with 'I understand' if you agree."

Genny's eyes meet and hold JP's. Chloe is obviously reading from a note. Below her flat tone, Genny can hear fear.

JP is shaking his head wildly and his eyes are huge and terrified. She thinks hers must be as well. But she can't refuse to come for her sister. She can't risk Chloe's life to protect her own. And she has to give an answer.

"I understand," she replies as confidently as she can. "And I love—"

The line goes dead before she can finish.

Genny sets down the phone and turns to JP, pressing a finger against her lips. She dashes inside and grabs a pad and pen from the phone table. Jotting down the address, she tears off the paper and shoves it in her pocket. Then she returns to JP.

"I have to go out," she says to him. "You can stay here if you want. I'm sure I'll be back soon." On the pad she writes: *Wait here for Q & C. Tell them everything.* She hands JP the phone.

He's scowling. Grabbing the pad, he scribbles: *I'm going with you.*

Genny shakes her head. *No*, she writes underneath. *They'll kill her. I can't risk it.*

I can't let you go alone. They'll kill you, he writes back, underlining the second *you* three times. He looks as panicked as she feels.

She takes the pad back. *Trust me. I have a plan. Wait for them. You'll hear from me soon.*

Before he can write more, she leans in and kisses him. "Love you. See you later." Then without another word, she goes inside, slips on her sneakers, and heads out.

As she walks to the bus stop, she feels both terrified and excited. She may not have been doing this for years, but she's confident she's strong and capable of killing vampires. Frowning, she realizes she's forgotten her mother's stake in her room. But that's okay. She can make one, like Quinn showed her. Since there's a good chance she's being watched right now, she stops and breaks off a lower branch from a dead tree. It's pointy enough for a makeshift stake, and she tucks it inside her jacket. It might not help. If what Quinn had told her is correct, and Darius, or even Kellan himself is holding Chloe, this hunk of wood probably won't do much. However, the sharp knife she'd slipped into her pocket on her way through the kitchen might. And if not, she will have back up. Just not right away.

Quinn had predicted this, that if the Assembly had Chloe they'd use her to lure Genny out, too. He is going to be furious when he learns she's gone on her own anyway, but she also knows he will understand why. She just hopes JP can as well.

Genny had told JP he'd hear back from her soon, but she hadn't told him that it will probably be through Quinn. Her connection to Quinn is her secret weapon, much more useful than any knife or broken stick. JP isn't going to like it, but Chloe's safety is all that matters right now. She'll deal with his reaction once this is over.

If they survive to talk about it, that is.

Chapter 16
Smothered Hope

Forty minutes later, the bus drops Genny off at the corner of a deserted intersection in an unfamiliar part of Toronto. It's eerily quiet. The only sign of life she spots is a black cat slinking off into the distance. All the buildings and warehouses seem to be abandoned. Just like in the movies, it looks exactly like the sort of disused industrial area to hold a hostage.

Once she orients herself on the city map she'd grabbed on her way out, she walks half a block east, then turns onto Marsden Road. The first address she sees is number 3000. All of Marsden is lined with huge warehouses. It might take a while to find the right one.

It's a cloudy evening and shadows are everywhere—shadows so deep pretty much anyone or anything could be hiding in them. Based on the message Chloe had read to her over the phone, Genny assumes she's being watched.

As if to confirm her suspicions, she suddenly feels Quinn's presence nearby, and panic spikes. *No,* she thinks as firmly as she can at him. *You have to get away! If you're spotted, they might kill Chloe. They might kill you. Please go back to Cassandra and JP. I'll tell you what's up as soon as I know, and then we'll figure out how to rescue her.*

Genny hopes he'll listen, although she knows it won't be easy for him to let her walk into such a dangerous situation alone. Not for the first time she wishes they could communicate both ways, but this is a lot better than being completely cut off. *Be careful,* she adds. *Don't let them see you. I'll be in touch soon.*

The tingle vanishes and Genny exhales a relieved sigh. She is relieved, but she's suddenly also a little nervous. Now she's truly by herself. Hopefully if all goes to plan, she won't be for long. She slips her hands into her pockets as she walks. The night is warm, but she's glad for her jacket. Stashed inside are the stake and knife. Hopefully one or both of them will be useful.

At last she locates number 3115. It's a wide, white building with no windows facing the street. She walks along the side to the back, as instructed. There are a few windows here, but they're high up and dark. She stops to listen for voices, but can't detect any. Anyone else would think they're alone, but Genny knows better. Something malevolent is watching her, and has been since she got off the bus. She doesn't need to feel a tingle to know this. It's unsettling, but it doesn't matter. Let them watch. She looks around again. Though she can't spot anyone, she raises both middle fingers and swivels so anyone observing will be sure to see.

This is undoubtedly a trap, but what choice does she have? If it's the only way to help Chloe, she'll willingly hand herself over. They may want her dead, but they won't kill her right away. Not until they get whatever information it is they want from her. From what Quinn had said earlier, she assumes she'll have to answer to Kellan, or even Lillabeta herself, before they decide to actually end her life. So there'll be some time. Time for what, she's not sure yet, but with her friend's help, they'll figure it out. Genny doesn't feel like dying tonight.

As she comes around the corner at the back of the building, she hears a soft snicking sound. A door she hasn't even had time to notice swings open right beside her. Before she can react, a hand snakes out over her mouth and she's hauled inside.

Instead of panicking, she manages to stay relatively calm. Getting inside is what she wants, after all. Hopefully whoever has grabbed her will take her straight to Chloe.

I'm in, she thinks at Quinn. She doesn't tell him she's already lost control of the situation, confident it will only be temporary.

Genny is dragged down a pitch black hallway—at least she assumes it's a hallway from the flat echo of her captor's determined footfalls. They go down some steps, through another door, and a few moments later she hears the unmistakable clang of metal being slammed against metal. She's rudely pushed forward and stumbles, landing on her side on cold concrete.

"Ow! No need to shove," she admonishes as she gets to her feet, although it hadn't really hurt much.

"Oh my God! Genny?"

"Chloe?" She reaches out blindly until she finds her sister in the dark. Chloe wraps her arms around her and squeezes so tight Genny can barely breathe.

"Thank God you're alive," Chloe murmurs.

"I'll let you two catch up," a man sneers, punctuating the comment with a snort. Genny recognizes the voice from the phone call. The metal bangs again, presumably locking them inside what she assumes is a cell. Next she hears a squeak of door hinges and a thud. Have they been left alone? If so, she doubts it will be for long.

"How many are there?" Genny whispers, although she knows it's futile. Someone will definitely be listening.

"Three. I think."

This is not the first time Genny's been in such a position. Not even the first time recently—how screwed up is that? Like before, she walks forward with outstretched hands until one of them hits a metal bar. Definitely a cell. She feels along them until she finds the sliding door. When she tests it, it doesn't budge. The déjà vu is unreal.

I'm with Chloe, she tells Quinn. *We're locked in, for now. There are at least three vamps.* "All three vampires?" she asks her sister out loud.

"I..." Chloe stops. "I don't know! How can I tell? Darry..." She trails off with a sob.

Genny finds her and pulls her into another hug, one hand stroking Chloe's hair soothingly. "I know, hon, and I'm so sorry. I just found out about him from Quinn not long before you called. If we'd only realized sooner, we could've warned you."

"I c…can't believe it was all a lie. He was just…" Sniffle. "He was just *using* me!"

Genny pulls back a little, wishing she could see her sister's face. "Did he hurt you?" If he did, she will hurt him right back. The vamp who'd grabbed her hadn't been smart enough to go through her pockets for weapons.

"No. He didn't, like, bite me or anything, if that's what you mean. He just…it was like he turned off the sweet Darry I knew and became someone else. He's totally not my Darry anymore. It scared the crap outta me." She shudders. "He's so mean now."

Genny knows this is partly her fault for not teaching Chloe about auras. She should have prepared her sister better. Darius may have used her and broke her heart, but Genny intends to ensure he never hurts anyone ever again. "Don't you worry. He'll pay for what he did. I promise you."

When Quinn returns to Genevieve's house, he can hear Cassandra, Dawn, and JP talking in the backyard. JP is telling Cassandra that his family will help them in any way they need. Quinn doesn't linger back to listen, though. He has to let them know what Genevieve had told him and then figure out how best to help her. The first thing they need to do is move to a closer location, so when she's ready they can get to her in seconds. This would be a heck of a lot easier without an immortal slowing them down, but Quinn knows JP will insist on coming. He can't very well fault the guy for it, because Quinn would do the same if their roles were reversed.

He goes around the house. The moment he steps onto the deck, all three pairs of eyes turn to him expectantly.

"Did you find 'er?" JP asks, jumping up. When he doesn't spot Genny behind Quinn, he sits back down with a sigh. "Clearly not," he adds.

"I know where she is," Quinn says, trying to mask his reluctance to admit it. Not because he doesn't want them to know, but because how he knows will inevitably lead to questions he'd rather not answer. "She's locked inside a warehouse with Chloe. There are at least three vamps that she's aware of. They'll be watching the perimeter for us."

"Lookouts-schmookouts. We can take 'em. Let's go," Cassandra says, getting to her feet. He can tell she's itching for a fight.

"You could tell all that from listening?" JP asks him. "Or did you sneak in after Genny and then come back and get us?"

"Not exactly. I—" He stops, his gaze shifting away from JP and going blank.

Quinn? You guys can come, but don't get too close. They can't know you're near until we're ready. You were right about Darius. Oh and Chloe's okay.

"She says we should come," he tells them once Genevieve finishes. "She wants us close, but not close enough to be spotted. Chloe's not hurt."

Cassandra is staring at him. Her brows bounce up. "You blanked out for a few seconds there, bud. Like you were listening. But she's too far away for you to hear her, isn't she? You two have some way to communicate that I'm not getting?"

Quinn glances at JP, then back to Cassandra. He clears his throat unnecessarily. "We...she..." He trails off with a sigh. Admitting the truth might cause problems between Genevieve and JP, and she has more than enough to deal with right now.

"'Ow is she telling you this stuff? Can you actually 'ear?" JP asks. He's frowning, but he doesn't look angry, exactly. More like confused. And concerned.

Nodding, Quinn meets JP's eyes. "Yes. I hear her in my head. Telepathically. We don't know why, and it doesn't work both ways."

"You hear her thoughts?" Dawn asks. "Like all the time? Jeez, *that* must get annoying."

"No. Only when she wants me to. She can think a thought at me and I'll hear it. I assume it's because of a spell, but we don't know who did it, or why."

JP's frown deepens. "Are you serious? You two 'ave some sort of mental connection? Is this new?"

Cassandra is still looking at Quinn. Her brows are furrowed and he knows she's thinking about the tingling sensation Genevieve gets when he's around. He hopes she doesn't ask if the two things are related. Talking about their strange link will only serve to make JP more agitated, and they all need to maintain clear heads right now.

Instead, she says, "We can discuss this stuff later. Right now, we need to get going. Especially since one of us can't move at vamp speed." She looks directly at JP as she says this.

"You're right, we should go." JP picks up the cordless phone. "I'll tell my family to meet us there."

Once he's off the phone, they head out. As they step off the deck, JP shoots Quinn a suspicious look. Quinn can't really blame him. Of course JP is suspicious. Suspicious that he hasn't been told the whole truth. Suspicious about why his girlfriend has been keeping secrets from him. Quinn exhales a sigh. He doesn't know what Genevieve has told JP, but he's pretty sure their connection is something she's kept to herself. It's probably going to make for a tense conversation once all this is over. He doesn't envy her that.

But first things first. They need to ensure Genevieve and Chloe's safety. At any moment, she could tell him she needs his help immediately. His top priority is to get to her as fast as possible.

As they approach the bus stop, Quinn stops. "You and JP take the bus," he instructs Cassandra. "Dawn and I will speed there. We'll wait for you near where you'll get off." Turning to Dawn, he asks, "You know where to go?"

Dawn shakes her head.

"Stick with me, then."

Before they leave, he hears Cassandra sarcastically say, "Fine. Just abandon us." Then they're gone.

Genny and Chloe huddle together on the floor of their cell, their backs against the wall. They're no longer talking, just sitting lost in their own thoughts. Chloe's head leans on

Genny's shoulder, her breathing now slow and even. Genny can tell she's exhausted.

It's Genny's fault Chloe is even in this mess. Since their parent's had died, she's always played kind of a maternal role to her younger sister, but lately she's been so wrapped up in her own stuff that she's left Chloe to do her own thing, barely telling her the most basic details of what's been going on. Genny should have been paying closer attention to her sister. If she had, she'd have figured out Chloe's new boyfriend is a vampire weeks ago. And he'd be dead already and neither of them would be trapped in here. If they get out of this alive, she needs to start being a better sister. Chloe deserves it, and frankly, their lives might depend on it.

The overhead lights abruptly come on, startling Genny. Chloe lifts her head from Genny's shoulder to see what's going on. Blinking, Genny looks around. They're in a windowless room—below ground, presumably—with a simple kitchen along one wall. The bars of their cell are so shiny and clean she can only assume it had been recently built.

A man approaches them. Genny's eyes haven't yet adjusted to the light, and because he's backlit she can't make out his features. He holds a smoldering cigarette between his fingers. The acrid scent of the smoke hits her and she scrunches her nose. It's unpleasant, yet also familiar. But from where?

"Is he a vampire?" Chloe whispers as Genny gets to her feet.

Focusing on the outline of the man's face, she tries to see his aura. She can't detect any reddish glow, so she assumes he's not a vampire. She thinks she might see a bit of something around his ears, but in this harsh light it's difficult to be sure. "Don't know," she mutters.

He comes closer. "Bonsoir Geneviève."

She knows that voice. Stepping forward, she grips the bars. "René?"

Why is he here? Had JP brought his family along on the rescue mission? But it's too soon. She hasn't given Quinn the signal yet. He's going to screw everything up.

René dips his chin in a nod. "I am sorry. Truly. I wish it did not have to be this way."

"What way?" she asks, confused.

Instead of responding, he turns his face just enough for the light to hit it. He looks kind of sad.

Suddenly Genny gets it. Her eyes narrow. "Wait. You sold me out?" She hears Chloe scramble to her feet behind her. "Why would you do that? I don't understand."

He takes a long drag on his cigarette and sighs out a plume of bluish-white smoke. "I 'ave my reasons. Extremely old, painful ones. Perhaps, if there is time, I will even explain them to you."

"If there's time? What does that mean? What's gonna happen?"

Before René can answer, the door opens again and a tall, blonde man who looks like he's not long out of high school enters the room. His hair is cut short at the sides, but left longer on top and his nose is long and slightly hooked. It's faint, but she can see a pale reddish halo around his face. Chloe grabs the back of Genny's shirt and she understands this is Darius.

"The General will be here shortly," he tells René.

René goes to a cupboard and pulls down a cup. After filling it from the tap, he brings it over and offers it to Genny. She frowns, but takes it. Though she's sure he didn't slip anything into it, she does not take a sip.

"Why are you giving them water?" Darius asks with a sneer. "They are not our guests. They are prisoners. Condemned. There is no need to offer refreshment."

"I assume they will be questioned," René replies with a shrug. "A dry throat is not conducive to talking. Or were you planning to kill them before he arrives?" He asks this last sarcastically.

Darius turns to Genny and Chloe, smirking as he scans them from top to bottom and back. "They are to be kept alive. For now. But if they cause any trouble, that does not mean they cannot be...punished." His grin is sadistic as he approaches their cell. "Immortal girls heal quickly. I'm sure the General would understand."

Genny shudders. She can't help it. It's obvious he's imagining all the things he'd enjoy doing to them. Inside her jacket she can feel the length of the stake pressing against her ribcage. Would it work on Darius? Quinn had said he's quite old. Her flimsy stake probably wouldn't even make a dent in his skin. But the knife might. She intends to try the second she gets the chance.

"Get the fuck away from us," she spits at him. Her words come out cold and commanding, masking the terror beneath.

Darius laughs. "You are not as nice as your sister." He takes another step closer.

"You heard her," Chloe says. She no longer sounds sad; now she sounds as angry as Genny. "Don't you dare lay a finger on us."

"Now, now. That's not what you said to me last night, if I recall correctly." He leers at Chloe and Genny feels a strong urge to rip his head off.

She slips an arm around her sister and draws her back from the bars until they're against the wall again. "Ignore him," Genny whispers, not caring if Darius can hear. "He's just trying to rile us up so we'll do something he can claim he had to punish us for. Don't give him the satisfaction."

Chloe still looks angry, but she nods. Genny's so furious she feels like she might actually explode. She remembers how amazing it had felt to plunge that stake into Gruhn's back, the high she'd gotten from it, and she craves to do it again. Killing Darius is now her top priority. He needs to pay for what he's done to Chloe. She's tempted to reach for the knife, but stops herself. No point in tipping her hand early and losing whatever small advantage she might have.

"I would listen to her if I were you," René advises Chloe. He still looks unhappy. Good. He should be. He's the one who got them into this mess. Genny doesn't understand the whys or hows yet, but she knows this is his fault.

And JP's, she realizes with a sinking feeling. JP has been telling his mom and uncle all about Genny and her family since the night they'd met, information René has clearly been passing to the vampires he'd claimed to hate so much. That's why she'd been kidnapped, why Gruhn and Darius had been sent, why they're locked in this cell right now. They'd probably already known her whereabouts before Cassandra had even told them.

Does this mean Marie is in on it, too? What about JP? Could all three have just been pretending all along? Had she been a fool to put her trust in any of them?

No. There's no way JP would betray her like this. He loves her. He hasn't been faking. She's sure of it. But still, he's the main reason René knows so much, and why Chloe had been targeted. And taken advantage of. Genny grits her teeth against her fury, trying to tamper it down so she can call it back up when she needs it.

Darius and René are talking softly over by the door. Try as she might, Genny can't hear what they're saying.

It's JP's uncle, she thinks hard at Quinn. *René has been feeding the Assembly information about us all along. He's here. I haven't seen the third vamp yet, but he's probably on lookout duty. Stay nearby. And please be careful.*

The more she thinks about it, the angrier she gets. She doubts JP is in on this, but she can't be quite so sure about his mother. Even if it's only René, the treachery cuts deep. He'd listened sympathetically to her, told her how evil vampires are, assured her over and over that they are arch enemies of immortals, and how it's Genny's life's mission to eradicate them. Now it turns out all along he'd been working with the Assembly behind her back.

But why would he betray his own people? It makes no sense.

She notices René nod at something Darius says to him. He then returns and unfolds a chair, taking a seat only a few feet from their cell.

Genny can't help herself. She has to know. "Tell me why you betrayed my family. What possible reason could you have to want us all dead? What did we ever do to you?"

With a sigh, René glances back at Darius. The tall vampire is leaning against the far wall. His eyes appear closed, presumably listening for anyone approaching. She has no doubt he can hear every word they say.

"It 'appened a very long time ago," René says, his expression now thoughtful. "Nearly two centuries ago, in fact. Much like most tragedies, this one began happily. I was a young man of twenty-three. Back then, by twenty-three, most men would undoubtedly be married with several children already. But I was not. I knew I 'ad all the time in the world for things like that and I was content with my life. How naïve I was, in retrospect. One morning I was out in the woods…" He pauses. "I believe you say *hunting*. I was 'unting deer. The sun was not yet risen. Deer tend to be most active at sunrise and sunset, did you know that?"

Genny shakes her head. He sounds a lot like JP when he's telling a story. It's a bit surreal.

"To my surprise, a woman appeared. My first reaction was fear—as I 'ave explained to you, we are told from a young age to be wary of strangers in the dark, to watch for vampires. But she…" René stops and a smile creeps across his features. "I was in no danger."

"Was she a vampire?" Genny asks. Chloe moves forward to stand beside her at the bars.

Nodding, René says, "Oui. But she was not like the creatures I was taught to fear. She was not evil. She was as curious about me as I was about 'er. She did not attack me. We walked and talked. She even assisted with taking down a large—I am sorry, I do not know the English word—a male deer, we say *cerf*—before she needed to go. We made plans to meet up again the following day."

"What was her name?" Chloe pipes up. Genny can hear the curiosity in her sister's voice and knows she is thinking of her own experience with Darius.

"Pascale," René tells them softly, that bittersweet smile still playing on his lips. "I used to sneak off and meet 'er as often as I could. Our feelings for one another grew, and before long we were deeply in love."

Genny frowns. This sounds nothing like the René she'd thought she'd known.

"We had to hide our relationship, of course," he continues. "My family and friends would not 'ave understood. Even now, nothing is changed. My people would do now the same as they did back then."

"What did they do?" Chloe asks.

"They killed her." His voice quavers. This clearly still causes him pain to talk about, even after all this time. Clearing his throat, he adds, "Specifically, your great-great grandmother, Anne Bourreau, killed her. Right in front of me."

The pieces suddenly click into place. "And you've been feeding the Assembly information on my family ever since, haven't you?" Genny accuses. "Helping them take us out one by one until there's no Bourreaus left?"

Before René can answer, the door flies open again, this time so hard it bangs off the wall. Three male vampires enter. Two of them are large and older looking. They appear to be bodyguards for the third, who looks even younger than Chloe. He's dressed in all black: black suit, black shoes, black button-up shirt, black tie. His eyes are also black, but his hair is brilliant shock of flaming red, spiked up in sharp points. He reminds Genny of a more polished version of Johnny Rotten. Maybe that's the look he's going for?

René gets up and goes to greet him. "General Lahaine," he says, dipping his chin in supplication. Even with the new information about his lost vampire love, Genny is astounded to witness it.

"General," Darius says, doing the same. The respect is clear.

So this is Kellan. Quinn had described him as cold and merciless. Ignoring the others, he strides toward her, his gaze trained right on hers. She'd been wrong about his eyes. They aren't black, at least not completely. The pupils are blood red.

If you ever meet him in person, do not look him in the eyes. Quinn's warning. Because Kellan can plant suggestions in people's minds. Quickly she averts her gaze.

"Geneviève Bourreau, as I live and breathe. Well, I suppose I do neither, but you get the point," Kellan says with a fangy smile. "You've proven to be a difficult one." His tone is low and soothing. Although he pronounces her name the French way, he has not a hint of an accent.

"Yeah? Well you've proven to be a royal pain in my ass," Genny replies. She's pleased to note she still sounds strong.

Kellan laughs. It even seems genuine.

"Stay back," she murmurs to Chloe. "Don't look him in the eyes." To Kellan, she says, "You look like you're barely old enough to shave. How old *are* you, anyway? Older than Darius?"

An amused, but definitely not kind smile crosses his face. "Oh, I'm nowhere *near* as old as Darius. But I am his superior officer. Age has nothing to do with rank."

It's difficult not to stare into those red eyes. She tries to focus on other parts of his face. Like his left ear, pierced with a small gold hoop. The thought flickers across her mind that the piercing must be constantly trying to heal. "You didn't answer my question," she says.

"My age is no concern of yours. However, since you are not long for this world, I will deign to answer. I am 461 years old. I was a young man of seventeen when I was gifted with this life, working on my father's farm in Shropshire."

Something about the lilt of his voice makes the hairs on the back of Genny's neck rise. "You consider it a gift?" she asks.

"The greatest gift I have ever been given. I was not well suited to the life of a farmhand. This life, however, I am ideally suited for."

Even without making full eye contact, just being near him gives Genny a wash of dread. It feels like their situation is hopeless, and she's tempted to just give up. She struggles against it, some part of her aware that these feelings aren't really her own. Kellan is sending her despair to make her feel like resistance would be futile.

When she doesn't comment further on his origin story, he says, "The Grand Mistress will be here soon. She wants to see you for herself—the girl who has given us so much trouble. And the sister, of course, who gave us no trouble whatsoever."

Behind him, she hears Darius chuckle. Then Chloe whimpers.

"Look at me," Kellan commands her.

Fight it, Genny thinks. *It's not real. You have to fight it.*

But the hopelessness is pervasive. What's the point in fighting? Fighting this will only prolong their suffering. It seems like it would be a lot easier to just give in.

She knows she's losing. But before she surrenders and locks eyes with him, she has just enough time to think one thought at Quinn.

Now!

Chapter 17
Head On

"Do you have a plan?" Dawn asks Quinn as they wait. She looks worried. She's right to be.

He sighs. It's been driving him crazy that he doesn't, and can't, until Genevieve tells him what she wants. There's no need to worry Dawn any more than she already is, though. "Not a fully formed one yet. But we'll outnumber them. I think we'll be fine."

"I don't know how to fight," she admits.

Quinn considers this. He knows she's worried she'll be a liability. "You're stronger than you realize, but try to stay out of it if there's any fighting. Stick close to Cassandra and you'll be fine." He knows he doesn't have to tell her this last bit. Sticking close to Cassandra has become second nature for Dawn.

With a screech of brakes, the bus stops at the corner and Cassandra and JP disembark. A car following behind pulls onto the side of the road behind the bus shelter and three immortals Quinn doesn't know get out. These must be JP's relatives.

Cassandra leads the others to where Quinn and Dawn are concealed behind a tall fence. Quinn eyes JP and his family curiously. While he and Dawn had been waiting, Genevieve had told him that JP's uncle is the one who'd betrayed her to the Assembly. Quinn doesn't know if the other Levoyants are in on it or not, but he intends to keep an eye on them. Then there's JP. Although he hardly knows the guy, he suspects JP is innocent. From all he's seen and all Genevieve has told him about their relationship, Quinn believes JP would never deliberately do anything that might endanger her.

Speaking of JP, he steps forward and gestures toward his family. "Please meet my mother, Marie, my brother, Thierry, and my sister-in-law, Deanne. They want to 'elp, and I figure three more immortals tips the odds in our favor." With a look behind him to the others, he adds, "And this is Cassandra, Quinn, and Dawn." Quinn notes he doesn't introduce them as his friends. Or Genevieve's. Perhaps it's implied. Perhaps not.

Quinn bobs his chin politely at the newcomers, while Dawn steps forward and shakes each of their hands in turn. JP's brother can't quite conceal his distaste when Dawn touches him. Quinn hopes Dawn hadn't noticed.

He moves closer to JP. "Can I speak with you in private for a moment?"

JP frowns, but follows him away from the others. "Did you 'ear from 'er?" he asks. He looks worried.

"Yes. Once."

"And?"

Quinn drops his voice, although he doubts the other immortals can hear from this distance. "She found out who's been passing details about her and her family to the Assembly. Your uncle."

"René?" JP looks and sounds incredulous.

Quinn nods.

"Not a chance," he snorts. "You must've 'eard wrong. René *hates* vampires. He would never."

"She said he's been feeding them information all along. I don't know anything more, or who else might be involved. That's why I'm telling you privately." Quinn directs his gaze over JP's shoulder toward the others.

Following Quinn's stare, JP glances back. He shakes his head. "Not possible. None of them would do that. My mother and Genny's mother were best friends. And my brother is as 'onorable as myself."

"If your uncle betrayed Genevieve, he's presumably been betraying the Bourreaus for decades. And he might not be acting alone. That's all I'm saying. I know this is hard to hear, but if we want to get them out safely, we need to be careful who we trust."

A defiant look comes over JP's face. "I trust my family. The bigger question remains: why should I trust you?"

Shrugging, Quinn starts to turn away. "For the same reason I know I can trust *you.* Because neither of us wants to see her come to any harm. I don't really care what you think of me, but I should hope by now you've figured out that I would do whatever's necessary to keep her safe. Just like you would. So if you could put aside your personal feelings about me for tonight, it would be in her best interests."

Quinn has taken three steps back toward the others before he hears JP mutter, "Fine."

"So what do we do now?" JP's brother Thierry asks them. "Just wait 'ere for some kind of signal?" He's regarding Quinn warily.

It makes sense that JP's family doesn't trust them, but Quinn hopes they can temporarily ignore their misgivings in order to help Genevieve and Chloe. He notices JP doesn't tell them about René. It doesn't matter. They'll find out soon enough.

Before Quinn can reply to Thierry, he gets another message from Genevieve. *Fight it. It's not real. You have to fight it.*

There's nothing further and it only takes him a second to realize this hadn't been meant for him. She'd been thinking it to herself. Which means Kellan must be there. This is bad. Very bad. Kellan wouldn't come alone. He'd bring at least one lieutenant. So there's now minimum five vampires and one immortal to deal with. They comprise three vampires and four immortals. Under normal circumstances, he'd think they could take them. But Kellan Lahaine is not a normal vampire. He's not big, but he's fast, agile, and extremely strong. And there's another problem. He has never known of a vampire as skilled at hypnotism as

Kellan. Quinn only hopes—and if he's being honest with himself, prays—that Lillabeta herself doesn't show up. Because if she does, hope will do them no good whatsoever.

"Kellan's here," he says softly, turning to Cassandra and holding her gaze. She's the only one who truly understands how serious this is.

At first a slight frown creases her forehead, but it quickly vanishes and is replaced with a confident smirk. "I can deal with Kellan."

Quinn is about to reply when he hears Genevieve say, *Now.* Just that one word, nothing more, but this time he's sure she meant to send it.

It's time to go.

Kellan's deep red pupils remind Genny of the dot of blood in her palm after she'd stabbed herself to see how fast she'd heal. They widen, then shrink to pinpoints, then widen again. How is he doing that? Is it just an illusion, a trick of the mind? She can't seem to look away.

"That's better," he murmurs.

His voice reminds her of something from a long time ago, back when she'd been small. It's soothing. She can no longer remember what she's supposed to be afraid of. Her fists loosen their grip on the bars and her arms fall to her sides.

She vaguely registers a clang as the cell door is thrown open. A cool hand takes hers and leads her out into the room. Some part of her brain registers that it feels a bit like Quinn's hand. Minus the surge of electricity. The thought makes her frown. This isn't right.

"Genny, no!" a familiar voice cries. She frowns, trying to identify it. Wait. Yes. It's Chloe. Genny's jaw twitches, but she doesn't speak.

Someone goes past her into the cell. The tall vampire. What's his name again? She can't recall.

"Get your hands off me!" her sister says indignantly. Genny thinks she should probably turn around to see what's going on. But she doesn't. It feels like too much effort.

The hand guides her across the floor to an empty chair and helps her sit. She's still staring into those twin pools of blood.

"Are there any other Bourreaus alive?" the soothing voice asks. She knows she should remember the name attached to that voice, but it's also out of reach.

"No Bourreaus. Only Duponts," she says in a monotone.

"Your mother is dead?"

"Yes."

"Her entire family is dead except for you and your sister Chloe. Correct?"

Genny nods. "Yes. All dead. Killed by vampires. Just us left." Is that her voice? It barely sounds like her.

"Do you know any vampires?"

"Yes."

"What are their names?"

"Quinn. Cassandra. Dawn."

There's silence. Not really—in the distance there are sounds of movement, other people in the room. But they don't matter. The only thing that matters is the voice. The silence seems to stretch out until Genny is nearly desperate for him to speak again.

"Cassandra Veld and Quinn Sinclair?" he asks at last.

"Yes." Has she ever heard Cassandra's last name before? She tries to hold onto it, but it slips away. Whatever. It doesn't matter either.

"Who is Dawn?"

Before Genny can reply, there's a crash.

"Don't move," he instructs, and then the red eyes vanish. She stays still, waiting for them to return. People are yelling. Someone screams, but it's cut short. She hears a thump, like something heavy hitting the floor.

She doesn't look over. She just continues to stare at the spot the red eyes had been. They'll be back. She knows they will. She just needs to wait.

And wait she does. Right up until the moment cool fingertips brush the side of her face.

"I'm only going to say this once," Quinn tells the others. "So listen well. The second we move all talking stops. You need to be as silent as possible."

JP and his family nod their agreement.

"Cassandra and I will take care of any lookouts. The rest of you stand clear. Once we reach the back of the warehouse, I want Dawn and Deanne to stay outside and keep watch while we go in. Dawn will listen to what's happening, and if we need them, we'll let her know."

"Works for me," Dawn says. Deanne just nods again. Quinn doesn't have a clue how useful she might be in a fight, but he thinks Dawn will feel better not waiting outside alone. He also suspects Cassandra would prefer Dawn stay out of any potential fighting.

Quinn focuses on the ones going in with him. "Cassandra, you're on Kellan duty. You're the strongest and most likely to keep him occupied for any length of time. I'll take out the bodyguards he'll have brought with him. Whichever of us is next free, which I assume will be me, will take on Darius. Thierry, locate your uncle, restrain him, and get him out of there if you want him alive. Marie, since you know how to fight, you can help me with the vampires. And last but most important, JP, you're on rescue duty. Get the girls free, out, and as far away from here as possible." His eyes hold JP's. "Got it?"

"Got it," JP says. Both his tone and his expression are grim.

"One more thing," Cassandra pipes up. "Kellan is easy to recognize. He's got red spikey hair and his eyes are black with red pupils. Under no circumstances should you look him in the eye. His super power is hypnosis, and I'd lay odds he can use it on immortals. I've seen it work on vampires. So avoid looking at his face."

"Yikes," Dawn mutters.

Cassandra smiles and drapes an arm around Dawn's shoulders. "Don't fret. This is the fun part." Dawn doesn't look convinced.

"Questions?" Quinn asks. When no one replies, he says, "Good. Silence until they know we're here." He speeds off with Cassandra and Dawn right behind him. The rest will arrive soon enough.

Cassandra circles the warehouse. When she returns, blood drips from her fingertips. She holds one up and licks it clean. One lookout, now deceased.

They're in front of the only rear door. Quinn raises a hand, palm forward to Dawn to indicate she should wait for the others. They're nearly here. He can hear their footfalls on the asphalt. If any vamps inside are paying attention, which they surely will be, they'll hear them, too. They need to move now, before their cover is blown.

As he braces a foot on the door, Quinn picks up Kellan's voice. The General is talking softly, and Quinn can't make out all the words. Suddenly he hears his own name, and right after Genevieve says "yes." She sounds calm, agreeable even, and Quinn frowns. It's unlikely she would be either of those things. Not under these circumstances.

Unless she'd made the mistake of looking into his eyes.

Just before he breaks in the door, he hears Kellan ask, "Who is Dawn?" Then he and Cassandra crash through and all Hell breaks loose.

A large vampire meets them in the hallway. Quinn is laser focused, tearing into the vamp's chest and removing his heart before the big guy can utter a word. Two down. That should leave three, maybe four to go.

They speed down some steps and through another door. A second vamp Quinn doesn't know rushes them, and Quinn makes short work of him, too. Dropping the bloody heart to the floor, he looks up to see Kellan approaching and quickly averts his eyes.

"Well, well. If it isn't the two traitors," Kellan says with a sneer. "Trying to play white knight? But why? Why would you betray your own kind for these pathetic humans?" With a slight turn of his head, he glances over at René. "Unless? Perhaps my answer lies right in front of me?"

"I know how much you love the sound of your own voice, but could you please just shut the fuck up?" Cassandra says to him, squaring her shoulders.

They trade further insults, but Quinn has stopped paying attention. He has more important things on his mind.

Scanning the room, he spots Darius by a shiny new cell. He holds Chloe in front of his chest like a pint-sized shield, one hand clamped over her mouth. Chloe's eyes are huge and terrified. For good reason. Darius could rip her head from her shoulders in a second if he chooses to. But Quinn's sure he wouldn't dare without Kellan's explicit order. He hears JP and the others come into the room behind him, but he doesn't turn around. He's finally spotted her.

Genevieve sits on a chair by the far wall, completely still, staring straight ahead at nothing. Her expression confirms his suspicion. Kellan got to her. Hopefully he hadn't had time to do any mental damage before they'd been interrupted. Quinn goes straight to her, crouching so he can look into her eyes. She appears to be in some sort of trance. It doesn't seem like she even notices him. Concerned, he strokes her cheek.

With a start, her eyes widen and then focus on him. "Quinn?" she breathes. She sounds like she's just woken up. Which he supposes she has.

Dropping his hand, he exhales a relieved sigh. "You okay?"

Her brow furrows, but she nods. "I think so." Her eyes shift away from his and widen as she registers what's happening behind him. She jumps to her feet and he rises as well, turning to follow her gaze.

Cassandra and Kellan have evidentially reached the end of the talking stage and begun fighting. It's actually a thing of beauty to behold. Each lunge and block, attack and swerve, leap and dodge looks like a meticulously choreographed dance. Every move seems elegant and effortless, but Quinn isn't fooled. He knows even the slightest falter could mean death for Cassandra. He has to be ready to jump in and help the moment she needs him. But that moment is not now.

Genevieve gasps softly, her fingers closing around his arm. She's staring at Darius, who still has a firm grip on her sister. Marie and a nervous-looking JP are approaching them from the front. Genevieve and Quinn come from behind.

"I wouldn't try anything," Darius says to JP and Marie. "Or she'll be dead before her cute little ass hits the floor."

Quinn notices Genevieve reach inside her jacket and wonders if she's brought her mother's stake with her. On impulse, he decides to distract Darius so she can make her move. "An empty threat," he tells the other vampire. "You know as well as I do she's to stay alive until the Grand Mistress arrives. *Your* life, on the other hand, means little to them." It's a bit of a bluff, as he's not certain Lillabeta is even coming, but it's a safe assumption. She would want to meet the last two Bourreaus before they die.

Bristling at the suggestion, Darius sneers, "I beg your pardon? I am one of Kellan's most valued lieutenants. You and Cassandra, however? You have betrayed the Assembly. I will parade your heads on spikes for the Grand Mistress to spit on." As if to prove his point, he spits in Quinn's direction. It hits the floor at his feet, a few droplets of spray landing on the toes of his boots.

"Let her go," Quinn commands. "Put her in the cell if you must, but release her unharmed. If you have a problem with me, then face me head on. Don't hide behind the human girl like some trembling child."

Darius lets out a primal growl, baring his fangs and shoving Chloe to the side and back into the cell. In a motion faster than any human eye can see, he flies at Quinn. But Quinn is expecting this, and he can move just as fast. He dodges to the right and sticks out a foot. Darius should have been agile enough to evade it, but he does not, tripping and landing with both palms on the floor. Before he can jump back up, Genevieve throws herself on his back and drives a hunk of wood into him. Quinn hears it snap off in her hands.

He rushes to assist, pinning Darius's head between his thighs and bracing his knees on the other vampire's biceps, correctly assuming that the stick she'd used hadn't penetrate deep enough to reach the heart. JP also tries to help, but a flailing kick from Darius' unsecured leg sends him flying. Quinn grabs the protruding end of the stick in Darius' back, knowing he and Genevieve won't be strong enough to hold him down for long. There's not much left of it, mere splinters remain embedded in the flesh. Darius growls again, pulling one arm free from Quinn's knee and batting away his hand. In return, Quinn squeezes his thighs together, increasing the pressure on Darius' skull. The old vampire screams. Marie and JP jump on and the four of them manage to keep Darius from rising just long enough for Genevieve to pull a shiny steel knife from inside her jacket. With both hands, she presses it into the back of Darius' neck, and his scream turns into a roar. Quinn braces his hands on top of hers to help push the blade through the thick skin.

But Genevieve doesn't need his help. "This is for Chloe. Enjoy Hell, asshole," she says softly and matter-of-factly.

Quinn could not be more proud of her as she gives the knife another hard shove until it clangs against the concrete, separating Darius' head from his shoulders. The head rolls to one side, empty blue eyes staring at the cell where his former girlfriend looks on in horror.

"Get the girls out of here," Quinn says to JP as he stands up.

JP looks shocked by what he's just witnessed. When he registers Quinn's words, he nods. He reaches for Genevieve's hand, but she pulls free.

"I'm not leaving until this is done," she tells him, bending to retrieve her knife. Droplets of blood fall from its tip to floor as she focuses back on Cassandra and Kellan. "Otherwise, it will never end. Take Chloe and go. I'll find you later."

She walks away from them, studying Kellan's movements. Quinn glances back at JP. He looks even more miserable than he had before, and Quinn doesn't envy the conversation he and Genevieve will undoubtedly need to have later. JP sighs, then goes to Chloe and helps her to the door. Quinn spots Marie and Thierry in the far corner with a now-unconscious René. One of them must have knocked the spy out. Quinn wishes he could have witnessed it.

He joins Genevieve to watch the fight. Though they're both at the ready, they don't jump in to help. Cassandra is still holding her own, but Quinn can tell she's wearing down. Her focus is starting to waver. Just a wee bit. No one else would probably notice, but no one else knows Cassandra the way he does. Kellan, on the other hand, looks the same as ever. Surely he must realize the three of them will have the advantage once they team up. He's never seen Quinn or Genevieve fight, though. Perhaps Kellan assumes Cassandra is his only worthwhile adversary. He's about to be proven wrong.

Cassandra's eyes flick toward Quinn and he braces himself to join the fray. Before he can make his move, however, an icy breeze blows over his skin. The fighting comes to a sudden halt as everyone turns to look at the new arrival.

Genny spins around to find a petite woman standing by the door. No one, not even the vampires, seems to have heard her come in. It's like she's just appeared out of nowhere.

She's incredibly beautiful, in an ethereal kind of way. She wears a white dress barely a shade lighter than her skin. Her platinum blonde hair is braided and twisted into a crown. It makes her seem taller, more authoritative. Genny has the fleeting thought that this woman—this creature—could not go out in public and blend in. No one would ever mistake her for human.

This must be Lillabeta. Though not large of stature, she has an instantly commanding presence. Her eyes, black with red pupils like Kellan's, scan the room until they land on Genny. Then her red lips curve into an icy smile. She glides across the floor toward Genny and stops in front of her. How ancient *is* she? Older than Darius, Genny would bet. Maybe by quite a lot.

Genny wonders if those red eyes can hypnotize the way Kellan's can. She makes a point to focus on the vampire's chin.

"Geneviève Bourreau," Lillabeta says. Her cold tone suits her cold look, Genny thinks. The vampire tilts her head to one side like she's studying some interesting new life form. "At last we meet. I have heard so much about you."

Balling her fists at her sides, Genny says, "From René, I assume?"

"Yes. From René. He has been extremely helpful over the years."

"I assume you're Lillabeta? The Vampire Queen?"

A flicker of annoyance passes over Lillabeta's face, but she immediately replaces it with the same frigid smile. "I am the Grand Mistress of the Vampire Assembly," she corrects. "But Queen is an apt enough title." She's still looking at Genny curiously, like a child might examine a bug they've trapped in a jar. It gives Genny the heebiesjeebies, and she draws in a breath, forcing herself not to shudder.

Genny flicks her eyes sideways to Quinn. She can tell he doesn't like this situation at all. He'd been hoping they'd get out before Lillabeta showed up. With both Lillabeta and Kellan here, it might not matter that they're outnumbered. She suspects if they decided to, the elder vampires could end her and her friends in seconds.

"What do you want from me?" Genny asks. She's trying to sound brave, trying to hide her fear.

"At the moment, nothing. I must apologize for our rudeness, but unfortunately we must pause this conversation for now." Lillabeta beckons to Kellan, and he's at her side in an instant. "General Lahaine and I have some rather pressing business to which we must attend."

"*What*?" Genny frowns. Has she heard wrong?

"Until we have the pleasure of meeting again," Kellan says to her with a slight bow.

"You're seriously just leaving? After all this?"

His dark brows bounce suggestively as he gives her a twisted grin. "So sorry to disappoint you, my dear. But do not fret. I guarantee we will see each other soon." He extends an elbow to Lillabeta and she links a pale hand through it. "Shall we?" he says to her.

"Wait," Genny pipes up. "What about René?"

Lillabeta briefly glances to where JP's brother holds René. He'd found a piece of cord and bound his uncle's hands. René stirs, his eyelids fluttering. He's starting to come around. "Oh yes," she says with clear apathy. "His usefulness is now at an end. You may do as you wish with him."

Then, just like that, she and Kellan are gone.

The temperature in the room seems to rise a few degrees the second they vanish. Astounded, Genny turns to Quinn. "What the hell just happened?"

"A fucking miracle," Cassandra replies, joining them. "Well, more like a temporary reprieve. But still. We got lucky. We won't next time."

Marie and Thierry help René up the stairs. Cassandra, Quinn, and Genny follow.

"What will happen to him?" she asks Marie when they step out into the fresh air. It feels like heaven in her lungs.

"He betrayed our people. He'll be taken back to Lentemps to stand trial. Either JP or I will let you know more tomorrow, once I make some calls." Marie turns to Quinn. "Where is JP? He left with Chloe?"

Deanne comes around the corner with Dawn. "They went to the bus stop. They're waiting for you there."

"Thank you." With that, Marie and Thierry slide their arms around René and walk away. Deanne leaves with them.

Dawn moves to Cassandra's side. "I heard most of that, but one of you needs to give me details. What exactly happened in there?"

Looking to Quinn and Genny, Cassandra seems to make a decision. Instead of launching into an explanation, she says, "I'm hungry. And I guarantee Dawn's hungry. I'll tell her everything on the way to find dinner. You guys don't mind, do you?"

Genny shakes her head. "Go. I'll just slow you down. Thanks for all your help tonight."

"You sure?" Dawn asks doubtfully. "Are you okay?"

"I'm fine," Genny reassures her, although it's a lie. "I'll talk to you tomorrow."

"Okay. Give Chloe a squeeze for me."

"I will."

Cassandra offers a hand to Dawn, who smiles as she takes it. They zoom away, leaving Genny alone with Quinn.

She turns to find him watching her wearing his patented concerned look. "You're not fine," he says softly. "How could you be?"

Her throat tightens. Breaking eye contact, she starts off toward the sidewalk. "I don't wanna talk about it. Not..." She pauses, drawing in a breath, trying to tamper down the emotions threatening to overflow. "Not right now."

He falls into step beside her. "I get that. But can I just say one thing?"

Stopping, she turns and looks up at him.

"You were amazing in there. In front of powerful vampires who could break you in half faster than you could blink, you never even hesitated. I was *so* proud of you. And you should be, too."

At his words, her fragile control snaps, and tears begin trickling down her cheeks. She's been strong long enough, strong for Chloe, strong for everyone. Finally she doesn't have to be strong anymore. She can just be a terrified twenty-one year-old girl who'd nearly lost her sister, nearly lost her own life, nearly lost everything tonight. And, though she's grateful her loved ones aren't hurt, the worst part about all this is that it's *still* not over. Their lives are still in danger, and they will have to face Lillabeta and Kellan all over again at some point. What if he manages to hypnotize her again? What if she's not strong enough next time? What if they kill someone she loves?

"Hey, hey," Quinn says. He starts to reach for her, but drops his hands at the last moment. She can tell he wants to console her, but worries he'd be crossing a line.

He needn't worry. Genny doesn't consider whether she should or shouldn't do it, she just steps forward, slides her arms around him, and presses her cheek against his chest.

Quinn freezes for all of a second, then pulls her closer, one hand stroking down her hair. "It's all right," he murmurs.

It's not, she thinks at him. *After everything we just went through, it's still not all right. I don't know if it will ever be all right again.*

"No," he agrees. "It's not. But it's better. The traitor has been caught, and won't be able to share info about you with them anymore. There are four less vampires in the world to kill humans. Your sister is no longer in danger from Darius. You cut off his head, ensuring he'll never hurt anyone ever again. Our problems aren't over, but we bought ourselves some time. And that can only be a good thing."

Genny lifts her face to look at him, but she doesn't pull back from of his embrace. "That's literally the most positive thing I've ever heard you say." She can't help a small smile. "Did you get hit on the head tonight?"

Quinn laughs, and her smile grows wider. "Guess I must have."

As they look into each other's eyes, as they hold onto each other, Genny feels the pull she's been trying to ignore for weeks now, and it scares her. It terrifies her more than

Lillabeta ever could. It represents something she's been refusing to even let herself think about, much less identify. Something huge and overwhelming, yet still distant enough that she's been able to pretend it's not there. So far, anyway. But in moments like this, it's becoming harder and harder to pretend. And she needs to. Because she has no idea what will happen if she ever lets herself acknowledge it.

Reluctantly Genny steps away from Quinn and resumes walking. Her feelings for him are confusing and complicated, but she loves JP. Although she's worried about that, too. After everything she's learned tonight and what had happened, and nearly happened, to her sister, she and JP need to have a serious conversation.

But not tonight. That can wait until tomorrow.

A month ago nearly everything in her life had changed. And Genny has a feeling deep down in her gut that something major is about to change again.

Chapter 18
The Hardest Walk

When the phone rings the next afternoon, Genny is still in bed. She fumbles for it without opening her eyes.

"Hello?"

"Bonjour, Genny. My apologies if I woke you?" It's Marie.

"That's okay. It was a long night, and I didn't get to bed until nearly four. But I should get up." She pauses as she recalls why Marie is likely calling. "So what's going to happen to, uh, to him?"

"Thierry and Deanne will leave tomorrow to take my brother-in-law back to France. René will stand trial in Lentemps, as I believe I mentioned last night. I do not know if JP told you this, but we 'ave our own laws and our own legal system."

"Immortals, you mean?" Genny frowns. "How can you do that?"

"Transgressions are not reported to the human authorities. We deal with them ourselves. If one of us ends up in a situation involving police, we take care of that, too. We look after our own."

Genny takes that to mean they bribe the necessary people to make problems go away. "So will his trial be like normal trials, with lawyers, a judge, and jury?"

"Kind of. I apologize for not explaining all of this to you earlier. Sometimes I forget you were not raised in our world. We have a Régent, Martin Temple. The rare times a trial is necessary, the Régent serves as judge and questioner, taking into account any witness testimonies. The accused will also be able to speak in his own defense."

Genny is still a bit sleepy, but she grasps on to the witness part. "Does that mean Chloe and I will have to go to France to explain what happened?" Good thing she already has a valid passport from a planned trip with her ex that had never happened.

"Yes. All of us will. Well, all of us immortals. Your…um…your vampire friends will not be required."

"But they were there. They saw more than I did."

"I realize this. But due to their nature, any testimony they might give would not be considered reliable."

Of course not. Because they think vampires can't be trusted. Sighing, Genny says, "Chloe and I can't really afford a trip right now."

"Oh, there is no need to worry. All your expenses will be covered."

Genny can tell she won't be able to get out of this, so she'd better make the best of it. "Really? Well I do want to see where my family's from. Any idea when the trial might be?"

"The preparation process can be quite time consuming, and in summer it can be difficult to gather all the Elders together. Perhaps next month. Perhaps longer. You will be given ample notification. I suggest you both write detailed accounts of everything you recall now, so you do not forget any important facts when the time comes."

"That's a good idea." Genny's mind turns to another thing weighing heavy. "Have you spoken to JP today? How's he holding up?"

There's a brief pause. "JP is understandably quite distraught. You should give 'im a call."

"I will," Genny promises.

"Before I go, I want to say 'ow sorry I am about everything. If I 'ad any idea at all of the deception…"

"I know. It's not your fault. I can't imagine how upset you must be."

Marie clears her throat. "I loved your mother very much. We were like sisters. To learn that she died because of René? I cannot comprehend it."

"That actually reminds me of something. How come you didn't know where Chloe and I were after our parents died?"

There's a pause on the other end of the line. "You'll 'ave to ask your grand-mère that. But I suspect your mother knew her death was coming and took steps to protect you. She was a mage, as you know. She undoubtedly put some sort of concealment spell on you both. I never knew where Agnes lived, and when I asked at the funeral, she was quite vague. We actually believed she'd taken you girls far away. It was a shock to learn you were raised in Toronto all along."

"I bet it was. Even with René's betrayal, I'm grateful to know you and your family. It helps me feel closer to my mother."

"We are glad to know you, too. But what René did? It was treason of the highest order. Rest assured, 'e will be severely punished."

"I hope so." Genny feels her fury start to rise again. "I can't...can't really talk about it. Not right now. It just makes me too angry"

"Oui. Moi, aussi—me, as well. Later, we will speak further. Take care of yourself."

Genny tells Marie goodbye and replaces the receiver. Instead of calling JP, she lies back down and closes her eyes. She will never forgive René for betraying her family, for getting not only her parents killed, but every ancestor before them. He had allied with Lillabeta and Kellan to end the slayer line.

And if it hadn't been for her friends last night, he might have succeeded. It's not like Genny had been much help, after all. To her deep shame, she'd been far too quickly indisposed.

An image of Kellan Lahaine pops into her mind, all spikey hair and creepy black and red eyes. Just the thought of those inhuman eyes staring at her makes her shiver. She'd known not to look into them—Quinn had warned her explicitly—yet somehow she'd done it anyway.

I nearly got my friends killed, she thinks. How many times has this exact thought crossed her mind over the past six weeks? Too many. And Dawn really had died. What if Kellan hypnotizes her again next time they meet? She remembers how easy it had been, how soothing it had felt to just give in to him, how his eyes and his voice had become the only things she'd known, the only things that she'd cared about. She would have done anything he'd asked of her—let Darius kill her sister, watch her friends get torn to pieces without lifting a finger to help them. Hell, she likely would have killed them herself if he'd told her to. She'd made a stupid mistake and her friends had nearly paid the price. And she despises herself for it.

Kellan had even walked away from her, yet breaking eye contact hadn't released his thrall. She knows she would have waited there for him even if it had taken hours. Or days. And God knows what horrible things he might have made her do once he'd returned.

So how did I break out of it?

She tries to think back. The first thing she remembers seeing when she'd come back to herself had been Quinn looking at her worriedly. Cool fingers had stroked her cheek. Had the jolt from his touch released her from the hypnosis? But why? Because of the spell that connects them? Whatever it had been, she'll have to thank him next time she sees him.

Her stomach rumbles, so she heads downstairs to find something to eat and to check on her sister. Gran has gone out, and Chloe is curled up on the couch with a book in her hands. It's not even open.

After grabbing a croissant from the bread bin, Genny comes into the living room and moves her sister's legs aside so she can sit beside her. "How're you feeling?"

Chloe sighs. "How d'you think? My boyfriend turned out to be a vampire who just pretended to like me so he could kidnap me and use me as bait to lure *you*. And after threatening to torture us both, he used me as a human shield. And then you cut off his head. Right in front of me. So, you know, not so great."

"I do know," Genny says, rubbing her sister's knee. "The whole thing sucks. I wish I had a memory wiping super power so I could take it all away for you."

Chloe shakes her head. "Even if you could, I wouldn't want you to. JP's mom told me what happened after we left. Those other two vampires—the spikey-haired one and some other one with a weird name—"

"Lillabeta."

"Yeah, her. The ones who want us dead are still out there. And someday they'll come back to finish the job. I *need* to remember. No one's ever gonna use me like that again."

Genny considers this. "No. They definitely won't." She faces her sister and takes a deep breath. "Hey Chlo, can I ask you a really personal question? I totally get if you don't wanna answer, but it's been bugging me."

"What?"

Chloe's eyes look tired and Genny wishes she doesn't have to ask this. But she does. "Did you and Darry…you know?"

"Did we what?" Chloe asks, frowning. "Have sex? Is that what you're asking?"

"Did he take advantage of you? Because last night he made a few comments that made it seem like it."

Chloe's cheeks redden. "No. I mean, well, almost. He wanted to the other night. He was really into it, and I nearly did, but…I changed my mind. Then he started getting mean and aggressive. He rolled on top of me and pinned me down so I couldn't fight back. I don't know *what* he would've done if his phone hadn't rang. I was a complete mess. He sure wasn't who I thought he was." Her voice grows softer as she speaks, ending in little more than a whisper.

Trying to hide her anger, Genny says, "I'm so sorry that happened to you. If it makes you feel any better, he'll never hurt anyone ever again."

"You made sure of that." Chloe grabs Genny's hand and squeezes it. "My sister, the vampire slayer. It still sounds so crazy."

Genny smiles. "I know, right? Can you even imagine what our lives might be like if Mom hadn't died and could've told us about all this and trained us and stuff? Sometimes I try to imagine what she'd think about everything, what advice she'd give me."

"What do you think she'd say?"

"I don't know. I never saw that side of her. I only know what Marie has told me." Then Genny recalls their earlier conversation. "That was actually her on the phone a few minutes ago."

"Yeah? What will happen to JP's uncle?" Chloe squeezes Genny's fingers.

"Thierry and his wife are taking René back to Lentemps to be charged. He'll stand trial there. You and I will probably have to testify."

At this, her sister perks right up. "Does that mean we get to go to France?"

Genny nods. "It looks like it. Not right away though. In a month or two. They'll let us know. So at least we have that to look forward to, even if the trial itself probably won't be much fun."

Finally Chloe looks happier. She sits up and swings her feet to the floor. "We're going to France! That's the best news I've heard in a while."

"Glad I could cheer you up."

With that, Genny finishes the last of her croissant and heads upstairs to jump in the shower. Once she emerges, she returns to her room to get dressed. There's a note on her dresser in her sister's messy scrawl: *JP called.*

Her eyes shift to the phone, but she doesn't reach for it. She thinks about how JP unknowingly fed information about her and her family to René that was then passed along to the Assembly. Information that had almost gotten her and Chloe killed. And had definitely gotten Chloe hurt, both emotionally and physically. Her sister had nearly been raped. If things had gone even a tiny bit differently last night, people she cares about would have died. People she loves.

Anger again flames up inside her. She understands JP hadn't meant to do it, but his actions still had consequences. Real, serious consequences. And Genny knows she's still too upset to discuss this rationally with him. She needs more time to process everything and decide how she wants to move forward.

Crumpling the note, she tosses it into the wastebasket and crawls back into bed.

It's not yet dark, but Quinn has been awake for a few hours already. Currently he's sprawled across his bed writing in his journal. He wants to document every detail he can recall of the previous day, so that when he reads this entry years from now he'll be able to relive each moment, both good and bad. But mostly the good. Though some parts had been tense, the good had far outweighed the bad.

With a soft sigh, he drops his pen, rolls onto his back and closes his eyes, thinking of one particular moment from last night. He knows it's not helpful to play it over and over in his mind like this—if anything he's only making things worse—but he can't seem to stop himself.

A rap on his bedroom door interrupts his musings. Before he can say *come in*, Cassandra flings it open and sits beside him on the bed. He knows she's been trying to reach any of her contacts at the Assembly. From her expression, it seems she's had no luck.

"Nothing?"

Cassandra shakes her head. "All the numbers I have are suddenly out of service. Can't imagine why."

"Looks like we're back to just us again." Quinn can't help the small smile that surfaces.

She doesn't look quite as pleased about it. "Seems so."

"Maybe it's not such a bad thing?" he says. "I mean, what did the Assembly ever do for us? Other than use us to do their dirty work? I for one won't miss them."

She considers this. "We have targets on our backs now. We'll have to be extra vigilant."

"What else is new?" He shrugs. That's just the life they lead. He suspects any so-called protection the Assembly had claimed to offer had been just lip service anyway. Lillabeta and Kellan don't care who gets killed on their missions, so long as the job gets done. Underlings are expendable and replaceable.

"True. Just let them try to come after us. Bring it on." Her grim grin disappears. "D'you think it's time for us to move on?"

Quinn darts a glance down at his closed journal. He doesn't even have to consider the answer. "This is my home. I'm staying."

Smiling, she says, "Me, too. Wherever you are, I am."

"And wherever you are, I predict Dawn will also be. It's not just us two anymore. And I'm glad. It's good to see you happy."

Cassandra's smile widens into a full on grin. "I am. And you're...well, okay, not *happy* exactly, but...you're happier. I guess that's all I can really ask for."

He snorts. She's right. But she's also wrong. He *is* happy, more than he's been in a very long time. "You convinced me to join the Assembly all those years ago because you wanted us to make connections. Well now we have connections right here. Dawn. Genevieve."

"And JP," Cassandra adds.

He shrugs. "Sure. Although I doubt he'd agree."

"The two of you are gonna have to learn to put up with each other if you intend to stay friends with her. He's a big part of her life."

"I know."

She holds his gaze. "They love each other."

"I know."

"So let me ask you this one last time: should we go?"

He doesn't look away. "No." No matter how much JP doesn't like him, doesn't like his connection to Genevieve, Quinn isn't going anywhere. Not unless she asks him to. The simple truth is that he needs to be close to her. Even if she can never look at him in quite the same way he looks at her, he won't walk away. He can't.

"Fine. So we stay. And you deal." She flashes him what he assumes is a sympathetic smile and gets up to go. Pausing at his open door, she says, "Have you spoken to her today?"

He shakes his head. "Not yet. I was planning to call later."

"Dawn already beat you to it. We're going over. You joining?"

"I'll be right down." Once she leaves, he tucks his journal back into its spot on the shelf. All these decades he's spent with Cassandra, it's mostly just been the two of them. Now their wee family has expanded. Quinn has spent the last 112 years thinking himself an outsider, trapped watching from the fringes and longing for the human life he used to take for granted. But he realizes he's no longer stuck on the outside. He's a part of something vital now. And even though some parts are still painful, he wouldn't trade it for anything.

Genny has been avoiding JP's calls for two days now. She's not any less upset, and she still doesn't know exactly what she wants to say to him, but it's been weighing on her for long enough. So on Friday she calls in sick yet again, tells Gran she's going out for a while, and walks to his place.

Since she hadn't let him know she's coming, she's not even sure he'll be home. As she knocks, a part of her actually hopes he won't be. But a moment later he pulls open the door looking like he's just gotten out of bed. He wears only basketball shorts and his thick black hair sticks out in all directions.

"Oh hi." He's clearly surprised to see her. Dragging a hand over his head in a futile attempt to tame the mess, he adds, "I wasn't expecting you."

"I know. And I'm sorry I haven't returned your calls. I just needed some time to process everything that happened." He's still standing there staring at her, so she adds, "Is it okay if I come in?"

"Right. Sorry." He steps out of her way, and Genny walks past him to the living room to take a seat on the couch.

"Can I get you a coffee?" JP asks.

"I'm good, thanks."

"Do you mind if I grab one for myself?" He doesn't wait for her answer, just heads straight into the small kitchen. She hears the sound of a cupboard door being opened and closed.

A minute later the smell of coffee hits her and she pipes up, "Actually, do you have enough for two?"

She hears a chuckle. "Already on it." Soon he brings out two steaming mugs and sets one on the table before her. It's instant, but she doesn't mind.

"How're you doing?" she asks tentatively.

JP takes a sip of coffee, then glances down at his chest, realizing he's still shirtless. "Be right back." He disappears down the hall and returns pulling down a blue t-shirt. "'Ow am I doing about what?" he asks as he sits in the chair. "My uncle betraying us or my girlfriend lying to me?"

Genny frowns. "What've I lied to you about?"

"Oh, just the usual. The details of your relationship with the vampire." He's staring her in the eyes, challenging her to try to deny it.

With so much more important stuff on her mind, she'd actually forgotten Quinn would've had to tell the others he'd been getting messages from her the other night. Sighing, she says, "Right. That. I'm sorry. I know I promised I wouldn't keep things from you anymore, but that? It's something I still don't fully get. Neither of us does."

"So what? That's *exactly* why you should've told me. It's undoubtedly some sort of spell, and you know full well Maman and myself know the 'istory of your family. Remember? Your family which included quite a few mages? I should've been the *first* person you told! And I keep asking myself why you didn't. What are you concealing?"

"Nothing! It's just..." Genny stops with another sigh. "You're right. I should've told you."

He leans forward, bracing his forearms on his knees. "So why didn't you? After everything we discussed before, you still chose to keep this from me."

"Because it would've upset you, and made you even more jealous than you already were! And because it's..." She trails off, breaking eye contact.

"It's *what*?" JP's tone is getting frosty and she doesn't like it.

She hadn't planned to say this, but her mouth opens and it just falls out. "It's *personal*. Our connection? It's...it's *ours*. Mine and his. And I didn't feel like sharing it with people who wouldn't understand. If that makes me an awful girlfriend, so be it." She looks back at him, her temper flaring. "Happy now?"

He sits back in the chair, his expression miserable. "No. Far from it. I maintain that you should've told me, and I'm 'urt that you purposely chose not to. You two have this *thing* between you that you claim I can't possibly understand. But you don't even try to explain; you just conceal it. 'Ow do you think that makes me feel?"

Genny reaches for his hand, but he pulls it away. "I didn't mean to hurt you," she says. "I was actually trying to avoid that. But when I went after Chloe, my ability to contact Quinn was the only secret weapon I had. And if I'd told you, you undoubtedly would've told René, and then the vampires would've known. They would've killed Quinn weeks ago." Her gut drops at the mere thought. "And then I would've been completely cut off from you guys. Not telling you more than likely saved all our asses."

His brows fly up. "You're not seriously blaming me for what 'appened?"

"I know you didn't do it on purpose. But you shared information about me and my family that nearly got us killed."

"That was *not* my fault! They already knew about you. Quinn and Cassandra told them after 'e saw you at the club that first night. And you told René stuff about yourself, too. He fooled *all* of us!" Now JP looks both hurt and angry.

"Quinn never told anyone where I lived or that I had a sister. He only told Cassandra he'd spotted an immortal. The Assembly knew everything else from your uncle. How many times did you casually talk about me around him? A lot, I bet. He knew Chloe was applying for a job at The Second Cup. They sent Darius there to charm her. Jesus, JP! She was nearly raped for God's sake! And the other night she came this close to dying!" Genny holds her thumb and forefinger about a quarter of an inch apart, her fingers quivering with rage. "And I nearly did, too. Kellan hypnotized me. If Quinn hadn't showed up when he did, I don't know what might've happened!"

Much of JP's anger drains from his face. "I didn't know about those things. Although I would've if you'd bothered to call me back. I'm so sorry, Gen. I really am. René's betrayal didn't just 'urt you. He 'urt us all."

"I know." Genny takes a deep breath to try to calm herself. For a few long seconds they just look at each other. A sick sense of defeat creeps over her.

JP leans forward in the chair again. "So now what? Where do we go from 'ere?"

Another sigh. Too many sighs. And she doubts they're done yet. "I honestly don't know," she admits.

"Do you think you can you forgive my part in my uncle's treason? And can you stop keeping secrets from me?"

"It's not that simple. Your uncle is responsible for my entire family being killed."

"I am fully aware of that. What 'e did is unforgiveable."

"Completely," she agrees. "I hope he gets the death penalty."

JP visibly recoils. "Immortals don't believe in capital punishment." He looks horrified.

"Well they should. How many immortals are dead because of him? Fifty? A hundred?"

He doesn't answer. He looks defeated. "I just don't understand why 'e would do it. It makes no sense."

Sitting back, Genny says, "That one I can answer. He did it for revenge. One of my ancestors killed the woman he loved."

"*What*? How could you possibly know that?"

"He told me, before Kellan showed up. Long ago he had a secret love affair with a vampire, and she was slain by a Bourreau. In retaliation, he swore revenge on our family. He started working with the Assembly to make sure all slayers were wiped out." Genny knows she's oversimplifying René's story a little, but that's the gist of it.

"That's not possible. You must've understood wrong. René would never. My oncle despises vampires."

"He's a good actor," she says with a shrug. "He fooled everyone."

JP's mouth opens and then closes again. "René really told you that? That 'e loved a *vampire*?"

Genny nods. She can tell JP is realizing he really doesn't know his uncle, and it's a tough revelation.

"That's...wow." He shakes his head. "Maman won't believe it."

"It will all come out at the trial. She told me the other day we have to go to France to testify. So that should be interesting."

JP waves this off. "Judiciary proceedings move slowly in Lentemps. I wouldn't pack a suitcase yet. It could take a few months." After a moment, he adds, "Remember when we talked about going there together someday? Who would've guessed it would be for this reason? But at least I can still show you the library and 'elp you learn about your family. If you still want me to, that is?"

Instead of replying, she reaches for her mug and at last takes a sip. The coffee is now lukewarm and tastes bitter. Seems appropriate really. She sets it on the table, but doesn't raise her eyes back to his. Try as she might, Genny can't see a way to smooth this over. There is too much between them right now, and it feels overwhelming. It feels broken. Maybe irreparably.

Neither of them speaks for what feels like several minutes, but is probably only a few seconds. Finally she exhales a puff of air and breaks the silence. "You asked me earlier where we go from here?"

He nods.

"I think…this is hard to say, but…I think we should take a break."

It's definitely not what JP had been expecting. His eyes flare. "You're joking?"

Tears threaten to rise, but she holds strong. "We're both clearly having trust issues right now. Maybe it's for the best if we—"

"*What*? Break up? Because you blame me for crimes my uncle committed?"

Getting to her feet, Genny says, "No. Because right now every time I look at you I think about the fact that my sister was almost raped and killed because of what you told him. Accidentally or not. And because you clearly don't trust me to be faithful. Without trust, we don't have a relationship to try to save."

"You're the one who's been keeping secrets. Repeatedly. Can you really blame me for wondering if you 'ave something to 'ide?"

Genny turns to him. Her throat is starting to ache and she needs to get out of here. She can't look into those sad brown eyes for much longer or she'll completely break down. "I didn't want this. I really didn't. I do love you. But I can't. I just can't." Choking up, she heads for the door.

JP follows her. Before she can pull it open and escape, he says, "Can't what?"

"Do this anymore."

Genny walks blindly, rivulets running down her cheeks and blurring her vision. JP hadn't come after her. Although most of her is glad he hadn't, there's a small part that can't help feeling a little disappointed.

She doesn't have a destination in mind; she only knows she's not ready to go home, not ready to tell Chloe or Gran or anyone else what had just happened. They will only offer comfort and well-meaning advice, both of which are sweet, but at the moment Genny wants neither.

Swiping away the tears, she realizes she's on the path to the park where she and JP had sat the day he'd told her she's an immortal. Although the sun is shining, the park is mostly empty. She takes a seat on the same bench and digs in her pocket for a tissue.

Did that really just happen? Did we really just break up?

She dries her face and blows her nose. Her chest hurts. It feels too tight, like it's holding in all the sobs she refuses to let out.

Her heart is beating fast. Too fast. Putting a palm against her chest, she feels its insistent throb below her fingers. Is this where the phrase *broken-hearted* comes from? Though she knows it's just hyperbole, the way it aches feels like it might actually be broken. She can hear her breath wheezing in and out. Deep inhales. Slow exhales. It doesn't help.

This is all wrong, she thinks. *I need to fix this.*

Her eyes wander across the grass to the path she'd stumbled down. She could go back to his apartment, bang on the door, throw her arms around him, and be in his bed not long after. She doesn't need precognition to know this is true. Standing, she even turns in that direction.

But then she remembers Darius holding Chloe in front of himself like a shield, stroking his thumb over her sister's cheek, burying his nose in her hair. The disgust that rises in the back of her throat makes her sit down. Quinn and Cassandra may have told the Assembly about Genny before they knew her, but Quinn had sworn he'd never said a word about her sister. The vampires had known details about Chloe because René had told them, plain and simple. Genny's also not without blame in this. She'd told René things, too. But she's positive she hadn't said a lot about her sister. Who knows how much The Assembly had learned simply because she and JP had been dating?

She's aware she's being a little unreasonable about the whole thing. JP hadn't done any of this on purpose. He just talks a lot when he's excited, and he'd been excited about meeting her. He clearly feels terrible about it, but it's her baby sister who'd had horrible things done to her because of his loose talk. Fair or not, Genny just can't get past it.

And then there's the Quinn situation. If she gets back together with JP, she'll feel obligated to spend less time with Quinn, because it makes JP so uncomfortable. Knowing her friendship with Quinn bothers him could mean at some point she might be forced to choose between them. She doesn't know if she could do that.

Maybe, if she and JP can manage to stay friends and spend time together in the group, they will figure out how to get past all this. Because she can't stand the thought of losing either of them. It may be selfish of her, but it's true.

At that, the tears overflow again, and this time she doesn't fight the sobs that accompany them.

Chapter 19
The Dog End of a Day Gone By

When Dawn hangs up the phone, Quinn comes over and sits beside her, looking at her with raised brows. Although he knows it's impolite to eavesdrop, he couldn't help overhearing much of her conversation with Genevieve.

Dawn meets his eyes and nods. She looks sad. "Poor Genny. They broke up. But she doesn't wanna talk about it. I offered to go over, but she said no. She just wants to be alone right now."

"I get that," he says. And he does. He gets it, but he also knows how much she must be hurting. He'd been able to feel her pain from her faint voice on the other end of the phone. She'd told Dawn she doesn't want company, but he doesn't know if he can just sit back and do nothing. Not when she's in so much pain.

He forces himself to go upstairs and try to journal his thoughts, but he's unable to focus. After a few long, meandering sentences, he puts it aside with a sigh and returns to the living room. It's now empty. Good. No one is around to question where he's off to. He laces up his boots and heads out into the night.

She may not want company, but he can't stand the idea of her sitting up in her room alone and hurting. He has to at least try.

But not yet. First, he goes to his favorite hunting trails to walk and think for a while. And to feed. A fox, this time. The blood tastes wild and gamey, a little bitter, but it does the trick. It's not human blood, but it will nourish him for now. He heals the fox and it runs into the underbrush, whipping its tail from side to side. Quinn watches it go with admiration. Foxes don't feel remorse, or duty, or love and hate. They do as they please from birth until death, surviving on instinct alone.

Sometimes Quinn thinks that would be easier.

Sometimes.

Slowly he makes his way back through the streets to Genevieve's house. Before he even gets close enough to see it, he hears her voice in his head.

Not tonight. I know you just wanna check in, but I'm fine. Well, I'm not, but I'll be fine. I'll talk to you soon, I promise. Don't worry.

How can he not worry? It's impossible. Although he's a bit disappointed, he will respect her wishes. He turns and heads for the subway instead. Maybe he'll go downtown and see if anything interesting is going on.

Several hours later, Quinn is on his way home. It's been an uneventful evening—he just hadn't been able to get into loud music or talking to strangers. Not that he's normally particularly into it, but these things can sometimes provide a needed distraction. He'd forced himself to go to a club, and had made a few dutiful attempts before giving up. It's no surprise, really. It's become increasingly difficult to turn his brain off lately.

As he approaches his house, he suddenly stills. Someone is in the backyard. Their breathing is mostly even, but every now and then it hitches. It sounds like a human. For a second, he wonders if it might be her, come to talk to him after all. But no. He'd spent an entire night lying beside her, listening to her breathe, watching her sleep. He'd recognize her anywhere, and this is not her.

So who is in his backyard?

He comes around the rear corner of the house and is surprised to find JP sitting on a patio chair. He's leaning forward, elbows on his knees, face bent down into his hands. Quinn can tell he's distraught. JP doesn't look up.

Moving silently is one of a vampire's greatest skills, and if Quinn chooses, he could vanish back the way he'd come and JP would be none the wiser. There's little point in delaying this, though. The man came here for a reason.

"JP," he says evenly. "Why are you here?" But Quinn's not stupid. He can guess.

JP's head bobs up. The moment his gaze lands on Quinn, his expression morphs from surprise to anger. "Why do you *think* I'm 'ere?" he growls, rising from the chair. He towers over Quinn, over half a foot taller. To most people this might be intimidating, but Quinn is not most people.

Quinn spots something protruding from JP's shirt pocket, something long and thin, and he exhales a sigh. He knows JP is hurting, but sympathy only goes so far. Quinn has no intention of putting up with any stupidity. He decides to try to diffuse the situation before JP does something foolish that will only embarrass himself and make Genevieve even more upset with him.

"I can see you're agitated, but let me stop you here. Walk away now and she never has to know you came. If you insist on some sort of confrontation, she will learn about it. And I doubt that will help your situation."

JP's mouth twists. "Because you two don't keep secrets from each other." It's a statement, not a question.

Quinn frowns. He chooses not to reply, but he takes a step closer. He can tell that below the anger JP is also nervous. He's been taught his whole life to fear the evil vampire, after all. But nervous people sometimes make rash decisions. Quinn needs to be careful.

"See, that's the whole problem right there," JP continues. "She's honest with you, but keeps important facts from me. 'Ow can I compete when I don't even know the damn playing field? I can't." A single tear escapes and slides down his cheek, but his voice doesn't crack. "Your strange connection to her gives you the advantage. By all rights she should despise you, should've killed you 'erself long ago. But she didn't, because of your fucking connection! If it wasn't for you, we'd still be together. Things would be the way they're supposed to be."

JP stops to draw in a breath, and although he's kind of expecting it, Quinn is still a bit surprised when the other man lunges at him. He tries to dodge, but doesn't quite succeed. They fall to the ground, JP on top of him, a wooden stake clutched in one fist and aimed at Quinn's chest.

Quinn's limited patience with this situation has now run out. He shoves JP off a little harder than he intends and sends him flying toward the back door. There's a slam as the door flies open and Cassandra appears just in time to catch JP by the shoulders before he lands on the concrete step.

"Boys, boys. Fighting over a girl? It's not the Victorian era anymore. Women get to choose who they want to kiss these days." She releases JP, who, instead of being contrite, flies at Quinn again.

"You *kissed* her?" he yells, stake once more raised.

With one swipe, Quinn knocks it from JP's hand and grabs him by the upper arms. "*Enough*. I did not. Nor have I ever tried. Cassandra was just attempting in her own way to make a point."

In vain, JP tries to shake himself loose of Quinn's grip. "She forgave *you* for 'elping murder 'er own parents, so why can't she forgive me for something I didn't even know I'd done?"

Quinn's entire body goes rigid. He hadn't known Genevieve had discussed that with JP, but of course she would have. He's well aware that he doesn't deserve her forgiveness for his role in her parent's death. Though they've gotten past it, that subject will always be a sore one. "You should stop talking now," he says icily.

JP's eyes flare. Perhaps he's finally realized the position he's put himself in. "It's not fair," he moans, head drooping. Another tear slips loose. "She…she dumped me." His voice is now little more than a whisper.

"I heard. And I'm sorry," Quinn says.

"No, you're not."

Quinn lets go of him and steps back. "Fine. I'm not. But I don't like to see her in pain, and breaking up with you hurts her. A lot."

"Does it?" JP asks, He sounds suddenly hopeful. Had he really assumed she wouldn't feel anything? That she'd just walk away from him totally fine? If so, he doesn't know her very well.

"Come inside," Cassandra says to them. "Before you wake the neighbors." She holds the door open and JP, at last looking sheepish, walks inside. Quinn follows, raising a brow to Cassandra and silently thanking her for breaking the tension.

"Did you drive here?" she asks JP.

He shakes his head. "Bus."

"Good. I'm pouring you some whisky and you're going to sit your ass down and drink it. And hopefully it'll help you calm down. Got it?"

JP nods. There's no anger left in his face. Only sadness. He flops into the papasan like all the life has drained out of him.

Quinn sits on the couch facing him. "If it makes you feel any better—and I realize it probably won't—I didn't ask her to keep anything from you. We didn't discuss it and make a choice to be secretive."

"She said…" JP stops to clear his throat. Cassandra hands him a glass containing a generous inch of liquor and a single ice cube. Taking a drink, JP grimaces, then continues. "She said it was personal. Your connection. That it was between you two, and other people—me, presumably—wouldn't understand. Do you 'ave any idea 'ow it feels to have your girlfriend tell you she's got a deep personal connection to another man that you couldn't possibly understand?"

Quinn frowns, but doesn't reply.

"It feels like shit. It feels like there's a part of 'er I'll never know, because it's only for you. And then she has the nerve to tell me she can't trust *me*. Which is fucking *rich*, don't you think?"

Cassandra takes a seat beside Quinn. Quinn doesn't ask where Dawn is, but she must be upstairs. "Why can't she trust you?" she asks JP. "What happened?"

JP breaks eyes contact, looking down at his glass. He takes another sip and makes another face. "Because of my oncle René. Because of all the things 'e found out about Genny and Chloe from me and then told the Assembly. But none of us 'ad any idea about René! I never would've told 'im *anything* if I'd 'ad even the slightest suspicion! My oncle fooled us all. It wasn't my fault, but she says she can't even look at me without thinking of what almost 'appened to Chloe. And I can't blame 'er. I can barely look at myself right now." Tears again threaten to spill over.

Quinn glances at Cassandra. He has no idea what to do in this situation. He's not about to hug the guy who'd just tried to stake him, and he doubts Cassandra will, either.

But she surprises him. She goes over to JP and kneels in front of him, setting a hand on his knee. "Hey. Shit happens, okay? Breakups happen. They suck, but it's life. I agree, the René business wasn't your fault. But could maybe some of the other stuff be because you acted jealous and made her feel like she had to hide her friendship with Quinn from you? Is that possible?"

JP raises his face to her. His eyes are still glossy. Sighing, he relents. "Maybe."

She straightens up and returns to the couch. "I don't envy ya, bud. It's a tough situation. But if she asked you for space, my advice is to give it to her. Don't contact her for a bit. Give her time to miss you. Maybe you two can still work things out. You never know."

The smallest of smiles emerges. "You think so?" JP asks.

"Hey, stranger things have happened. Just in the past week, in fact."

JP downs the rest of the whisky and sets his empty glass on the coffee table. He turns to Quinn. "Do you really need to tell 'er about this?"

Quinn looks to Cassandra again, who shakes her head the slightest bit. She's right. Genevieve would be livid if she found out JP showed up here with a stake and attacked him. What would that help, other than to make her feel worse?

"Fine," he agrees reluctantly. "This can stay between us. But if you ever try that crap with me again, I can promise I'll make you grateful for your accelerated healing." Quinn tries to sound threatening. The soft snort from Cassandra doesn't help.

Standing, JP smiles. "I would expect nothing less," he says to Quinn. He starts for the door, but turns back. "Thanks. I know we're not friends, but you didn't 'ave to go easy on me, or listen to me whine, or agree not to tell Genny I made an ass of myself. You didn't 'ave to do any of that, so thanks."

"No bother," Quinn tells him. It's not totally a lie, although he could have done without any drama tonight.

Without another word, JP leaves.

"Well, that was weird," Cassandra says to Quinn. "But at least it ended without bloodshed. He'll be okay." She finishes off her whisky and heads for the stairs.

Quinn stays where he is for a few moments. It's doubtful he and JP will ever particularly like each other. Quinn's fine with that, but he doesn't wish the guy any harm. Anyone who loves Genevieve as much as JP does is okay in Quinn's book. And if they do get back together, he'll do his best to support it.

It won't even be that difficult. If she's happy, so is he.

It's been a week since the breakup. Genny had cried off and on for a couple of days, but now she mostly just feels numb. At first, she had little interest in seeing her friends, and no interest at all in talking about it, but today she's finally feeling a bit better. Dawn and Cassandra, with some help from Chloe, have managed to convince her she should go over to their place for a movie night. To their surprise, she'd agreed. She's wallowed long enough. Although she misses JP like crazy, and keeps having to stop herself from calling him, it's time to start getting on with her life.

Cassandra picks Genny and Chloe up, and once they've settled on a couple of vampire movies from Sheppard Video—Cassandra picks *Fright Night*, while Genny and Chloe will not be swayed from *The Lost Boys*, with its cast of drool-worthy hunks—they head over to the house.

The moment Genny walks in the back door, her eyes lock on Quinn descending the stairs to meet them. He stops at the base of the steps and regards her cautiously, and she flashes him a small smile. It's possibly her first genuine smile since the day Chloe had been kidnapped, and it feels a bit weird, like her facial muscles don't quite recall what to do.

When he sees it, he relaxes. Sometimes they don't need to speak, either mentally or out loud, to know how the other is feeling.

"Who wants popcorn?" Cassandra calls from the kitchen.

"I do!" Chloe exclaims. She and Dawn flop onto the couch. As far as Genny knows, her sister has never been here before, but she props her feet up on the table like she's at home.

Genny goes into the kitchen. "Need any help?" she asks Cassandra.

"Sure. Watch the pan for me while I make us some drinks. Once those two test kernels pop, we add the rest and take it off the burner." Cassandra opens a cupboard and starts pulling down glasses and bottles. "Taking orders. Who wants what?"

Once the popcorn is ready and everyone has drinks in their hands, they all settle into the living room. Chloe, Dawn, and Cassandra are on the couch, while Genny and Quinn take the chairs that flank it, angled toward each other.

As Cassandra pops *The Lost Boys* cartridge into the VCR, Chloe turns to Genny. "So who will you train with now?"

It's a valid question. With her and JP no longer together, Genny doesn't feel comfortable asking Marie to continue her training. Before she can reply, Cassandra flops back down beside Dawn and says, "We'll train you."

Genny's brows draw in. "You will?" But she can already see that it's a great idea.

"Of course," Quinn answers. "Who better to train you how to take down vampires than us?"

"Makes sense."

Cassandra reaches for the remote control and hits Pause. "Wanna start right now? I'm game."

Chuckling, Genny says, "Maybe tomorrow. Tonight I just wanna watch some dumb Hollywood vampire movies with my friends and not think about real life."

Quinn's eyes meet hers across the room. "Real life can wait until tomorrow," he agrees.

As if on some unspoken cue, they all pick up their drinks. "Here's to putting things off to tomorrow," Cassandra says loudly, raising her glass in the air.

"Hear, hear," Dawn agrees.

"And to dumb vampire movies with hot boys," Chloe pipes up.

"And to friends," Genny adds just before she takes a sip. She's so grateful for them. Even though she's still hurting, still angry, still worried about so many things, she doesn't know what she'd do without the support of the people in this room.

As the opening notes of "Cry Little Sister" start up on the television, she sits up straighter in her chair. Her problems with the Assembly are far from over, but she is not some weak, terrified little girl. She's a slayer, like her mother had been before her, and her grandmother and great-grandmother before that. But with one huge difference. She's a slayer who does not kill indiscriminately, and understands who her real enemies are. Knowing Quinn has taught her important lessons her mother never would have been able to. She's incredibly lucky to have him—all of them, actually—in her life.

Thank you, she thinks at him. He glances over at her, his pale gray eyes reflecting the glow of the television screen, and smiles that small smile that means he understands.

"You're welcome," he mouths.

She relaxes back into the cushion and tries to focus on the movie. Her problems will still be here tomorrow, but she doesn't have to face them alone.

Chapter 20
Oblivious

August 2, 1994, Sydney, Ontario, Canada

The bell over the door rings and Johnna looks up to see an older couple come into the bookstore. She's been sitting on the floor in the back corner rearranging a lower shelf. Now she jumps up, brushing dust from her trousers.

She greets them with a cheerful smile. "Good morning. Welcome to Becca's." It's been a quiet morning so far, but maybe these folks will actually buy something.

"Hello," they both respond. Johnna lets them have a look around without attempting to make small talk. She's not very good at it, anyway. Instead, she goes behind the counter and takes a seat on the stool.

After browsing for a while—at least the wife does, the husband makes a half-hearted attempt, but mostly looks bored—they come up to her with two books.

"Does Rebecca still own this shop?" the lady asks as Johnna punches her purchases into the cash register.

"Yes, she does. She's out running errands today," Johnna replies, tucking a loose strand of auburn hair behind one ear. Rebecca Cross is the owner of Becca's Book Nook. She's also Johnna's housemate. Although Rebecca is quite a few years Johnna's senior, Johnna considers her a close friend. Rebecca had helped her rebuild her life here in the village of Sydney when Johnna had been lost and alone. For the past thirteen years, Rebecca has let Johnna live with her, and in exchange for this kindness, Johnna helps out at the store. It's a good deal, and she leads a simple, yet contented life. Mostly.

The woman's blue eyes crinkle at the corners. "I knew Rebecca when she was a girl about your age. Back then, she helped her mother run the store. Is Mrs. Cross still alive?"

"No, unfortunately she passed away several years ago." Johnna places the books inside a brown paper bag and slides it across the countertop. "Here you go."

"Thank you so much. What about you, dear? Are you a relation?"

Shaking her head, Johnna says, "No, just a friend."

"Did you grow up here? What's your family name?"

For a moment, Johnna stills. This is a question she dreads getting. She'd give anything to know the answer. "I'm not from around here. My last name is Doe." It had been the name the nurses at the hospital and the police who'd questioned her had given her. She'd been brought into Emergency, extremely dirty and a little bloody, after a kind man had found her one icy winter morning walking barefoot along the side of a rural road. Her clothing had been in charred tatters, yet by some miracle, she'd suffered no injuries. She couldn't recall what had happened to her, where she lived, or even her name, so they'd checked her in as Johnna Doe. Once she'd been released, she'd decided to keep it. It's as good a name as any.

"Doe, huh? Any relation to Peter Doe?" the husband asks.

"I'm afraid not. You two have a lovely day."

They both smile at her as they leave, turning down the street toward the pub on the corner.

With a soft sigh, Johnna returns to re-organizing the store's small travel section. Instead of by author like the other sections, she's decided to sort these books by location: Albania to Wales and about twenty other countries in between. The *Discover Albania* book has been here longer than she has. Apparently not many people in this town are looking for travel guides for that country.

Johnna lingers for a moment on *The Backpacker's Guide to France*. A lovely image of green rolling countryside with a crumbling stone castle in the distance graces the cover. It's beautiful, and for a fraction of a second something scratches at the back of her mind. When she tries to grasp for it, it vanishes.

She puts the book back with a frustrated sigh. This has happened to her a few times lately. She doesn't know what triggers it, but that split second of familiarity she sometimes gets gives her optimism that some of her memories may start to return. Wishful thinking, she knows, after all these years, but she can't help it. There has to be someone, somewhere who wonders what has happened to her. After all these years, chances have gotten slim that anyone is still looking for her, but it's not impossible.

One thing Johnna knows for certain about herself is that she's stubborn as hell. She refuses to let go of the hope that someday she'll remember.

That night, Johnna finds herself studying her reflection in the bathroom mirror for far too long. This is not an uncommon occurrence.

Someone out there must know this face.

It's the same thought she always has every time she's looked at herself over the past thirteen years. Someone must know her. Had she left behind brokenhearted parents who'd assumed she'd run away? Do they still think of her? Worry for her safety? Miss her? It's logical to assume she would have had family, yet no one has filed a Missing Person's Report with the Ontario Provincial Police looking for a woman of Johnna's description. Not back then, and not since. She checks in with them a few times a year, even after all this time.

She turns and starts the water running in the bathtub. Rebecca has gone to bed early, but Johnna isn't sleepy. A hot soak will help relax her. Probably. Becca always claims it eases her aching back after a long day at the bookshop. Johnna's back doesn't ache, though. It never has.

Her eyes steal back to the mirror again as she waits. They'd told her at the hospital that she'd been about twenty.

If the doctors had been right, that would make her around thirty-three now, yet her deep green eyes have no wrinkles at their corners. Her hair is still thick, reddish-brown with not a single strand of gray. Though she has only a few photos of herself, she looks basically the same in each of them. These little things have her wondering if she'd actually been younger than people had assumed. Becca often teases her that her family must be blessed with amazing genes. Johnna brushes this off with a smile, but sometimes she wonders.

Turning off the tap, she adds some lavender sprigs to the water and slips into the tub. The bath is hot. Really hot. Just the way Johnna likes it. Becca has also chided her more than once about her scalding hot showers, saying she can't understand how Johnna can stand them. Johnna just laughs, although she doesn't really get the point. The hot water doesn't hurt. It actually feels wonderful, relaxing, and even sort of rejuvenating. She assumes Becca must be over-sensitive.

Leaning her head back against the tub's edge, she closes her eyes, inhales deeply of the soothing lavender, and tries to empty her thoughts. It doesn't work for long. She can't help thinking of that little scratch at the back of her mind when she had looked at the French travel guide. Might she be French? She doesn't speak French, at least she doesn't think she does. Maybe she's not even Canadian? Could she have been visiting from France when whatever happened to her had happened? If she'd been traveling alone, maybe there had been no one to raise any alarm about her disappearance? But that doesn't track either, because surely someone back home would have known she'd been here and contacted local authorities when she hadn't returned. Yet no one had.

So many questions. Johnna has no answers for any of them.

She lifts her right leg above the water. The only clue she has to her identity is a tattoo of a black cross on her left hip. It's small, only about three inches long. The top portion of the cross is rounded. If you examine it closely, it sort of looks like a human figure with arms outstretched. As she traces her finger over its surface, Johnna again wonders about its significance. Had she been religious? Had she attended church? If so, which denomination? If she's French, does that mean she'd been Catholic?

More unanswerable questions. It's so frustrating to not know who she is. At times it feels like it might drive her crazy.

Johnna is well aware that her memories may never return. She knows this, but she can't help noticing that the peculiar scratching at the back of her mind has been happening more and more often lately. Maybe someday it may just dig its way right through.

And if she does remember, then what?

Will finding what she's lost bring her joy or despair?

Turn the page for a special preview of the next book in the Forever Twenty-One series

MORE THAN JUST BLOOD

Available late 2021

MORE THAN JUST BLOOD
Chapter 1
No Love Lost

August 20, 1994, Paris, France

A vision in white, the Grand Mistress of the Vampire Assembly drifts into the room. She moves so gracefully she appears to float above the marble tiles.

The moment he sees her, Kellan Lahaine extinguishes his cigarette and gives her his undivided attention. Though he's been waiting for a while, he's not irritated by her tardiness. The truth is he cannot take his eyes off her. Lillabeta is perfection in stark hues of white, black, and red. Snug white gown that flows out below her waist, gleaming white hair she wears in a long braid draped over one shoulder, and flawless alabaster skin. Her kohl-rimmed eyes meet his as she takes a seat across from him. They are nearly identical to his own: jet black with red pupils, unlike any other vampire he's ever met. He has no idea why, has never asked, nor particularly cared. And her lips...Kellan's gaze darts to those plump, ruby-red lips. He's been at Lillabeta's side for over four hundred years and in all this time she's never once failed to captivate him.

No human could ever fascinate him the way she does. He'd grow bored of them before even a single month passed. But Lillabeta is as far from human as a vampire can get. It's not just her ethereal beauty, although no human could compare to that, either. She may be cold and ruthless, but Kellan knows the real her, the side she shows only to him. He'd do anything she asked of him to stay in her favor. He has, in fact, done pretty much everything, and he does not regret a single moment.

They're on the upper floor of a neoclassical apartment block. Former apartment block, actually—the Assembly has owned this building for the past sixty years. It's now a walled-off and guarded compound, and what suites haven't been converted to conference rooms are no longer rented to humans. A High Council meeting is about to begin two floors below, but as often happens, the Grand Mistress had wished to speak privately with him beforehand. High Council meetings, which are comprised of Lillabeta and her six most trusted advisors, used to be an uncommon thing, Lately they seem to happen several times a month.

"My source has heard rumblings," she says by way of a greeting. Her voice is high and clear as her strange eyes hold his. "The immortals are up to something. I believe they may be preparing to strike."

This is not the topic Kellan had assumed she'd wanted to discuss. He snorts. "What source? Our inside man now rots away in their prison. Or dead. You told them to do as they wished with him."

At his scoffing, her face hardens. "True," she replies, her tone a degree cooler. "Losing René Levoyant was unfortunate, but it could not be helped. However, as you are aware, he was not my sole informant."

Although Kellan will always defer to Lillabeta's decisions, he's confident enough to speak frankly to her without fear of repercussions, a privilege granted only to one other. "An attack on us seems doubtful. They have no true slayers left, which means we both outskill and outnumber them. Such an aggression would be suicide."

She doesn't look appeased. "The Bourreau girl took out Darius, and she was trained by a non-slayer." One pale eyebrow arches. "Or have you forgotten?"

"I have not. She did not do it on her own, though. She had help from Sinclair." Kellan scowls. "Filthy turncoats, both Sinclair and Veld. I admit I did not foresee that. I cannot imagine how she managed to sway them." There is nothing special about Geneviève Bourreau. She's just a regular immortal human, perhaps a bit more defiant than some, reasonably attractive, sure, but otherwise rather ordinary in Kellan's far from humble opinion. No reason he can see for them to put their eternal lives at risk for her. Except there clearly is one. And he intends to find out what it is.

"Ah yes. The traitors. You have taken care of them." Lillabeta says this as if it's an understood fact. Cassandra Veld and Quinn Sinclair betrayed the Assembly. Therefore they exist no more.

"I've been meaning to discuss that with you, actually." Kellan tents his fingers on the table in front of him. "I'm sure you'll agree that, as they are confidants of the Bourreau girls, allowing them to live—for now—could be to our advantage."

Lillabeta's eyes narrow a few millimeters in the merest hint of a frown.

"I've sent a couple of my men to Toronto to keep an eye on them," he continues. "From a discreet distance, of course. Veld is a skilled tracker, so they have been warned not to get close. I receive reports of what they're up to, which for the record is very little. Of note, Geneviève is no longer training with the Levoyants. Instead, she now trains with the vampires."

The Grand Mistress is displeased, which Kellan had expected. "Treason is an act punishable by death. The traitors know this. Why did they not go into hiding? Why stay where they know we can find them? It is suspicious."

"You're correct, and I've considered that. It *is* odd, and something I intend to find out. For now, knowing their movements could prove useful. Let them sit there in fear, constantly looking over their shoulders. They can't even use magic to hide—all their mages are long dead. So it doesn't matter if they stay or flee. They are mere fruit for the picking whenever we choose."

Squaring her shoulders, she says, "That may be, but I still do not like it." There's a note of petulance to her tone. Sometimes in moments like this Kellan thinks he still sees hints of the human girl she'd once been so long ago. Such glimpses are rare, and he locks each one away in his memory banks for later consideration.

"Then why didn't we kill the Bourreau girls a few weeks ago when we had the chance?" he asks.

"Make no mistake, they will both die. As you well know, there were more pressing issues that needed our attention."

He does well know, because those issues are not yet fully resolved. They concern an enemy far more worrisome than the two surviving Bourreau girls. But Lillabeta seems to consider both threats equally problematic, so he listens calmly to her concerns.

"You're correct," she declares suddenly, surprising him. "The girls are untrained and not a true risk at the moment. Geneviève Bourreau can spar with her vampires all she wants. When the time comes, she will pose no threat to us." The expression on Lillabeta's face says that by *us* she means herself. She intends to personally destroy the last of the Bourreaus. And Kellan will be by her side to witness their deaths with grim satisfaction.

"Not yet," he ventures. "Perhaps someday she might."

"We shall ensure they do not live long enough for that day to come. For now, do your job and dispose of the traitors, as is their due. I don't care how. Just see that it is done."

"As you wish," he concedes, dipping his chin in supplication.

"It is the law. They betrayed me. They die. You should have had them executed weeks ago." He bristles inside at the disapproval in her voice, but his face remains impassive.

"Of course. I wanted—" Kellan's words are cut short by a cool hand covering his mouth and the simultaneous press of a curved blade to his throat. A scimitar. *Fuck.*

Lillabeta offers an amused smile as she looks up at the woman standing behind him. "Hello Juliette."

The blade vanishes and Kellan spins to face the dark assassin. "Bloody hell! Was that really necessary?" Juliette and Lillabeta are the only two creatures on this planet who are capable of sneaking up on him. He doesn't mind when Lillabeta deliberately startles him—it usually amuses him—but he's always found Juliette unsettling. The assassin has an uncanny talent for making herself disappear into the background. When she chooses, she's unseen, unheard—a virtual ghost. And her skill with weaponry is absolutely unmatched. It's no wonder Lillabeta keeps her happy. Juliette has the well-earned reputation as the most dangerous vampire on earth.

The burst of laughter that erupts from Lillabeta at his irritation is child-like at best, venturing into unhinged territory at worst.

"Grand Mistress." Juliette bows. She is dressed in tight-fitting black leather, and her black curls are cropped close to her scalp. Glancing at him with eyes as dark as her ebony skin, she simply says, "Kellan."

He frowns. She should refer to him by rank, not by his given name. It's disrespectful, as had been the pantomime of the knife to his throat. Yet Kellan does not correct her. Juliette's message is clear. She answers to the Grand Mistress and the Grand Mistress alone.

"I didn't realize you would be joining us," he says. Inside he adds, *you complete and utter freak.*

"I summoned her," Lillabeta tells him coolly.

"Did you now?" Kellan wonders why she hadn't mentioned it. Perhaps she enjoys the rare chance to witness her General and longtime companion caught off guard. Then he reconsiders. No perhaps about it.

"I did." Lillabeta gestures with one lily-white hand toward an empty chair. "Please have a seat, Juliette. I have a mission for you."

About The Author

J.S. Eades lives in southwestern Ontario, Canada, with her family. An avid traveler and scuba enthusiast, she can often be found under the warm waters of the Caribbean.

The second book in the Forever Twenty-One series, MORE THAN JUST BLOOD, should be out in late 2021.

Connect with me
Website: www.jseades.com
Facebook: AuthorJSEades
Twitter: @JS_Eades
Instagram: @jseadesauthor

Dear Readers
Thank you so much for reading my novel. If you enjoyed it, would you please take a moment to write an honest review on Amazon or Goodreads.com so other readers can find and hopefully enjoy it, too? Even just a few sentences would mean a lot to me.

Thanks!
J.S. Eades

Other Books by J.S. Eades

PROMISES AND OTHER BROKEN THINGS

(Amelia and Declan book 1)

Amelia York seems to have it all: a great career, good friends, and she's married to her high school sweetheart. Starting a promising new job is just another step in the life she has all figured out. The intense connection she develops with a handsome co-worker, however, threatens to derail all her well thought-out plans.

Declan Kavanaugh's whole world revolves around his daughter. Overworked and under-appreciated both by his wife at home and his colleagues at his family's firm, the stress is starting to get to him. Making friends with the pretty new accountant comes as a surprise, but he finds time spent with Amelia is like the breath of fresh air he so desperately needs.

Neither of them wants any complications in their lives—and the last thing they want is to fall in love.

But as they discover, sometimes no matter how much you fight it, life has other ideas.

THE FINE ART OF FORGIVENESS

(Amelia and Declan book 2)

You don't always get what you want.

Amelia York knows this all too well. Her entire life has been torn apart and she's lost nearly everything that matters: her job, two of her closest friends, her father, and most devastating of all, the man she loves. Though she's gotten good at pretending she's fine, inside she's still shattered. All she wants is to move on and rebuild. She never thought it would be easy, but she didn't expect it to be this hard. And an impulsive decision at a friend's wedding throws a surprise wrench into her life that makes it even harder.

Declan Kavanaugh considers himself a damn good salesman, but he's got no pitch capable of convincing himself the choice he made was the right one. He promised to be there for his family, but he's hurting. And he misses *her* more than he's willing to admit. Can a miracle give him the second chance at happiness he craves? Or is he doomed to always destroy everything he cares about?

Things never turn out quite the way you think they will. But sometimes you might just get what you need

AGAINST ALL ADVICE

Giving advice is easy; taking it, on the other hand...

Evie Colville has one goal: earn a college scholarship to escape from small-town Sutterton. Between studying and working in her dad's coffee shop, she doesn't have much free time. None for a boyfriend, that's for sure.

Then she meets Alistair.

Alistair fled to his uncle's after the woman he loved brutally betrayed him with his own brother. The last thing he wants is another relationship. And after what he's gone through, he has zero tolerance for lies.

Evie, however, is keeping a big secret, not just from Alistair, but from everyone in town. Along with her other responsibilities, she's also the clandestine author of the local paper's Miss Lonely Love advice column. And recently she's been corresponding with a frustrated young man who has sworn off women for good.

Falling for each other is the *last* thing either wants. There's no possible way they could make this work.

Is there?

All books available at most online retailers.

www.ingramcontent.com/pod-product-compliance
Lightning Source LLC
LaVergne TN
LVHW020706110826
845149LV00012B/2130
* 9 7 8 0 9 9 3 9 5 8 2 3 6 *